The mark of the lion

Even in her shock, Rani realized that she was in danger. She knew that she needed to escape from these rebellious soldiers, from men who would attack their own sworn brothers.

Rani whirled toward her stallion, desperate to remount and escape.

"Stop!" Bashanorandi's order flamed across the twilight chill. In a flash, Rani saw that he held Mair close to his chest; she could make out a steel dagger leveled against the Touched girl's throat.

"Let her go, Bashi!"

"She's not going anywhere, and neither are you. . . ."

Don't miss Rani Trader's first exciting adventure . . .

THE GLASSWRIGHTS' APPRENTICE
Mindy L. Klasky

THE GLASSWRIGHTS' PROGRESS

Mindy L. Klasky

A ROC BOOK

ROC
Published by New American Library, a division of
Penguin Putnam Inc., 375 Hudson Street,
New York, New York 10014, U.S.A.
Penguin Books Ltd, 27 Wrights Lane,
London W8 5TZ, England
Penguin Books Australia Ltd,
Ringwood, Victoria, Australia
Penguin Books Canada Ltd, 10 Alcorn Avenue,
Toronto, Ontario, Canada M4V 3B2
Penguin Books (N.Z.) Ltd, 182–190 Wairau Road,
Auckland 10, New Zealand

Penguin Books Ltd, Registered Offices:
Harmondsworth, Middlesex, England

First published by Roc, an imprint of New American Library,
a division of Penguin Putnam Inc.

First Printing, July 2001
10 9 8 7 6 5 4 3 2 1

Cover design by Ray Lundgren
Cover art by Jerry Vanderstelt

 REGISTERED TRADEMARK—MARCA REGISTRADA

Printed in the United States of America

PUBLISHER'S NOTE
This is a work of fiction. Names, characters, places, and incidents either are the
products of the author's imagination or are used fictitiously, and any resemblance to
actual persons, living or dead, business establishments, events, or locales is entirely
coincidental.

To Jane Leigh Johnson,
who listened to too many stories
about child armies in the north

ACKNOWLEDGMENTS

Rani Trader's continuing story would not have been possible without the support and guidance of numerous people: Richard Curtis (agent extraordinaire, who fielded more questions with more patience than anyone should have to do), Bob Dickey (who, along with the rest of my Arent Fox family, has supported me every step down this long road—and I'm not just saying that because he's my boss), Laura Anne Gilman (whose editorial guidance made this finished book much better than the one I initially wrote), Deb Givens (who pitched in to read page proofs at the last minute, over a holiday weekend), the Johnsons (who gave me a West Coast home while I was making not-quite-final edits), Bruce Sundrud (who read each chapter as it evolved and who remained on call for emergency medical questions till the end), the Washington Area Writers' Group (which really is not the Writers' Group from Hell), and, of course, my family (who have put up with my crazy stories longer than anyone.)

Finally, I want to give special thanks to Frank Patry and Sharon Keir, who created my website out of whole cloth and helped me to find the perfect look when I had no idea what I wanted. Their handiwork is on the web at: www.sff.net/people/mindy-klasky.

1

Rani Trader swung down from her tall bay stallion, taking a moment to pat the animal's muscled neck and catch her breath. The wind had torn at her lungs as she raced to the top of the rise, and she gasped for air, more than a little surprised that the past two years had given her the skill to ride so wildly. Behind her, several riders were strung out, flung across the tall grass like discarded chessmen. At the distant edge of the long, long plain, Rani could just make out the top of the City's tallest tower, already flecked with gold in the late-afternoon light.

Rani's thoughts were not on Moren's towers, though. Instead, all of her attention was focused on Gry, the master falconer of Morenia. Rani's heart pounded as she stepped closer to the cadge that the falcon-master had set on the hilltop. Gry had left Moren early that morning, transporting by cart the sturdy birch enclosure and two prize falcons.

When Rani saw her kestrel's red-and-brown feathers, stark against the weathered supports of the cadge, she caught her breath. She was so pleased by Kalindramina that she scarcely spared a glance for the other raptor perched inside the enclosure. That bird was a peregrine, a falcon that merchant-born Rani would never be permitted to fly.

"Is she all right?" the girl asked the master falconer as she leaned over the kestrel. "Did the trip hurt Kalindramina?"

Gry snorted his gruff laugh and pulled at his right ear out of long habit. "Nothing will hurt that little falcon, my lady. She's too mean to be hurt. It's no wonder the king doesn't fly kestrels!

I expected you to get here earlier in the day, though." He weakened the implied criticism with another laugh.

"I wanted to." Rani frowned. This was the first day in ages that she had managed to break free from her obligations in King Halaravilli's court, free from the endless parade of ambassadors and nobles, guildsmen and soldiers, all intent on bringing the greatest glory to the kingdom of Morenia. Rani could barely remember the time, only a couple of years before, when she'd been afraid to leave the City walls, when she'd feared bandits and plague and all manner of disaster outside Moren. Now, scarcely a morning passed that she didn't dream of escaping the palace and all her courtly obligations. She took a deep breath, filling her lungs with the sweet aroma of autumn grass.

And she wasn't even supposed to be free this afternoon. Rani had promised to work on her embroidery. Nurse frequently assured her that she'd never find a husband if she did not master neat, even stitches in her handwork. Bristling against the injustice that made her old enough to waste her days entertaining visiting nobles but young enough to be subject to Nurse's jurisdiction, Rani had nodded in reluctant agreement and promised to try harder. Promised, that was, until Nurse had bustled out of sight.

Of course, Rani justified, Nurse *might* have relaxed her vigil if she'd known that Kalindramina was ready to fly. Even though the old woman knew nothing of falconing, Rani might have convinced her that the small raptor was a needy creature in the world of the Thousand Gods, a poor soul that required human contact. Besides, Rani could have explained, she herself must learn to watch over man *and* beast if she were eventually to count herself a good guildmistress.

For Rani held the future of the glasswrights in her hands, as surely as she had recently gripped her stallion's reins. It would likely take decades, but the former apprentice intended to rebuild the guild that had been destroyed two years before. The stained-glass makers had fallen victim to rumors and lies, to the king's mistaken belief that the artisans had been responsible for the Crown Prince's assassination. The new king, Halaravilli, had held true to his word, though, and he had sent a notice throughout his lands that the glasswrights had been forgiven, that they could return to Moren. Unfortunately, few of the guildsmen had trusted the royal proclamation. They remembered bloodshed and torture; they remembered betrayal and death.

Rani was determined, though. Even if she temporarily had to leave the comfort of Morenia, even if she had to travel to some distant land to learn her craft, she *would* see the glaziers return to Hal's court. And years from now, Rani would be responsible for her own master craftsmen, for the journeymen and apprentices. Of course, she'd also need to watch over their horses, over the cats that she would keep in the granary to chase the mice, over the caged birds that would inspire the masters with their song. A kestrel would fit well into the menagerie.

If Rani learned to manage the wild raptor.

Drawing her thoughts back from the beasts that would eventually sleep by the hearth in her own guildhall, Rani stretched her fingers toward Gry's hound. Soon, she would learn how to hunt with her own dogs. For Kalindramina's first flight, though, Rani would rely on the falcon-master's experienced hound to flush autumn-fat grouse from the brush. The dog sniffed at Rani's hand curiously, but he jumped back toward his master as another horse gained the crest of the low hill.

A young woman clung to the reins, sawing back on her mount's mouth as if she would decapitate the poor beast. The girl's shoulder-length hair was whipped by the wind of her passage, and her narrow features were pulled into a grimace. "Ye might've waited fer me!" she squawked, before Rani could step forward to help her. "Ye might remember that some o' us aren't used t' perchin' on a cursed animal's back!"

"And you might remember that you're supposed to be a lady, Mair." Rani grinned. "You promised His Majesty that you would stop squawking like a Touched hen every time you speak."

"And *you* promised His Majesty that you would stay within sight of the city walls when you go out riding. There's a whole lot of lying going on in the royal palace, isn't there?" Mair's retort was quick, but Rani noted that her companion slipped back into the cultured tones of the court. Two years of living in the palace had smoothed Mair's rough brogue, but Rani was still a little surprised every time she heard the Touched girl speak in the round, soft tones of Morenia's nobility.

Of course, Mair was a quick student. That skill had kept her alive for more than sixteen years, years that had been astonishingly rough in the City streets. Mair refused to talk about her childhood, about the parents who had abandoned her to her life among the City's teeming population of lawless, casteless children. All that Rani knew was that Mair had gathered a group of loyal Touched around her, children who were willing to lay down their lives for their leader. In exchange for that devotion, Mair had kept her troop safe and warm and fed, even when the King's Guard had tried repeatedly to drive out the group of casteless urchins.

"Cursed beast! Stand yer ground!" Mair swore at her mount as it shied away, and she sawed at the animal's tough mouth with arms that trembled on her reins. Rani's falcon, Kalindramina, shifted her talons on her bow-shaped perch, ruffling her feathers at the disturbance. The peregrine, though, remained aloof beneath its buckskin hood.

"Mair," Rani chastised, "don't frighten Kali. You know you won't get anywhere if you manhandle your horse like that. Hold the reins firmly, and don't pull sideways."

"Mind your own horse," Mair snarled, and Rani swallowed a laugh as she turned her attention back to the falcon-master, who had watched the entire exchange with an indulgent smile. "Gry, can we fly Kali now?"

The old man's eyes darted to Rani's hand as she pulled on her heavy buckskin falconing glove. He tugged at his ear and gazed out across the plain toward Moren. "We'd best wait for the prince, my lady. He'll be offended if we start without him."

"He could have been here already, if he didn't ride like a noble reviewing his troops," Rani grumbled. "Besides, the prince already knows that his Maradalian will fly well. Please, Gry! I don't want to look like a fool in front of him."

The falcon-master glanced at the hooded peregrine, perched next to Kalindramina on the sturdy cadge. He tugged at his ear again, and a frown creased his forehead. "It's not a contest, my lady. You must respect the bird, as she's learned to respect you. You're not competing with Prince Bashanorandi today." Shaking his head in rebuke, the falconer stepped away from the two girls, becoming unusually interested in the raptors' jesses, the strips of leather that tethered them to their perches.

"She's *always* competing with Bashi," Mair noted dryly to the back of Gry's head as she finally slipped to the ground from her jittery mount. "You know, Rai, you were wrong to speak so harshly to the soldiers when we rode through the city gates."

"They were taking too long to pass us through. They *know* we're allowed to come and go. They were only dragging their feet because Bashi was there, too."

"They were doing their job."

Rani glared at Mair. "So, it's come to this? You're going to tutor me in being kind to *soldiers*?"

Mair grimaced at Rani's sharp tone. "I'm telling you to be kind to *people*. I don't care what caste the men are, they don't deserve the cheek you offered them."

"Cheek! I haven't been cheeky a day in my life!"

"Call it what you will. Some of us adapt better to our life in the castle than others."

"You take that back, Mair! I didn't do anything wrong with the soldiers!"

"Of course not." Mair paused. "My lady," she added sweetly.

"Mair, if you want to criticize me, do it outright."

"You'll know when I criticize you, Rani Trader."

The words bit hard, spiced with deep-rooted anger, and Rani blinked back sudden tears. "You used to call me Rai."

"You used to act like one of the Touched."

Rani spluttered, digging for an answer, but no retort came easily. Instead, she glared at Gry's back, taking in the falcon-master's supposed interest in one of the joints of the portable cadge. Gry had been born one of the casteless Touched, like all of the nobles' servants. Through the years, he had worked hard to gain his employers' trust, to earn his success as master falconer. Rani looked away from the silent condemnation of his still back, turning her attention to the four soldiers who finally drew near the top of the gentle rise. "My lady," called the captain, bowing slightly from his saddle. "It's dangerous for you to ride alone."

"I'm not alone!" Rani exclaimed, and her voice was sharper than she intended. She swallowed hard and forced her words into a less shrill register. "I rode with my lady-in-waiting, Mair. And I rode to the king's own falcon-master. Besides, we were never out of your sight, Farantili."

"Much good it would do me, if I had to watch enemy troops ride out of those trees and carry you off." Farantili nodded his grizzled head toward the copse that bled across the bottom of the hill.

Rani covered a shiver of concern with scornful words. "What enemy would come so close to Moren? We're near enough to hear the Pilgrims' Bell from here. By all the Thousand Gods, you worry too much, Farantili."

"I'm paid to worry, my lady." The soldier's words did nothing to ease Rani's roiling temper, especially when he edged his horse between hers and the trees. "I'll send one of my men down to check out the woods, before you fly the kestrel."

"Farantili, that's ridiculous. It's already getting late in the day. If we have to wait for your scout, we won't get back to the city until after dark."

"Of course, my lady. We should turn back now. You can practice your falconry another day."

Mair did not bother to disguise her smirk of amusement as Rani yelped in frustration and whirled on Gry, ready to plead her case to the master. Before she could speak, though, the last handful of horsemen rode up. Farantili bent low in his saddle, and Gry swept into a deep bow, but Rani scarcely inclined her head.

"Bashi," she murmured, and she watched anger flare across the prince's pale face. Prince Bashanorandi had no use for childish nicknames, particularly names that had been bestowed by the current king, when both boys had lived in the royal nursery.

"You had no right to leave me back there!" Prince Bashanorandi scowled as he fought to rein in his feisty brown stallion. "You *know* that Hal would not want us riding this far from Moren's walls. He'd have your hide if he saw you jump that creek! When will you stop to think, Ranita? You're not a merchant brat any longer."

But you're a brat, all the same.

No, Bashi was not fool enough to utter those words, not in front of the master falconer and the soldiers. Nevertheless, he thought them so clearly that Rani's hands curled into fists as expressive as Kali's talons. She bridled at the bitterness in Bashi's superior tone, even as she tried to remind herself that the past two years had not been easy for the bastard son of two proven traitors.

Bashi had been indirectly implicated in the plot to assassinate Morenia's Crown Prince. Many thought that the bastard should have been executed like his scheming mother and father. King Shanoranvilli, though, had mandated from his deathbed that the boy he had always known as his youngest son should live. Even after the heartbroken old man died, Halaravilli had not withdrawn that sanctuary. In fact, Hal had left Bashanorandi the title of "prince," figuring that the appellation might help rein in the rebellious youth.

But Bashi had continued to be difficult, refusing to assume any responsibility in administering the kingdom. Hal had rapidly found himself snared in a paradox: he could have forced his so-called brother to act as a councillor, to be responsible for Moren's day-to-day administration, as was typical of a Crown Prince. But everyone knew that Bashi *wasn't* the Crown Prince. He wasn't of Morenian royal blood at all.

The situation was frustrating, and Hal took out his aggression with his sometime brother in a thousand ways, berating Bashi in the dining hall when the youth arrived late for supper, ridiculing Bashi's notions for a feast day honoring all the Thousand Gods.

And Bashi took out his anger in ways that were safe, especially by tormenting the lower-caste Rani. The prince had arranged for her apartments to be on the darker, southern side of the palace compound, and he had snagged the best palace seamstress for himself. He had even managed to snare the treasured dinner place at Hal's right hand.

Rani was forced to grit her teeth and accept the ignominy. She was, after all, a merchant girl who only teetered on the edge of the noble caste. Now, painfully aware of all the limits on her rights, Rani harnessed her self-control. "I didn't leave my escort 'far behind,' my lord. You must not have noticed that we're at the top of a hill. The soldiers could see Mair and me, as we rode to this vantage point."

"A lot of good it would have done, if you'd been attacked."

"And who's going to attack us, this close to the City?"

"Ranita, you know there've been tales of marauders," Bashi sneered. As his face twisted around his superior words, he looked younger than his fifteen years. "Even if you *haven't* been allowed in council meetings, you can't have missed the stories in the streets."

"You may be frightened by tales meant for children, O Prince, but *I* am not. I know the difference between a monster that lurks beneath a child's bed and an invading army."

"No one said that it would take an army," Bashi answered hotly. "A single soldier with a sharp blade could kill you, before you even knew that you'd been taken."

Mair cut in before Rani could spit out a reply. "Aye, Prince Bashanorandi. A single blade is all it would take to cut down any of us. That's why we all must stay united. Against our *true* enemies." Mair accented her pious declaration by settling her right hand on the hilt of the dagger she wore at her waist, contrary to the delicate customs of the noble caste. There were, after all, advantages to being one of the casteless Touched.

"Now, now," interrupted Farantili. The grizzled soldier had let his wards argue among themselves, accustomed to their squabbles. When hand touched steel, though, he apparently deemed it time to intervene.

"Lady Rani, Lady Mair." Gry took advantage of the broken hostilities to regain the young people's attention. The master falconer added the noble title to the girls' names, as if he were accustomed to following the polite form of address with only a few syllables, instead of a noble's long name. "It *is* getting late in the day. If these falcons are going to fly, they should do it now, before dark. It can be hard enough finding them at noon, once they've taken their prey in the high grass."

Rani bit back a sharp reply, swallowing her inclination to claim that *she* had been ready to fly the falcons hours before. Instead, she turned her back on Bashi, stepping toward the falcon-master with a nervous energy. "Do you really think Kali's ready, Gry? Do you think she'll come back?"

The old falcon-master shrugged, and his brows beetled ominously. He tugged again at his ear. "If I didn't think she was ready, I wouldn't have brought her out here. There's no way of knowing for sure, though, until you try."

"But—"

"You've trained her, haven't you? You've been around my mews long enough to understand that this kestrel won't be acting like a dog. She won't come back out of love for you. She's still a wild beast."

"I know that!" Rani protested, fighting the hot blush that stole across her cheeks as she heard Bashi choke on a guffaw. "It's just that after all the time and energy we've put into training her . . ."

The master falconer squinted as he settled a hand on the cadge. "She flies to your lure, doesn't she?"

"Of course."

"And she's stopped bating when you hold her on your fist?"

"Yes." Rani fought back a grimace, remembering her frantic struggle the first time the falcon had tried to fly away from her gloved hand, even though the bird had been held close by the leather jesses around her talons. Rani's face had been batted by the tips of the falcon's wings, and she had waved her arm in reflexive fear, upsetting the poor kestrel even more. Rani had been grateful for the thick cuff of her buckskin glove as Kali dug in her talons above her would-be mistress' wrist.

The master falconer persisted. "And you know your kestrel's hunting weight?"

"Yes." Rani struggled to keep doubt from her voice. Hunting weight—that had proven to be the hardest part of the discipline of falconry. Rani had held Kalindramina within minutes after the bird was first caught in Gry's snare. The little falcon had fought with the power of all the Thousand Gods, desperate to be free. Rani, though, had followed the master falconer's instructions with trembling hands. She had slipped a long band of leather about the wild bird's body, pulling the noose tight to cinch in the kestrel's desperately flapping wings. With Gry's help, Rani had managed to settle a hood over the falcon's head, barely cinching the soft buckskin tight before the bird's cruel beak could slash through the leather.

Kalindramina had quieted then. She had stopped thrashing her wings, and her talons had ceased their frantic opening and closing. Nevertheless, the kestrel's heart had pounded, quivering faster than an infant's as Rani pressed her fingers against the bird's breastbone. "Aye," Gry had crooned. "You feel that? D'you feel the meat on her? We'll let her lose a little of that flesh, so that she'll fly when we ask her. A hungry falcon is a trapped falcon. A hungry kestrel stays to eat. A hungry bird can be recaught."

Rani had checked the breastbone again, and one more time, before she was certain that she knew the feel of Kalindramina's full-fed weight. Then she had nodded, and Gry had taken the kestrel away to the mews.

Now, a breeze picked up on the hilltop as Rani pressed a gentle finger against her bird's chest. The girl had grown accustomed to the miniature thunder that pounded behind the deceptively fragile cage of bones. Kali's heart yearned to fly free, to soar above the grasslands. The falcon longed to bank against the wind, spying the ground, watching for prey. Rani nodded to Gry, registering the weight of the hungry kestrel. "Aye. She's ready to fly."

"Let's fly her then." The bowlegged falconer waited for Rani to step up to the cadge. The girl took a deep breath before settling the falcon on her gloved fist. She fumbled with the hood for a moment, but then Kalindramina was blinking in the late-afternoon light, cocking her head to the side as she looked at Rani. The girl drew in her breath sharply, snared as always by the beauty of the tiny feathers that fanned out from the falcon's eyes.

Bashi pushed past Rani to the cadge. As he reached for Maradalian, he grunted, "Aye, let's go."

Rani squealed her protest. "No!"

"Gry." Bashi's single word held an entire argument.

"Bashi, you can't!" Rani complained. "You know Maradalian will catch the prey. She's faster than Kali, and larger. It's not fair!"

"The Thousand Gods favor the fast." Bashi stripped off his peregrine's hood, settling the bird on his gloved fist with brutal efficiency.

"My prince," Gry began, clearly uncomfortable. "You know how important it is that Kali succeed on this first flight. The bird is too valuable to break on a whim."

"Oh, all right!" Bashi exclaimed. "You have my word. I'll keep Maradalian on my fist until after Kali has flown."

"But—" Rani began to protest.

"Surely Gry has taught you enough about falconing that you understand Maradalian won't have a chance? Your kestrel will have the advantage of height and speed as she drops toward the prey."

"I *know* that!" Rani snapped, irritated that Bashi was instructing her as if she were a child. "It's just that—"

"What? You think that Kalindramina is too weak to hunt, even with the advantage of height?"

"No! I only . . . Please—" Rani began again, but this time she was cut off by the soldier, Farantili.

"Perhaps, Your Highness, we should simply wait for another day." The guard addressed his comment to Prince Bashanorandi as he looked morosely at the lengthening shadows.

"Ranita?" Bashi bowed toward the former apprentice, ceding her the choice with a twisted smile.

"No," she answered miserably. "Let's get this over with."

Gry waited a moment for her to confirm her decision with an unhappy nod, then he whistled at his hound. The little dog had watched the exchange with growing excitement, whining softly as both falconers settled their birds on their wrists. Now, he understood his mission, and he coursed out over the grassy hillside, nose low to the ground as he ranged back and forth. Rani followed, taking long strides in her riding leathers, remembering to croon softly to Kalindramina. The little kestrel *was* fast enough to get the prey, even if Maradalian were competing. Rani knew that. She just had to repeat it to the falcon a few times.

Bashi crashed behind them, the grass rustling loudly against his legs. Gry came next, then Mair and the soldiers.

An excited hush fell over the humans as they watched the dog. The sun was visibly lower in the sky, and the hound had covered half the distance to the shadowy copse of trees before he found his prey. Just as Rani was preparing to offer up a special prayer to Fairn, the god of birds, the little dog finally snapped to attention, all of his canine energy focused on a large tuft of grass. Gry nodded tersely and waved his hand, indicating that Rani should move around to the far side of the tussock.

Rani complied, aware that her heart was beating almost as fast as her falcon's. She watched the hound, hoping, praying that the beast would remember its training, would wait until Kali was ready. The dog quivered with excitement, but he stayed low in the grass, head pointing at the hidden grouse like an arrow.

Rani's fingers were slick with sweat as she loosened Kali's jesses. She clenched the muscles in her arms and tossed the falcon gently skyward. The kestrel did not hesitate; instead, she caught a puff of breeze and began to climb above Rani, circling to use the wind to her best advantage. Rani caught her breath. This was the moment when Kali could choose to fly away, could choose to find her own meal, her own prey to satisfy the hunger that burned in her belly.

The kestrel did not flee, though. Instead, she reached a comfortable height above her mistress, banking into the wind and settling her wings against the draft, managing to stay even with scarcely any effort. Rani watched for only a moment, until she was certain that the kestrel was waiting on, and then she shouted a harsh command to the dog.

The hound leaped forward as if propelled by a spring, barking as grouse exploded from the tussock of grass. The birds flapped their wings desperately, struggling to clear the ground, to escape the slashing canine teeth. Rani's heart leaped into her throat, almost strangling her with its sudden pounding. Her glance flashed from the dog to the grouse to Kalindramina.

As if Rani were staring through a tunnel, she saw the falcon's wings pull in toward its body. The sleek red-and-brown feathers moved with precision, calm and quiet despite the turmoil on the ground below. Rani imagined she could see the kestrel's sharp eye; she felt it measure the distance to the grouse, calculate how far the slow prey could travel while the falcon plummeted. Then, Kali's talons were extended, and the kestrel plunged from the crystal sky.

Kalindramina never caught her prey.

Even as Rani watched, an ebony lightning bolt flew from the earth into the sky. The grey-and-white arrow caught Kali in the middle of the kestrel's plunge, knocking the bird aside. Feathers exploded in midair, and Rani's heart was sheared by her falcon's furious cry. Even as the grouse fluttered to safety, Rani tried to decipher the scene before her. The hound took up an excited barking as Rani ran forward. The girl ignored the dog, ignored the rough grass, ignored everything except the whirlwind that tore across the ground.

Maradalian, Bashi's peregrine, screamed from the tall grass, struggling to lift its prey to safety. That kestrel prey, though, thrashed about, shrieking its own desperate cry. "Kali!" Rani added her panic to the melee. "Gry! Stop them!"

The old falconer, though, understood the danger of getting between two fighting raptors. He knew too well their razor talons, their tearing beaks. Gry held his ground. Maradalian was the larger bird by far, and more experienced in flying with jesses attached. Kali was struggling to fight her way free, screeching her rage, flapping her red-and-brown wings.

Rani reached into the avian whirlwind, leading with her buckskin glove. Maradalian slashed at her with a sharp beak, and Rani swore, grasping at the bird with both hands. Before the peregrine could react, Rani sucked in her breath; Kali had caught her unprotected left palm with a dagger-sharp talon. "Gry!" Rani panted again, desperate for assistance.

The falcon-master could not move, though, before the kestrel fought its way free from the ground. Even as Rani grasped at Maradalian's jesses, Kalindramina took to the sky. The red-and-brown bird pumped her wings hard to gain height, and Rani thought that she must be injured to labor so hard. "Kali!" she gasped, but the kestrel only circled once before she flew off to the east, pushing toward the copse of trees.

Rani raised her bleeding hand to her mouth, sucking at the jagged wound even as she watched her treasure disappear into the sky. Blood flowed freely from the slash, and the salty taste on her tongue made her stomach tighten.

Even as she fought the urge to gag, Gry stepped forward, managing to slip a hood over Maradalian's frantic eyes. The falcon-master stood still for a moment, blinking in disbelief, and then Prince Bashanorandi stepped forward to claim his falcon. His face was pale as he settled the bird on his gloved fist, and he sucked breath between his teeth when he saw the jagged slash across Rani's hand. For just an instant, he looked precisely like a fifteen-year-old boy caught breaking the rules.

"Bashi!" Rani spat. "You did that on purpose!"

"Don't be ridiculous!"

"You wanted to kill Kali!"

The prince's tongue darted over his chapped lips. "I never wanted any such thing! I held back until Kalindramina had the height." His gaze followed the course that the kestrel had flown, and he shook his head. He swallowed hard before adding plaintively, "I assumed she'd have the skill to catch her prey." Bashi settled a protective hand against the dark grey feathers of his now-calm peregrine, then he reached into a pouch at his waist and pulled out a kerchief. "You're bleeding all over. Wrap your hand with this."

Rani wanted to throw the cloth at his feet, but she dared not. Mair stepped forward to bind up her wound, not bothering to disguise a hateful glance toward the prince. Bashi became absorbed with his peregrine's feathers, and he muttered, without looking up, "You have to admit, Rani, Maradalian didn't have much of a chance, flying from my fist."

"I don't have to admit anything, you bastard!" Rani sucked in her breath as Mair knotted the kerchief across her palm.

Prince Bashanorandi paled still further, and his lips turned to grim stone. Maradalian sensed his tension, and the peregrine bated, trying to fly from his gloved fist, only to be pulled up short by her jesses. Bashi soothed the bird mechanically before he turned back to Rani. When he spoke, the words were pulled out of him like wool thread stretched on a spindle. "So you would remind me, merchant girl. Every single day, you would remind me."

Rani saw the raw anger in Bashi's eyes, recognized that the better part of his rage was because Mair and the soldiers had witnessed their altercation. For just an instant a chill crept up Rani's spine. Before she could reply, Bashi spun on his heel and marched up the hill toward the cadge. Gry followed close behind, but the soldiers waited until the girls were ready to make the climb. Rani lingered for a long moment, staring east into the gathering nighttime gloom, toward the copse where Kali had disappeared.

Mair whispered, "Don't even think about it, Rai."

"She might be there."

"Why would she? She's frightened and hungry. And free."

"That kestrel is my responsibility, Mair. She might get tangled by her jesses. I trained her for four months—"

"Lady Rani," Gry called from the cadge. Even in the dim twilight, Rani could make out the falconer's impatience as he helped Bashanorandi settle Maradalian on a perch. The stocky man's voice was harsh as he spat out his frustration with Rani, with the royal prince, with the loss of one of his birds. "It's not likely that Kalindramina stopped at the trees. She'll be far away by now."

"I have to find out for sure."

"It's getting late, Lady Rani!" The falconer tugged at his ear as if he would rip it away from his skull. "King Halaravilli will be angry!"

"Aye, Gry. Bashi should have thought of that before he flew Maradalian."

The falcon-master shrugged. "Bashi wasn't thinking."

The prince moved before Rani could realize what was happening. Pulling a curved dagger from the top of his boot, Bashi slashed his blade across the side of Gry's throat. "My name is Bashanorandi, you Touched dog!"

Gry cried out and sank to his knees, even as Rani shouted the falcon-master's name. In a glowing ray from the setting sun, Rani could see Bashi's face, could make out the momentary horror etched across his eyes. The prince was clearly astonished by his own action, and his right hand trembled on his curved knife. Bashanorandi looked up at Rani, reaching toward her with his empty hand, grasping like a child.

"In the name of Fen, what have you done?" Rani croaked the question before she could think.

She saw Bashi register her words, saw him absorb the name of the god of mercy like a slap across his face. His cheeks flushed crimson beneath his ginger hair, and before Rani could speak again, he had whirled on the stricken falcon-master, drawing back his fine leather boot to sink his toes hard into the falconer's side. The stocky man curled up reflexively, the action making blood spurt from his throat. He pleaded with the prince, making a horrible gurgling sound.

"Your Highness!" barked Farantili, sprinting to the hilltop. "Leave him be!"

Bashi drew back, trembling with rage. Rani stared at the prince in amazement, unable to comprehend what he had done. Mair's eyes blazed in the twilight, and she rushed to the master falconer, tugging at her cloak in a futile attempt to rip it into bandages.

"Stand back!" Bashi ordered. He snatched at Mair's arms, dragging her away from Gry. "Don't get near that Touched dog!" Even as Mair fought against the prince's grip, Farantili stepped forward. "Soldier! Don't even think about helping him!"

"He's a finer man than you'll ever be," Farantili grunted, falling to one knee beside the stricken falconer. Gry's hands and feet twitched, and his body began to spasm.

"Leave him!" Bashi's throat tore on the shout, and he fumbled for his curved blade. "That's an order, man!"

For just an instant, Farantili stared up at his liege, his eyes dark with unspoken emotion. Then, the soldier turned back to the falconer, and he began to mutter soothing words, trying gently to view the wounded man's gaping throat. Bashi gasped in disbelief, and then he raised his curved blade. "To me!" he cried, flashing a glance over his shoulder at the other guards.

There was a moment's hesitation, while loyalties fought among themselves, and then a tempest broke over the hillside. Metal clanged against metal. Horses whinnied in panic, the sound high and chilling on the twilight breeze. Maradalian bated from her perch, fighting her hood and jesses. One of the soldiers crashed into the cadge, splintering the birch supports.

As Rani watched, Farantili was shoved to the ground amid the shambles of the cadge. Another soldier stepped up, menacing the fallen fighter with a short sword. Rani cried out, desperate to stop the bloodshed, but before she could make herself heard, another guard was cut down, bellowing as his hamstring was sliced by one of Bashi's loyal men.

Across the now-trampled grass, Rani could make out the sound of bones crunching. Two soldiers pinned Farantili to the ground, pressing his spine against the shattered birch uprights from the cadge. One of the pair straddled Farantili's chest and began to pummel the man's head, starting with closed-fist blows and ending with a simple rhythmic pounding. Farantili's limp neck hit the earth again and again and again.

Even in her shock, Rani realized that she was in danger. She knew that she needed to escape from these rebellious soldiers, from men who would attack their own sworn brothers, who would sanction the murder of a defenseless master falconer. She was not safe among men who would beat one of King Halaravilli's soldiers to a pulp and butcher another like so much meat.

Rani whirled toward her stallion, desperate to remount and escape.

"Stop!" Bashanorandi's order flamed across the twilight chill. In a flash, Rani saw that he held Mair close to his chest; she could make out a steel dagger leveled against the Touched girl's throat. As if to emphasize the command, Mair dropped her own blade. The prince kicked it into the high grass.

"Let her go, Bashi!"

"She's not going anywhere, and neither are you."

Even in these dire circumstances, the words rang falsely. "Are you going to keep us on the plain all night then? Like children lost in the countryside?"

"You may pretend this is a joke, Rani, but I assure you it is not." Bashi twisted Mair's arm behind her back, and the girl's lips tightened over her teeth. She refused to cry out, but her look spoke volumes to Rani. "You will not go running to Hal with stories of what happened here. I don't want my men to hurt you, Ranita, but I'll let them if they must."

"*Your* men? Those are King Halaravilli's soldiers." Rani tried to force certainty past the image of Farantili's bloody head, past the moans of the hamstrung guard.

"These soldiers are loyal to *me,* Ranita." Even as Bashi made his pronouncement, one of his guards grabbed for Rani's arm. Without thinking, she spat in the man's face. He bellowed in rage, snatching for his sword, but his fellow grabbed Rani and pulled her, hard, against his chest. Through the Morenian livery, she could feel a hardened leather breastplate, a foreign design that poked against her spine. The full armor was stranger still because there was no reason for the soldier to be wearing it, not for an afternoon ride within sight of the City. The man she had spat at swore and wiped at the mess on his face.

For just an instant, Rani thought her eyes deceived her in the twilight gloom. When the man pawed at his face, he left behind a tracery around his eyes. Only when Rani blinked did she real-ize that the man had not *covered* his face with the strange de-sign. Rather, his wiping motion had removed a layer of color, a coating of flesh-colored paint like the cosmetics that Nurse was always thrusting at Rani. Beneath that false color, Rani could now make out a distinct tattoo, the careful outline of a lion be-neath the man's left eye.

She caught her breath. She'd heard enough in Hal's court for the past two years to know that the northern soldiers tattooed themselves at birth, dedicating their lives to their warrior existence. A northern soldier, then, from Amanthia. From the executed Queen Felicianda's homeland.

"What have you done, Bashi?"

"That's Prince Bashanorandi to you!" Bashi nearly screamed his rebuff, pulling hard on Mair's arm. The Touched girl tried to bite back her cry of pain, but a little of the sound leaked into the clearing.

"My lord Bashanorandi," Rani forced herself to say.

Bashi nodded, apparently placated. With a curt gesture, he passed Mair to one of his soldiers. "Kill her, if that one takes a single step amiss."

"Yes, my prince." The soldier locked his arm across Mair's windpipe, settling a long, curved dagger against her side. A curved dagger, Rani finally registered. Curved like the knives of the northern troops.

"What are you doing, Bash—, Prince Bashanorandi?"

"Once, I thought I'd wait to show my strength, but you've made that impossible. Get on your horse."

"What?"

"I know you're not stupid, Ranita. Get on your horse."

"I'm not riding anywhere with you."

"I'll kill you here and now, if I have to." Watching the pulse beat fast in his throat, Rani understood that Bashi was not making an idle threat. "I'm not going back to Moren, back to Hal. But if I sent you back to Moren directly, I'd never have time to get to Amanthia, before you'd have Hal's soldiers after us. I just might convince my brother to ransom you two sorry excuses for courtiers, though. Parkman, get the creances."

The lion-tattooed soldier strode over to the toppled cadge, swearing as the frantic Maradalian flapped her grey-and-white wings. The man extracted two long leather leashes from the collapsed structure. He snapped the creances between his fists, testing their strength as he turned back to his liege.

Bashi's eyes glinted in the last of the sunlight. "I don't want to do it, Ranita. I don't want to order you killed, but I will if I have to." The girl had no doubt that he *would* follow through on his threat. "Mount up now. We have a long ride ahead of us."

With a warning glance toward Mair, Rani turned back to her stallion. She grunted as she pulled herself onto her high saddle, trying to ignore the slash of crimson that painted the leather as her wounded hand opened again. Somewhere in the struggle of the last few minutes, she had lost her rough bandage.

Bashi jutted his chin toward Rani, and the soldier snapped the creances once again. "Lash her to the stirrups."

Rani immediately set her heels, ready to kick the horse and flee back to Moren. Before she could act, though, Bashi barked a command to the soldier who held Mair. The man tightened his grip on Mair's arm, twisting hard and pulling the limb high behind the Touched girl's back. The crack of splintering bone was audible above the rustle of the high grass, and Mair cried out through her clenched teeth. "Don't even think about riding off, Ranita. I'll kill her before you're out of earshot."

Certainly Bashi would use more violence to gain his way. The prince's face was coated with a sheen of sweat, and his hands clenched and unclenched repeatedly in the twilight. Mair began to moan softly, although she tried to swallow her pain. Rani sat still as Parkman tightened the falcon's leash about her, lashing first one foot to her stirrup then passing the leather beneath her stallion's belly and binding the other. "Get her hands, too," Bashi barked, and the soldier complied, using another length of leather.

Staring at Bashi with bitterness, Rani only just remembered to hold her tongue as the prince nodded and ordered Mair released. It was a simple matter for Bashi to have the Touched girl bound, to have her tied to her own mount. Then Bashi's soldiers seated themselves on their own horses. The prince glanced around the plain nervously, his eyes lingering on the dead falcon-master, the murdered soldier, the maimed one. The falcons' cadge was crumpled on the ground like a skeleton. Maradalian stood amid the ruins, blinded by her hood, uncertain of the disaster around her.

Bashi nodded to Parkman and pointed his chin toward the hamstrung soldier. "Get rid of that one, and let's get out of here.

We can get to the coast by sunset tomorrow and find a ship to sail north, to Amanthia. With any luck Hal won't find this till then. We can demand ransom for the girls when we arrive in my mother's homeland."

Before Rani could protest, the soldier dispatched his onetime brother, slashing the man's throat with one even motion. Then the guards fell into formation, one riding at Rani's left side, one riding at Mair's right. Two of the armed men followed behind, flanking their prince. When Rani hesitated to spur her stallion, the soldier beside her drew his sword. Before she could decide whether she would take a stand, Mair swayed in her own saddle, moaning as the movement jarred her injured arm.

"You've got to help her!" Rani cried to Bashi. "At least let me put her arm in a sling."

"After we've ridden. You can help her after we cross the Yman."

"The river is two hours from here!"

"Then it will be two hours before her arm is set."

Rani heard the determination in his voice. In a flash, she remembered the Bashi she had first met when she arrived in the palace. That prince had been a spoiled boy, a noble who accepted his royalty with an unseemly arrogance. He had manipulated nurses and guards, played upon his supposed father's heartstrings. Now, he had these four soldiers bound to him, and nothing would convince him to take pity on two low-caste girls.

Sighing, Rani touched her spurs to her stallion's flanks. Mair moaned through lips that were grey in the twilight, but she jigged her own horse forward. As the riders moved east into the unfolding night, a breeze picked up, blowing from the distant city walls. Rani could just make out the rhythmic clang of the Pilgrims' Bell, summoning the faithful to Moren's safety, to the haven of King Halaravilli, to the lost comfort of home and hearth.

2

Shea had put too much salt in the soup. She had thought there were still three potatoes left, that they would absorb the extra salt. It was only when she clambered down to the dank root cellar that she learned that she was wrong. There were no more potatoes. And there was too much salt.

She was getting old. Too old to remember if she had any potatoes.

When Shea called the orphans to sit at the long table, she expected them to complain. After all, her children were still learning to follow the course appointed for them by the skies. They were still striving to live by the stars that had shone over their births. Her skychildren were not perfect.

The five lionchildren, though, stoically raised their bowls of salty water to their cracked lips. They drank like good little soldiers. Five tattoos peered at her over their wooden bowls, lion-brown constellations curving beneath each left eye.

The nine sunchildren managed as well, sighing in discontent, but drinking down their supper. Only a few rolled their eyes, wrinkling the rayed tattoos high on their cheeks, symbol of the sun that had shone over their births.

The flock of four owlchildren took the opportunity to discuss the logic of the situation. Should Shea have expected there to be more potatoes? If not, then had she acted properly in preparing the soup? On and on, the owls jabbered at each other, their own tattoos glinting black against their cheeks.

Shea merely watched them and listened, thinking of her own

children, who had come to her so late in life. Her own dead lionson, her lost daughter. Her lost swangirl. Like Serena.

Just six years old, the orphaned swangirl Serena was the problem during supper. She perched at the head of the table and wrinkled her nose at her bowl of tepid brine. One of the sunchildren
tried to forestall a tantrum by giving Serena his portion of acorn
bread. The swangirl took one look at the dry crust, and a crystal tear trickled past the silver wings tattooed beneath her left
eye.

That tear made Tain, the oldest sungirl, rush over to comfort
the swanchild. As Tain crooned soft words, the lion captain, Hartley, glared at the other children. He made a show of mopping
out the salty dregs from his bowl with his own bitter bread. The
other children followed his example. Shea's heart went out to her
oldest orphans, to Tain and Hartley, who were almost ready to
take their places in the warring, wild world.

As Tain cleared empty bowls from the table, Shea rested a
hand on Hartley's arm. She spoke awkwardly. "Thank you."

"I was only doing my job," the lionboy growled. It still surprised Shea that he spoke with a man's deep voice. He had already lived fifteen years. Fifteen years, all in the shadow of King
Sin Hazar's wars, of the Uprising and the battles that followed.

"You do your job well. It's a comfort knowing that I can trust
you."

The boy was clearly pleased by the praise, but before he could
answer, Tain approached. "I'll get the children into bed. We should
get the suns up early tomorrow, if we're going to forage in the
northern clearing."

"Aye," Shea agreed. "It's a long walk."

"I still don't think it's safe," Hartley protested. He had argued
every morning since Shea had proposed the journey to the distant part of the forest. "My lions can't guard all of us so far
from home."

"Well, we can't just sit here and starve," Shea said. She might
only be a sun, she might not have been born under a star-sign,
but she knew about providing for her children. "Besides, it's just
the suns and the lions who will go. We'll send the owls and Ser-

ena to the village for the day. Father Nariom can teach them more
of their lessons."

"The village isn't safe either! Sin Hazar's men could come
through at any time!"

"King Sin Hazar's men have not passed this way in over a
year, Hartley. They're staying far to the north. They're preparing
to do battle across the sea, in Liantine."

The boy shook his head. "They may fight across the ocean,
but they'll come here to gather up soldiers for the Little Army.
They're still set on punishing us for the Uprising. You know the
rumors—you've heard them in the village!"

"If stories had any value, then bards would give feasts all year
round."

"Shea, my lions have been talking about nothing else. Everyone knows that the Little Army grows near." Shea forced herself
to laugh, as if she had not heard the desperate tales. "You know
King Sin Hazar needs us, Shea. He needs children." Hartley re-
cited the lessons he'd learned, the lions' catechism that he'd been
taught when he first met other lionboys around the village foun-
tain, when he had first begun to learn how to fight, how to protect his homeland. "After fifteen years of fighting the Uprising
against our pitiful, rebellious province, the king had hardly any
grown men in all Amanthia. The Little Army, the army of children, will help King Sin Hazar reclaim his power in the world.
King Sin Hazar will be able to capture Liantine to the east, and
he'll bring power and glory to his united kingdom of Amanthia."

Of course, Shea knew these truths. She knew about the endless battles that King Sin Hazar had fought, that he planned to
fight. She knew that her tiny corner of Amanthia had led the rebellion against its king more than twenty years before, that it had
planted the seeds of the civil war that had torn all of Amanthia
for nearly a generation.

Shea's province had rebelled because it had been forced to
pay too many taxes. It had been forced to provide soldiers for a
royal army overseas. It had been forced to forfeit the peace and
comfort of quiet country life. It had had no choice but to fight

against its own king decades before. A lifetime ago. Many lives ago.

And it had lost.

The king was not through punishing Shea's land. He was not ready to forgive the rebellious province that had cost him so many skilled fighting men. Instead, he continued to fight, continued to harvest children for his Little Army.

Shea made her voice reassuring. "King Sin Hazar may have great plans for his united Amanthia, but we're too far from the capital for him to notice us yet. We'll be safe for a while longer."

"You can't *believe* that!"

She shrugged. "I believe that I have to feed my children. And I believe that the owls need to learn. I can't teach them how to debate, and you can't either. We'll send them to Father Nariom in the village and trust to the Thousand Gods."

"I'll trust to my lions," Hartley grumbled. "I'm sending two with the owls."

"That's a good decision." Shea smiled at the boy.

She wondered if she was saying the right thing, wondered if she was raising him properly. She asked herself such questions every day, about all the lions, and the owls, and her sole little swan.

Shea wished that her husband, Bram, were still alive. But he had died years before, felled by a fever during the Uprising. Bram had died before the last rebels had been carted away, the rich manor fields salted.

Before Shea could lose herself in the memories of everything she had lost over so many years, Tain began to tuck the orphans into their beds. The oldest sungirl listened to the other sunchildren say their prayers, watched the children bow to the west and thank the sun for serving as their guide and inspiration as they toiled in the fields. Taking her cue from Shea's practiced supervision, Tain ignored the fact that no fields had been planted that year. She ignored the fact that they'd eaten their seed corn in the middle of winter.

Hartley put the lionchildren to bed, two to a cot, head to toe. Before he ordered his soldiers to sleep, he had them salute the sky. The Lion had risen early, hovering over the horizon in a dim spray of stars.

The owlchildren found their own way to their cots. They clustered into a tight knot to continue debating the ways of right and wrong, knowledge and ignorance. At last, they fell asleep, arguing about how they could know with certainty that the Owl would return to the night sky in seven days, as the constellation was supposed to do.

That left Shea awake with the swangirl, with the one child who stubbornly refused to sleep at night. Serena paced back and forth through the dark hours, already restless with the longing that should have carried her to the Swancastle. If the Swancastle were still receiving fosterlings. If there had been other swans nearby, to teach Serena the ways of right and wrong and decision-making. If the traditions of Amanthia had not been toppled in the Uprising.

Shea could not help but think of Larina, her own beautiful, lost swandaughter. More than twenty years before, Shea had labored through the night, pushing to bring Larina into the world while the Swan was still in the sky. Before Hartley and Tain were born in their distant villages . . . Before all the adult men in King Sin Hazar's kingdom had been wiped out by the Uprising and the plague of war . . . Before the orphans had found their way south from their war-ravaged pockets of Amanthia, before they fled the tattered remnants of the Uprising and discovered Shea. Long ago, Larina had crowned just before the Swan sank below the horizon, and Father Nariom had laughed as he tattooed silver wings beneath the newborn's eye.

Shea sighed and forbade herself to think of Larina's beautiful face. She thrust down the familiar sorrow and frustration as she shuffled off to her closet and her cold, empty cot. She prayed her nightly prayer to all the Thousand Gods that King Sin Hazar's madness would end, that the man would give up his idea of using children as his army to rebuild the strength he had lost in the Uprising, of using children to conquer the eastern kingdom of Liantine. If King Sin Hazar forfeited his mad plan, little Serena could go live in the Swancastle with whatever swans remained in the kingdom.

If only Serena were already grown . . . If only Serena could take charge and issue orders to lions and owls and suns, all alike. If only Serena could save the skychildren . . .

The next afternoon, Shea spread out her ragged blanket in the clearing, easing herself to the hard ground and calling the sunchildren to her. The boys and girls left their tattered baskets on the edges of the blanket and scrambled over each other, tumbling like puppies to be near the woman.

"Hush," Shea smiled. "We must rest now, while the sun is highest in the sky."

The children settled down quickly, exhausted by their search for berries, for roots, for anything edible in the picked-over woods. Dor, the youngest boy, climbed into Shea's lap, and she rested a soothing hand on his head. The child turned about to trample her skirts flat, and then he sighed deeply, wriggling toward his dreams.

Bees buzzed in the afternoon air, exploring the sweet autumn fruit in the baskets. Shea's eyelids grew heavy, and her head bobbed forward. She started awake twice, automatically noting both times that the lionchildren stood on the edge of the clearing. Of course, in these straitened times, the three young soldiers had no true weapons, but they gripped stout sticks, and they looked watchful.

Sometime later, Shea woke from a deeper sleep, startled by a rustling noise. She knew immediately that something was very wrong. A young man stood before her, dressed in ragged azure clothes. Blue. The color of King Sin Hazar's army.

When the youth saw that Shea was awake, he leaped forward, settling his cold dagger against her throat, where the skin sagged. His long hair was pulled back in a tight braid that stretched the skin around his eyes, twisting his face into a grimace. A vicious scar burned above his left cheek.

For a single dream-instant, Shea thought that she was looking at her own son. "Pom." Shea spoke softly, as if she feared to wake the sleeping children. This child had the same straight hair, the same nut-brown eyes. He had the same gawky frame of youth, of bones grown long before his body could fill out. Fifteen years old, she thought. Fifteen at most.

"Quiet, hag!" The boy swallowed his words in a growl, and Shea came fully awake, remembering that she was alone in a field with her orphans. Remembering that her Pom was grown. Grown and gone and dead.

Dor stirred in Shea's lap, shaking himself awake like a puppy. When he opened his eyes, he saw the dagger at Shea's throat, and he cried out, waking the other suns.

"Hush, little ones," Shea soothed. "This visitor doesn't mean us any harm."

"I'll show you harm!" the youth menaced, stepping back so that he could wave his blade. "I'll show all of you the meaning of the word!"

"Nonsense." Shea set Dor aside and clambered to her feet. She longed to look about for the lions, for her protectors. What could have happened to the guards? Had Hartley let them fall asleep? Well, all she could do was try to buy the lions time to recognize the danger, to save the skychildren. Shea stretched a soothing hand toward the warrior-child's scarred cheek.

Her heart twisted as she saw that his birthright tattoo had been scraped from his face. She ached for the skychild he had once been. She had heard tales of the king's Little Army. She knew that King Sin Hazar took all sorts of skychildren and turned them into fighters. Scraped away their tattoos, trained them in the camps. The Little Army was an abomination, a twisting of the sky-signs and the fates that men were meant to live by.

"What were you before the war came, lad?"

"I'm a soldier now, a soldier in the troops of King Sin Hazar."

"Aye," Shea answered gravely, as she had answered Pom's own brave declarations when he went off to join the king. "I can see that. But what mark did the king carve from your face?" The youth glared at her with hatred, and she had to fight to keep her voice even against her own fear, her own disgust for a king who could mutilate a child, for a child who would fight within such a system. "It can't have been a swan's wing—you're too harsh for that. I don't see you with the owl-sign, either, no deep thoughts for you. Perhaps the sun, but then you'd know better than to fight a lonely woman and her children. I'm betting on the lion, then. I'll wager you're a lionchild."

The youth's knife wavered as he listened, and she saw the acknowledgment spread across his face. She remembered assuring her own Pom, when he first learned about his place in the world, when he first learned that it was his lot to fight, to make war. Pom had been reluctant to go to the village, to work with the few ancient warriors who stayed at home during the Uprising, who stayed to teach children the ways of the lion. "Aye, son, there's nothing to be ashamed of. We need lions, to be strong and brave and true. Lions protect old women and their babes. There's no shame in being a lionboy."

"I'm not ashamed!" His face darkened around his puckered scar.

"Aye, aye! That's good and proper." She hastened to reassure him. She wanted him to set down his knife, to stop waving the weapon about. "Why *should* you be ashamed, fighting for good King Sin Hazar?"

As Shea spoke, the boy's lower lip began to quiver. Shea looked at his torn and filthy uniform, short in the sleeves, well above his ankles. A ratty dragon was frayed across his chest. The child's face was pinched; he looked hungrier than her own orphans.

She realized that this child-soldier was too far from any army to be a loyal scout. What had made the boy flee the king's troops? What had made him run away, after he'd been taken in, after he'd submitted to the loss of his birthright, to the scraping away of his skychild fate? Having survived such an attack, such a brutal uprooting, how much did the lionboy now hate and fear his king?

With a scarce-thought prayer to Wain, the god of fate, Shea plunged ahead: "You don't need to stay with King Sin Hazar, son. You can join my children and me. We've all sorts of creatures with us. Swans and owls and suns. And plenty from the Lion."

The youth snarled and lunged forward, leveling his knife against Shea's throat. "I've *captured* you! You're just trying to confuse me!"

"Not at all, young man. I never try to confuse my children." Shea raised her chin, drawing on an impossible stock of bravery. A lion threatening a sun . . . There was nothing in all of Shea's experience to explain a world gone so mad. "Toss away that knife, son, and have some of our food. Tain, bring this boy our berries." The lionboy's eyes darted to the baskets beside the oldest sungirl, and he swallowed audibly. The tendons in his neck stood out like blades of grass. The sunny fragrance of the fruit hung in the clearing, like a ribbon in a flirting girl's hair. "They're ripe," Shea crooned. "Full of juice. Sweet."

The youth lunged for the baskets. As he thrust his hands amid the berries, Shea's three lionchildren finally appeared from the edge of the woods, sticks and stones at the ready. "Drop our berries!" Hartley cried.

The soldier boy complied, but not before he'd been hit hard across the shoulders and the backs of his legs. Hartley turned to Shea, his face blazing red with more than the afternoon sun. "My lions and I . . . We saw a boar, at the edge of the woods. We were going to bring back fresh meat." The lion swallowed hard and refused to meet Shea's eyes. "It got away."

Before Shea could decide whether to offer comfort or remonstration, Hartley whirled on his prisoner. "What's your name, boy?"

Berry juice ran over the enemy boy's fingers like blood. Hartley had to raise his stick, brandishing it like a bludgeon, before the youth spat, "Crestman." Before he could say more, Hartley snarled a command, and the lions secured him with their own ragged clothes, gagging him with harsh bonds.

That night, Shea waited until the sunchildren were asleep, until Serena was walking her restless swanwalk on the roof, before she summoned together the lions and the owls. Crestman sat across the room, lashed to a chair. He had managed to fall into a fitful sleep, obviously exhausted by his days of travel. Shea cast a glance toward the boy, then she addressed her children. "The king is getting closer. Crestman must be a deserter, but King Sin Hazar's recruiters are probably not far behind. We . . . we have to decide what to do." She swallowed hard. Decision wasn't her job. She was a sun, after all.

"Can there be any real question?" Hartley demanded. "If you give that Crestman to my lions, we'll make sure his trackers never find us. We can leave his body far from here. The king's men won't be able to ask us difficult questions about one of their deserters, even if they *do* find us."

"He's still a child," argued Torino, the eldest owl. "You know the teachings of the Thousand Gods. We cannot kill a child."

"Who says he's a child?" Hartley replied. "He's old enough to travel across the countryside on his own. He's old enough to join King Sin Hazar."

"He can't be any older than you are!" Torino retorted.

"And perhaps *I'm* not a child," Hartley countered. "Besides, that Crestman was ready to kill Shea." Hartley raised a hand to the tattoo on his cheek, using his blunt fingertip to emphasize his lion-power.

"He didn't kill her, though." Torino did not back down.

"You owls are supposed to be the thinkers!" Hartley rounded on the owlchildren, and Shea heard the boy's anger at himself, anger that his lions had let Crestman creep into the clearing. Hartley and his lions had failed the skychildren, and the breach could have been deadly for them all. "You're supposed to be the ones who find answers!"

One of the youngest owls climbed to her feet. "We're owls, Lion. Don't you doubt that." She turned to her fellows. "Come on, then. Like Father Nariom taught us, down in the village. Premise: We may kill to protect our safety."

"Counterpremise," another owl responded immediately. "No child may be killed."

"Premise," hooted a third child. "Children who fight for King Sin Hazar threaten our safety."

"You don't know that he *was* fighting for the king!" squawked one of the youngest owls. "Shea says he was deserting!" The debate disintegrated into childish argument.

Shea raised a hand to her aching eyes, shaking her head as she stumbled to the doorway of the small house. The night was flooded with light. The moon was full, so brilliant that it nearly drowned out the Lion.

As Shea listened to the wind in the trees at the edge of her clearing, she was carried back to a time when all the skychildren had known their places. Back when Bram and Pom and Larina had still been alive, when she had not been responsible for this motley crew, for this tangle of right and wrong and maybe. Long ago, the king had been a good man, a man who provided for his people, even if he did sit on his throne, leagues and leagues away. No one had feared the king in those days, before the Uprising.

Shea closed her eyes, and she remembered Larina's childish laughter, her joy at the world around her. The little girl had thrown her arms around Shea's neck each morning, her silver-marked cheek smooth against Shea's sun-starred one. Even now, the woman could feel Larina inside her breath, inside her bones, and for just an instant, Shea heard her daughter whisper in her ear. "I love you, Mummy. I know you'll always be here for me."

Before Shea could answer, she was jerked back to her cottage. For an instant, she thought it was her own dreams that had pulled her, but then she heard the muffled cry again. She was at Crestman's side before the other children could reach him.

The young soldier was lashed to the one sturdy chair in the hut, his arms pulled tight behind him. A rag was bound across his eyes, and a gag slashed his parched lips. He moaned and rocked his chair back and forth, dreaming.

"Hush," she crooned, resting her chapped hand against his cheek. "Hush, little lion. It's all right. You're in my hut, here with your brothers and sisters. You'll be fine. You'll be safe."

Crestman quieted beneath her soothing touch, never fully waking. Shea sat by his chair long into the night, rocking back and forth and thinking of Pom. Thinking of her lost son, who had been among the first wave of children sucked into the whirlwind of King Sin Hazar's schemes, after the Uprising had been put down. Shea thought of the wise men in the village who had first decided to rebel against their king because of taxes, because of cold, hard *money*. She thought of starvation and honor and helpless, hopeless children.

The next morning, Hartley confronted Shea as Tain served up bowls of acorn porridge. Shea knew the gruel was bitter, but at least she could put something in each of the small bellies beneath her roof. She scavenged an extra bowl and started to carry it to Crestman.

"The prisoner may not eat." Hartley's voice was flat.

"Nonsense! He's a growing boy!"

"He's a growing boy who would have killed you. You risk our safety and your own if you feed him."

"Hartley, I can't let him starve to death. I'd be no better than King Sin Hazar."

"Torino," Hartley appealed.

The owl chimed in immediately. "The lion speaks the truth, Sunwoman. That soldier intended to kill us. To kill us and steal our food."

"But what—" Shea almost stopped, overwhelmed by the notion that she—a sunwoman—was debating an owl. "What if he *wasn't* deserting? I thought he was. It looked like he was. But what if he was just gathering troops to bring to King Sin Hazar?"

"Is that any better?" Torino cocked his head to one side, and he sounded honestly curious about Shea's thoughts.

"That means he's not a bad person. He's merely trying to do as his king commands. He's merely trying to recruit for the Little Army."

"But his king would command him to take all the boys. And Serena, too."

Of course King Sin Hazar wanted the boys—whatever their sky-sign. And he wanted Serena. He wanted all the swanchildren in Amanthia, all the potential leaders from Shea's rebellious province, even though the Uprising was over, had been over for years.

Poor Serena. The pale, moonstruck child was sleeping even now, huddled in her tiny private room beneath the eaves. The sun's strong rays were too great for Serena—how could the swan-girl possibly survive King Sin Hazar's military camp?

"Very well," Shea acceded after a long minute's indecision. The words tasted bitter in her mouth. "To save my children."

Hartley nodded his approval. "All right, then. Let's get everyone organized. We'll head to the stream and try to catch some fish. The trout should finally have begun their run."

"Watch your step, Lion!" Shea snapped. "We sunfolk know about gathering food, not you lions. Have you already forgotten what happened when you decided to hunt a boar?"

Hartley looked abashed, and Shea swallowed the anger that constricted her throat. First she was arguing with an owl, and now she was angry at a lion! What was the world coming to? What evil had King Sin Hazar worked, even in her own house?

There was no sense in making Hartley look foolish, especially in front of the others. "You're right, though," Shea said after an uneasy pause. "Fish would be sweet on the tongue."

Only when Hartley had gathered the children together did Shea decide not to accompany them. "You go ahead, Hartley. Take the owls along with the suns. They all need sunlight and fresh air. No, no, Torino. No arguments. Take your owls and play your debates by the brook. Tain, keep an eye on everyone."

"But aren't you coming?" Tain seemed concerned.

"I have things to do here. This house doesn't take care of itself."

Hartley frowned. "I can't spare extra lions to guard you."

"Nonsense. You need to leave someone to watch over Serena, in any case."

"But there's an additional risk, with the prisoner."

"With a fifteen-year-old boy, tied to a chair? I may be a sunwoman, Hartley, but I'm not daft. I can take care of myself." Hartley grumbled, and he left his two best lions to guard the cottage. He glanced back with every step, but he led the other children toward the distant riverbank.

Shea made sure that the lions left behind were busy scanning the horizon before she ducked back inside her cottage. She was moving to the hearth before she knew it, looking down at Crestman.

Crestman. Such a sturdy name for so young a soldier.

Hartley had tightened the youth's gag, and the rough cloth sawed into the corners of the young lion's mouth. His blindfold had slipped off sometime during the night, and he glared at her, his scarred cheek livid in the gloom beneath the rafters. Shea thought of Pom, of the way her son had raged when she had punished him for stealing boiled sweets in the village. "*I* had nothing to do with this, child. The lions protect us. You should remember that much, from the days before you cast your lot with King Sin Hazar. Now I'll feed you, if you swear to stay quiet. If the lions outside hear you, I'll have Hartley to answer to. Do you promise?"

She held a bowl of porridge so that he could see the food he was missing. She imagined his belly clenching in hunger. Berries were no meal for a growing boy. Besides, he'd eaten their meager hoard hours before. At last, Crestman nodded. She set the bowl on the floor as she loosened his gag.

"Let me go!" he whispered as soon as he had worked spit back into his mouth.

"I can't do that, boy."

"They'll kill me!"

"And King Sin Hazar will kill us all, when you lead him here. Kill us or steal my boys for the Little Army." Shea kept her voice quiet, fighting for reason as if she were an owl.

"I won't lead him here. I promise. You were right. I *was* leaving the king's army. I don't want to be a soldier anymore."

"He'll find you, though. He'll track you down and bring you back to his camp."

"But I won't tell about you! I promise!"

"You'll have no choice. We've heard stories about the king, about what he does to the children who desert him."

"No worse than what your lions will do to me!"

"They'll do what they need to. They'll do what's best for all of us."

"For all of *you*. Not for me." Crestman's voice broke across his harsh whisper. "You know they'll kill me." His eyes brimmed with tears.

"I know nothing of the sort. Father Nariom has taught my little owls well. They'll think on this and decide what is right. Now, are you going to eat or not? I need to sweep the floor."

For a moment, she thought that Crestman would send her away. Then, the boy's belly rumbled, loud enough that she could hear it in the close room. "I'll eat."

She fed him the bitter gruel, using the spoon to wipe spilled porridge from his chin. She ignored the tears that trickled down his cheeks, silver against the scar from his missing tattoo.

The sun was setting by the time the other children returned to the cottage. Shea heard them before she saw them; their voices bounced off the trees. When the group emerged from the forest, they were in high spirits, singing and whooping. Four of the children held strings of fish—lithe, silver trout that danced in the dying sunlight.

Shea crowed praise for her charges, lavishing compliments as Tain cooked supper. She longed to give some of the flaky fish to Crestman, but she dared not. She had replaced his gag at the first sound of the other children, and now she tried to ignore the guilt that tugged at the back of her mind.

Hartley turned to her when everyone had finished eating, after the children had sucked the sweet flesh from heads and tails and fins. Shea's belly tightened at the grave expression on his face. "We've decided. Crestman must die."

"No!"

"We have no choice. If we let him go, he'll likely be caught by King Sin Hazar's men. When they're through torturing him, they'll come after us. At the very least, they'll take Serena and conscript my lions. They might take *all* the boys. They might burn down the house. They might kill us all."

"So we'll keep him. We'll make him one of us!"

"We can't trust him, Shea, and I don't have enough lions to watch him every day. The owls finally agreed. We'll take him down to the stream and drown him. It will look like an accident, in case any of King Sin Hazar's soldiers come through here later."

"He's just a boy!" Shea exclaimed in anguish, and the words sounded oddly familiar, as if she had wailed them in the past.

"He's a soldier."

"Did all of you agree to this?" Shea rounded on the other children. Tain returned her stare placidly. Some of the younger suns looked abashed, but the lions all stared back without blinking. Shea caught a couple of the owls tilting their heads, studying her as if she were some curious specimen.

Torino stepped forward and nodded deferentially. "All of us discussed it. We owls debated it for the better part of the day. There are no alternatives—the soldier must die."

"Crestman! Say his name, at least."

Torino shook his head. "His name has no meaning. He's the enemy. His death will enable us all to live."

Shea looked at her charges. Hartley gazed back with the solemn expression he used when he assigned his lions their guard posts. Torino blinked hard, but his face betrayed no emotion.

I want things the way they were, Shea thought. I want my own son and daughter. They were *good* children. They would know right from wrong. Shea raised her chin, and announced, "I want this brought before the swan."

"What!"

She had surprised Hartley. "I want to take this to the swan. Let the swan make the decision."

"Shea, you know that the Swancastle is empty. King Sin Hazar came through there first of all, when he began assembling the Little Army. You told us yourself that your own daughter was taken."

She set her jaw against the memory. "We have our own swan. We'll ask her."

"Serena?" Hartley almost snorted his surprise.

"Serena."

"Don't be ridiculous! She's a child—"

"Serena," Shea repeated firmly, feeling the rightness of what she demanded.

"Fine." Hartley squinted in the dim light and nodded to Tain. "Fetch her downstairs."

Only a moment later, the oldest sungirl led Serena into the room. The little swan's pale features were creased into a frown, and her nose twitched at the lingering aroma of trout. She had eaten her share, along with the better part of Tain's portion, before she had gone up to her room.

Crestman was hustled upright, his hands bound tight behind his back. His mouth was still lashed tight with the gag. Hartley appointed two lions to stand beside the soldier. "The prisoner is to stay silent," Hartley snapped. "If he so much as sneezes, kill him. Do you understand?" The last question was directed at the trussed-up child-soldier, not the guards. Crestman merely glared at the older lion.

Hartley turned back to Serena. "Swangirl," he said, and he made a stiff, formal bow. "We would have you decide a matter of justice."

Serena sniffed again, but a light of power kindled at the back of her eyes. "Aye?"

"The lions and the owls have concluded that this prisoner must die. The sunwoman thinks his life should be spared. What do you say?"

Serena's voice went soft with wonder. "You want me to decide?"

Hartley responded gruffly, but his words were laden with ingrained respect. "You're the swan. The only one we have."

Shea forced herself to step forward. She must speak out against her lion. Hartley was wrong; Torino was wrong. Tain, too. They were only children. She was an old woman, and she knew what was right. Shea swallowed hard and worked her throat to get past a lifetime of belief. "Serena, Crestman does not deserve to die."

"*Crestman,*" Hartley's voice grated over the lionname, "is a traitor to his people. He came to kill us. He raised steel against the sunwoman as the children gathered berries. He belongs to King Sin Hazar. We have no idea what deviltry he learned in the Little Army's camps. He probably knows a dozen ways to kill you, swangirl."

"He's just a boy!" Shea cried, and now she remembered the first time that she had wailed those words. She remembered receiving the terrible news that Pom had been cut down in King Sin Hazar's camps. Her only son had been murdered in the barracks of the first corps of child-soldiers, killed when he refused to go along with some brutal Little Army training regimen. Learning of her loss, Shea had cried out even before she realized that she was alone, that she had lost both Pom and Larina, and Bram so long ago. For just an instant, she had pictured herself kneeling in the middle of King Sin Hazar's camps, on her knees among the children who served the king's cause. She had seen herself holding Pom's body, stretching out his boy-arms and his boy-legs.

But she had never seen him. She had never learned what King Sin Hazar's troops did with Pom's body, although she had heard the rumors about archery practice and the children's ravenous hounds. Shea swallowed hard, knowing that she needed to plead her case, knowing that she needed to make Serena understand. The words would not come, though. Shea could only manage, "Serena, he's a child."

"We're all children!" Hartley spat. "We're all children, and if you let that one live, then all the rest of us may die."

Serena looked from Hartley to Shea and back again. A look of wonder brightened her pinched face. "You'll do whatever I say?"

"Aye," Hartley vowed promptly.

"Aye," Shea managed after a much longer pause. Serena was a swangirl. Swans must be obeyed. That was what Shea had always believed, before the Uprising. Before the Little Army. Before children had their tattoos carved from their faces.

"Then I say the soldier . . . dies." Serena's eyes grew wide at the release of pent breath from the children. She smiled as if she'd just discovered a new game. "Kill him at dawn."

All through the night, Shea lay on her cot, listening to her own slow breathing. She had been a fool to bring the matter before Serena, before a six-year-old child who had no concept of life and death. What had Shea been thinking? Why had she thought that Serena would have the maturity, the grace, of a grown, trained swan? Certainly, Serena was not *evil,* she just did not recognize

the power that she held in her silver-winged tattoo. She had had
no swans to teach her, to show her the way.

It had taken Shea hours to get the excited children into bed,
to calm them after the confrontation on the hearth. She had finally resorted to brewing a posset, surreptitiously adding a fistful
of slumberleaf to the dregs of the day's thin milk. She covered
the taste of the sharp herb with a generous dollop of honey, the
last in the bare pantry. Even Tain had not suspected her duplic-
ity.

Now, Shea dragged herself to the door, grabbing her ragged
shawl against the night's chill. The Lion was low in the sky.

Sunchildren gave way to the sky in all things. So many suns
were born, born to toil in the daylight hours. Born to a hard life
of labor, simple, good labor, like the simple, good light of the
sun.

Sun, then Lion, then Owl, and Swan, that was the order of the
stars, the order of the world. That was the truth that Shea had
lived since she was a girl. She had taught that truth to Hartley
and Tain, to Pom and Larina, to all her skychildren.

Another star rose on the horizon, the first tip of the Swan's
wing unfolding into the night. Shea closed her eyes and took a
deep breath. As she exhaled slowly, she turned back to the cottage. The floor creaked as she walked toward the hearth, but she
knew that the drugged children would sleep through any disturbance.

Crestman was watching her, his eyes glinting above his gag.
His scar stood out against his pale flesh, glistening reminder of
King Sin Hazar. As Shea knelt beside the youth, she could smell
the sweat on him, the cold, adult fear that slicked his flesh beneath his bonds.

"I can't let you go back to the king," she hissed into the still
night. He blinked, as if he understood. "I can't let you lead that
man to my babes."

Shea thought of the river that flowed through the woods, the
cool, clear water that could steal this boy's life. Her hands shook
as she knelt beside him. She could not trust him alone in the
world; he'd surely bring King Sin Hazar's men. Even if the boy

did not intentionally seek out the king's soldiers, he'd be found, tortured.

He needed help. He needed Shea.

The lion's eyes were bright as she tugged at his bonds, and she shook her head as she slipped off his gag. "Silence, boy," she hissed. Then, almost to herself, she muttered, "It's time we changed things."

Change. So much would be different. The other children would be on their own. Alone. Abandoned.

No, she told herself. Not abandoned. Shea had trained Tain and Hartley. She had raised her oldest sundaughter and lionson to protect her other children. She had prepared them, in case she died in the night. Shea's brood could survive without her.

If the king's men did not come and take them. If Crestman did not harm them.

Shea had no choice.

She would have to decide which road to take. She would have to decide when they should eat, when they should move, when they should lie low. So much would be frightening, and terrible, and necessary.

Shea picked free the last knot, and then she helped the lion to his feet. She steadied him as the blood flowed back into his legs. "Wait a minute. Wait until you can feel your feet."

Ignoring her, Crestman bolted for the door. He stumbled on his blood-starved limbs, though, and she caught him before he fell. Her fingers were tight on his arm as she jerked him around to face her. "I'll have none of that, lionboy! If we're going to survive on the road, you'll listen to me." Shea swallowed hard and raised her chin. "You'll do as *I* say."

Crestman stared at her for a long minute, and she read the emotions on his face as clearly as if they were stars in the sky. He wanted to speak out. He wanted to remind her that *he* was a lion, that she was only a sun. He wanted to put Shea in her place, a laborer, a worker. Not a thinker. Not a soldier.

Shea stood her ground, though. She tightened her grip on the lionboy's arm, her fingers pinching until she felt bone. At last,

Crestman nodded, a single, taut bob of his head that told her he understood. He knew that things had changed.

They disappeared into the forest as the Swan crested over the horizon.

3

Rani stood on the deck of the ship, looking out at a shoreline that seemed a lifetime away. As the ship pitched forward, Rani was forced to grab for the railing to keep her balance. For the past three days, whenever the sailors had bothered to speak to her, it seemed that they commented on how smooth the ocean was. In fact, the wind had been still enough the previous day that the captain had been forced to employ his sweepers, teams of four men who walked giant, hinged oars back and forth across the deck, driving the boat forward through the water. The shuffle of the seamen's feet had been drowned out by the songs they sang, stirring chanties like soldiers at their drink.

Today, though, the wind was back, and the ship lurched up the coast with a renewed speed. Rani's belly turned as the craft crashed down into yet another ocean trough. The salt smell of the ocean spray hung at the back of her throat, sharp and caustic.

That morning, Mair—despite her broken arm—had forced Rani to gnaw on a slice of rough bread. Rani had given in after only a few minutes of cross argument. Despite the agony of being tossed on the ocean, she *was* hungry. She had even managed to keep her rebellious belly under control as she chewed the tough crust. Managed, that was, until Mair passed her a slice of ripe cheese. The creamy texture of the stuff made Rani's skin crawl, and when the musky odor hit her nose she scrambled out of the tiny cabin, desperately climbing hand over hand for the deck and the railing and the open water that carried away her meager breakfast.

Now, Rani stared into the freshening breeze and forced herself to take deep breaths. Seven days, Bashi had said. Seven days from Moren to Amanth, the capital of Amanthia far to the north. They had already been traveling for three—they were nearly halfway there.

"Feeling any better?"

Rani turned to see that Mair had crept up behind her. That was another problem with this cursed ship. It creaked so much, and the wind thumped against the sails so loudly, that Rani could not hear anyone approach. "Not much," Rani admitted. "I can't understand why you aren't as sick as I am."

"You sound as if you'd like me to be." Mair's tone was exasperated, but Rani only shrugged. The motion was easier than speaking. There was a long pause, and then the Touched girl said, "I thought it would be cooler up here. It's so close in that cabin, I thought I'd faint."

Rani turned to look at her friend sharply. The cabin had been warm, but the deck was actually chilly. Immediately after being sick, Rani had settled a cloak over her shoulders, and she was alarmed to see that Mair bore no protection against the stiff breeze. "You'll catch cold."

"Not I." Mair grimaced.

Rani brushed the back of her hand across the other girl's brow, ignoring her own angry scab from Maradalian's talon. "You're burning up!"

"I'm better than I was." Mair shrugged off the attention like a restless child. "It's just a bit of fever. Nothing important."

"Nothing important!"

"It's just because of my arm, you know." Mair shrugged with one shoulder, only to make a face against the obvious pain that the movement caused her.

"It still hurts, then."

"A little," Mair conceded.

"I knew that cursed soldier didn't know what he was doing! How could you let him set your arm?"

"What else was I supposed to do? You don't have the strength to have done it, especially when your own palm was still bleeding. 'That cursed soldier' may not have known the first thing about medicine, but at least he did what I told him to do."

Rani's belly flipped again as she remembered their rest stop at the edge of the River Yman. At least Bashi had been true to his word—he had let them stop and set Mair's arm. But even he had not been prepared for the pain the injury caused her. The prince had blanched almost as white as Mair when the girl cried out, and he had nervously scooped up water from the river to bathe her face. Rani had pushed him aside, though, before he could provide that service. She did not want him anywhere near her friend, anywhere where he could work more harm. She did not want to hear that he had not meant to hurt them. He had not meant for everything to spin out of control.

"But will it heal properly?" Rani asked, forcing her voice to a calmness that she did not feel.

"How can I know?" Mair let her voice shrug and spared her shoulders. "I've done all I can. After all, I'm just a Touched brat from the City streets, not a chirurgeon. Maybe Bashi will let us see a healer in Amanthia."

"Something to look forward to." Rani spat into the water. "That and getting off this miserable boat."

"We might be wishing for this boat, before all this is over." Mair looked back at the coastline, at the shore that unrolled beside them. It was odd, Rani thought. They were close enough to see the land, close enough to see the distinct line where earth met sea. But they might as well be leagues and leagues away for all the good it did them. They could not make out any settlements along the water's edge, and they were too far away to see any people. They were as lost as if they wandered in a forest.

As if to underscore their isolation, the seamen took that opportunity to sluice down the deck of their creaking craft. Bashi had explained to Rani the first night that they had boarded the boat—the ocean water made the wood swell, tightening the joints and keeping the craft seaworthy. Rani understood the logic, but she deplored the need. The tang of the ocean water, fish and salt, was enough to raise acid again at the back of her throat. The water seemed to leach out the stench of the tar that sealed ropes and joints about the craft. Resignedly, Rani clambered onto a coil of rough hemp, trying unsuccessfully to keep her leather soles dry. After she had helped to steady Mair against the sea bath, Rani turned back to the deck and the railing.

The breeze of their passing really *did* make her feel better, she reminded herself. Breathe deeply. Again. They would gain the shore eventually.

Rani forced herself to watch the ocean water split open by the boat's prow. The craft created an ever-changing wake, a constantly emerging pattern that Rani could never hope to capture in the stained glass that had been her work, that remained her dream. The sea leaped and swirled like billows of white lace, like the fine garments of the delicate wardrobe that Rani had eschewed in King Halaravilli's court.

Squinting into the froth, Rani could make out dark shapes that skipped across the ship's wake. At first, she could not decipher what she was seeing—there were only dark shadows against the white, white water. Then, Rani cried out in surprise.

The shadows were fish!

Almost against her will, Rani found herself smiling. The giant fish leaped over the boat's wake, skipping on top of the water, then diving deep beneath the craft. The morning sun glistened on their sleek bodies, reflecting off their black-and-white flanks. When Rani leaned out over the prow, she could see that each fish had a long nose; each appeared to grin at his fellows as the creatures slipped through the boat's feathery wake.

"Look!" Rani exclaimed to Mair, but before the Touched girl could step up to the prow, Prince Bashanorandi strode forward, pushing his way to the point of the ship's deck. Rani had long since stopped being startled when the prince materialized from nowhere on the ship. Besides, she was so taken with the playful beasts that she was willing to set aside her anger momentarily.

"Bashanorandi." She nodded in greeting. Since the violence on the hillside, she had been careful to give Bashi his full name.

Mair was not so forgiving, though. The Touched girl shifted her arm in its sling, wincing at the pain as the ship chopped its way through a particularly high wave. "Your Highness," she gritted through set teeth. "Rai, I beg your pardon," she said, pointedly turning her back on the prince. "I'm going belowdecks for a rest. The air is not as fresh up here as I had hoped."

Rani stared after her friend, her jaw loose as she watched Bashi register the insult. What was Mair thinking? How could she dare be so rude to Bashi when he commanded the troops that held them captive? Even as Rani admired Mair's courage, she shook her head in despair. It would do no good to anger Bashi now. Not when he held the only key to their bonds. Not when he was the one who would decide if they would go forward into unknown lands or back to the comfort of the City.

Prince Bashanorandi stared after the Touched girl with a look of true hatred in his eyes. "You'd do well to stay away from that one, Ranita Glasswright."

"What do you mean?" Rani exclaimed, momentarily forgetting that Bashi called her by her guild name out of mockery. "She's my friend!"

"She's no friend to anyone but herself. She's Touched. You know they can't be trusted."

"She's the only family I have, Bashanorandi." Rani's anger was stirred by the prince's superior tone. "Surely you haven't forgotten how difficult it is to live without family."

The jibe was a deep one. Rani had lost her family two years ago, but the fault had not been her own. Her brother had dragged her mother and father and all her siblings into the king's dungeons, and not one had emerged alive. But that was different from Bashanorandi's loss. Rani's family had only been *accused* of being traitors. In truth, *her* family had been innocent victims.

"I forget nothing, Ranita Glasswright." Bashi managed to keep his tone steady, even casual, but Rani saw the pulse that beat strong in his throat.

This time, Rani registered the cruel teasing of her guild name; she heard the prince's certainty that she would never succeed in rebuilding the destroyed glasswrights. She made her voice cold, almost as cold as Mair's had been. "She's my friend, Your Highness. She stood by me when no others would. Surely even you understand the value of that?"

Bashi looked as if he'd been slapped. His pale blue eyes blinked as he measured the passion in Rani's voice. "What do you mean? I understand the value of friendship. I understand the value of faithful friends. Do you realize that I have lost them all, Ranita? Do you realize that I used to be a prince among men, and now I'm nothing but an outcast traitor, despite the fact that I've done nothing to earn men's distrust?" The prince spoke without any of his usual haughtiness, as if he were truly inquiring about Rani's thoughts, about her beliefs.

Bashi's tone gave Rani courage to answer from her heart. "You can't understand faithfulness, Bashanorandi. Otherwise, you'd never tell me not to trust a girl who has *proven* herself my friend. You'd never advise me not to trust a girl who has been injured in service to me. She's beside me! She rose up from her own sickbed even now to make sure that *I* was all right."

"I'm saying you can't trust a brat who was bred in the streets and will do anything to put food in her own mouth."

"And you think that your own twisted birth makes you so much more trustworthy?" Rani retorted before she had a chance to think about her words.

Bashi's eyes blazed beneath his ginger hair, and he reached out to grab at Rani's face. He caught her chin between his fingers, pinching hard through the flesh to her bone. "I had no control over my birth! I chose neither my father nor my mother, and I did not ask to play out that farce in King Shanoranvilli's court."

The prince's fingers dug into Rani's flesh as if Bashi intended to sculpt new bones for her. Rani looked into the youth's eyes with terror, wondering what he would do, how he would focus his anger. She longed to point out the complete illogic of his argument, to show him that he was merely proving what she herself had said. Bashi had had no say in his life, and he'd been scarred. Mair, too, had not chosen to be Touched.

But Rani dared not speak. She dared not make any attempt to force words past Bashi's iron grip. Tears pricked at the corners of her eyes, unbidden. The sign of weakness only tightened Bashi's fingers more, and his wrist trembled. Then, like a drunken man pushing away more wine, the prince thrust Rani away, shoving her toward the railing that protected the boat's prow.

Rani clutched the wooden support and forced herself to take deep breaths. She forbade herself to raise a hand to her face, to finger the bruises that she knew would be swimming to the surface of her flesh. Instead, she concentrated on quieting her rebellious belly, on breathing past the pain in her jaw. She let the breeze of the ship's passing carry away her tears.

"Ranita—" Bashi began, and she felt him step nearer. There was a note of panic in his voice, a true fear that appeared to spring from deep inside his mind. She did not want to hear a prince's fear, though. She did not want to hear an awkward apology. She did not want Bashi to change from evil to good, and possibly back again.

Rani forced herself to gaze out over the prow. Incredibly, the sleek black-and-white fish still frolicked in the wake, oblivious to the angry drama played out above them. When Bashi did not leave, Rani finally managed to speak, determined to shatter the heavy, awkward silence as if it were a piece of flawed glass. "Look at the fish."

"They're dolphins," the prince answered dully. Nevertheless, even he could not ignore the leaping creatures, and Rani caught a loosening in the tension across his lips. "They're all through these waters. They're not fish, though."

"Not fish!" Rani snorted, losing her resolve in a rush of disdain. "Of course they're fish. They've got fins and a tail!"

"Stick to things you know, Ranita Glasswright. Dolphins bear their young live, like a bitch or a sow."

"What difference does that make?"

"According to Epidemian the Philosopher, no fish bears its young alive. The dolphins are smarter than fish, too. They've been known to guide lost fishermen home to their ports."

"According to Epidemian," Rani sneered. "You're quite the scholar, aren't you?"

"King Halaravilli saw to it that I was educated. The king does not want to be shamed by a bastard brother's ignorance."

Rani looked away from Bashi's bitterness, letting her eyes

roam toward the coastline. She regretted her rash words, if only
because they had sparked Bashi's anger once again. Rani attempted to build a bridge to her captor. "King Halaravilli is not
ashamed of you."

Bashi barked a harsh laugh, and for an instant, Rani could see
the vulpine lines of his cheekbones, the heritage of his traitor
father. "Lies do not become you, Ranita Glasswright."

"Why do you call me that? My guild does not exist anymore."

"What else should I call you? You're no longer a merchant.
Even if you consort with the Touched, you're not one of them.
Would you rather be a soldier, like that traitor Farantili? Or should
I bow before you and call you a noblewoman?"

Rani's stomach tightened as she thought of Farantili, of the
grizzled soldier who had done nothing wrong, who had had no
reason to pay with his life. She forced herself to ignore the scorn
behind Bashi's last question as she stated: "I think of myself as
Rani Trader. That was my name the longest. That's what I will
call myself until my guild has been rebuilt."

"What do you trade then, Rani? What do you barter?"

Rani stared down at the water, wondering how she could answer the question. She had made her family wealthy by finding
patterns in their wares, by setting their goods out to best advantage. Now, she struggled to find the pattern, to find the logic in
Bashanorandi kidnapping two common women and dragging them
north. She spoke without being certain of what she would say
before she formed the words. "Let us go, Bashanorandi."

"What?"

"Let Mair and me go. We aren't worth anything to you. Amanthia won't set any stock in us. We're not nobles. You can't ransom off a caste-skipping merchant and a Touched girl. Set us
ashore and go on your way. We'll hardly delay you, and you can
travel faster if you don't have to keep us under control."

Bashanorandi looked at her for long enough that she believed
he was considering her plea. Before he could answer, though,
one of the sailors approached. The seaman bowed as he drew
near, and his frown furrowed the tattoo of a sun that sprawled
beneath his left eye. The man's skin was so sun-dark that his tat-

too was almost lost, just more wrinkles in a deeply lined face. He swallowed hard, then spoke directly to Bashi. "I beg your pardon, my prince. You asked to be informed when we approach any of the coastal towns. Riversmeet is just beyond that point of land. It will be in sight shortly."

"Thank you." Bashi nodded curtly and dismissed the sailor with a wave of his hand. "Parkman!" he called, glancing past Rani toward the ship's main mast.

Rani had not paid attention to the soldier who stood behind her, even though the fighting man was the one who had murdered Farantili. Bashi had his soldiers about him all the time on the boat, as if he feared for his safety. Or as if he believed that the guards would bolster his status as he headed into a strange land. Now, Parkman stepped forward, settling one meaty hand on his short sword. He squinted in the morning light, wrinkling the tattooed lion beneath his left eye. "Yes, my lord?"

"Take Ranita Glasswright belowdecks. Make sure that she stays there until we've passed Riversmeet."

"What!" Rani squawked, already feeling her stomach clench. She whirled to face Bashi, but he had turned back to the boat's prow and the foamy swath the vessel cut through the ocean. "My lord! Why are you doing this?" When Bashi did not reply, Rani turned on the soldier. "What have I done? Why am I being punished?"

Parkman glanced uneasily at Bashi, but when the prince remained silent, the soldier grumbled a reply. "We'll be coming on a city, when we round that point. His lordship does not want to risk your sending a message."

"A message? Who, exactly, would I be signaling? And with what?"

"His lordship won't take the risk."

Rani started to sputter, even as the soldier reached for his short sword. Before the curved weapon could clear its oiled scabbard, though, Bashi stifled a groan. "Just go, Ranita."

"I'll be sick down there."

"Nonsense. The sea is quite smooth."

"Perhaps to you," Rani argued. "To me, it feels like I'm trying to stand on a slatted cart pulled by a team of unmatched oxen. Please, Bashanorandi!"

Bashi flicked a quick blue glance toward Parkman. "Now. Man, take Ranita Glasswright belowdecks and make sure that she stays there. Mair, too."

Desperate to avoid the stinking hold, with its hot, stale air, Rani clutched at the wooden railing, scarcely flinching as her grip stretched the scab across her palm. "Please, Your Highness. The breeze is the only thing that helps! Just let me watch the fi—, the dolphins! I promise—"

As if in response to Rani's plea, the dolphins chose that moment to leap clear of the ocean. For just an instant, the four marine acrobats were suspended in the air, curving in an impossibly graceful arch above the water.

This time, though, Rani saw that the sleek black-and-white creatures were not alone in the sea. As she watched the lithe bodies return to the water, a darker shape loomed out of the shadow of the boat, gliding-up from the darkness.

Rani watched in horror as the shadow solidified into a silver-flanked body. She could make out a yawning mouth, with line after line of pointed white teeth. As Rani cried out, the giant shark snapped at one of the dolphins, sawing at the black-and-white flesh for one terrible instant. The foam from the boat's prow ran crimson, then the shark disappeared beneath the craft. The other dolphins took only an instant to recover from the danger, then they swam out to sea, their arched backs laboring beneath the suddenly chilled sun.

Rani stared at the patch of water that had flowed red. Already the shark had disappeared, and the playful dolphin was nothing but a memory.

Bashi's voice rang out across the prow. "Parkman, take her below, or I'll find a man who can."

Rani turned away from the cruel ocean and made her way to the ladder and the rolling, stinking darkness belowdecks.

*   *   *

King Halaravilli slammed his fist against the council table, scattering the rolls of parchment that littered the surface. "Dammit, man! I *know* we aren't prepared to invade Amanthia!"

This cursed council meeting had gone even worse than Hal had anticipated. The royal councillors were little more than ill-bred children, each squabbling for a piece of honey bread that he thought should be his, and his alone.

Hal resisted the urge to run his fingers through his unruly dark hair. The gesture would only make him look ill at ease. Ill at ease and juvenile and unprepared to deal with the senior lords in his kingdom . . . He stifled a sigh and forced his voice to an even tone. "I'm not suggesting that we raid the north. I'm only suggesting that we need more information. We need to send a trusted agent to parley with Sin Hazar and determine his demands."

Determine his demands. Check his hands. Ride the lands.

The singsong rhymes rolled about in Hal's skull. He'd spent years protecting himself behind a facade of idiocy, building up wall after wall of inane babble. Now, he knew enough to not speak aloud the rhythms that rolled behind his eyes, but he could not silence the voices, could not still the beasts that had gnawed through his brain for seventeen years.

"Your Highness," Duke Puladarati spoke as if he were chiding a wayward toddler. "This may not be the time to send someone north. We don't know that Sin Hazar was even involved with the abduction."

Hal whirled on the duke. The silver-maned man had long fought his king in the council chamber, questioning each and every decision that Hal attempted to make. The entire court knew that Puladarati had chafed at King Halaravilli's emancipation the year before. Of course, a duke was powerful in the realm, but a regent . . . A regent had been able to command the entire kingdom.

Now, Hal let some of his frustration with his erstwhile protector bleed through his protest. "We've been through this a thousand times! We can't *know* that Sin Hazar was involved until we send an emissary. We can read the signs, though. We can recognize the marks of a curved dagger blade. And we know that

Bashanorandi has allies in the North—your own men intercepted the letters from Sin Hazar's court, this past spring."

This past spring. Long talking. Who's plotting?

"And *your* men were the ones who determined that those letters were nothing more than a distant uncle expressing concern for his nephew. Your Highness, I'm not trying to debate with you." Puladarati held up his hands in protest, as if he would ward off Hal's anger. The burly man was missing the last two fingers of his right hand, mute testimony to the battles he had fought long ago, at the side of Hal's father. "You know as well as I that the letters to Bashanorandi did not speak of any plot to spirit him north. We can't *know* that Sin Hazar was behind the . . . events on the hill."

"Events? At least call them what they were! The *murders*. My knights were murdered within sight of my city. My falcon-master was cut down, an afternoon's ride from my mews!"

Puladarati shrugged, the motion moving his hands enough that Hal's attention was dragged to the two missing digits. What had Hal ever given to the kingdom of Morenia, that these council lords should follow him? What battles had he fought to gain their faith? Who was Hal, to order around the entire King's Council?

King's Council. Denounce all. Cat's pounce—.

Enough.

"My good duke Puladarati. We know that you are only trying to counsel us in our hour of need." The dozen lords at the table all leaned closer. Hal rarely lapsed into the royal plural. "We are concerned, though, that we may not act properly in this, the first major confrontation of our rule. You know that we value your counsel, Your Grace. We value the counsel of all our lords."

Hal sat back and watched the tension begin to defuse around the table. Not for the first time, he wished that his father had allowed him into the council chamber when Shanoranvilli had still been alive. Hal might be able to fight these battles better if he'd been permitted to watch an admitted master at work. The lords at the table were like a nest of rats, all tossed into a sack. They were too busy clawing their way to freedom to worry about whose flesh they tore on the way out.

And of all the rats, Duke Puladarati was the oldest, most yellow-toothed beast, the scratched and scarred warrior who patrolled the largest section of the rodent waterfront. If Hal could convince Puladarati that he could rule competently, the rest of the council would fall into place. Of course, if Hal could sprout wings and fly to Amanthia, he could overlook Sin Hazar's palace and dispense with any further debate in council. Wings and Puladarati's cooperation. Each was as likely as the other.

"So." Hal bargained for a few more moments, looking up and down the table at his expectant lords. "Let us review what we know." He steepled his hands in front of his chin, echoing a gesture that he had seen his eldest brother, Tuvashanoran, use. Before Tuvashanoran had died. Before the crown had passed to Hal.

Clearing his throat, King Halaravilli forced himself to continue. "First. We know that Prince Bashanorandi has received correspondence from his uncle, from Sin Hazar. We know that the letters *we* intercepted did not contain direct incitement to rebellion; however, we cannot be certain what letters we did not receive."

Very good. None of the lords jumped in to interrupt. Hal continued. "Second. We know that Bashanorandi traveled to the hilltop three days ago. He went to fly his falcon, taking advantage of the clear weather, and the fact that falcon-master Gry was already transporting a bird for Lady Rani and Lady Mair."

There was a shuffle of discomfort at the council table. *What?* Hal wanted to cry out. What bothers you so much about *names?* Of course, he knew that his loyal lords were made uncomfortable by his adding the honorific "lady" to the short names of a merchant and a Touched girl. Hal stifled a sigh. Now was not the time to change the traditions of a kingdom. Now was not the time to struggle with the beliefs of centuries. Hal had another mission at hand—saving his stolen loyal vassals while protecting his kingdom from invasion. He continued.

"Third. We know that the party on the hillside was attacked, apparently after L—, after Rani flew her falcon, because that bird has not been found. Two guards were killed outright, and three were taken captive, along with Prince Bashanorandi and the two . . . girls. Are we in agreement?"

"No, Your Highness." Hal stifled an oath and whirled to his right, to a spot halfway down the council table. He had not expected the full agreement of his council, but he had hoped to get further in his argument before his men contradicted their sworn liege lord.

"Aye, Tasuntimanu. And why do you disagree?" Hal fought to keep his words steady, although he was doubly upset when he realized the identity of the speaker. In other hallways, in other councils, Tasuntimanu was Hal's sworn brother—both were members of the Fellowship of Jair. The existence of that shadowy group, though, was not known to most of the lords who crowded the council table. In fact, most of Hal's sworn retainers would have been scandalized to learn that their lord and master had offered up his loyalty to another organization, to a group of individuals more powerful than the Crown, than the divine right of kingship bestowed upon the house of Jair by all the Thousand Gods.

Because of the Fellowship, Hal knew Tasuntimanu. He knew that the older man was high in the ranks of that other body. Hal heard Tasuntimanu speak at the council table, and he listened to the voices of others, to advisors who would never be, who *could* never be admitted inside the council chamber. Swallowing hard, Hal pressed forward for enlightenment. "Go on, Tasuntimanu. Tell me why we are not in agreement."

"Your Highness,"—the earl inclined his head respectfully, exposing the bald spot in the middle of his thinning mud-brown hair—"you must understand that the days are growing short, that autumn is almost over, and winter will soon be upon us."

"Of course I know the time of year." Hal barely swallowed his impatience.

"And you know that most of us must return to our holdings, to supervise the final harvest, to make sure that our people are secure against the approaching winter."

"Aye."

"Then, surely, you understand that we would be foolish to

abandon those plans, those *necessities*, to ride after three captives, three *children* who are not even of noble blood."

Hal heard the indrawn breath of his other councillors. Tasuntimanu's disdainful words went to the heart of the single greatest battle Hal had fought since stepping to the throne. Even as Hal had struggled to get his council to recognize his power, to support him as their liege, he had fought to protect the people who had been loyal to him in the bitter confrontation that had set him on the throne. Hal had fought to protect Rani and Mair, even though they had no noble status. Hal had even fought to preserve Bashi's royal treatment, constantly reminding the council that the old king, Shanoranvilli, had commanded such a thing.

Tasuntimanu's outspoken stance, though, was all the more disturbing to Hal because the earl discussed other members of the Fellowship. Rani and Mair were both sworn to the organization; they were sisters to the earl who spoke against their rescue. They were sisters to Hal.

Swallowing hard, the king forced his voice to remain even, forced himself to remember that he was the one who wore the golden fillet of Morenia. Whatever might pass between him and Tasuntimanu in the Fellowship's shrouded meeting house, however higher Tasuntimanu might be in that shadowy hierarchy, Hal was king in this room. As king, Hal set his words into his council chamber, letting the chill of fear that surrounded his heart frost his words. "You forget yourself, my lord."

"Do I, Your Highness? With all respect, my liege, I forget nothing. You see, I remember that Bashanorandi is not even a prince by our reckoning. I remember that he is the rebellious son of two executed traitors. I remember that Rani Trader is a merchant—and scarcely that. She sold that birthright to join a guild so rebellious against your crown that it had to be physically dismantled, stone by stone. I remember that Mair is a Touched brat, sprung from who knows where, born under the sign of who knows which god. In the name of Jair, Your Highness, do you believe that I forget anything?"

In the name of Jair. There. Tasuntimanu was not jousting with a tipped lance. He was summoning Hal to a true battle, calling into play the power of the Fellowship, the oaths that Halaravilli had sworn when he was only a prince, when he was the outcast younger son of a king who showed him neither favoritism nor respect. Tasuntimanu drew upon Hal's bonds to the Fellowship of Jair.

"I understand your concerns, Tasuntimanu, and all the counsel that you would offer me." Hal hoped that he loaded the words with enough certainty that the earl would grasp his double meaning. There would be time enough, after the council meeting, to determine why Tasuntimanu was prepared to sacrifice Rani and Mair. Time enough, after Hal had cemented his own plans. He cleared his throat. "Nevertheless, my lords, this is a matter we have visited before. I have told you, I have told all of my people, that Prince Bashanorandi is to be honored in Morenia. My father, King Shanoranvilli, recognized the prince as his son and honored Bashanorandi from his deathbed. I would not be forsworn to my own father, blessed be he by all the Thousand Gods."

Hal paused to make a religious sign across his chest, a sign that the rest of his council aped. Peering up from his piously averted gaze, Hal noted which councillors took longer to fall into the platitude than others. Three men were notably slow in acknowledging Hal's gesture, three plus Tasuntimanu. Fine, then. At least Hal still held the majority of the council. At least five men still believed in the divine right of kingship. For today.

"Besides," Hal continued, deciding that there was no time like the present to force his game. He dripped heat over his words. "The house of Jair does not only rule to protect the nobility. We have watched over all of Morenia for decades, for centuries! We bear responsibility for *all* of our subjects, for merchants and guildsmen and even the Touched. We can hardly stand by and watch a raiding party steal away our loyal subjects and do nothing!"

Hal gauged the council's reaction to his fiery speech and fought an inward wince. Certainly, the nobility of the land understood that it had an obligation to the Thousand Gods, a destiny to keep Morenia safe and loyal to the gods. Nevertheless, no king had ever bothered to protect a handful of low-caste folk before. No one had waged war for a Touched girl and a caste jumper.

Well, Hal had not been king before.

Besides, he wasn't ready to wage war. Not yet.

Hal softened his tone, bringing his voice down to a wheedling conspiracy. "My lords, I'm not suggesting that we storm Amanth. I'm merely stating that we should send a *letter,* an envoy demanding to know by what right Sin Hazar has taken our people. I only want to ask him what right he thinks he has to send armed men onto our land! What right he thinks he has to ride to within a day of our City walls! Gentlemen, I do not want to fight Sin Hazar. I merely want to question him—for Morenia. Not for a dishonored prince. Not for a merchant girl. Not for a Touched girl. For Morenia. For the Crown. For me!"

Hal's voice rose as he spoke, gaining conviction with the rhythm of his words. For just an instant, he might have been harnessing his singsong messages of the past, he might have been drawing on the strength and power of his old mental games. He drew straighter as he spoke, and he flung back his shoulders. As he proclaimed the last two words of his litany, he pounded his fist against the table, striking the dark oak with enough force that the wood shuddered for a long moment.

Hal looked down the council table, catching the gaze of each of his advisors in turn. Some stared at him with frank amazement, clearly taken aback by the child-prince who had been rumored an idiot for years. Others looked back with wary agreement, narrowed eyes, and shrewd appraisal. All of them, though, were focused exclusively on their king.

Looking each man in the eye, one by one, Hal said, "Let all of you who are with us stand beside us now. And if you are against the Crown of all Morenia, let us know now, that we may count the traitors in our midst."

For one instant, there was silence in the chamber. Hal's heart pounded so loudly in his ears that he wondered if the other lords could hear it. He forced himself to breathe, first one long breath, then another, and another.

Just as Hal was wondering if he had made the greatest mistake of his life, there was the sound of a chair being pushed back, of wood scraping across stone. The jagged rumble was echoed again and again, and then all the council lords were standing, pounding their hands against the oaken table, proclaiming their fealty to good King Halaravilli. Hal swallowed hard and forbade his eyes to shed their sudden hot tears.

"Then, my lords," he continued after a moment, "we are decided. We will send an embassy to Sin Hazar and remind the dragon that the lion of Morenia has awakened from its slumber."

Hal regained his seat at the head of the table and watched as his councillors followed suit. Some of the men were wary, clearly resentful of the sudden groundswell of support that Hal had inspired. Nevertheless, the remainder of the council meeting went smoothly. Hal declared that he would work with a scribe and send a messenger that afternoon. After a brief invocation of all the Thousand Gods, Hal sent his noble retainers on their way.

Perhaps he should have led the way from the council chamber, sweeping through the halls with the power and the prestige that had been his father's, that had been his elder brother's. But Hal could not bring himself to make the walk back to his apartments, not immediately, not while his first council victory still pounded through his blood.

Instead, he sent his councillors away and held back, sitting in his chair at the head of the table like a man awaiting a feast. He was just reaching up to his brow to remove the heavy golden fillet when he realized that he was not alone. The eldest of the councillors, Lamantarino, was completing his shuffle to the door.

Hal started to swear under his breath, embarrassed at almost being caught like an irresponsible schoolboy. As if he could hear that faint sound, the ancient man turned to Halaravilli with a wheeze and a sigh. "You did a good job here today, Your Highness."

Hal's immediate reaction was one of pleasure. He *had* done a good job, and without any overt support from anyone at the table. After he swallowed his first flush of pride, though, Hal was disturbed by the old courtier's praise. It hardly became the king of all Morenia to be complimented by a mere baron. No matter how old that baron was. No matter how close a friend that baron had been to the king's father.

"My thanks, Your Grace. I was guided by the Thousand Gods."

"Ach." The old councillor shuffled back toward the table, leaning his crepey hands against the dark wood and pausing for a moment to catch his breath. "You were guided by your thoughts, and your brains. Give the gods their due, but don't forget to take your own." Hal almost grinned. He was proud of his accomplishments, and he was loath to give away all the credit. "Be careful, though, Your Highness. You mustn't show a glimmer of weakness."

"Weakness! Do you think I'm weak, my lord?"

"I think you're young." As if to emphasize his statement, Lamantarino paused, fighting for breath against a sudden wheeze that rattled his chest. When he could speak again, his voice was higher, wispier. "I think you're young, and not well used to fencing a roomful of opponents."

"I've had good fencing instructors."

"You've had instructors who were good enough for a junior prince. It was Tuvashanoran who was supposed to sit at this table."

For one instant, Hal could see his elder brother, standing strong and proud in the cathedral on the day that he was to step forward as Defender of the Faith. The old king had not been ready to transfer the crown yet, but he'd been eager to bestow a mantle of responsibility on Tuvashanoran, on the eldest son who was beloved of all the people. Thinking of Tuvashanoran, thinking of the black-fletched arrow that had destroyed a proud, able man, Hal's throat tightened. He managed to say, "Yes."

Lamantarino nodded, or maybe it was only that his head shook with palsied age. "You come from the same blood, King Halaravilli. You can rule with the same power." The old man started to shuffle back toward the heavy doors, but he turned toward Hal one more time. "Your father always kept one rule in mind as he handled his advisors."

"What was that?" Hal could not admit that he had scarcely spoken to his father about the council. Until the calamity of Tuvashanoran's death, Hal had not spoken to his father about anything concerning rule and kingship.

"Let them think they're the noble stag, but treat them like the coursing hounds." The old man laughed at the puzzled expression on Hal's face. "I never said they were words of wisdom, son. But your father lived by them. Treat them like they're coursing hounds."

Lamantarino started to laugh again, but this time his amusement turned to a choking cough. Hal seized a nearby goblet and rushed across the chamber flagstones. He held the pounded silver against the old man's lips, gently raising the cup so that Lamantarino could drink.

It took a moment, but the baron managed a single swallow, and then another, and another. He settled his hand against Hal's, pushing away the cup with gnarled fingers. "You're a good man, King Halaravilli. Don't forget all you've learned as you begin this chess game with Sin Hazar."

"I won't, I won't forget anything."

"Just keep in mind who you're playing here. You're not just matching yourself against Sin Hazar. It's your own men in the fray. Your own men who have to understand your moves."

"I'll be certain that they do." *As soon as I understand them myself,* Hal thought.

"They have to know why Prince Bashanorandi is important. They have to understand about the girls."

"It's not about the people, you know. It's about my entire rule. It's about whether Morenia will accept me as king."

"Oh, I know, sire. I know what's at stake here. Just make sure that they do, too."

Hal bowed his head and made a holy sign across his breast. "Blessed be Jair, the First Pilgrim. May he guide me in the ways of righteousness."

The old man snorted. "Jair has little to do with this, son! Ruling a kingdom takes common sense and a firm hand on the reins. The Pilgrim may serve as a guide, but he'll not be much help keeping your council under control."

Hal bit back a laugh, surprisingly pleased to hear such bluff words. Shrugging, he offered the old councillor his arm, and the two nobles left the chamber. As he walked, though, Hal wondered if he would be able to make the others understand why he must save a bastard prince, a caste-changing merchant, and a wayward Touched girl. And even if the king succeeded with his council, there was still the Fellowship of Jair to convince. Hal did not look forward to that confrontation.

4

Shea had been a fool to think that she could lead Crest-man to safety. She did not know the first thing about traveling through the countryside. She'd only seen one map in her entire life, on the wall of the Greenwood Inn in the tiny village near her cottage. That map had been drawn by a traveling man, as payment for all the ale he had drunk. Everyone in the village joked that King Sin Hazar's roads could not run as crooked as the drinking man had drawn them. Everyone knew that the map was a joke, a game.

And now, Shea was pinning her life and the life of the boy on that game. She knew that they must travel south, away from Sin Hazar's capital of Amanth. She must escape the king's long reach if she dared to walk beside one of his deserting soldiers, one of his stolen captains.

As long as she was traveling toward the south, Shea also knew that she would go east. East toward the ocean, toward the Swancastle. She needed to see that massive fortification, needed to see the magical place that she had turned to all her life, in times of strife and mystery, in times of need. She needed to see the place where the nobles of her province had first rebelled, where the Uprising had been born. The Swancastle had cost her her son, her daughter, the peaceful life she had known and loved.

Shea was afraid of the Swancastle, and of the ocean beyond it. She had never seen the moving, seething water, but she had heard tales. In fact, she had heard tales about so many things along the road—the dark forest through which she walked, the ravening hordes of the king's riders. Shea had heard of wild beasts, too, voracious animals that would snap up a sunwoman with two short clicks of their jaws.

Crestman did not seem afraid. He walked beside her like any sullen youth, like her own son had, before he had gone off to fight. She judged him to be fifteen years old. A difficult age. A stubborn age.

"Make sure that you gather enough wood," Shea remonstrated with Crestman, as they started to settle in for the evening. "It's going to be cold tonight." Her back ached as she eased herself to sit on a fallen log. The day had been long, and every muscle in her body protested the abuse of walking, walking, walking endlessly beneath the forest canopy. The autumn chill settled in her bones. Already, it seemed like a lifetime ago that she had taken her babes to harvest the last autumn berries, centuries since she had lazily fallen asleep in the warm sunlight of the clearing near her cottage.

"I'm working as fast as I can," Crestman grumbled, shuffling his feet through the rotting dust of years-past leaves.

"No, you're not. It will be dark soon."

"I'm not a sunboy, for you to order me around!"

"No, you're not," Shea repeated, disapproval spicing her back-handed agreement. "If you were, you'd listen to what I have to say." Shea huffed and pulled herself to her swollen feet. She dug about in the shadows to the side of the path, stooping low to lift the loose branches that had fallen by the roadside. They were on the very edge of the forest; this would be the last night that they could sleep beneath its protective branches.

It took only a few moments to shame Crestman into helping her. At first, she refused to let the boy carry the wood that she had gathered. She dragged it back to the forest's threshold, to the place where they would pass the night. She relented, though, when she felt a sharp pang in her back. She had to take several deep breaths before she could see clearly again, and even then it was difficult to find a comfortable sitting position, difficult to find a way to sleep in the cold, dark night. She was too old for this adventuring.

She was too old, and too frightened, and too ignorant. She

should be jostling her children's children on her knee, sitting in front of a warm fire. But she had no choice. She needed to be on the road, with her newest ward. With Crestman.

The next day, they were almost caught by soldiers twice. Perhaps the men had seen the smoke of their fire on the horizon. Whatever the cause, the horsemen were thick on the road. Crestman was responsible for watching for riders. He'd cry an alarm, and the two travelers would leave the road, roaming across wild-grown fields until they could crouch in weeds. If Shea had realized how close the soldiers were before she began this foolish journey . . . If she had known the danger that she was in, with her skychildren, with all her precious lions and suns and owls, with her one little swan . . .

As the last of the soldiers rode off and the sun began to set, Shea decided that she should turn back. She should return to her cottage and her children. Who said that Hartley and Tain would be able to protect the children? Even now, they might all be hungry and cold. They might need her.

Shea started to turn around, but she realized that she might put the children at greater risk if she returned. Who was to say that the soldiers were not tracking them this very instant, playing with her like a cat with its prey, waiting for the nighttime, for the next day, to take her captive? Who was to say that Shea would not lead King Sin Hazar directly to her children if she turned around to save them?

Better to press on, then. Better to keep moving toward the Swancastle.

At least Crestman seemed to be gentling a little under her ministrations. Of course, he still cried out in his sleep—that she was unable to stop. If Shea startled him awake from a nightmare, he woke grasping for his knife. He also shied away from anyone touching his face—Shea had learned that lesson inadvertently, when she'd reached out to rub away a smear of berry juice from his cheek. He still kept his hair pulled tight in a soldier's clout, emphasizing the harsh lines of his hungry face.

Bit by bit, though, like a sparrow growing accustomed to taking bread crumbs, Crestman began to relax around her. During the day, he let his hand stray from the curved knife that he kept tucked into his leather belt. Once, when Shea slipped in a muddy rut in the road, Crestman hovered over her, a look of anxiety twisting his face where annoyance had played only the day before. When they were caught in one of the frequent autumn downpours, Crestman no longer hesitated to pull close to Shea, to take shelter under her oiled cloak.

The morning after the heaviest downpour, though, Shea had her first true fight with the boy. Not surprisingly, it was about their destination.

"Why go to the Swancastle?" Crestman had complained. "There aren't any swans there, anymore. The castle lies empty."

"You've been there?"

"Aye." Crestman looked uncomfortable, as if he wanted to forget a bad dream. "My unit trained on the castle grounds."

"Trained? What do you mean? What did you learn at the Swancastle?" Crestman refused to meet Shea's eyes, but his fingers strayed to the scar that melted beneath his eye. "Is that where they did it, then? Is that where they cut away your tattoo?" Crestman only tightened his belt and hefted his meager pack. "You can't ignore me, boy! You answer your elders when they speak to you!"

Crestman would not reply, though. Shea's anger flashed behind her eyes, as sharp as the pain in her back, and she badgered him for a few minutes more. "Are the troops still there? Does King Sin Hazar use the Swancastle to train his Little Army?"

"I don't know! Stop asking me questions! I don't know who's there now! I just know that the king's troops fought long and hard for it, to take it from the rebels years ago. After the Uprising, Sin Hazar decided to use it to train his armies."

Fought long and hard . . . That's right. King Sin Hazar had paid in blood to defeat his rebellious swans. He had extracted a toll as well, though. Now, more than ever, Shea *had* to go to the Swancastle. Now that she was free from protecting her orphans, she had to see where the Uprising had been born, where her world had been turned upside down. She had to see the place that had spawned the battles that cost her Pom. Pom, who had

died in the Little Army's first camps, who had fallen learning
how to protect the king's loyal swans in the precarious years just
after the Uprising. Pom, who had been learning how to protect
his way of life. . . .

By the time they'd been a week on the road, Shea had grown
tired of fighting with her lionboy. Crestman's initial obedience,
his early sense of gratitude, had faded away like stars bleached
by the morning sky. The farther south they moved, the more
Crestman challenged every statement that Shea made. She needed
to explain why they started at a particular hour of the morning,
why they traveled down a particular fork in the road. She needed
to justify why they stopped to fish at a particular rill, why they
could not eat those particular mushrooms. She needed to prove
every decision, every choice.

And she did. She stood up to the lionboy, as if she hadn't
spent her entire life acting on decisions made by others. She stood
her ground, as if the sun had burned away her old self, crisped
her ancient identity and blown it away with the autumn winds
that came with increasing frequency. Shea had become a different person from the meek sunwoman who had lived her entire
life one day's walk from a village, from the comfort of Father
Nariom, from the familiar skycastes.

Now that Shea was not acting like a sun, she had freedoms
she'd never dreamed of. Once, while they wandered, they came
across a stand of curling sweetleaf. Shea knew that she should
harvest the dark green leaves, stow them away for future use and
throw the seeded fruit far over her shoulder, to spread the patch
of the precious herb. She did not care to, though. She would have
no time to use the sweetleaf, no time to bake, or even to boil the
herb down to its sticky syrup. She walked on, ignoring the tug
at the back of her mind. She might be a sunwoman, but she was
no fool. She'd do what needed to be done, here and now, not
just what she'd been raised to do.

Another time, a couple of days later, she and Crestman were
skirting the edge of a village. Crestman had spent the better part
of the morning complaining about their food, or more precisely,
their lack of sustenance. Shea had listened to him with a mother's

concern at first, but then she had grown tired of the sulking boy. Certainly he was hungry. So was she.

"Why can't we go into the tavern, Shea?" Crestman was still whining as the village faded behind them.

"We don't know who's in the tavern, boy. We don't know what we'll find."

"We'll find food and drink, we know that much."

"Aye, and how would you buy it, boy?"

"You have two copper pennies."

"How do you know that?" Shea tried to keep fear from her voice, letting anger wash her words instead.

"I know things," the boy replied stubbornly.

Before Shea realized what she was doing, she whirled on the lionboy, catching his throat in her rough hands. "You don't go prowling through my pockets, boy. Awake or asleep, I'm the closest thing you've got to a family on this road. You sneak on me while I'm sleeping, and you just remember what I can do to you. I may have saved you from my children, but I'm not above slitting your throat and letting the crows eat your liver if you do ill by me."

As Shea spoke the words, she believed herself; she believed the rage that trembled through her fingers. Crestman must have believed her as well, for he dropped his grumbling and complaining, not even looking over his shoulder as the village faded from view. That night, Shea removed the two copper coins from her knotted kerchief, sliding them into the cracked leather of her shoe.

Shoes proved to be a problem again, only two days later. Shea had never worn her shoes for as long as she had on the road, and she'd rubbed blisters on the very first day of their expedition. She had tended to her feet carefully that first night, breaking the angry, watery bubbles and binding the tender flesh with soft cloth ripped from her underskirts. She'd hobbled a bit for the next couple of days, but her feet were beginning to heal, at least enough to let her focus on the other agonies of a body not used to walking, to the hard labor of living on the road.

Crestman, though, did not have as easy a time. Certainly, the boy was used to travel, accustomed to lean provisions and sorry accommodations. He was a growing child, though. Shea noticed him limping after the first couple of days, when her own pained feet had stopped burning and settled into a dull ache.

"What is it, boy? What's wrong with your legs?"

"Nothing."

"Nonsense. I can see that you're limping. No reason to lie to me."

"There's nothing you can do to help." Crestman set his jaw and continued walking, visibly steeling himself not to limp. Shea did not have a chance to follow up until they reached a stream later in the morning. She pointed out some fleshy mushrooms growing along the edge of the creek, and she frowned as Crestman lurched toward the food. When he came back, he slipped in the wet earth, and he swore loudly as his feet twisted out from under him.

"Watch your words, lionboy."

"I'm not a lion," he responded reflexively, swallowing hard and offering her the newly harvested mushrooms. They smelled of good, clean earth. Shea brushed hers off against her skirts and began to chew, grateful for the food in her belly.

Crestman sank down beside her and raised his own mushroom to his lips. He had not begun to eat, though, when Shea darted out a hand, snaking it around his ankle. The maneuver sent her own food flying, but she caught the boy tightly. Her fingers crashed against the end of his leather shoes, jamming hard against his toes.

"Ow!" Crestman exclaimed, and he twisted to get away.

Shea only tightened her grip on the boy's leg, using stiffened fingers to test the shoes. There was no question—Crestman's feet were jammed into the leather; his toes were hard up against the front edge of the unforgiving leather. "Well, no wonder you're limping, boy! Why didn't you say something?"

"What was there to say?" Shea's ungentle ministrations had brought hot tears to the boy's eyes. "I'm a soldier in King Sin Hazar's army."

"Not anymore, you're not. Not when you're wandering through

the countryside with a sunwoman. Not when you're sneaking beside a riverbed, trying to avoid detection by His Majesty's troops. If we're going to travel together, you can't lie to me."

"I haven't lied! I haven't said a word!"

"There are lies in silence, boy. Sometimes worse lies than speech." Shea shook her head and let the youth go. "Take off your shoes."

"What? I'll never get them back on again!"

"I said, take them off." Shea's voice toughened as she spoke, until her words sounded harder than the water-tightened leather on Crestman's feet. Swallowing his grumbling complaint, the boy complied, easing off the cracked shoes. He handed them to Shea.

Shea managed not to gloat over Crestman's ill-disguised look of relief, the easing of pain in the tight lines of his jaw, his temples. Instead, she drew her long knife, the only weapon that she had taken from her cottage. The blade was sharp, but she still needed to fight with the stony leather. She set her own jaw as she sawed through the toes at the front of each shoe. When she handed them back to Crestman, he looked up at her in disbelief.

"My feet will freeze!"

"You'll wrap them in cloth. You'd be a cripple if you wore those things much longer."

"They were good shoes!"

"Good for a child, perhaps. You're not a child anymore, Crestman." She spoke the words in a chiding tone, but they made the youth stand taller. He wasn't a child. He was growing to be a man. "We'll see if we can get you new ones, when we arrive."

"Arrive where?"

"Wherever we find ourselves," Shea finally responded. The answer sufficed to get Crestman to wrap his feet with more bandages, torn from the last of her underskirts. When they walked away from the stream, the boy moved awkwardly at first, growing accustomed to his new, open-toed footwear. It only took him a few strides, though, to fall into a soldierly swagger. Shea swallowed a smile and let him take the lead for the rest of the day.

Their newfound companionship made Crestman's behavior doubly shocking when the boy lashed out at her, less than one day from the Swancastle. They had stopped to drink by a stream, grateful for the cool water after a morning of walking along a high, dry road.

"Stay here," Crestman insisted. "I'll go on ahead and let you know what I find."

"Nonsense. We'll walk together, as we have so far."

"It's dangerous. I'll go first."

"You're only a boy."

"That's not what you said the other day. I'm a soldier in King Sin Hazar's army!"

"Not anymore." Shea set the words down stubbornly. She had almost grown accustomed to speaking back to lions. How a few days on the trail could change a good sunwoman like her . . . "You're not anything anymore, Crestman. You're eager enough to point that out when you think it will work to your advantage. I won't let you go on alone."

"And how will you stop me?" The boy's face had flushed crimson, as if he were stained by the leaves of the trees that flirted across the road. He steadied his voice by settling a hand on his knife hilt.

"I'll box your ears, if I have to. You're not so old that I won't treat you like a child if you insist on acting like one."

"You wouldn't dare!"

"I wish we were back at the cottage, lionboy. You'd talk to Hartley, then. You'd know that I don't make idle threats."

"You're only a sun."

Shea moved faster than she'd thought possible. Her hand darted out and grasped at Crestman's fleshy earlobe, twisting viciously as she jerked him close. Even as he opened his mouth to protest, she curved her hand into a cup. She clapped the side of his head with all her force, setting free her nervousness, her fear, her hatred of this frightening, unknowable life.

Her own fingers stung with the force of her blow, but she kept her grip on the boy's ear as he tried to twist free. Her hands were strong, wiry after years of laundering and scrubbing, plucking chickens and shelling peas. "Only a sun, boy?" she asked, but she was not certain if she said the words aloud, or if she only thought them.

Crestman's cry was wordless, a gasping protest like a toddler who startles itself by falling down a steep slope. Shea shook her stinging fingers and grimaced at the boy. "You asked for it, you did! I've told you to listen to me. I've told you that I'm the one leading us. I saved your life, you miserable brat!"

Shea heard the words tumble from her lips, scattering across the clearing like shards of broken pottery. She wanted to scramble after her anger, gather it up in her trembling hands, but it was too late. The words were spoken, the blow delivered. Shea shook in the morning sunlight, remembering the last time that she had struck Pom, the last time she had raised her hand against her own flesh and blood.

That had been the day when Pom announced that he was leaving her, that he was riding to the Swancastle. She had protested then, told Pom that he could not leave her alone and unattended in the woods. Pom had stood up proudly, drawing himself to his full height as he must have imagined warriors doing for generations before him. Shea had flung herself at him, rage tightening her hands into fists. She had pounded on her son's chest, beating at him with wordless fury. She could not believe that he would abandon her, could not imagine that he would let his own mother live alone and unaided in the woods. . . .

Shea could remember that fury as if it had only beat in her veins a moment before. Lionboys. They were all fools. They all claimed that the stars drove them, forced them onto distant paths. They all claimed that the skychildren were bound by the fate of their births. Well, Shea knew better now. She knew that a sun could make decisions, could decide her fate, even if she wasn't born under one of the night signs.

Why didn't the lions listen to their mothers? Why didn't they do what was right? Why didn't they let the old order of the world work?

"Crestman," Shea began, uncupping her hand. The young soldier took a step away, lowering his head and shaking it, like a bull tossing away flies from its ears. "I didn't mean—" she began, and fumbled for words. "I thought that . . ."

Shea trailed off, helpless to explain what she had thought. Maybe if she were an owl she could have explained. Maybe then, she would have had the words to tell this boy that she had not meant to harm him. She stepped forward and grasped for his wrist with her rough, callused hands.

Crestman leaped away as if her touch burned him, and his cry of protest broke through Shea's foggy misery. Before she could say anything, though, she saw that Crestman had drawn his dagger from the sheath at his waist. The curved blade glinted in the malevolent sunlight, and Shea stepped back in surprise. "Boy! No need for steel!"

Before she could continue with her startled exclamation, Crestman hissed and jerked his chin toward Shea. No, not toward her, she realized with a sick flip of her belly. Past her. Over her shoulder. Shea forced herself to breathe, forced her numb fingers to scramble toward the kitchen knife that hung at her own waist. She turned about slowly.

Shea and Crestman were quickly surrounded. A company of soldiers had weapons trained upon them, curious crossbows that nestled along their forearms. The archers were *children,* every one of them peering up at Shea with young eyes that knew too much. Each boy's hair was lashed back from his face, savagely woven into a warrior's clout.

Even as Shea struggled for a breath, she could make out the tips of the arrows set in the miniature weapons. The bows might be small, the archers might be young, but Shea had no doubt that the glinting iron arrowheads could gouge out her life.

Even as she registered the threat, an icy cage clanged shut around her heart. Her breath froze in her lungs, and she clutched at her torn and soiled dress, clawing at her chest to unlock the iron bars, to make the pain disappear. Her fingers buzzed and jangled, as if she'd slept with her head across her arm for too long. She fought for another breath, and another, but the tingling in her hand crept up her arm.

She never should have boxed Crestman's ear, she thought absurdly. She never should have beaten the boy. A gasp escaped her lips, sounding suspiciously like a sob. She stretched her tingling hand toward the scarred lionboy, muttering his name as she fell to her knees.

Crestman's only answer, though, was to grip her by her hair. His fingers twisted cruelly against the nape of her neck, and he forced her to stay upright in the leaf mold along the path. Shea cried out, pushing feebly against his hand, but she was no match for the boy's strength. "Crestman!" she gasped, but he only twisted harder.

As if in reply, the pain beneath her breastbone leaped higher, cutting off her breath, forcing her to gasp like a trout dangling on a line. A child's voice piped across the clearing. "Keep your arrows trained on both of them! This may be a trick!"

Crestman swore, a more vicious oath than any he had used while he sought sanctuary with Shea and her skychildren. "Don't you recognize me, boys? I'm one of you! I'm a soldier in King Sin Hazar's army. I'm helping this woman. I'm trying to help her breathe!"

As if to reinforce his claim, Crestman gave one last vicious tug to Shea's hair, pulling her upright. The motion forced some air past the metal bars that enmeshed her chest, but her heart squeezed again, forcing that hard-gained breath from her lungs. Black clouds roiled up from the edges of her sight, and she toppled forward to the grass. The last thing she saw before the world faded to starless night was Crestman's twisted face and the blood that snaked from his boxed ear to his filthy tunic.

Shea heard people moving around her before she was able to open her eyes. There were grunts and the sound of shifting bodies, the angry murmur of orders. She could make out the smell of a rich stew, and her belly clenched at the aroma of meat. There was also the ripe aroma of fresh-baked bread, powdery and clean.

Shea wondered who had drugged her, and what potion they had used. She was so tired. . . . Tired like when she'd brought her son into the world. Like when she'd birthed her swandaughter,

fast and furious, bringing the girl forth while the stars still shone
auspiciously in the sky. Then, she'd had the ladies from the village to help her, to lift her head, to feed her rich broth.

There were no comforting women's voices in the room, though,
and no infant nestled in swaddling clothes by her side. Of course
not, Shea thought. Of course there were no infants. She was well
past that foolishness. Catching a deep breath and holding it in
her lungs, Shea forced her eyes to open.

And when she'd looked around her, she almost wished that
she could go back to sleep, back to her strange, confused dreams.
She was in a cottage, a single room with a large hearth and a
crackling fire. This cottage, though, was nothing like any room
she had ever seen before.

The wooden walls were lined with books, leather-bound tomes
more precious than all of Father Nariom's treasures back home.
A table sat beneath the one window that Shea could see, and it
was covered with dusty glassware and piping, looking like the
rejected remnants of a lamp-maker's wares. Another table lurked
in the shadows of one corner, and it appeared to be covered with
dusty jars. By squinting, Shea thought that she could make out
bones inside the jars.

The rafters were strung with wreaths. Shea could decipher
dried apples and braided onions and various herbs. Mixed among
the foodstuffs, though, there were more ominous hangings—long
curved blades and military banners stained with a muddy brown
that looked like dried blood.

As Shea turned her head, she could peer at another shadowy
corner, which was dominated by a tall, wooden stand. On the
crossbar of the stand stood a bird, a bird that Shea had never
seen before in the forests of Amanthia. The creature was feath-
ered in brilliant blue. Its body was the size of a chicken, but it
was longer and more streamlined, like the shape of a sparrow. It
had a sweeping tail, lush with the same azure feathers as its body.
As Shea blinked, the bird spread its wings, and she could see
that its under-feathers were a pearly grey, the same grey that
traced around the creature's yellow eyes. Shea watched it raise
one foot to its mouth, cleaning its four claws with a cat's me-

thodic care. The bird's tongue was thick and black and flexible, like a snake. When it had finished grooming its foot, it started preening its massive blue-and-grey wings. Only when the creature had finished that task did it turn about on its stand, thrusting its neck forward and crying out in a child's voice, "Feed me! Feed me now!"

Shea started at the talking bird, raising trembling hands to make a protective sign in front of her eyes. Surely she was being punished by all the Thousand Gods, punished in a place where even the birds spoke aloud. She closed her eyes and started praying to the gods, praying for deliverance from this creature, from her certainly imminent death.

"Shea!" The old woman heard her name, but she refused to open her eyes, refused to see the demons that the Thousand Gods had sent to torture her. "Shea! You're awake! We've waited so long!"

Shea thought that she recognized Crestman's voice, and she felt his fingers on her arm. There was nothing for it, she couldn't live the rest of her life with her eyes clenched shut. If the Thousand Gods were going to strike her down, punish her for leaving her children alone and unattended, she might as well accept that punishment now. She forced her eyes open, ordering herself to ignore the momentary exhaustion that threatened to send her spiraling back into the starless darkness.

When she blinked, she could make out the lionboy, his face pale in the shadowy hut. He brushed his hair back nervously, fighting back wisps that had escaped from his battle-braid. The action drew attention to the scar high on his cheekbone. "Shea, you had us worried!"

"Us?" she managed to croak, and the single word taught her how dry her throat was. She realized that her body craved water—cool, sweet water—even more than her belly twisted around the aroma of the cooking food.

"Me, Shea. Me and Davin and Monny and the others."

"I—I don't understand." Shea heard the plaintiveness in her voice, the rough edges like tears that haunted her words. Afraid that she would break down, afraid that she would cry in front of the child who was her charge, Shea forced herself to utter one more word: "Water."

For just an instant, Crestman looked confused. She saw a hundred stories flit across his face. He looked like her own children, when they came in from the fields, alight with some new tale, some new observation. She knew that she should listen to him, she should hear what he had to say. That would make her a good mother. That would make her a proper sunwoman. She was too tired, though. Too tired to hear. Too tired to speak.

She felt Crestman's arm around her shoulders, supporting her head. A clay mug was raised to her lips, and she swallowed gratefully, once, twice, three times. The boy tilted the mug a little too quickly, and precious water trickled down the corner of her mouth, escaping her eager lips. "That's good, boy," she said, though, when she had drained the cup. "You're a good lion, Pom."

She knew there was something wrong there, that she had made some mistake. She was too tired, though, to correct herself. There was time enough to do that after she had slept. After she had dreamed. . . .

The next time that Shea awoke, it was nighttime in the cottage. She could turn her head toward the window, but she could make out nothing but inky darkness. The wood fire still burned on the hearth, but now it was little more than embers, glowing coals that sent out the smoky scent of wood. Shea glanced at the talking bird, but it was asleep, blue head tucked neatly under its azure wing.

Shea was thirsty again, and her belly burned with hunger. She caught a deep breath against the back of her teeth and pulled herself into a sitting position.

"Cor!" A child's voice startled Shea, and a twinge shot through her chest. Her breath was already short, and she felt as if a band were tightening around her flesh, a broad strip of leather soaked in water and left to dry and tighten in the cottage's close air.

"Hush!" she replied automatically, as if she knew the person who had spoken, as if she knew who she might be awakening in the hut.

"I'll not be quiet! You can't order me about!"

Shea eased an elbow beneath her, steadying herself as she rolled over on her pallet. A young boy sat beside the fire, rubbing sleep from his eyes with a grimy fist. The child's bright red hair had worked loose from his soldier's braid; it stood out from his head like flaming straw in a just-harvested field. His face was spattered with freckles, across the bridge of his nose and down his cheeks. In fact, the only flesh spared the sprinkling of dark flecks was the smooth patch beneath his left eye. A scar, carving away the child's birthright.

"Who are you, boy?" Even as Shea shrugged herself upright, past the shortness of breath, past the pain in her chest, she realized that she had seen this child before. He was the one who had faced her in the clearing in the woods, the one who had leveled an iron-tipped arrow toward her heart.

"You're the visitor here," the child pouted. "You should name yourself first. That's what Davin says."

"Davin? Who's Davin?"

"Name yourself first."

Before Shea could reply, she heard a familiar voice. "You might as well give him your name. He won't be quiet until he's won." Crestman's voice was filled with resignation, but Shea barely managed to smother the joyful smile that tried to twist her lips. Crestman was still alive. Alive and well enough to speak.

"My name is Shea," she said to the redheaded boy.

"I'm Monny." The child beamed his satisfaction at having won the little battle. Shea noticed that his eyeteeth were overlong in his mouth, as if he were a wolf. Nonsense, she told herself, shaking her head at her lingering exhaustion. There was nothing sinister about the child. He'd just lost his milk teeth, and the adult replacements were too big for his mouth. Shea forced herself to focus, to think reasonably.

"Thank you, Monny," she said. "Where are we? What happened to me in the woods? Did you shoot me?"

"Shoot you! Why would I do that?"

Crestman answered before Shea could puzzle out an explanation. "You fell, Shea. You clutched at your chest and fell, before any of the children could shoot you."

"I didn't imagine them, then? There are more?"

"Aye." Again, Crestman answered. Shea could see that Monny did not like being ignored. The younger boy shifted from foot to foot, and his fingers curled into fists at his side. "More than a score. They're outside, though."

"Outside? It's too cold for boys to sleep outside."

"It's not too cold for the troops of King Sin Hazar!" Monny responded eagerly, looking as if Shea had questioned his birthright. "We sleep outside *every* night. That makes us tough for the king. That makes us good soldiers for him."

"But you shouldn't—" Shea began to protest, but Crestman cut her off.

"You won't get anywhere arguing with him. He serves King Sin Hazar. He's proud of his service."

Shea heard the message behind Crestman's words, the warning that she was speaking with the enemy. Only as Shea leaned back on the pallet did she realize just how much danger she might be in. She'd been found on the road with a deserter from King Sin Hazar's troops, found by the king's own soldiers. Why was Crestman still alive? Why hadn't he been bound and carried off to the king's justice?

"Here." Monny thrust a bowl toward her, apparently oblivious to the questions that floated through the old woman's head. "Davin said you should eat when you awaken. Not too much, and not too fast, but he said you'd be hungry."

"Who is this Davin?" Shea asked again. She started to reach for the bowl, but her hands trembled too much for her to grasp the thing. Crestman came and sat beside her. She let herself lean against him, at the same time wondering what could have happened to her, how she could have become so weak. Crestman reached for Monny's wooden bowl, but the child pulled it back.

"Davin said that *she* was to eat, not you."

"I'm not going to eat it, boy. I'm going to feed it to her."

"How can I trust you? You were hungry enough when Davin gave you your own bowl."

"I'm a captain in King Sin Hazar's army, boy. You can believe me now, or you can believe me when I've taken stripes out of your skin."

"So you say," Monny muttered, but he let the larger boy take the bowl. "You say you're a captain, but so far, we've seen nothing to prove it."

"I told you this woman would back me up, when she awakened." Shea heard the sharp edge on Crestman's voice, as sharp as the elbow that he surreptitiously dug into her side. This exchange was important. She should concentrate. Crestman glared at the boy. "Do you always doubt your king so obviously and so vocally?"

"Goodwife." Monny turned to Shea. "This one's been telling stories. He says you would vouch for him when you awakened."

"Aye," Shea agreed. "But let me eat a little, first. We've been over a week on the road." Even as Shea offered up her excuse, she realized that she might already be contradicting some story that Crestman had told. The lionboy, though, did not tense as he raised her bowl, and his face remained smooth as he fumbled at a small table beside her, lifting up a wooden spoon.

"Aye, let her eat, Monny. She'll tell you our story soon enough. She'll tell you all about our journey from the north. She'll tell you about being nursemaid to the king himself, to King Sin Hazar and to Princess Felicianda, when they were children. She'll tell you all about her life in the castle."

Shea nodded, not even able to wonder at the stories she would have to spin. Instead, she chewed on the piece of meat that Crestman eased into her mouth. The venison was tough, but full of flavor, and her mouth flooded with water as she worked the morsel around with her tongue. As she swallowed, she felt a tendril of strength begin to uncurl, easing its way into her limbs. Her arm still felt strangely numb, but her fingers and toes were beginning to thaw. Crestman fed her a bite of potato, which she chewed thoroughly, and then she felt obligated to answer at least one of the questions that floated behind the young Monny's eyes.

"Aye, child. This one tells the truth. I come from the castle, from the Sw—"

Crestman started to choke, as if he were the one eating the tidbits of stew. Even as the lionboy coughed, bouncing Shea up and down on her pallet, she realized the mistake that she had almost made. Of course, if she were the king's nurse, she would not have come from the Swancastle. She'd be from Amanth, far to the north. There was nothing in the made-up tale that told why she'd been walking to the Swancastle, though. Nothing at all.

"Careful, boy," Shea said, and shifted as if she would ease the choking Crestman. He glared at her in the dim light of the cottage, and she wanted to apologize, wanted to tell him that she was not one for spying and telling tales. She was a sunwoman, after all! What could he expect?

"And you, Grandmother," Crestman said, filling her mouth with another bite of meat. "You be careful as well. It was an honor for the king to entrust you to my care, and I'd fain not disappoint him by your starving now. Finish chewing. Then we can talk."

"Aye," Shea said around the morsel of venison. When she had swallowed, she picked her way across the treacherous field of nettles that the lionboy had strewn before her. "The king wanted me to be safe, after all the years I gave him. He was sending me south, away from his own city, where his enemies will attack first." She felt Crestman relax a little against her side. She must have guessed right, then. That must be their story.

Monny sank back on his heels, looking appeased for a few minutes. Shea took advantage of the child's silence to finish the bowl of stew. Only when she had chewed the last bit of a carrot did Crestman set the bowl on the floor beside her cot.

"Rest now, Grandmother. You had quite a start out there, on the road. Those boys had no right to terrify an old woman with bows and arrows."

"I *told* you," Monny complained loudly. "We didn't know who you were. We were out on maneuvers. We thought that you were attacking the Swancastle!"

"Attacking the Swancastle!" Crestman exclaimed scornfully. "An old woman and a single captain in the king's army. What sort of attack do you think that would amount to?"

"Davin told us to," Monny whined.

"Who is this Davin?" Shea asked one more time, even though the waves of fatigue were beginning to swamp her again.

"He's *Davin.*" Monny shrugged, as if there could be no other answer.

"He's—" Crestman started to say, but he was interrupted by the crash of the cottage door on its hinges and the swirl of autumn-cold air that swept into the room.

"He's standing outside the cottage, listening to an old fool and two children babble away into the night."

"Davin!" Monny leaped from his crouching position by the fireplace, flying across the cottage to the ancient man who entered. Along with dusty robes and a long crooked staff, the old man brought the scent of autumn into the room—cool crisp air, tinged with crumbled leaves and dark earth. "We've got them here! We've kept them as prisoners!"

"Prisoners!" The old man snorted through his nose, and the child crumbled before the ancient disdain. "Are they chained, your prisoners?"

"Well, no—"

"Are they bound with magical spells?"

"No, but—"

"Are they hamstrung so that they cannot run away?"

"No, Davin, but—"

"Have they sworn loyalty to King Sin Hazar, and let the blood oath flow from their veins?"

"No, but we thought—"

"I have." Crestman set the words amid Monny's protest, steady and even. "I've sworn my loyalty to the king."

The calm statement silenced the thundering old man, settling his beetling brows over his night-black eyes. Davin blinked and shrugged and suddenly seemed to be nothing more than an old, old man, pottering about his cottage on a cold autumn night. "So," he said at last. "You're staking claim to the king's army, then, are you?"

"I've been a member of His Majesty's troops. I've been a captain."

If the old man caught the past tense of Crestman's words, he said nothing. Instead, he gestured vaguely toward Shea. "And what about the woman?"

"The king entrusted her to me. She was his nursemaid when she was young. He was afraid that she would starve along the road, so I brought her with me. I gave her some of my dried beef while we traveled. I kept her alive." Crestman's voice was growing strong with his story, and he dared to look the old man in the eyes. "She would not be here, if not for me."

"And you, old woman. What do you say?" For the first time, Shea was pinned by Davin's gaze. At first impression, the old man's eyes were mild enough; they watered at the corners, as if stung by the wind that blew outside the cottage. She could sense the power in those deep pits, though, the raw energy that flashed far beneath the surface. She automatically looked for his tattoo, to see if she confronted a lion or a sun, a swan or an owl, but she could make out nothing in the flickering firelight. The wrinkles around the old man's eyes were too deep, his face was too worn to provide the familiar signposts of Shea's world.

She wanted to tell him that Crestman spoke the truth. She wanted to rely on the lionboy's stories to pull them out of this disaster. She wanted to find herself spirited away from the murderous child, Monny, from the strange talking bird that even now had awoken and shifted from foot to foot on its wooden perch.

But when Shea looked into those eyes, she found that she could not lie. She was snared by Davin's age, by the power that emanated from him like the ripples of a stone dropped into a pond. "I don't know, lord. I don't know what's the truth any longer."

"The truth is what you make it to be."

Shea heard the words, but she did not understand them. They sounded like the sort of thing Father Nariom said, like an owl's hooting.

"I don't know how to make things, lord. I'm a sunwoman. I raise my children. I find food. I keep a clean house."

Crestman stepped forward, settling a firm hand on Shea's arm. "You did those things in the king's household, Grandmother."

Shea blinked, confused. She'd never been in the king's household. She'd never been farther north than her little cottage.

Davin turned his piercing gaze on the lionboy. "You set your game pieces on an unsteady board, boy."

Crestman's reply was immediate. "I play no games, lord. I haven't played games since I set aside my toy sword for a real blade."

There was a long moment, while the only sound was the fire crackling on the hearth. Then, the old man exhaled slowly. "It's been a long night. The stars are bright, and I stayed out to see the Owl rise. The Owl will watch over the next phase of my work. My work for the king." Davin shuffled toward his hearth, letting his ragged cloak fall onto the packed-earth floor, as if he were an absentminded child who did not care where he set his belongings. "Monny! Bring me some ale. And you'd better tell me that you've kept some stew for an old man."

"Yes, Davin!" The boy was prompt to answer. Shea could hear the relief in his voice, his joy that he'd done right in bringing Crestman and Shea to the cottage. Or at least, he had not done wrong.

"We'll wait until the morning," Davin grumbled, as Monny tugged off the old man's boots. "We'll decide what to do with our prisoners in the daylight."

5

Sin Hazar rubbed his hands, sliding his fingers over the dead chill of the cabochon-cut rubies and emeralds set into his rings. A draft seeped through the stone chamber, blowing across the packed-earth floor deep beneath the castle. It was unnecessary to continue holding war strategy sessions here—the Uprising had been crushed for more than seven years. The days of secret planning against rebellious nobles were long past. Nevertheless, the planning had begun here when Sin Hazar needed to fear spies and traitors. Habit kept the soldiers gathering in the bleak stone room as they began to plot their campaign against Morenia.

Habit or tradition. That was the problem with these noblemen—every one of them was snagged by the dead branch of *tradition*. We can't fight a war as winter approaches because no Amanthian had before. We can't feign war against the Liantines over the ocean to the east because no Amanthian had before. We can't raise an army of children, because . . .

An army of children. They were wrong there. Sin Hazar *could* raise an army of children. Could and had.

Certainly the Little Army was not going to march for days and then pitch battle against that southern upstart Halaravilli. The child soldiers would never take a battlefield by sheer force, and the advantage of surprise—the startling appearance of bloodthirsty, screaming babes—would only last for one battle, or at most two.

But there were other advantages to the Little Army.

Sin Hazar looked up from the map that he had been studying, from its grim message that Sin Hazar needed a deeper treasury. Money. Mercenaries. Supplies. With scarcely a conscious thought, the king of all Amanthia raised a broad finger to the swan's wing that stretched across his cheekbone, reinforcing the royal command behind his question: "What word from Teleos?"

"Your Majesty." Al-Marai, Sin Hazar's older brother and the most senior general in Amanthia, bowed deeply before answering. The king braced himself for yet another round of argument. "May I speak plainly?"

Sin Hazar nodded once, tautly. It would not do for his own brother, for his own *general* to fear him. Honor him, yes. Respect him, certainly. Recognize the power of his swan tattoo, of course. But fear did not have a place on a battlefield. At least not on one's own side of the bloody, trampled earth.

Al-Marai narrowed his eyes to a squint above his curling chestnut beard. The grim expression crinkled the lion tattoo that sprawled across nearly half his face. "You know that the men despise Teleos. They hate what he stands for and what he does. That hatred is weakening them as your tools. Is it necessary for us to continue doing business with that pig?"

"Are you saying that your soldiers are ready to rebel because I choose to conduct business with a particular merchant?"

"Of course not, Your Majesty." Al-Marai ducked unhesitatingly into a bow, folding at his waist as if that were the most natural reaction in the world. Of course not. But that *was* what Al-Marai had implied. Sin Hazar continued to gaze at his brother, at the greatest commander in all of Amanthia. The grizzled warrior grimaced at the map, avoiding his liege's eyes. The soldier fidgeted with the belt that held his sword about his waist, finding ways to occupy his fingers, his eyes, his mind. But Sin Hazar could be patient. He knew the compelling power of silence. At last, Al-Marai shifted from foot to foot, slamming a hand against the map board so hard that three of the pieces toppled to their sides. "He *is* a pig!"

"You may call him a pig, Al-Marai, or say that he eats the flesh of boars, or say that he couples with swine. Debase him in any way you see fit. The fact remains that he is the man who fills our coffers. I need hardly remind *you* of the expense of horsing and housing and feeding my men-at-arms."

"Nay, Your Majesty." Al Marai swallowed hard, mastering his fury. He inclined his head and spoke through set teeth: "I know the costs of war."

"Then perhaps you'll help me pay a little of the toll." Sin Hazar pinned his brother with a steely gaze. "I asked, what news from Teleos?"

"He says that he can take another hundred before the new year. In the spring, he's prepared to take as many more."

"Two hundred? That's all?"

"Sire! That's two hundred more of your subjects shipped overseas!"

"Two hundred children who would otherwise starve come spring! Al-Marai, I need hardly remind you of the facts. Every child who boards one of my ships for Liantine lives longer than he would live in the countryside. Every child who serves his king abroad plants a seedling of support over the sea. Every child who is given to Teleos will come back to reward us a thousandfold."

"Yes, Your Majesty." Al-Marai bit his lower lip. He swallowed hard, and when he spoke again, his voice was pulled even tighter. "There's more, Sire."

"Aye?" Sin Hazar refused to spare his brother more than the single word. The man should know better. Al-Marai was the one who had taken the coin gained from those children and transformed it into a winning army at home. He was the one who trained the children before they left, who inspired their passion and their confidence. Al-Marai made certain that the Little Army would stay loyal to its king, even in a strange land, even in the midst of adversity.

"Teleos is willing to buy more than two hundred boys."

"You just said—"

"He'll buy girls as well. He'll pay for them, the same as soldiers."

For just an instant, Sin Hazar was knocked silent, surprised enough that he did not bother to reprimand Al-Marai for cutting him off. The possibilities unfolded like a rare flower blooming beneath a chilled midnight moon. Girls . . . The kingdom was filled with *girls*—suns, lions, owls, even swans—who would never find a husband, not with all the men and boys gone or killed. Girls who would become more of a risk than they were worth once they realized they would never find a husband, never bear babes.

"What does he want with them?"

"What does one ever want with girls, Your Majesty?" Even with distaste creeping across his words, Al-Marai managed to keep his voice dry. "I suppose he'll keep *some* of them as soldiers. He said they need not be trained, though. No more so than the girls who already tag along beside the camps, in whatever unofficial capacity."

"Girls . . ." Sin Hazar said aloud, turning the concept about in his mind. The word felt smooth beneath his thoughts, like coins cascading between his fingers. Why had he never thought of it before? Why had he passed up the possibility?

Before he could follow the thought, a guard hurried into the stone chamber, bowing deeply before his king. "What is it, man?" Sin Hazar snapped.

"You have visitors, Your Majesty."

"I'm the king. I always have visitors." Sin Hazar was frustrated at being disturbed, interrupted before he could work out the import of Teleos's new offer.

"You'll want to see these, Sire."

Sin Hazar shot the man a probing glance. "Will I?" Whatever his frustration, Sin Hazar trusted his household lions. He shrugged his robe off his shoulders, the better to display the dragon-chased azure doublet that he had chosen for the day's formalities. "And who is so important?"

"Prince Bashanorandi, Sire."

"Felicianda's bastard?" Sin Hazar heard a surprised note creep into his own voice.

"Aye, Your Majesty. He's just come from the harbor."

"Is he traveling as an ambassador from Halaravilli?"

"I don't think so, Sire. He has a handful of soldiers with him— our men." The guard brushed the tattoo on his right cheek, silent explanation of his words. "There are two girls as well. No one in Morenian livery."

So. That gambit had paid off at last, sending lions to Morenia. Sin Hazar had almost given up on Bashanorandi. He had debated before deciding to send lions south in the first place. If the men had been discovered, if they'd been unmasked as Amanthian soldiers, then that upstart Halaravilli would have pitched a diplomatic tantrum. Nevertheless, Sin Hazar had argued with Al-Marai, the risk of sending a dozen men was minimal. A dozen men, dispatched alone or in pairs . . . It was worth the gamble.

Now, Sin Hazar resisted the urge to turn to Al-Marai, to gloat over his success. Which of his lions had been successful in penetrating the Morenian court? Well, time enough to learn that. Even more intriguing was the question of why Bashanorandi had come north. He could just as easily have used the lions to consolidate power in Morenia, to build up his own loyal corps.

Sin Hazar ran through a handful of scenarios. Bashanorandi had come to stake a claim as the childless Sin Hazar's heir. He had come to plead for assistance in his internecine battle against Halaravilli, to beg reinforcements for his fledgling rebellion. He had come with battle plans and passwords, ready to betray his so-called brother.

Of course, there was no reason to trust a half-breed bastard. No reason to trust a boy whose mother and father had both been executed as traitors.

Not that Sin Hazar had any complaint against Felicianda's attempt to deliver the kingdom of Morenia to her ancestral home, to her family line. No—Sin Hazar's only concern was that his sister had *failed*. She had always been given to complicating things, Felicianda had been. No reason to ride in a straight line, she'd always thought, when a looping jaunt could be done instead.

Grinning ferally at Al-Marai, Sin Hazar nodded to his soldier. "I'll see them here."

By the time the guard had led the trio into the stone chamber, Sin Hazar had taken a stand beside the detailed map. He lifted a token in his hand, a marker that represented ten horsemen. The piece moved easily between his fingers, over, under, over, under, soothing with its familiar feel. While Sin Hazar had initially planned on being engrossed in the map when his visitors entered the chamber, he decided at the last instant to scrutinize their approach.

He raised a jeweled finger toward his swan tattoo, as if he were smoothing away a momentary itch. The movement was not lost on the three southerners, all of whom obediently followed his pointing finger. He saw each of them acknowledge the silvery swan wings that spread across his cheeks. Sin Hazar remained focused on the boy, though. On his nephew.

Bashanorandi had not yet reached his full man's size. Certainly he had his mother's height, but at . . . what was it? . . . fifteen years of age? . . . he had yet to fill out in his shoulders and across his chest. The boy wore Halaravilli's colors, although the livery looked like it had been slept in for a fortnight. Simple clothes, Sin Hazar noted. No velvet. No silk. As if Bashanorandi were nothing but a poor relation. Well, even that was not *quite* the truth, was it?

The Morenian crimson clashed with Bashanorandi's auburn hair. Ah, yes, the auburn hair that had also been the gift of his mother. That, and his blue eyes. The shape of the boy's face, though, was more delicate than Felicianda's had ever been. The boy's chin came to a point, and his eyes tilted up just the slightest bit. The vulpine expression made him look vulnerable. Legacy of his traitor father, Sin Hazar supposed.

Sin Hazar flicked his gaze across the boy's companions. Two girls. One, scrawny with the pinched look that came from a lifetime in the streets. She had one arm bound up in a sling, held awkwardly across her chest. The other girl was better fed and lacked any outward sign of injury, but she was more ill at ease, looking about the stone chamber as if she expected guards to throw her in a dungeon at any moment. Neither of the pair looked worth a wasted heartbeat. The king turned his gaze back to Bashanorandi.

"Cousin." He kept his voice low with the one word, not tinting it with a hint of welcome or distrust. He watched Bashanorandi register the two syllables, and confusion was apparent across the youth's face. Should he respond with a familial greeting to this man he'd never met? Should he reply as nobleman to royalty? As prince to king? Sin Hazar hept his eyes steady on the boy, purposely not giving him any sign of a proper resolution.

"Your Majesty."

Excellent! Sin Hazar might have gloated, if he had not been so intent on keeping the boy off-balance. So, Felicianda's bastard son would address him as a king, as a liege lord. *That* could make things simpler. "We trust that you had an easy journey to our court. If we had known of your intention to visit your mother's homeland, we would have prepared an escort from the harbor."

"I—We did not know that we'd be coming until we'd already taken ship." The boy paused, clearly waiting for Sin Hazar to say something. The king did not oblige. "We—that is, I, um, I wanted to see my homeland. I wanted to see my mother's country."

"The times are rough for traveling, between the approaching winter and the rebels on the open seas. We trust that you encountered no difficulty?"

"No, Your Majesty. Your men protected us all along the way."

"*Our* men?" Sin Hazar raised his eyebrows and tilted his head in a study of surprise. "Do you hear that, Al-Marai? This youth apparently believes that we dispatched our soldiers to the south."

"Impossible, Your Majesty." Al-Marai stepped forward without hesitation, settling a hand on the sword that swung at his waist, as if to remind the trio of southerners that they were deep in enemy territory. "Sire, if we were to send armed lions into another kingdom, we could be accused of unbridled aggression."

"So." Sin Hazar pinned the youth again with his own steely eyes, fully aware that the boy was struggling to take in his Uncle Al-Marai's broad chest, to comprehend the threat implied by the massive sword, by the brawny arms. Before Felicianda's bastard could speak, Sin Hazar purred, "Are you certain they were *our* men?"

"Yes, Your Majesty. That is, I thought . . . The guards . . . They came to me in the castle, posing as new members of the royal guard. They said they came from you."

"They *said* . . ." Sin Hazar let the second word trail off, weaving a rainbow of meaning into the single syllable. What would the boy do with *that*? Demand that the king acknowledge his own men? Question the reality that was before his very eyes, in the shape of the tattoos on the soldiers' faces?

"Yes. Er, I thought that you sent them because of my mother. Because of Queen Felicianda."

"Ah, our poor lost sister, blessed be her name before all the Thousand Gods." Sin Hazar made a religious sign across his chest and bit back a smile as the boy belatedly followed suit. Out of the corner of his eye, the king noted that neither of the girls saw fit to invoke a blessing on dear, dead Felicianda. "So. You claim to travel with our soldiers. And who are these delicate flowers that you bring with you?" Courtly language—neither of the girls bore the slightest resemblance to a blossom. Well, the shorter one might, the one with some meat on her bones—but at most she resembled the bloom of a thorn tree.

Bashanorandi seemed surprised by the king's compliment. "These flowers?" He cleared his throat and made a half bow. "May I present to Your Majesty, um, Ranita Glasswright and Mair."

Ranita Glasswright. Sin Hazar's spies had told him all about that one. She was the girl who had sent Felicianda's tottering plot crashing down, disclosing the conspiracy to the old king of Morenia. Fascinating, that Bashanorandi traveled with her, with the one he must blame for his orphaning. Interesting, as well, that he named her by her guild name, when she had apparently jumped about among castes like that Jair the southerners held in such high esteem.

And Mair. Sin Hazar had not heard her name before. The single syllable told him a great deal, though. She was one of the casteless, one of the . . . Touched. It was odd enough that a prince would travel with such a girl. That he would obviously dislike her so intensely . . . Well, this game just might prove entertaining enough for all the long winter nights.

King Sin Hazar inclined his head, first toward the guild brat, then toward the Touched wench. "My lady Ranita. My lady Mair." He noticed his nephew stiffen at the honorifics. Ah. Anger could have many sources—Sin Hazar was willing to bet that Bashanorandi's was based on jealousy. The king of all Amanthia added, "We trust you'll find all to your liking as you stay in our court."

Ranita Glasswright glanced at Mair, as if she were seeking permission to speak, but when she stepped forward, she held her head high. "We thank you for your hospitality, Your Majesty. Nevertheless, we would be most honored if you could return us to Morenia immediately. We will only require a small escort as we journey south, and that only until we reach your border."

"What, my lady? You've scarcely arrived in our fair city. You must take some time to appreciate the riches of our northern realm."

"Begging your pardon, Your Majesty." The guild refugee ducked her head in a charming, rustic bow. "We are honored by your promise of hospitality, but we must insist upon returning to King Halaravilli. We traveled here against our wills, Your Majesty, even at great personal pain to my companion, to Mair."

Sin Hazar slitted his eyes as he glared at Bashanorandi. The boy might only be a bastard prince, but he should have better control over his subjects than *that*. How could he stand by and let this girl tell her tales? Even if they were *true*, a guildsman should have enough fear of a prince to keep her mouth shut.

Bashanorandi might have been thinking the same thing, but he held his tongue. Instead of replying, or defending himself, he glared at Mair. So. The guild girl spoke, but the Touched wench was blamed. Fairly? Or because Bashanorandi hated her? So much fun Sin Hazar might have. . . . "Cousin? What say you to these accusations?"

"Please, um, Your Majesty. I brought Ranita and Mair here for their own safety. They had raised steel against me, against my men. Your men, that is. They knew that I rode willingly with your soldiers, Your Majesty, yet they sought to stop me. I had no choice but to bring them."

"One *always* has a choice," Sin Hazar purred, watching as his nephew took his meaning, as the boy blanched.

"If I had slain them," Bashanorandi replied after a long pause, "then Hal would have chased after us with all the men at his disposal."

Hal. How intriguing. The boy called his brother by a Touched name. Or a god. Or nothing more than a childhood nickname. . . . Sin Hazar almost smiled. His spies had brought him tales of the deep valley of hatred between the southern boys, hatred that could so easily be harnessed in support of Amanthia's cause. "And so you stole these ladies?"

"It was more like . . . borrowing, Your Majesty." The prince was earnest in his reply.

"And if we choose to kill them now?"

"Your Majesty?" Bashanorandi barely whispered the words.

"If we choose to execute them? If we choose to label them enemies. Traitors. Spies."

"Then I would be forced to challenge Your Majesty to combat. These women are under my protection."

Brave words, Sin Hazar thought. Brave words when the speaker was little more than a child, surrounded by well-fed, well-rested men-at-arms in a court leagues and leagues from so-called home. Perhaps there was more to this prince than Sin Hazar had thought at first. Perhaps Felicianda's whelp could be used wisely.

The king kept his steady gaze on the boy, knowing that his own dark eyes frightened men. Sin Hazar was blessed with the ability to delay blinking, a childhood skill well harnessed against fighting men. The effect, he knew, was to make him seem like a cat, like a ferocious predator who could stare down an enemy for as long as that action took.

The boy stood up to the attention better than Sin Hazar had expected. For nearly a full minute he gazed at his uncle, then he maneuvered his hand to rest on the hilt of his sword. When he spoke, his voice was deadly still. "Your Majesty, I came to you because you are my kin. I came because I believed the stories that I heard at my mother's knee. I expected you to welcome flesh and blood. If I was mistaken, then you should not hold that against my companions, against Ranita Glasswright and Mair."

Sin Hazar startled all three of the southerners by clapping his hands loudly, again and again. "A fine speech, cousin! Fine words! You speak bravely." Sin Hazar watched as his compliments lent steel to the boy's spine. "Your mother would be proud of you, son!" The endearment made the boy's eyes shoot toward Sin Hazar's face, searching the king's gaze for some inner meaning. Sin Hazar let his own features relax into a smile. "It must have been very hard getting the ladies here, to Amanthia, if they did not even understand the danger they were in down south. If they did not even know enough to protect themselves."

"Your Majesty—" Ranita Glasswright leaped to the bait, eager to clarify the record.

"We were speaking to our nephew, Lady Ranita."

"But you weren't—"

"We were not addressing you."

"Your Majesty—"

"Really, we don't know what insubordination Halaravilli suffers in his kingdom, but we can assure you that we do not permit guildsmen to tell us how to rule. In Amanthia it is customary to wait until your king has asked for your advice before you offer it."

"You are not my king!"

"You are on our soil, in our castle, surrounded by our men-at-arms!" Sin Hazar let a little of his true rage leak into his words. The child was insufferable! Not only did she think that she knew better than her elders, but she somehow thought she had free license to say whatever came into her mind! Sin Hazar jutted his chin toward Al-Marai. "General, if this one speaks another word before we leave this chamber, you are to have her gagged, bound, and thrown into our dungeons."

Ranita Glasswright drew breath to protest but clearly thought better of her rebellion when Al-Marai stepped forward with a simple bow, inclining his head and resting his hand on his sword. The king waited for a long moment, testing her, measuring her stupidity. When the brat remained silent for several heartbeats,

Sin Hazar softened his gaze and permitted his nephew the scantest of smiles. "You have traveled long and hard. Let us offer you the meats of our table, cousin, and when you have filled your belly, a bed in our house." The king set a hand on the boy's shoulder and felt the young flesh quiver, like a hound trembling beneath its master's touch.

"Your Majesty!" It was the other girl who spoke, the one whose arm was in its awkward sling. "We have asked for your protection. We have asked that you return us to Morenia."

The king bit off his annoyance. He had not forbidden that casteless wench to speak. "All in good time, Lady Mair. All in good time." Sin Hazar took a couple of steps toward the doorway of the stone chamber, driving his nephew forward with the weight of his hand. He let it seem an afterthought that turned him back to the two girls. "In the meantime, you should make yourselves comfortable in our castle. We will send women to you, to tend to your needs. Guards! Al-Marai, attend me."

Sin Hazar left the two girls in the stone chamber, surrounded by the toys of war and a handful of soldiers in royal livery. The king would be true to his word. He would send women to look after Lady Ranita and Lady Mair. But that would be *after* he broke bread with his nephew.

After he began to explore the benefits of his three new hostages.

Halaravilli, King of Morenia, stood in the drafty entrance of a ramshackle hut, cursing himself for not grabbing a warmer cloak. Nearly three months had passed since he'd last masqueraded as a Touched youth, slipping out of the palace through the secret corridor that Dalarati had shown him so long ago. Three months ago, the summer sun had beat down on Hal's head as he made his way through the City streets, worming into the narrow byways of the no-man's-land between the quarters.

Now, a chill wind blew through those same streets. A promise of snow teased the air, and Hal would not even have considered leaving the palace compound if he had not found the slip of parchment lurking beneath his morning cup of mulled wine. Even

as he unfolded the message, he knew what it would say. There
was no need to question his manservant about the parchment's
provenance. Even though Hal was only seventeen years old, he
had lived long enough to know that the servant would have no
idea how the message had appeared on the tray. The Fellowship
of Jair wanted things that way.

And the Fellowship had certainly lost no time in summoning
him. Hal had only taken his stand against Tasuntimanu in the
council room the morning before. The earl must have run directly
to the Fellowship's hierarchy. Hal, sipping his mulled wine, had
nodded as he read the neat words: "The Pilgrim Jair watches over
all his children, even from the darkened hallway, even as the sun
draws nigh to noon."

Hal knew from earlier cryptic messages that the Fellowship
had moved its safe house only a fortnight before. The newest
meeting place was a tiny hut in a nondescript street. Hal just
hoped that whoever he was supposed to meet would show up
promptly at noon. The streets would be even colder when the
sun began its early trip to the west.

Blowing on his fingers to warm them, Hal could not help but
think of the tales Rani had told him about the Brotherhood of
Justice. She had witnessed some of their meetings in similar ramshackle huts; she knew how members of secret cabals could be
betrayed in the dark passages where Hal's own soldiers did not
patrol.

A chill crept down the king's spine as he thought of the con-
niving traitors that Rani had almost joined, of the headman's axe
that had closed their tale. What would Hal's loyal councillors do
if they discovered their king skulking in dark alleys, making deals
with shadowy forces? How quickly would they have him imprisoned, executed?

Nonsense. Hal was the king. He could hardly commit treason
against himself.

He was only thinking such morbid thoughts because he was
tired, because yesterday's council meeting had worn him out. He
was tired and nervous at the proposition of defending his actions
to the Fellowship of Jair. Tugging at his filthy cape, Hal resisted

the urge to look up and down the dingy street. The King's Guard would throw a fit if they learned their liege lord slunk through the City in common trews and a grimy shirt, looking for all the world like a ragged Touched boy, roaming free from his troop for the first time in his life.

There was no reason, though, for the guard ever to find out. With luck, no one would come to check on Hal until well after the sun had set. The king had carefully fostered a rumor born during his days as an odd junior prince in his father's court, a rumor that served him better now that he was seventeen than it had ever done him as a child. Hal let all around him believe that he sometimes suffered gripping headaches, pulsing agonies that left him incapable of speech, unable to gather his wits about him. His only salvation in the midst of those seizures, he lied, was sleep—uninterrupted sleep in a completely darkened chamber.

He knew that he played a dangerous game. No sane king would deliberately foster the image of himself as an invalid. But no sane king would deliberately join an underground cabal of people from all the castes, working toward some mysterious, unknown goal. Hal had had no choice, when he had made his initial decisions. He needed to guarantee that he could escape the palace when necessary. He needed freedom to fulfill his obligation to the Fellowship of Jair, to meet his debt to the brotherhood that had helped him gain his throne, that had stood by him when he was weakest and most subject to attack.

Hal owed the Fellowship. He had sworn his fidelity as a member of the shadowy coalition. The Fellowship, in turn, had sent members to watch over him, to help him, to protect him. One of those members, Dalarati, had died to further Hal's cause, cut down in the bitter struggle with the Brotherhood of Justice.

The Fellowship might be dangerous, but it had accepted Hal when no one else would. Hal paid his debts, no matter the cost, no matter the games that he needed to play with his court, the charades of illness that he needed to create.

"Speak, Pilgrim, and enter." The cathedral bells had just begun to toll noon when Hal finally heard the whisper at his ear, through a bolt-hole that grated open in the door of the rotting hut. He stepped forward before he could question the wisdom of disappearing, anonymous and alone, into a structure of questionable integrity with an unknown stranger.

"Blessed be Jair the Pilgrim, who protects the lion from the flood." Lion. Flood. Hal was certain those were the passwords. Nevertheless, he knew a moment of heart-clenching fear that he had remembered incorrectly, that the Fellowship had changed its passwords since he had last heard. Or worse yet, that it was not the Fellowship that waited within the crumbling building. If even one of Hal's enemies had learned of the existence of the shadowy body . . .

Hal imagined a heavy sword suspended over his bare neck, a wicked Amanthian blade curving toward his blood. He should have slipped on armor beneath his Touched garb. He should have protected himself before he risked his life and his kingdom. He should have told someone—anyone—where he was going.

Where he was going. The threat was growing. His blood was flowing.

Catching his breath, Hal swallowed the blossom of panic, forcing himself to count to twenty. He had only completed half the count, though, when the door swung open. "Come, Pilgrim, and enter the house of Jair."

House of Jair! Not likely!

Nevertheless, Hal's relief washed over him like a wave of scorn, and he drew his cloak closer as he strode down the narrow corridor. He tried to tell himself that he pulled the filthy garment closer to protect it from the sticky walls, but he knew that he sought comfort in its woolen warmth. He may not have been waylaid by assassins *this* time, but there was still danger in the hut. Who knew how Tasuntimanu had twisted his story of the council meeting?

Hal was shown into a room as grim as the outside of the building. A low fire crackled on a flagged hearth, but the flue did not draw well, and smoke had stained the wall to either side of the flames. A three-legged stool crouched beside the fire, close enough that Hal expected the seat's occupant to be flushed with heat. She wasn't, though. She was pale, pale white, like an insect writhing under a stone in the royal garden.

"At least ye still remember 'ow t' follow a direct order when it drops into yer lap." The cracked voice made Hal jump, and he bit back a curse.

"Glair." Well, at least the Fellowship was not going to waste Hal's time with minor officials. Contrary to all order in the rest of the City, the Touched crone was a high commander in the Fellowship of Jair, the most senior member of the brotherhood that Hal had ever met.

The ancient Touched woman barely acknowledged his greeting. "Boy, d' ye realize 'ow serious this is? 'Ave ye thought on why I summoned ye 'ere?"

Boy. Under other circumstances, Hal would have resented such a familiar address from a subject, especially from one of the Touched. He might even have had the disrespectful wretch tossed into the royal dungeons, to contemplate caste and station in society. Coming from Glair, though, the word was little more than a statement of fact. Hal was not a nobleman in this hut. He was merely a foot soldier in the Fellowship's army, a pawn who knew next to nothing about the organization's master plan. The king of all Morenia forced himself to take a steadying breath before he looked the ancient crone in the face. There was no reason to make up a tale. To fear the jail. To admit he'd failed. "Yes, Glair. I understand why you are concerned."

"Concerned? Ye think I'm *concerned*?" The old woman's voice broke on the word, and her head shook with more than her usual palsy. "Only 'n idiot would think I'm *concerned*!"

Only an idiot. Hal had spent the better part of his life called that. He refused to let one old woman's taunts draw him into an angry retort. He forced his voice to a steady register, ignoring the unnatural ringing in his ears, the whispering rhymes that swirled just beneath the surface of his thoughts. "You have to understand, Glair. I have a greater master than my own personal beliefs, than my own faith in the Fellowship. I cannot decide, alone, what I think is right and what is wrong. I must act for the good of all Morenia, for all my people, and not just the Fellowship of Jair."

"*Just* th' Fellowship o' Jair!" The old woman's voice squeaked on the exclamation, and she pitched forward with the force of her words. "Do ye even 'ear th' words ye say, boy! Do ye even 'ear 'ow stupid ye sound? Th' Fellowship o' *Jair*, we are! Th' First Pilgrim, boy! We're th' ones 'oo got ye on yer throne, even when they said it couldna be done, even when they said all o' Morenia was lost to that scheming she-dog, Felicianda!" Glair spat into the flames, but some of the spittle stayed on her bruised lips, glistening like a slug's slimy trail.

Hal's belly twisted, and he fought the urge to back out of the chamber. Steeling himself, he cut into the old woman's torrent of scorn. "Glair, what accusations has Tasuntimanu leveled against me?"

"Tasuntimanu?" She screeched the name like a madwoman. Not for the first time, Hal wondered at the wisdom of letting a Touched woman hold such high office in the Fellowship. The Touched were casteless, they were nothing in the City hierarchy. Surely some could be trained, brought into service for nobles and the wealthiest of merchants, but most Touched were parasites, sucking life out of the City. That was why they were driven from the streets regularly, why Turning Out Day was necessary. That was why the oldest among the Touched grew mad, crazed with the hard struggle of life. And that was why no decent folk associated with the Touched.

No decent folk, but the Fellowship. The Fellowship and the Thousand Gods. First Pilgrim Jair had been born a Touched brat.

Hal reminded himself that he had joined Glair's cause voluntarily, and he forced his voice to remain steady. "Aye. Tasuntimanu. I know he must have come running to you after our council meeting. There's no other reason you would have summoned me here, in broad daylight. There's no other reason you would risk exposing the entire Fellowship."

"So ye're not so foolish that ye don't realize th' risk we're takin', eh? Ye're not such 'n idiot that ye don't see 'ow ye're forcin' me t' put me own flesh 'n' blood at risk?"

"Glair, you knew there was a risk five years ago, when you took me into the Fellowship. I never hid the fact that I have loyalties to other causes, to Morenia, first and foremost."

"Th' entire Fellowship knows o' yer 'loyalties,' boy. But Dalarati vouched fer ye. 'E said we needed ye in our midst. That poor soldier would fall on 'is sword if 'e saw 'ow ye're abusin' th' Fellowship wi' th' power o' yer Crown!"

"Don't speak to me of Dalarati!" Hal bellowed, his anger mixing with fear and spewing out like acid. "Dalarati knew the king I would be! The rest of you were only interested in *what* I was, the son of a king. But Dalarati knew *me*! If it weren't for Dalarati, I never would have cast my lot with the likes of you!"

"Cast yer lot! Th likes o' us! Dalarati was one o' us, boy, 'n' 'e gave 'is life t' further yer cause, gave 'is life *because* 'e was one o' th' Fellowship."

"I know what debts were paid to get me on the throne, Glair. I measure them every time I pass the headman's block." Hal's throat tightened around his words. He had not asked Dalarati to lay down his life in service to the Crown. That had been a mistake, the worst sort of lies and misunderstandings. Dalarati's death had been a terrible accident, a cost of waging war.

Waging war. Fight for more. Bloody gore.

No. That's what it had been—war. Hal had waged war against traitors who would have stolen his father's throne. Glair had no business questioning Hal's loyalty, no business drawing upon the death of a beloved retainer. . . . Hal forced himself to take a deep breath, stealing the chance to breathe a quick prayer to Plad, the god of patience; Hail Plad, cool my blood and still my mind and give me the patience to walk upon your holy path.

The words did not make him feel any better, but they broke the angry exchange. Hal tried again, forcing himself to keep his voice steady. "Glair, you must understand. I had to speak out in council. If I don't take a stand now, if I don't separate myself from Puladarati, I'll be pinned beneath his thumb forever. Yesterday's meeting was a battle for the type of reign I'll have. It was only a single skirmish, but it will shape the entire war."

"I understand, boy. I understand th' nature o' battles, 'n' I

know better than ye do, th' nature o' war." Glair dragged a claw
across her face, scraping back a few strands of glossy hair. "Ye
must trust me, though. Ye canna see th' lay o' th' land from where
ye're standin'. Ye dinna know what's at stake."

"Then tell me! Tell me what's so important. Tell me what is
worth having Bashanorandi poisoned against us at his uncle's
knee. What is worth dragging Rani and Mair—two members of
our Fellowship, Glair!—what is worth dragging them north,
against their wills, at the edge of a curved Amanthian blade?"

Glair stared at him, her rheumy eyes suddenly calculating. He
felt her measure his grimy clothes, his torn cape. He sensed the
calculation in her mind, her weighing him as a person, as a man,
as a king.

And he made his own calculations. After all, what *did* he know
about the Fellowship?

They had come to *him*, seducing him when he'd been frightened and angry and alone in his father's court. His older brother,
Tuvashanoran, had still lived, and the possibility of Hal's taking
the throne had been distant enough to be laughable. Dalarati had
been his bodyguard then. The handsome young soldier had been
the only person in the entire palace who had talked to Hal as if
the young prince were capable of thought. Back then, Hal had
worked hard to craft his facade of idiocy, to make people think
that he was too stupid to bother with, too hopeless to drag into
the swirl of deadly court politics. Hal had carefully cultivated an
idiot's stance, so that he heard all that happened in the palace,
learned the plots and subplots that eddied around him. Hal worked
to protect himself against his scheming stepmother, against Queen
Felicianda, who wanted nothing more than to see her own son
replace Hal in the line of succession.

All the same, though, the lonely prince had craved attention.
He had grown to look forward to his casual conversations with
Dalarati, to the easy answers that the soldier gave to Hal's questions. The soldier had joked with him, told the outcast youth stories about life outside the palace, about Shar, the Touched girl
who had kept Dalarati's barracks room clean, who'd kept his bed
warm.

When Dalarati had offered to spirit Hal away to a secret meeting, the lonely prince had gladly agreed. There was an excitement in being outside the palace compound, a positive thrill in learning things that Bashanorandi was not being taught. The Fellowship had immediately represented a place where Hal could be the person he knew himself to be—a thinker, an actor, a person who did things, rather than a younger prince who cowered and waited for things to be done around him. Hal had joined the Fellowship almost as a reflex, reciting his vows of loyalty calmly and smoothly, when all the rest of the world thought that the prince could do no more than babble singsong rhymes.

But even after Hal had embraced the Fellowship, he did not know all that it worked toward. He knew that Glair led the group, at least in Moren. He knew that every official meeting of the Fellowship was opened by a prayer to Jair, the First Pilgrim. He knew that the Fellowship had been opposed to its arch enemies, the Brotherhood of Justice, and that shadowy group of traitors had set in motion the tumultuous events that led to Halaravilli ascending the throne. And he knew that the Fellowship expected Hal to act in certain ways, to make certain decisions as king.

"Tell me, Glair," he pressed. "Tell me what is so important, so that I can decide wisely."

"I'll not be tellin' ye all our plans, boy. It wouldna be safe." Hal started to protest as the Touched crone shook her head, her hands clenching and unclenching on her rags, but then she seemed to reach some decision. "I'll tell ye this, though. We're not alone, 'ere in Morenia. Th' Fellowship is spread across th' lands, from th' Eastern Sea t' beyond th' mountains, 'n' north 'n' south as well. Ye think in terms o' yer kingdom, 'n' ye think in terms o' all ye know 'n' 'old dear, but ye're only lookin' at one tiny corner o' th' true picture."

"What is that picture, Glair?"

"We're th' Fellowship o' Jair. Jair was one man, 'oo lived 'is life through all th' castes." The Touched woman's words reminded Hal of the windows in the cathedral, the broad plains of glass that told the story of the First Pilgrim's life. Jair had been born one of the Touched, but his hard work and shrewd dealings had elevated him—first to merchant, then guildsman and soldier, finally to noble-priest. Glair continued, "'E 'ad th' power t' see what 'is people truly needed. 'E 'ad th' power t' join all th' world t'gether in their faith i' th' Thousand Gods. 'E's our model, boy. 'E's what we strive t' be."

"What do you mean? The Fellowship intends to unite all the kingdoms? The Fellowship wants to conquer all the nations?" For one instant, Hal saw himself as the king of a vast empire, a land that stretched as far as the maps had been drawn.

He recognized his folly almost immediately, though. Glair had not said that Hal would rule over the Fellowship's dream. She had not said that *Hal* would succeed. If anything, she was suggesting that Hal would be forced from his own throne, that he would be forced to step aside for the greater good of the Fellowship. Hal would be forced to proffer up his birthright, like a merchant buying his way into a guild. As Rani had done, forfeiting one life for another. Hal dared not let himself dwell on how Rani's bargain had turned out. "Is that what you mean, Glair? That the Fellowship will rule all?"

The old woman grimaced and shook her head. "I've already told ye more than ye should need t' 'ear. If ye're sworn t' th' Fellowship, ye should be able t' support us wi' what ye know. What's it t' be, boy? Are ye fer us, or agin us?"

"It's not that simple."

"Ah, but it is. As long as ye're in th' Fellowship, ye're like a soldier. Ye're given yer orders. Ye either follow 'em, or ye mutiny. 'N if ye mutiny, then ye pay th' price."

"You're threatening your king, old woman!"

Glair threw back her head and laughed, a throaty chortle that made the folds of flesh at her neck tremble like aspic. "I *made* ye king, boy! Now. Enough o' this. I'll ask ye once more. Are ye fer us, or agin us?"

Hal stared at the ancient woman, wondering who had made a Touched crone the power behind his throne, behind all of Morenia, behind—if he could believe her—the entire world. It was fruitless to protest, hopeless to rebel. His tone was exhausted as he pledged, "I'm for you, Glair. I'm for the Fellowship."

The old woman started to nod, but the gesture was lost in her palsy. "All right, boy—"

"I'm for the Fellowship," Hal interrupted, "but I'm *also* for Morenia. Before I swore my oaths to the Fellowship, I was born the son of King Shanoranvilli ben-Jair. I owe a debt to Morenia, to her nobles and soldiers, to the guildsmen and merchants who have followed me faithfully for the past two years. I can't just hand over my kingdom to the Fellowship, to let you do whatever you think right."

"Then what do ye intend t' do, boy?" She asked the question as if she were truly curious.

"I'll do what I promised my council. I'm sending a messenger north. I'm sending a letter to Sin Hazar, asking the meaning of his affront and demanding the return of my brother, Rani, and Mair."

"Ye 'ave no brother, boy. Yer brothers are all dead 'n' buried, the Brotherhood's traitor, Tuvashanoran, last o' all."

"My father called Bashanorandi his son, and I honor my father's memory. I won't compromise on this, Glair. I'm sending my messenger. When we hear Sin Hazar's reply, I'll come to the Fellowship. I'll seek your counsel then."

The old woman cocked her head as she looked at him, and he felt her measure his words like bread on a scale. "Aye," she said at last. "Ye can send yer one message. But ye'll listen t' th' Fellowship after this. When Tasuntimanu speaks in our name, ye'll take 'is counsel. Or ye'll pay th' price."

Hal ignored the threat. "I'll send my message."

Before Glair could add further qualifiers, the king of Morenia turned on his heel and left the ramshackle hut. He made his way through the city streets quickly, keeping to the shadows, drawing his ragged cloak across his face as he approached passages that were more populated. He did not know if Glair sent agents to follow him; he did not know how many members of the Fellowship of Jair roamed Moren's streets. He only knew that for the second time in as many days, he had taken a stand to rule his kingdom as he saw fit. He had stood his ground like a man, and he liked the feeling of that solid earth beneath his feet.

Exhilarated by his success, Hal only slowed his pace as he drew near the palace compound. It would not do to get caught now, discovered by some well-meaning guard or serving wench when he was so close to completing his mission. All he needed to do was keep to the shadows for a few moments more, wander down this alley, up against the back wall of the compound, and—

Hal made the last turn, expecting to find himself alone in the dimly lit passage that led inside the palace. Instead, there were two shadowed figures in the narrow street. They were men, by the breadth of their shoulders, and they stood with the easy stance of soldiers or noblemen trained at fighting.

Hal caught his breath, the better to hear their whispered words. "I tell you, the council won't tolerate many more scenes like the one yesterday." The speaker stepped back as he made his declaration, and his broad face was clear in the evening light, serious beneath his thinning, muddy hair. Tasuntimanu!

"Aye. The boy played us like we were his chess pieces. He's good, I tell you. That's what worries me. He's as good as his father ever was, maybe better." Hal could barely make out the words, but the tone was clear—the speaker did not intend a compliment by his comparison with the old king. The hairs on the back of Hal's neck rose in silent warning, and he sidled closer to the pair, determined to learn who joined Tasuntimanu to speak against him.

"His father is dead," Tasuntimanu muttered.

"Aye, may he walk beyond the Heavenly Gates." Both men made a religious sign before the unknown speaker continued, "We'll see if the boy has the skill to keep from meeting Tarn himself." Hal heard the threat behind the words, as clearly as if the god of death loomed over the pair in the alley. "He may have a chance, if he'll just listen to his elders. His elders and not his own, headstrong self."

The speaker chose that moment to raise a hand to his bushy hair, to scratch at some passing itch. In the gloaming light, Hal could see quite clearly that the unknown man was missing two fingers on his right hand. Tasuntimanu was meeting with Duke Puladarati, Hal's former regent.

Of course. The men's words made perfect sense. Of all the men in court, Puladarati was the "elder" who stood the most to lose by Hal's growing independence. It was even logical that they would be standing in the shadows, by the secret entrance to the palace. After all, it was Dalarati—a member of the Fellowship— who had taught Hal about the shadowy passage. Tasuntimanu would certainly know the secret as well.

Hal melted into the safety of the shadows. Even as he waited for the nobles to duck inside the palace, he wondered just how hard Duke Puladarati would fight to keep the power he had once tasted, the crown that had once been practically his. Hal wondered just how close he was to fighting for his life.

6

Rani looked down from the parapet, reflexively raising one hand to catch her hair against the tugging fingers of a wintry breeze. Her hair was not blowing in her eyes, though. Instead, it was pulled back tightly from her forehead, tugged into place beneath a tight-fitting headdress. Rani almost knocked the winged structure from her head as her fingers fumbled awkwardly with her odd costume. She swore under her breath and turned back to the scene far below her.

"Look, Mair!"

"I can see from here."

"Mair!" Rani looked up from the busy courtyard and took a step toward her friend. The Touched girl was as pale as the bleached cloth that framed her face, and she huddled beside the lion-tattooed guard who silently watched over the pair. Mair also wore one of the strange northern headdresses, and the ornate piece underscored how pointed her cheekbones were, how thin her face had become. "Mair, what's wrong?"

"Nothin's wrong, Rai." Mair swallowed audibly, letting her Touched patois leak past her chapped lips. "At least not like ye mean."

"Then what? Come look at the courtyard from here! It's filled with carts, like it's market day, or something."

"I believe you, Rai. No need t' look at th' obvious."

Rani turned back to the parapet wall. "There must be two dozen drays there! Just feeding those oxen would eat up a merchant's profit in no time. It's strange to hold a market now—everyone must be getting ready for winter." Rani watched for another minute before she exclaimed, "Wait! They're not setting up any market. These carts aren't *arriving*. They're leaving Amanth!" Rani leaned out over the low wall, craning her neck for a better view of the ground close to the tower.

"Rai, don't!" Rani turned to look at her companion as she registered the note of fear in Mair's voice. "Don't be leanin' over th' wall!"

The soldier smirked at the Touched girl's obvious terror, and Rani shot him a glowering look. "Mair, it's fine," Rani hastened to assure her friend. "I'm perfectly safe." Mair only shook her head, flattening her palms against the stone wall behind her. She managed to dart a glance at the railing, a look akin to terror. No, Rani realized, not *akin* to terror—*filled* with terror.

"What is it, Mair? What's wrong? Is your arm paining you?"

"My arm is fine." Nevertheless, the Touched girl hugged the splinted limb close to her chest, taking an unconscious step closer to the lionman.

"What, then?"

"Do ye 'ave t' stand so near th' wall? It's a long way down."

"Of course it's—" Realization finally dawned on Rani. "It's the height, then? You're afraid of the tower?"

Mair tried a weak grin, with little success. "Not much chance t' learn about towers, when ye're livin' i' th' City streets."

"But you were fine on the ship, on the deck when we sailed north!"

"I was fine so long as I stayed away fro' th' railin'! Do ye know 'ow far th' drop is t' th' courtyard?"

Mair, afraid of heights! Rani might have laughed, if the Touched girl had not clearly been so close to tears, so close to fainting dead away.

Rani had craved heights all her life, since she had first climbed the ladder to her bed in the shadowed loft above her parents' shop. As Ranita Glasswright, she had scampered over her guild's scaffolds like ivy tumbling over a wall. And now, to find Mair *afraid*! Mair had faced down the King's Guard; she had led a troop of children for years, keeping them safe from illness and starvation and Turning Out Days. Mair had even manipulated the

Fellowship of Jair, making her way into that hierarchy with scarcely a moment's hesitation. To think that the Touched girl could be afraid of fresh air and a little sunlight!

"Well, then," Rani finally said, surprised at the rush of warmth she felt toward her friend. "Let's just go inside."

Mair immediately turned to the stairs that led from the rooftop; she began her descent before Rani could even gather up the goblets they had brought to the open platform. Rani had never seen her friend so anxious to retreat. The guard chortled as they passed him, but he did not follow them down the dark, twisting stairs. There were other soldiers to watch over the prisoners once they were back in the tower.

In fact, even Mair might not have been so anxious to escape the parapet if she'd known what awaited them in their chamber. The girls were sharing a round room halfway up the tower. Guards were posted on the level below them, always a pair of stalwart men armed with pikes and swords like the fellow on the parapet. Rani could scarcely tell when the individual soldiers changed—each man was beefy and overfed, his hair cropped short to fit beneath his fighting helmet. Every one of Sin Hazar's guards bore a lion tattoo beneath his left eye. The guards had obviously been instructed not to speak to the southerners; every friendly overture from Rani had been greeted with stony silence.

Even without words, the guards managed to forbid Rani and Mair to leave the tower, blocking their way with weaponry. Sin Hazar had commanded the girls to get their rest. They were to recover from their arduous journey north. When Rani had insisted that she needed no rest, the king had merely brushed away her protest, like an unseemly crumb that had fallen upon his broad chest. "Your friend needs rest, then. She needs to recover from her injury." After that rebuff, it had seemed disloyal to Mair to continue to protest, and Rani had let herself be shown to her elaborate prison.

For that's what the room was. Surely, it was better appointed than other prison cells Rani had survived. The floor was strewn with fragrant rushes, rather than sodden straw. The fireplace drew well, and the soldiers brought in a steady supply of dry wood.

The food was tempting and varied, arriving still warm from the royal kitchens. Nevertheless, Rani had no doubt that she was a prisoner.

Therefore, she should not have been surprised to find someone inside her chamber when she and Mair entered from the dark stairwell. Prince Bashanorandi started nervously as the girls entered the room, looking like a child caught filching sweets from a shop.

"Bashi!" Rani exclaimed, before she could stop herself.

"Ranita." The prince bowed stiffly as he registered her use of his nickname. "Mair."

The Touched girl lashed out, anger crackling across her words. "What are you doing in our room?" Rani barely noticed that Mair's Touched speech had faded, replaced with the iron tones of court.

"It's hardly 'your' room, now is it? It belongs to my uncle, to King Sin Hazar." The prince eyed the girls, and a sheen of disgust oozed across his features, as if he smelled something rancid. Rani became aware of her headdress once again, of the awkward wings that weighted down either side of her head. She rubbed her palms against her sides, but the action only served to remind her that her clothes were not her own. Fine silk and velvet, certainly, but borrowed. The deep breath that she took to steady herself cut into her side, and she was forced to think about the tightly lashed girdle beneath her gown. Northern women wore strange attire, none of it comfortable.

"Why are you here, Ba—" Rani stopped herself before she could start another fight by calling the prince by his nickname. "Bashanorandi."

"Our benefactor sent me. He wishes to hold a feast in our honor, tonight. It's been a month since we arrived at his court. Four weeks since we came under his protection."

"I don't have a benefactor here." Rani's voice was cold.

"This is an honor, you fool!"

"This is a ploy! Don't you see how he's playing you, Bashi? Don't you see how he's manipulating you, with fine horses and jewels! Can you honestly be bought for a few bites of roast fowl?"

"No one is buying me, girl!" Bashi flushed crimson, and his words cracked off the stone walls.

"What's that on your hand, then?"

"This? It's nothing. It's a signet. I sent a letter to Hal this morning. I needed something to seal it, didn't I?"

Mair snorted, snagging Rani and Bashi's attention. "And you could hardly seal a letter to a king without using gold."

"I don't have to listen to you, wench!"

"I'm the guest of your precious king, aren't I?"

"Don't push me, Mair."

"Or you'll what? You'll order us to the dungeons?"

"I'll order you confined to this tower! I'll have them lock the passage to the rooftop! You can just sit here in your chamber and rot!"

"Go ahead, Bashi!" Mair was so angry that spittle flew from her lips as she spoke. "Chain the door above! That won't change anything! Rani and I, we still know where *our* loyalties lie. We still know enough not to bow down before a strange king!"

"I'm not bowing, you sl—"

"No, ye're not, Bashi," Mair interrupted before the prince could spit out his slur. "Ye're not bowin' at all. Instead, ye're kneeling, close enough t' fondle yer king's ballocks, ye are. Close enough t' take 'im in yer lyin' mouth 'n'—"

"Guards!" Bashi bellowed as he whirled toward the doorway, and his hands were clenched so tightly that his entire ermine-lined robe quivered like a living beast. "Guards!"

And then Prince Bashanorandi fled the tower room, hurtling down the stairs as if he were chased by the Thousand Gods. Rani could hear him exclaiming to the soldiers; his voice rising as he referred to "that Touched sow." Rani could not make out the soldiers' reply, and she waited only an instant before she turned to her friend.

"And you think that was wise?"

"I think it was necessary. Don't you see what's happening,

Rai? The king is seducing him, as certain as if he *were* a bedboy."

"He's the closest thing we had to an ally here, Mair. You shouldn't have made him so angry."

"If you think he's your ally, Rai, then you know nothing of war. He's not your friend. He never has been. He's the one who dragged us here."

"He's the only friend we have, now."

"We have each other, Rai. That's all. Don't be counting on anyone else, not anyone else in all of Amanthia. You remember that, until we're back home in the City. *No one* in Amanthia is your friend."

Rani sighed in disgust and stomped across the room. Her skirts tangled about her legs as she threw herself into a low chair, and she tugged furiously at the fabric. These cursed clothes, with their tight-laced underskirts—the nareeth, the Amanthians called them—and the pleated overdress, the balkareen. . . . No wonder northern women did little more than pick at needlework or pluck an occasional instrument! They could hardly breathe to do anything else. No self-respecting glasswright would find herself confined in such a cloth prison.

Rani sulked while the better part of a log burned away in the fire. She'd be cursed by all the Thousand Gods if she'd speak to Mair first. Rani hardly cared that Mair had offended Bashi—*that* had happened often enough when they'd lived in the south. No, the true problem was that when Mair alienated Bashi, she cut off one of the girls' few activities of interest. There was nothing to *do* in Sin Hazar's palace.

Rani had requested parchment every morning since their arrival, and she had been told repeatedly that writing tools would not be made available, that they were for owls only. Owls? It had taken nearly a fortnight before Rani understood that owls were another one of the strange northern castes. Now, Rani scarcely paused to wonder how Bashi had secured writing tools for his letter to Hal. He'd probably had an owl do his copywork for him, writing out his words. Sin Hazar would approve of such an arrangement—it would prevent any secret messages.

After Rani had failed to send a letter, she had tried to obtain permission to ride beyond the city walls. She was told, politely but firmly, that Sin Hazar would not permit his guests to take such risks. There were dangers in the countryside, and King Sin Hazar would fain not have Rani and Mair harmed while they were his responsibility.

The girls were not allowed to walk alone in the gardens; they were not allowed in the palace library. Rani had not been permitted to find Sin Hazar's glasswrights, to learn from her erstwhile guild members.

The girls were not even allowed to wander the palace hallways unattended. Once, the previous week, an ambassador had ridden into the courtyard—whispered palace rumor said that he was from lands to the distant west. Rani and Mair had been forbidden to see the man; their guards had become surly when the girls even tried to examine the magnificent destrier that had borne the nobleman.

Even Rani's attempts to educate herself about the northern court had borne little fruit. Amanthia was largely a mystery to its southern neighbor; Queen Felicianda had been an exotic visitor to the Morenian court. By watching Sin Hazar's palace staff and listening to snippets of gossip, Rani realized that some of the "truths" she thought she knew about Sin Hazar were merely tales.

For example, she had been told once, by her brother, that warriors in the north fought for the title of king, that there was no direct succession to the throne. Rani's brother had lied, though. Lied, or he had not been told the truth himself. Sin Hazar was descended from a long line of kings; his royalty ran deep in his blood, channeled beside his pride. And that royalty led him to issue edicts, absolute orders that were enforced by steel.

One such edict made Rani and Mair prisoners, and they stood little or no chance of communicating any message to Hal. And now, Mair had squabbled with Bashi, cutting off the girls' one solid line of communication with the king who held them captive. In the name of Plad, the Touched girl was insufferable when she thought she was right! Muttering a prayer to the god of patience, Rani finally stalked to the woven basket beside the room's one narrow window. As she leaned down to pick up the fancy needlework Sin Hazar had bestowed upon her, she heard the heavy door open lower in the tower.

At first, Rani could not identify the clanking sound on the stairs. Then, her ears picked apart the sound of a soldier's mail, of heavy boots on stone. She heard a man muttering under his breath, swearing to San, the god of iron. Only as the curse became clear did Rani understand the other noise, the clanking noise, the repeated, jarring, terrifying noise.

Rani leaped to the threshold of the chamber, just as the soldier swung by. He snarled at her as she opened the door, his angry leer twisted further by the lion emblem etched across half his face. "Back in your room, girl!"

"But—"

"Back in your room, or I'll put these on *your* door!"

Rani stepped back over the threshold, gathering her skirts close about her legs. The soldier clanked on up the stairs, lugging the lengths of heavy chain behind him. Rani did not need to watch to understand the sound she now heard. The chains were looped through the door's ancient wrought-iron fittings. She heard metal slide against metal, scraping like giant snake scales. Then there was a softer sound, a snick, and three sharp tugs.

Sin Hazar had ordered the tower door locked.

Rani would no longer be able to breathe fresh air from the parapet. She could no longer study the courtyard, look out at the surrounding countryside, imagine her escape to Morenia and Hal. She was trapped in the tower.

She only waited until the soldier had swaggered back down the stairs, accompanied by his fellow, who had stood guard above. Then she turned on Mair, her voice trembling with fury, or with the tears of betrayal. "I hope that you're happy now!"

"It had to be done." Mair was sitting beside the fire in a low chair. She hunched forward as she hugged her arms about her belly, and she rocked back and forth. "There was nothing for it. It had to be done."

"Aye, you couldn't stop yourself!" Rani spat. "As if you even care. You hated being on the parapet in the first place!"

"I had no choice. It had to be done." Mair rocked slowly and steadily.

"Nothing *had* to be done! We could have spoken with Bashi! We could have worked with him! Mair, not everything is a struggle! Not everything is a battle!"

Mair only shook her head and continued her rocking. "It had to be done."

Rani barely caught another exclamation before she could shout at her friend, bridling her exasperation but letting herself storm across the room to their window. Looking through its narrow slit, she could make out the sapphire sky of late autumn. A flock of geese flew across her narrow field of vision, and she could just hear their cries to each other. As Rani craned her neck to follow their progress, she saw the lead bird drop back and another forge forward, taking the point position in the formation. The geese disappeared toward the south, away from the cold, away from winter, away from certain death. Rani felt more enclosed than ever, more hopeless than she'd been at any time since her falcon, Kalindramina, had flown from her wrist.

The sunlight faded rapidly, and Rani set aside her needlework when she could no longer make out the faint stitches against the soft linen background. She was getting better, she decided, folding the square in her lap. Her stitches were more even, and the background was less puckered. Nurse would be pleased with her, if the Morenian woman could see what Rani had accomplished. Still, the handicraft was a waste of good time.

No more a waste, though, than spending hours dressing herself. With the sun setting, Rani knew that she only had a little time before Sin Hazar's feast. From past experience, she also knew that the northern king expected her to be robed in the complete finery of his court if she were going to come into his royal presence.

The first few times that Sin Hazar had granted the girls an audience, he had sent servants to help them dress. Mair had put an end to that, though, pulling one girl's hair when the hapless servant tugged a little too vigorously at Mair's own ragged locks. Sin Hazar had sent word that he would not have his household terrorized by uncouth southerners. Rani and Mair had been left to their own devices, then. At least they had been able to relax the robing requirements—with Mair's damaged arm, she *couldn't* pull the nareeth laces as tight as expected across Rani's hips.

Now, Rani rose and began to dress herself mechanically. First, the soft linen kirtle, draping her from head to toe. Then, the tight nareeth, already cutting into her flesh as she laced it snug. Mair came out of her stupor before the fire as Rani crossed the room, and the Touched girl reached up mechanically to snap the laces tighter. Rani reached up for the mantel and took a firm grip, and then Mair cinched the garment closer about her waist. "Breathe!" Mair ordered, and Rani puffed all the air from her lungs. Mair took advantage of that instant and tugged again, forcing Rani to cry out.

"Ow! That's too tight!"

"That's as tight as it's been all along."

"I can't breathe!"

"If you're going to masquerade as a lady of the north, you'd best look the part."

"I can look the part and still be able to swallow!"

Mair only shrugged and reached for Rani's balkareen. The ornate fabric draped across Rani's chest, pleated to cover her with the scantest modesty. The garment had a sash sewn in, which Mair folded with deft fingers, tying an elaborate bow across the small of Rani's back. "Raise your arms." When Rani had complied, the Touched girl twitched the tail ends of fabric into place, taking only a moment to smooth the dozens of tight, rigid pleats. "All right." She nodded at her handiwork. "Where's your headdress?"

Rani gestured toward the chest at the foot of the bed and watched as Mair retrieved the heavy ornament. Unlike the padded decoration that the northerners deemed appropriate for daywear, the evening headdress was a complicated affair of jangling metal, suspended over a framework wrapped with intricately woven fabric.

Rani sat on the low chair beside the fire and handed an ivory comb to Mair. The Touched girl unpinned her companion's hair and began to run the small teeth through snarls. "Ach!" Rani exclaimed. "That hurts, Mair!"

"It hurts to be beautiful. The king expects you in all your finery." Rani started to protest, but Mair tugged harder at a particularly stubborn knot. Rani fought the reflexive tears that pricked the corners of her eyes. She endured as Mair first combed out the tangles, then tugged roughly, yanking Rani's hair into two neat plaits. Those braids were piled atop her head and secured with long, wickedly sharp ivory pins. Rani bit her tongue as one of the pins grazed her scalp.

Mair settled the headdress carefully, weaving her fingers between the dangling ornaments. A clever arrangement of miniature clamps anchored the item to Rani's hair, tugging like a hundred babies' fists. Again, Rani sucked breath between her teeth. She could feel the flesh beside her eyes stretched tight, and she could only turn her neck partially to either side, for fear that she would upset the ornament.

"There," Mair proclaimed. "Fit for a royal feast."

"You shouldn't have put on the headdress. I can't help you dress."

"I'm not going."

"You must!" Rani cried. "You heard Bashi. This is a feast in our honor!"

"No one here wants to honor me. Besides, my arm hurts too much."

"Mair . . ."

"Go along, Rai. Just tell the guards that I'm not well."

"But—"

"Go, Rai. It's all going to be all right. In the name of Vir, all will be fine."

The god of martyrs. Not exactly the god Rani would have prayed to for comfort. Nevertheless, she swallowed hard and turned to the door. Before she left the chamber, though, she looked back at her friend. "I'm sorry, Mair. I shouldn't have gotten so upset, about the door being locked."

"It's all right, Rai. It had to be done."

Rani shook her head, but was kept from responding by the ominous metal jangle from her headpiece. She took the stairs slowly, afraid that she would trip on her unfamiliar skirts. The bone stays of her nareeth gnawed at her ribs, and she wondered if *she* was well enough to attend the feast.

Of course, the choice was taken from her as soon as she reached the landing, one flight below the chamber she shared with Mair. Four guards lounged against the stone walls, belatedly springing to attention as Rani's jangling headdress announced her arrival. "My lady," said the first man to regain his composure.

Rani could read a great deal into those two words. The man found her attractive. She saw the instant that his eyes took in her cinched waist, the way he measured the tight folds of the balkareen across her chest. She took another step, and the headdress set to jangling, and she watched his eyes dart toward the metal, then toward her bare throat. "My lady," he repeated, and he even managed a bow.

"Let us go to the feast," Rani commanded coldly, mustering all the disdain she had learned in Hal's palace.

The guard cleared his throat. "Er . . . Where is the other one? The Lady Mair?"

"She is not well. Her arms pains her."

"But His Majesty has commanded both of you to attend him."

Rani cocked her head slightly, listening to the headdress's jangling music. She settled one hand over her hip, managing not to wince as she added to the nearly unbearable pressure of the nareeth's stays. "I'll explain to King Sin Hazar." She twisted her words with the vaguest hint of a smile, and she watched the soldier melt into compliance. Two of the guards accompanied her down the hallway, and another stayed behind to guard Mair.

Rani marveled at the power of her costume.

It was as if Mair had cast a spell as she cinched tight the nareeth. Rani could feel the soldiers' eyes as she passed through the hallways; each member of the household guard snapped to attention as if he were on military parade.

When Rani was shown into the great hall, the musicians paused in their playing. King Sin Hazar already sat at the head of his great table, looking out at the room with palpable boredom. He stood, though, as Rani entered, and he quirked one eyebrow as she crossed the length of the hall. The flickering torchlight picked out the silvery swan wings upon his face, lending him a mysterious air.

Rani harvested glances from every nobleman she passed. More than one tattooed gaze strayed from her face; she was acutely aware of the balkareen's tiny pleats, of the grasping nareeth stays about her waist. A heat flushed over her cheeks, and she bowed her head, but that only caused her headpiece to jangle, as if she intended to summon yet more attention.

Bashi stood at Sin Hazar's right hand. He, too, had climbed to his feet as Rani made her way across the hall. Rani surprised a curious look on the prince's face, as if he had never seen Rani before, or as if he had met her only in the untrustworthy landscape of his dreams. Without her planning, her lips curved into the faintest of smiles.

"My lady Ranita." King Sin Hazar stepped forward, offering her his hand.

Inspired, Rani twisted herself into a curtsey, managing not to cry out as the motion forced the nareeth's bony fingers even deeper into her flesh. She could not keep from catching her breath, though, and her gasp tightened the balkareen's folds across her chest. She blushed as she caught the king's eagle glance, and she knew that he was measuring her unseen flesh with a practiced eye. "Your Majesty," she managed. The headdress jangled again as she straightened.

"We hardly dare ask, Lady Ranita, lest you think that we discount the value of your presence, but where is your companion, the Lady Mair?"

"She is not well, Your Majesty. Her arm pains her."

Once again, the royal glance knifed across Rani's body, and she knew that the king measured the precision of her stays. He knew that no servants had attended his prisoners. Mair's arm could not be as bad as she made it out to be. "We will send our chirurgeon to her again."

"No need, Your Majesty. There are some injuries that only time can heal."

"We would not have it said that we neglected a guest in our own house."

"There has been no neglect, Your Majesty." That was not enough. Sin Hazar still pinned her with his eyes. If only the king would blink . . . If only he would give Rani an instant's respite from his attentions . . . She felt compelled to say more. "Lady Mair and I . . . quarreled this afternoon."

"Quarreled?" The king almost choked on the word, and Rani could make out a sudden glint of merriness at the bottom of the deep pools that snared her.

"Aye, Your Majesty."

"Very well, then." The king shrugged and seemed to dismiss the matter. "If the Lady Mair does not care to join us . . ." Sin Hazar trailed off, then gestured to the empty chair at his left hand. "We will be more than honored by your presence, Lady Ranita."

Rani felt the king's hand as he assisted her to her seat; his fingers blazed hot through the layers of cloth and bone that swaddled her. His touch lingered as she settled herself carefully, gingerly shifting to ease her breathing as much as possible. Then Sin Hazar was summoning servants, and Rani found her glass filled with cool, clear wine. She drank deeply, ignoring the nareeth's pinch as she swallowed.

Maybe it was the magic of the feast—the roasted birds displayed with their feathers and the endless dishes flavored with rare and valuable spices from over the Eastern Sea. Maybe it was the attention that King Sin Hazar paid to her, his solicitousness as she inquired about each new dish, as he answered her like a courteous suitor. Maybe it was the gazes that she felt from every corner of the room—the noblemen who seemed drawn by the delicate folds across her chest, drawn like dust motes to a beam of sunlight.

Maybe it was the bone stays, keeping her from taking a single deep breath.

Whatever the cause, Rani was intoxicated before she had drained her first goblet. And Sin Hazar saw to it that her cup did not remain empty for long. The king ordered one servant to do nothing but keep Rani's glass filled, another to keep her trencher covered. She found that she could eat only a few bites of the rich, seasoned meats. Her heart pounded too hard for more than that.

But she could sip from her goblet throughout the long evening, through course after course, where each dish was followed by entertainment—jugglers and troubadours and a funny jester in parti-colored hose who told ribald stories. As the evening wore on, Rani forgot her resolution to remember the stories, to remember how she would fit the tales into panes of glass, once she had rebuilt her guild.

During the entire feast, King Sin Hazar remained attuned to Rani. She recognized the man's interest; she had spent too much time with her older sisters in the loft of her parents' shop not to understand the looks that the king cast at her tight-bound chest, at her jangling headdress.

Perhaps, if Sin Hazar were truly snared by Rani, she could negotiate for her release, for her traveling south with Mair, or at least for the right to send a letter to Hal. . . . Rani took another sip of wine and leaned closer to the king, daring to rest one of her hands along the sleeve of his golden robe.

Throughout all the frivolity and flirting, though, Bashi sat at Sin Hazar's other side, frowning like an old nursemaid. The prince ate from all the dishes as well, and he drank from his goblet, but he might have been sitting at a funeral feast for all the enjoyment he showed. As soon as the last course was served—a marzipan confection, with the almond paste fashioned into a magnificent swan—Bashi rose to his feet.

"If Your Majesty will excuse me," he muttered and bowed.

"Where do you think you're going, cousin?"

"I'm tired, Your Majesty. The Lady Ranita must be weary as well."

"The Lady Ranita does not seem weary, cousin." The king cast a pointed look at Rani. Confused, she withdrew her hand from his sleeve. Not knowing what else to do, she raised her goblet to her lips. When she swallowed, the room swirled crazily.

"She may not realize how taxing a royal feast can be, Your Majesty. Perhaps we should let her speak for herself."

Sin Hazar eyed his nephew gravely for a long minute, then turned to Rani. "My lady, your protector seems to believe that you would like to be gone from our table. What say you?"

Even with the wine swimming through her blood, Rani heard the threat beneath the words. She imagined Sin Hazar's outrage if she agreed with Bashi, if she said that she *did* want to return to her chambers. The king might punish Bashi, have him thrown into a prison cell. Or worse. "Your Majesty," Rani began, but she had to take a deep breath to concentrate. The action made her nareeth saw into her ribs, and she resisted the urge to wince. "Both Bashi and I are honored by the feast you have set for us. We fain would not leave until Your Majesty chooses to."

"Ha!" The king reached out with one long finger and traced the line of Rani's determined jaw. "Well spoken, my lady." He seemed to ignore the shudder that coursed through Rani at his touch, turning instead to Bashi. "Any other questions, cousin?"

"No, Your Majesty." Bashi sank back onto his chair, clutching his goblet and looking miserable.

And so, Rani stayed at the feast, sitting at the table until the wee hours of the morning. Once she realized how much the wine had affected her, she tried to keep away from her goblet. Nevertheless, she could not refuse the king's attentions entirely. She even rose from her chair to dance with Sin Hazar, although she begged to be excused after the first simple figures, admitting that she had never learned the intricate movements for the next music played.

At last, King Sin Hazar seemed to notice that many of his subjects slumped at the table. More than a few of the nobles had fallen asleep, victim to the warm room and the ever-flowing wine. Even Bashi was blinking furiously in his chair, rubbing his eyes with a fist when he thought that no one was looking. The king turned to Rani. "Our most gracious thanks, Lady Ranita, for joining us this evening."

"The pleasure was mine, Your Majesty." Rani was snared again by Sin Hazar's opaque gaze. It seemed as if the man would never blink, as if he would swallow her with the midnight pools of his eyes. Rani raised one hand to her neck, as if to fan her moist flesh, but Sin Hazar caught her fingers and bowed over them, brushing the lightest of kisses across her palm. Something quivered deep inside Rani's belly, and she suddenly wondered if she could remain standing in front of the court, in front of the king.

"Good night, Lady Ranita. Sleep well."

Before Rani could reply, Sin Hazar turned on his heel and raised a hand. Two guards detached themselves from the shadows along the walls. The king nodded and stalked back to the head of the table. Rani was just able to catch the beginning of an exchange with Bashi as the soldiers ushered her from the feast hall.

What had she been thinking? Of course Sin Hazar was not going to set her free! Of course he was not going to change his mind about his captive. Of course he was not going to move her from her tower room to the royal apartments. . . .

The hallways were chilled in the late night, and a wintry wind blew through the few arrow loops that they passed. Rani felt hobbled by her nareeth, and she wondered how she'd been able to walk all the way to the feast, how she had managed to *dance* with Sin Hazar. By the time she reached the chamber she shared with Mair, tears pricked at the corners of her eyes.

The soldiers saluted their fellows on the landing below Rani's room. All four escorted Rani up to her door, and they stood at attention as she stepped into the chamber. Rani closed the door behind her and waited for the clanking sound of four men descending the staircase. Only then did she look toward the curtained bed on the far side of the chamber. Mair, though, was waiting for her by the fire.

"So! You finally decided to return!"

"I wanted to come back earlier, Mair, but I couldn't. It would have been dangerous for Bashi. For me." Rani heard the frantic energy behind her words, heard her slurred speech.

"By all the Thousand Gods, you're drunk!"

"I am not! I only had a little wine, to prove my friendship with Sin Hazar."

"You're a fool! Did I have to tell you not to drink with the king? Any idiot would know not to! Especially not tonight!"

"What's so special about tonight?" Rani said crossly. She was fumbling with the balkareen that restricted her chest, but she could not manipulate the tight knot across her back. Mair swore under her breath and crossed the room. She made short work of the knot, and then she started to turn Rani about, gathering up the yards of silken cloth. "Wait!" Rani cried as the floor spun up to meet her. "What are you saying, Mair?"

"Ach! How much *did* you drink? And did you eat *anything*?"

"I couldn't eat. You pulled the nareeth too tight."

Mair swore again and stomped to the door. She tugged it open, making a great deal of noise, and stormed onto the landing. "Bring Lady Ranita some water," she commanded, when one of the lion-tattooed men leaped up the landing. "A pitcher of fresh water."

The Touched girl turned back to Rani, leaving the door cracked so that the girls could hear when the soldier returned. "Turn about, then. Let me untie the lacings."

Rani moved like an exhausted child. For just an instant, Mair yanked the lacings *tighter,* but then the unbearable pressure eased across Rani's ribs, her waist, her hips. For just an instant, she felt as light as a bird, and then her freed flesh started to ache. She hugged her arms about her, rocking slightly as she heard an iron tread on the stairs.

"Quick. Behind the curtains." Mair gestured toward the bed, and Rani complied, sliding the heavy velvet into place so that the guard would not see her undressed.

Even as Rani gulped fresh air, her drunken dizziness began to fade. She fumbled at the mattress beneath her, clutching her hands to steady her spinning head. There were large lumps strewn across the bed, as if a field of potatoes were planted beneath the linen sheets. Trying to ignore the tears that bloomed at the corners of her eyes, Rani quickly realized that the lumps were covered with cloth; in fact, they were huge knots of cloth. She barely managed to wait until she heard the door close before she leaped out of the bed.

"Mair! What—"

"Hush. Drink." Mair snagged a pewter goblet from a low table and forced a refreshing draught on Rani. "We don't have much time. Listen to me." The old crack of command was back in Mair's voice. Rani thought of the troop that the Touched girl had controlled in the City streets, the children who had eaten well and survived the worst that the King's Guard had to offer. Rani swallowed her protests along with her water, and she was rewarded with a steadying of her pulse, a slight retreat of the wine's vapors. "We're leaving the palace tonight. We're climbing down from the tower."

"We can't do that! It must be the height of a dozen men."

"I made us a ladder. Tonight, I ripped our dresses. I ripped our sheets."

"But I can't go tonight. I'm too tired." Rani thought of Sin Hazar, remembered his lips brushing across her palm. "It's too late."

"Don't be a fool!" Mair hissed. "Of course we have to leave when it's late. That's our only hope. And going tonight, when they think you've drunk enough to knock out an entire garrison, that might even work to our advantage."

"But what about your arm? You can't climb with a broken arm."

"It's better than I've made it out to be. I cinched your dress, didn't I?" Rani could not argue with that. She let her fingers gingerly test her waist. She'd be bruised in the morning, from the nareeth. "Come on, then," Mair grumbled. "Let me show you what I've done."

As Rani watched, Mair stepped back from the bed, pulling the knotted cloth with her. Hand over hand, she extracted the twisted fabric. Rani was amazed that there had been so much cloth to tear, so many sheets and skirts to turn into a rope. "But what about the lock? They chained the door this afternoon."

"I've picked it."

"You've what?"

Mair scrambled about the pillows, now shed of their satin coverings. She produced some ragged bits of fabric, stitched to gold braid. Rani recognized the headdress that she had worn only that afternoon. Mair twisted the cloth straps and revealed the long metal strip that had anchored the ornate decoration. "I picked it. That was she hardest part, shifting the chains without their hearing. Easier to pick a lock, though, than to dispatch a guard. That's why I pushed Bashi so hard this afternoon. I had to get that guard off the roof." Mair dropped the remnants of the headdress. "Men place too much faith in iron and locks."

Rani could do little more than gape. "Mair, this is madness! We can't just throw ourselves over the palace wall!"

"That's *exactly* what we can do. Those carts that you were watching are packed and ready to go. They must be planning to leave at dawn. All we have to do is hide beneath the load."

"All? Mair, you can't be serious!"

"I've never been more serious in my life, Rai." As if to underscore her words, Mair crossed to the fireplace, picking up a thin stick that was charred black on its end. "And if we're to succeed, we'll have to look the part. Close your eyes."

Uncertain what else she could do, Rani followed the command, shutting her eyes and catching her breath. The room tilted unevenly, but not as badly as it had done in the great hall. Water and fresh air and time were working their magic; the wine in her veins was being pushed aside by anticipation. By fear.

Even with her eyes closed, Rani sensed Mair moving closer, and then she felt the end of the pointed stick, sketching across her cheek. She only opened her eyes when Mair ordered her to do so, and she found herself staring into a mirror. Her face was reflected in the wavy surface, but now she sported a rayed sun, spreading under her left eye. "A sun!"

"Aye. We'd be suspicious as swans, and neither of us is fit to be a lion. I certainly don't know enough to be one of their owls. Besides, we've only seen a handful of those. There are bound to be a number of suns in the countryside, going about the business that keeps this palace running." As Mair spoke, she tilted the mirror toward her own face. She drew her own tattoo with quick, steady motions. "Try not to touch it. It'll rub off soon enough, but it might help us if we're stopped near the city. We'll have to redraw it often."

"Near the city? Where are we going, Mair?"

"I don't know yet. First, we've got to get out of here. Sin Hazar isn't about to hand us over to Halaravilli anytime soon. We're more valuable to him as captives, Rai. We're hostages."

"But his feast was lovely tonight!"

"Aye, and a nightingale's cage is made of finest gold."

Rani drew a deep breath to protest and felt the sore flesh beneath her ribs. Staring at the length of cloth rope, Rani realized that she and Mair truly had no choice. There would be no way to explain their shredded clothing in the morning, no way to justify the ruined sheets. The suns in Sin Hazar's employ would certainly report the escape attempt, even if the girls took no further action. Mair had decided for both of them.

"Give me your balkareen, Rai. I'll add it to the end here."

Rani handed over the fabric mutely, watching as Mair tore the cloth into thick strips, knotting them securely to the end of her rope. "What if it's not long enough?"

"It has to be. One way or another." Mair tugged the new length tight, barely favoring her bad arm. "All right, then. Anything that we should take?"

Rani glanced about the chamber and shrugged, seeing it with a clarity born of Mair's matter-of-fact determination. Certainly the bed had been comfortable. The chair was nicely carved. The threads of Rani's stitchery glimmered in the firelight. But there was nothing of true value in the prison room—no weapon, no coins, nothing to help two girls flee from the king of all Amanthia. Rani shook her head.

"Very well, then." Mair reached for her cloak, where it hung on a peg behind the door and offered Rani her own garment. "It'll be cold, tonight. We'll find better clothes on the outside."

Rani pulled the cloak over her thin linen kirtle, clasping it at her neck with a mechanical precision. She did not speak until they stood at the door. "Wait! Mair, we can't do this! We'll be up on the *tower*! You can't face the height!"

"I'll do what I have to do."

"But Mair—"

"Ye're wastin' time, Rai."

Rani swallowed her protest and took one last look around the room. Nothing. Nothing to keep her here. She nodded at Mair, who eased the door open.

The girls made their way up the stairs in silence, feeling for each stone step cautiously. The staircase twisted about itself, and after only one turn, Rani could no longer make out the light from the guards' flickering torches, now two levels below. She found herself leaning into the wall, fearful that she would miss the narrow inner lip of each step above her. Some were carved at irregular heights, and once she fell hard, banging her knee. She managed not to cry out, though.

Mair was true to her word—the lock had been cleanly picked. Mair guided Rani's hands over the iron chains, showing her where they lay, where she must step to avoid toppling the links. Then, before Rani could lose her nerve, the Touched girl eased the door open.

Mair only left them a crack to slip through, as narrow as possible, to keep from disturbing the torches several levels below. Rani caught her breath at the freezing air, but she stepped swiftly to the side so that Mair could close the door behind them. She shivered as the Touched girl darted to the edge of the parapet. In the starlight, Rani could make out her friend tossing the rope about the first merlon from the wall, cinching it secure. Better that they descend the tower in its own shadow. Better that they hide in the darkness.

Rani heard Mair grunt as she pulled the last knot tight, and then the Touched girl stood by the embrasure. She waved her arm once, looking like a ghost in the eldritch light. When Rani drew near, she saw that her companion was as pale as the linen strips she had tied together. Mair's breath came quick, and her palms were slicked with sweat as she pulled Rani's hand over to test the knot that secured the rope.

Rani lifted the cloth and fed it through her hands, taking a deep breath to prepare for stepping over the stone wall. "No."

Mair spoke close to Rani's ear, her voice scarcely audible. The Touched girl panted as she said, "I'll go first. In case th' knots dinna 'old. In case I dinna 'ave th' strength." Mair flapped her injured arm like a wounded wing.

Rani argued, "But I can anchor it for you once I'm on the ground. I can make it easier."

Mair shook her head furiously, barely mouthing, "I'm the weakest. Let me go first." When Rani still refused to step back, Mair leaned closer still, and hissed, "It 'as t' be done. If I'm to fall, don't let me go knowing that I've brought you down as well."

It has to be done. Mair was terrified, injured, and no doubt exhausted, but there was no other means of escape.

In the starlight, Rani could just make out Mair's progress down the rope. She saw how the Touched girl used the knots to support herself, how she found anchors with her feet and her fists. More than once, Mair let herself swing back toward the palace wall, easing some of the pressure of her descent by steeling her back against the stonework. Slowly, painfully, she made her way down.

Twice, Rani saw Mair start to slip, both times when she had put too much weight on her injured arm. Once, the Touched girl hissed between her teeth, loud enough that Rani could hear. Apparently no soldiers did, though, for no alarms shattered the wintry night.

Once Mair reached the ground, she tugged three times on the rope. Rani caught her breath and threw one leg over the embrasure edge. As she gathered the first knot between her fingers, she realized that she could not remember the name of the god of ropes. "Help me, Roan," she improvised, speaking to the god of ladders instead. "Help me to descend this crafting, made in your name and to your glory."

The prayer was unsettling, though, not least because Rani feared that the god of ladders would take offense that his special province was being impinged on by a hastily knotted cloth contraption. Rani settled her prayer into a simpler sentence: "It has to be done." She repeated the five words again and again, stretching for footholds, squeezing her hands together for a better grip.

She almost screamed when Mair's hand closed around her calves, but she managed to swallow her surprise and drop to the ground. She stumbled forward a step and was surprised to see that a few coils of the rope lay upon the ground—Mair's improvised creation had been more than long enough. Rani took only an instant to be grateful that she had not needed to cling to the slippery silk of her balkareen.

Before Rani could look back up at the tower, Mair tugged her deeper into the shadows. Rani followed obediently, skirting the foot of the building until they reached the courtyard. The drays were standing where the soldiers had left them, waiting for the oxen that would drag them out of the city gates.

The first three wagons that Rani checked were lashed down, with tarps stretched tight over the clear forms of barrels and boxes. Before Rani could despair, though, she heard Mair hiss from the next cart.

Rani could smell the autumn fragrance even as she approached. The wagon bed was deep, filled with new-harvested hay. The grass had dried partially in the field, but it still gave off the heady aroma of autumn.

Mair grinned at Rani and gestured toward the dray. Rani took only a moment to gather her cloak close about her flimsy garments, then she pulled herself up onto the wheel, throwing first one leg and then the other over the side of the wooden cart. She hoisted Mair up beside her, tugging hard on her friend's good hand, and then both girls were burrowing deep into their fragrant bed, creating a nest that was warm and safe and secure from the king's wrath.

7

Shea settled her hands on her hips, glaring at the carters. "You took your time getting here, didn't you?"

The leader flicked his gaze toward her sun tattoo; the man's own rayed mark was small and high on his cheekbone. "This entire journey has been cursed, goodwife. We were late leaving the city. The king's lions made us repack our entire load."

"That was a week ago! Couldn't you make up time on the road?"

The man bristled, and for a moment, Shea thought that she might have prodded him too hard. They were both suns, though. They both should have known their place beneath the sky. She should not need to fight with one of her own kind, just to do her own work, just to serve the Little Army.

The carter glanced at his men, who were unpacking barrels and crates from the wagons, and for just an instant, Shea thought that he might order them to stop their work. The man only shook his head, though. "Don't complain to us, goodwife. There were troops moving north, troops getting ready to sail east. We had to clear the road every time they came by."

"Well I've got troops here, too—hungry mouths to feed. I hope you've brought us enough supplies. My lions work up quite an appetite."

"There are no lions in Sin Hazar's Little Army." The man's flat statement deflated Shea. Of course there were no lions among the children. Their tattoos had all been carved away. They'd all been turned into casteless rogues, children without homes, without families. They were vicious little creatures fighting for their proper place in the world.

Not for the first time, Shea wondered if she were lucky that Davin had permitted her to stay. That strange old man had fed her potions mixed from herbs she'd never heard of, counting her pulse until he declared her cured of the strange heart-gripping pain that had felled her on the road. She'd thought that he would throw her out then, force her back on the road, with or without Crestman.

He'd done nothing of the sort, though. Instead, he'd muttered that she could sleep in an abandoned hut, one of a half dozen crumbling buildings that ringed his own sorry cottage. He'd accepted Crestman's strange story about how a captain in the Little Army came to be on the road, traveling with the king's old nursemaid. The ancient man had accepted Crestman's rank, too, and he'd ordered the other boys to give way to their new captain. Davin had not turned the pair over to King Sin Hazar's men— neither to the Little Army nor to the grown soldiers who rode through irregularly. Davin had chosen not to label Crestman a deserter; he kept both of the newcomers alive.

Shea had returned the favor by doing a sun's work, trying to straighten the old man's cottage into a decent space. She had whipped up clouds of dust and swept up droppings from that terrifying talking bird. She had sorted through rolls and rolls of parchment, trying to separate them into military projects and landscape sketches and endless pages of writing. She found herself baking bread for the boys, using their fine-ground flour to relieve their dull menu of gruel and salt beef.

Throughout the commotion, Davin ignored her, poring over his books and charts and muttering strange words to himself. Three nights in the past week, he'd stayed in the blacksmith's forge behind his cottage until dawn, shouting orders to the mute giant who pounded away at the iron, trying to match his master's strange specifications.

Every morning, Shea awoke, remembering that she had planned on fleeing south with Crestman. She had planned on escaping Amanthia, on leaving behind the famine, and the war, and a king

who was desperate enough to impress children into his army. She
was a sun after all—affairs of state were none of her business.
But then, every morning, Shea remembered the Swancastle.

The castle was just beyond the fringe of Davin's forest, an
easy walk from Shea's little hut. The first time she had emerged
from beneath the trees to see it, she was overwhelmed by its glistening snowy walls. The castle towered above her, easily the height
of ten men. The building itself was at the top of a steep hill; Shea
remembered the stories she had heard of suns toting cartload after
cartload of earth to the building spot. The walls gleamed in the
morning air, capturing sunlight and fracturing it into a thousand
thousand prisms.

Shea had fallen on her knees as she stared at the edifice that
had sparked the rebels during the Uprising, the building that would
have been a peaceful home to her own swangirl, to Larina, if only
the war had never begun. Even now, even knowing what the castle had cost her, Shea was bound to the ghosts of the swans who
had lived there, the swans who had rebelled against Sin Hazar
and dragged their province to defeat.

Thinking of the waste caused by her province's rebellion, Shea
felt the familiar weakness seize her chest, and she gasped for
breath. What was she doing here, arguing with carters in front of
the Swancastle? She should have been home in her own cottage.
She should have been surrounded by her own children, by *their*
children. Her greatest concern should have been whether or not
to give a grandson a bite of honey bread before supper. She should
not need to worry about feeding dozens of ravenous boys, about
filling their bellies so that they would have the strength for their
next maneuvers in the service of their king.

Shea shook her head. She was lost in the past. Again. She'd
get nowhere by fighting King Sin Hazar's cartman. "Go ahead,
then, man. All of you, get your supper, round the castle. On the
far side, there's a cook-tent. I'll unhitch your oxen."

The carter seemed willing enough to yield his argument, with
the prospect of hot food nearby. He whistled his handful of fellows across the grassy slope, and Shea turned toward the beasts

of burden. The oxen hung their heads low, snorting as if they were disgusted by the trip they had taken.

"Crestman!" Shea called, seeing her charge loitering near the haphazard tents that housed the division of the Little Army. "Give a hand, boy! Unhitch these beasts!"

The lionboy ignored her, pretending that he hadn't heard. Shea had seen his shoulders tense, though, and she scarcely hesitated before storming across the short distance that separated her from the children. She leaned close and whispered, barely taking care to keep the other boys from hearing. "I'll take away your toys, boy! I'll break that bow over my knee and toss it into the woods, even if it *was* made by your precious Davin!"

Crestman shrugged as if he did not care, but he left the ragtag group of boys. He preserved his dignity by taking his time to saunter with Shea, sighting at various birds and blades of grass with his wrist-braced bow. When they were out of earshot, though, he cast a quick glance over his shoulder, making sure that his fellows weren't watching. Then he hissed, "You can't do that! You can't order me around in front of my men!"

"Don't tell me what I can and cannot do, boy. You swore your loyalty to *me*, remember! You said the words easy enough when you thought your life hung in the balance."

"Hush!" Crestman hissed, with another backwards glance. "There are twoscore soldiers in the Little Army encamped here. If even one of them finds out that I deserted, do you think we'd last long enough to explain away our lies?"

"If you remember your oaths, there's no danger of their finding out."

"No danger, unless they hear your squawking. It's bad enough that I'm trapped with *them* again. I don't need you harrying me, too." Crestman continued to grumble, but he turned his attention to the oxen, unfastening their harnesses.

Shea ignored the boy's complaints. After all, her Pom had often needed to complain before he settled in to whatever tasks she'd set him. It was fine for boys to grumble, so long as they did not forget their chores.

Sure enough, Crestman began to speak to her again after only the briefest of sulky silences. "So, Shea, what supplies do you think are here?"

"From the looks of it, flour and salt. Maybe some lard. Some wine, to be watered down for the boys. Salt beef. Maybe some early apples."

"It's about time."

"I thought that you boys *enjoy* living by your own handiwork. I thought the Little Army liked eating what it can kill."

"Perhaps the Little Army does, but I know better. I'll eat from the king's larder and enjoy the honor." Shea joined in the boy's grim laugh. She, too, had been hungry. She, too, could appreciate the wonder of food that arrived, salted and cured, ready for the eating.

If only her orphans could share in the bounty. . . . If only Tain and Hartley could enjoy the richness in these casks.

Tain . . . Even now, the sungirl would be gathering the orphans together, getting them to offer up their daily prayers to the Thousand Gods. Shea hoped that they had been able to lay in some food against the winter, against the creeping cold.

Shea exhaled deeply, her breath fogging in the cool evening air. As she always did when she thought of her children, she wondered if she'd made the right decision. She could admit to herself that she had saved Crestman because he reminded her of Pom. Oh, she could make up stories that she was protecting her orphans from the shame of killing a child, from the sorrow they would feel when they grew and matured and realized the horror of their actions. But in her heart, Shea knew that she had not acted for the children. She had acted for herself. She had acted for Pom.

Even as Shea admitted the truth, she thought of Serena, the little swangirl that she had abandoned in her cottage. The child had been so pale, so slight. . . . By now, she might have succumbed to a cough or a fever. She might be nothing more than a shade.

Shea stared off in the twilight, and she could see Serena's wraith before her. The child stood beside the last wagon, holding on to the wooden side with a trembling arm. She was clothed all in white, as if Tain had managed to find a funeral dress for her.

Serena looked up when she realized that Shea was watching her, looked up with an expression of horror on her face.

"Serena," Shea breathed, stumbling forward. Even as she moved, the swangirl fell to her knees, her funeral gown billowing up around her like the finest of linen. She cried out and ran to her. "Serena, forgive me!" she sobbed. "Forgive me, child! I never should have left you! May Nome have mercy on my soul!"

"Please! Help me!"

Shea realized her mistake even as she registered the weak cry. The child who lay beside the wagon was larger than Serena; she must be twice the swangirl's age. Nevertheless, Shea knelt beside her, gathering up the white-clothed, shivering form. "Who are you, child? What are you doing in the king's wagon?"

"Please, Grandmother! Don't let the soldiers get us!"

"The soldiers won't get you, child. I'll keep you safe." Shea heard the words and wondered at her confident tone. What could one sun possibly do to keep this child safe from the Little Army? How could she keep *anyone* safe, in the upside-down world that her life had become?

Crestman had sprung to Shea's side at the first sound from the girl, and he eyed the newcomer cautiously. His knife was out of its sheath, its curved blade tilted to catch the best of the evening light. "Be careful, Shea! This may be a trick!"

"It's no t—trick." The girl's teeth chattered like dice in a cup. Her face was smudged with dirt, as if she had rubbed ashes into the hollows beneath her eyes. Her flesh looked blue beneath her flimsy linen gown. "I p—promise you, I can work no tricks." She took a few steps toward them, showing her empty hands. She favored her right leg heavily as she moved, and Shea could not help but glance down from the girl's face. The skirt of her white gown was filthy, covered with dark stains that looked black in the twilight.

"What is it, child? What happened to you?" Shea took a step closer, ignoring Crestman's hissed intake of breath.

"We needed to hide from—from some bad men. We sought refuge in these wagons. I was injured, though, as w—we escaped. They pushed their swords into the hay, through the cart's boards, to make sure no one was hiding there. Seven d—days of riding in these wagons has done me little good."

The girl's trembling fists closed around the once-white cloth of her skirt, and she lifted the fabric enough to show an angry gash along her calf, creeping up her thigh. Shea leaned closer, squinting to view the wound in the fading light, and she saw that the skin had been shaved from the child's leg, carved like meat from a bone. The wound was bloody; it had reopened with the girl's few steps.

Bad men had done this. . . . Shea did not need to be an owl to know that this child told only part of a tale. Bad men, seven days north of here. Bad men in King Sin Hazar's own city. The royal troops must have chased this child into the wagon. Shea only nodded, not disclosing how much she understood. "We?" she asked.

"Aye," the girl said, and her affirmative nod was almost lost as she shuddered convulsively from the cold. "My f—friend and I."

For the first time, Shea looked back at the hay wagon, and she could make out a pair of dark eyes staring over the side. Dark eyes and ragged hair, a pinched face. "Aye," she called to the other child. "And are you injured too?"

"Not cut, anyway." The face rose from the sideboard, proving itself attached to a girl's body, a girl also clothed in simple linen underclothes. "But hungry. And cold."

"Hungry and cold, we can solve. Climb down from there."

"Shea—" Crestman started to interrupt.

"Not now, boy."

"But Shea—"

"I won't hear your arguments, Crestman. On your oath before my hearth, I won't listen to you. Help that child down from the cart."

Crestman grumbled as he stepped forward. "Stupidest words I ever spoke," Shea thought she heard him mutter. Nevertheless, he reached up to help the girl. She ignored his assistance, though, swinging her leg over the side and clambering down with a maximum of independence, a minimum of grace. This child, too, had ashy smudges across her face, but now Shea could make out the remnant of rays, as if the girl had rubbed off a sun tattoo.

Crestman glared at the girls. "What are you going to do with them, Shea?"

"First we'll get them to a fire. Then we'll find some clothes and some food, some bandages to bind up that bleeding leg. We'll figure out what to tell Davin after the cartmen leave." It felt good to issue orders, good to solve problems like a sun. Shea turned to the first girl, the one who was injured. "Can you walk?"

"Aye." She said the single word decisively, but Shea saw a flicker of doubt cross her face. Well, they would see.

"And do you have names, girl?"

"Aye. I'm Rani. That's Mair."

"Rani. Mair." Shea nodded and gestured down the hill. "I'm Shea. Come along, then. Crestman, see what you can find among the boys. Bring us trews and shirts, and the warmest cloaks available."

"Cloaks! There aren't any extras!"

"How do you know that?"

"I'm their *captain,* Shea. You've forced me back to that."

"*I've* forced you? You're the one who staked a claim, out on the road." She saw Crestman's face darken, recognized a longer debate than these shivering girls had time for. "You may be their captain, boy, but I'm a sun. I have faith that you'll find cloaks, if you look hard enough. You managed to find new shoes for yourself, didn't you?"

For just an instant, she thought the boy would continue to fight. He drew a deep breath but then shrugged his shoulders. "Fine, Shea. But you're the one who'll be explaining to Davin."

"If Davin asks, I'll be happy to explain." She would handle *that* old goat when she needed to. "Come along, girls." She began to herd her charges toward her tiny hut. "And Crestman?"

"Yes?"

"Bring more firewood when you bring the clothes."

Rani squinted in the brightness of the midday sun. "Look, Mair! Look how close they're getting!"

She needed to shout to make herself heard over the battlefield noise, but she managed to limp a few steps closer to the Touched girl. Her leg was healing slowly; every time she placed weight on it, she risked ripping open the delicate scabs that tracked from her thigh to her ankle.

She could almost forget her injury, though, as she watched boys run back and forth on the ramparts of the Swancastle, screaming epithets at their brothers in the Little Army. Rani had watched the boys' officers exhort them before the mock battle began—the soldiers had been told to fight as if their very lives depended on their ability to defend the glistening white castle. This was apparently a vital test in the boys' training, a major hurdle before they could advance in the Little Army.

As Rani watched, she thought that this exercise was ridiculously wasteful. Boys' lives were actually at risk; they were endangering themselves as they both attacked and defended the castle.

Nevertheless, they were learning skills they would need in actual warfare. It was really the same thing, Rani mused, as entrusting an apprentice glasswright with the finest Zarithian cobalt glass. She might shatter the stuff, she might even slice open her palm with a dagger-sharp edge. But she'd certainly learn along the way. And if she couldn't handle the finest glass, she'd best learn early on. Before the guild had invested a great deal in her. Before her fellow glasswrights came to depend on her.

The children on the ramparts had taken their orders to heart. They had spared no weapons, hurtling down stones on their fellows, along with an occasional burning arrow. Nevertheless, they remained unable to kindle the heated oil that they had poured upon their companions only a few moments before.

Those companions, the rest of the division stationed at the Swancastle, went about their work as if there were no screaming hawks on the walls above them. The largest boys wrestled with the heavy stone shield that protected their fellows from oil and stones. The shield was made of slate, attached to a wooden framework with mortar. Even though the structure was massively heavy, it could be tilted at whatever angle the boys chose. The captain—

Crestman—Rani reminded herself, merely bellowed an order, and two boys tugged on a giant wooden screw. The screw was connected to the wooden frame with a complex system of ropes. The boys' motions tilted the shield up or down, left or right. Oil streamed off its surface, and rocks were deflected. Throughout the exercise, the boys beneath the shield chanted. "We're the Little Army! We're the Little Army!"

The chant kept the boys' true work moving in an orderly fashion. For while the stony shield was fascinating—and a military advantage in its own right—it posed nowhere near the threat made by the machine that worked beneath the shield. The boys had dubbed that engine the Eater.

The massive construction lived up to its name, tearing away at the earth beneath the Swancastle walls with angry metal jaws. Its teeth had been modeled after pitchforks, pitchforks turned into nightmare maws in the smithy behind Davin's hut. Rani had watched in the pale dawn light as the old man lectured the boys before they began their exercise. Davin had told the children that they were testing the latest of his inventions, the newest of his crafts. He boasted that if they were successful, he would build a bigger Eater, a monster engine that could chew away at the very seawalls of the Liantine cities across the ocean. If the Little Army succeeded, Sin Hazar could conquer his enemies before they even realized that battle had been engaged.

Not that the Eater needed to be much larger. In the course of one morning, the pitchfork teeth had chewed a deep hole beneath the Swancastle's wall. The earth that was taken from beneath the structure was ferried away from the excavation by a series of metal pails. These, too, had been fashioned in Davin's smithy, modeled after wooden buckets. Chains ran between the pails, chains that traveled over and under a complicated system of pulleys. The pulleys were turned by a rack of levers that ratcheted back and forth like the treadles of a loom. Boys pushed at the levers, moving them in time to Crestman's measured commands, to the measured cadence that the captain had barked, uninterrupted, since dawn. The boys' backs rose and fell as they hauled on the levers, looking like the crew of a laboring galley on a smooth green sea.

As the boys struggled on, Davin stood by Shea and the girls, raising scroll after scroll of parchment to better catch the daylight. Occasionally, the old man swore vicious oaths, throwing his rolls to the ground and stomping away. He never went more than a few feet, though, before he returned, nodding to himself, checking one calculation or another against some scrawled chart.

Crestman's voice had grown hoarse during the long morning, and by noon, he'd been barely able to squawk his orders. Once, Shea had ordered Rani to bring the boy a cup of tea, but he had dashed the drink from her hands, breaking his cadence only a moment to berate her. Rani gathered that a sun had no place on a battlefield, at least no place unless a soldier commanded assistance. She had stalked away from the stone shield, wincing as her healing leg almost collapsed beneath her. Once she gained the safety beyond the engines' creak, she had let Davin, Mair, and Shea know what she thought of such command tactics.

Davin had ignored her, consulting yet another of his mysterious scrolls and holding a notched curve of wood steady with the horizon. Mair had grinned at Rani's tirade. Shea, though, had crumpled, crinkling her face into a mask of sorrow. Rani watched as the old woman stared at Crestman with mourning eyes, as if she were a beaten dog. Maybe dogs were what these northerners needed, Rani thought cruelly— a new caste or two. Suns, lions, swans, owls . . . These Amanthians needed a bit more of a menagerie.

Even as Rani imagined Shea as a dog, she realized that she was being ungrateful. The woman had clothed her, after all, and dressed her wound. She had scrubbed the ashy markings from Rani's and Mair's cheeks and silently redrawn their tattoos, this time using ink from Davin's forbidden cottage. She had fed the girls hearty gruel and hot bread, fresh meat for the first time since they had fled Sin Hazar. Certainly, Shea's fare was better than the meager rations that Mair had managed to filch from the carters while they were on the road.

It was hardly the old woman's fault that Rani was left with a throbbing, oozing leg, with a wound that would certainly leave a nasty scar. The long cut itched fiercely as it began to heal, and even now Rani could feel that it had once again reopened beneath the rough fabric of her borrowed trews. There was nothing to be done for that, though. No gentler clothes could be found. Shea was the only woman with this branch of the Little Army, and she had only the homespun dress upon her back.

Nevertheless, Rani's frustration and fear began to ripen like tangible fruit. She and Mair needed to be back on the road. They needed to move south, away from Sin Hazar's capital. They needed to travel hard and fast, gain the Morenian border before Sin Hazar's soldiers could track them down. Feeling the slow seep of blood down her leg, though, Rani knew that she'd be traveling nowhere with Mair, at least not for a week more. Not until her wound had closed for good.

Rani's attention was drawn away from her itching leg as the boys beneath the wood-and-stone shield set up a cheer, breaking their own constant chant. Davin stiffened beside her as Rani demanded, "What happened, Mair? What did I miss?"

The Touched girl craned her neck, grimacing as she tried to make out the events across the field. "I can't tell for sure. Look at that mountain of earth, though!"

"How much longer can the walls stand?"

Mair was spared the need to respond by a sudden sharp crack. For one instant, the plain was frozen. The defending boys on the castle wall were poised like a child's dolls, their hands raised over their heads to throw ineffective stones, to light puny arrows. The boys beneath the stone shield were still as well, rooted beside their metal pails, beside the giant pitchfork teeth of their machine. Then, Crestman bellowed one more time. "Push!"

The boys by the pulleys grasped the wooden handles, grunting as they pushed the levers away from their sweaty bodies. The iron pails crawled away from the wall one more step, each dragging one more mouthful of earth from beneath the Swancastle.

Then there was a tremendous crack, as if the ground itself were being split by thunder. The boys on top of the wall scurried to safety, leaping away from the excavation and disappearing inside the keep. As Rani watched, the wall seemed to lurch toward her, moving of its own volition, like a rock monster from her nightmares. Then, Crestman's voice rose, sharp and urgent. "Back, men! Back from the wall!"

There was a frantic scramble, as boys scurried from beneath the stone-and-wood shield. Some ran like rabbits, intent only on placing the greatest distance possible between themselves and the Eater. Others looked over their shoulders as they fled, stumbling over their own feet.

Crestman, though, ignored his own command and stood fast beside the pulleys. When the last of the boys had darted from beneath the tilted shield, Crestman grasped two treadles on the pulley mechanism. "*Push!*" he bellowed, as if he were ordering some unworthy underling to work. He suited action to his command, grunting at the strain as he tried to do the work of half a dozen boys. The muscles in his arms knotted, and the cords in his throat stood out, shaking, vibrating. His face was pulled into a tortured mask, made more hideous by the tight skin around his eyes, where his warrior's clout stretched his flesh. "Push," he gasped, fighting to suit action to words.

For one instant, the Eater refused to advance, refused to consume one more bite of earth. Then, the pitchfork jaws ground into the soil, tore out the rich dirt. The iron spikes fed the nearest pail, and the chains groaned forward, pulling the iron container back, away from the wall, away from the Swancastle.

And the Swancastle fell.

Not the entire wall, Rani realized when her ears had stopped ringing. The gap in the curtain wall was probably no wider than six men riding abreast. That was enough, though. A troop of soldiers could scale the ruins, could break into the unprotected underbelly of the keep.

"Yes!" Davin shouted, his ancient voice made strong by his excitement. "It works!" The old man threw his scrolls to the ground.

"Crestman!" Shea wailed, and the old woman surged past Rani, ignoring the dust, ignoring the screaming, cheering boys, ignoring the stones that even now were coming to rest on the hillside.

The sun need not have worried, though. Crestman had leaped

back at the last possible instant, sparing himself from the undermined wall. Now he stood at the edge of the rubble that had once been a proud castle, shaking his head in amazement. He looked up at the ruins and opened his mouth, closing it sharply, as if he were trying to clear a ringing noise from his ears. He was still shaking his head when Shea fell upon him. "Crestman!" the old woman sobbed. "Are you harmed? Were you struck?"

"I'm fine, Shea," the boy croaked, pushing away her attentions. Crestman rolled his eyes in annoyance, glaring at Rani and Mair. Rani understood the order there—the girls were to gather up the distraught woman. They were to free the commander for his work. "I'm fine, Shea. Just let me finish. Leave me alone, woman!" he bellowed when she would not restrain her inquisitive fingers. As the old sun's face crumpled, Crestman turned back to the Little Army, harnessing what was left of his voice. "All right, men! Into the keep! Watch for traps and round up the traitors!"

The boys cheered as they surged into the ruins, drawing their curved knives and their strange, short bows.

The air was filled with bloodcurdling screams as the Little Army conquered its own, playing out the last act of its risky game. Even as chaos echoed above her, Rani found herself drawn to Shea. The old woman stood where Crestman had left her, still stretching a shaking hand toward empty space.

For just an instant, Rani remembered her own mother, standing beside the hearth in the large room behind their merchant shop. Deela Trader had reached for her eldest son, for Bardo, with precisely the same expression on her face. Bardo, though, had been in a hurry, heading out to the marketplace, or to a pub, or to some other, darker pleasure. Rani's mother had recognized her loss, recognized that her son was leaving behind more than the hearth where he'd been raised.

Rani shook her head, hoping that she never longed for anyone so desperately. Then, Mair stepped forward, grabbing at Rani's arm. "Cor! Did ye see that? An army o' little boys, 'n' they managed t' bring down a castle wall, all i' a mornin'! Rai! Did ye see!"

"Aye, Mair. I saw."

"Just think, Rai! Think what 'Alaravilli could do wi' one o' these!"

Rani thought, but she realized that Sin Hazar was prepared to do far more. For Sin Hazar had Davin. He had the Little Army. He said he was after Liantine, to the east. But Sin Hazar could change his tactics. He could change his goals. Sin Hazar could bring the Eater to Morenia any time he chose.

Mair was still chattering that night, as the Little Army gathered to celebrate its victory. "I've never heard a noise like that, Rai. Have you?"

"No, Mair. I've never heard a noise like that," Rani answered for the hundredth time.

Mair's amazement, though, was cut short by Davin, who loomed out of the darkness, as if he'd been conjured by the man-high bonfire.

"Little Army!" the man proclaimed.

"Da-vin! Da-vin! Da-vin!" The boys pounded on the ground as they shouted each syllable.

The old man flapped his hands in the air impatiently, signaling the children to silence. When the chant had trailed off enough that Davin could be heard, he cleared his throat. "Little Army! You've served your king well today! With your bravery and your hard work, you have tested the latest of my war engines. When you set sail for the east, you will be prepared to fight King Sin Hazar's greatest enemies. You will be armed with an Eater three times the size of the one that you tested here today. You will bring glory to King Sin Hazar in Amanthia and across the ocean!"

"To King Sin Hazar!" one boy shouted.

"To Amanthia!" cried another.

"In honor of your service, Little Army, I declare tonight a feast night. Captain Crestman! You may broach three barrels of wine to honor your king and liege lord! Drink to your liege as you complete your maneuvers at the Swancastle! Long live King Sin Hazar!"

"Long live King Sin Hazar!" The Little Army swarmed around Crestman, gathering him onto their shoulders as they stormed around their bonfire. For just an instant, a handful of boys stepped toward Davin, as if they would include him in the celebration, but the ancient man waved them off. The boys, more intent on celebrating than giving appropriate credit to their elders, quickly abandoned the attempt. Davin turned to walk down the hill.

"Your Grace!" Shea shouted, her voice almost lost in the boys' revelry.

"What?" Davin's irritation was clear to Rani as he turned to face the old woman.

"Your Grace, that wine needs to last all winter. You shouldn't have told them they could break out so much tonight."

"Don't speak about things beyond your ken, old woman. My Eater works. That's cause for celebration. Besides, that captain of yours needs to cement his bond with his soldiers. He needs to be their leader."

"He needs—" Shea broke off her own protest, and then started again. "I'm a sun, Davin, the only one you've got here. I'm trying to run this camp, as a sun ought, and I'm telling you there won't be enough wine to last until spring."

Davin barked a laugh as harsh as a fox. "These boys won't be here till spring. The king will send them over the sea before midwinter."

"You can't be serious! They're children!"

"What did you think we meant by the *Little* Army, woman? They're *all* children. They fight without fear of losing their own lives; they fight with more energy than grown men. They've never seen death, not on a battlefield. They'll use my engines to win Sin Hazar's war without a thought to what the battle might cost them." Davin scowled at Shea. "Don't get attached to soldiers, sunwoman. The Little Army is worse than lions—this division'll be gone in two months, your captain, too. More boys will take their place. There are always more boys."

The gruff old man trudged down the hill, tossing his black hood over his snowy hair and melting into the darkness. Rani saw the mother-loss spread over Shea's face, and she limped to the old woman's side. "Shea—" she began.

The sun fumbled at her rough dress, clutching the fabric across her chest. "I'm tired, child," she said, her eyes staring across at the bonfire. "I'm going to sleep."

"Shea, you can't worry about them. They're not sailing yet."

"I'm not worried, child. My Crestman will be fine. He's a captain. In the Little Army." Before Rani could think of a comforting lie, the old sun turned and staggered down the hillside. Rani thought that she should follow the woman, at least to make sure that she arrived safely at her cottage. Before Rani could move, though, Mair grabbed her arm.

Rani turned back to the bonfire, only to see Crestman swaggering toward the girls. "So," he croaked, his voice still hoarse from his morning's exertions. "You're lucky to have been here today. You got to see our enemies' nightmares."

"We're honored," Mair said dryly, and Rani looked at her friend in amazement. Hadn't the Touched girl been crowing for the better part of the evening? Hadn't she been amazed by Crestman's feat?

"You were very brave, to push the levers the last time," Rani said. She delivered the compliment as an offering to Shea, as the words that the old woman might have said, if she could have stayed beside the bonfire.

Crestman grinned at Rani, but there was no mirth in his expression. The firelight glinted off his teeth. "I'm their captain. Davin's seen to that. With a pair of leather shoes and the power of command, he's seen to that."

Before Crestman could elaborate on his grim words, a shout went up from the fire. "Captain! Captain, it's time to judge the prisoners!"

Crestman took a deep breath, letting his eyes travel down the hill to the darkness that had consumed Davin. "Excuse me, ladies. Duty calls."

"Captain!" Mair snorted, as the boy stalked away. "He doesn't know the first thing about leading a group of children! He's only doing this because Davin ordered him to."

"Hush!" Rani said, taking a step closer so that she could hear what transpired by the fire. The boys had fed four huge logs onto the flames, stoking the bonfire higher than it had been when Davin addressed them. For just an instant Rani imagined capturing the scene in glass, building spikes of red and orange and yellow in a lead framework, tilting the planes of color so that sunlight would make them glow.

In the bonfire's light, Rani could see that the victorious soldiers, the ones who had manned the Eater, had smeared their faces with something—earth from the fallen Swancastle? Ash? Something streaked dark across their cheeks, covering the scars where their tattoos had been carved away.

As Rani watched, one of the younger boys danced up to Crestman, reaching up to daub the dark substance across the captain's face. Crestman accepted the attention earnestly, lowering his head so that he could bear the same marks as his men.

Only when he was decorated did he turn to the dozen boys who huddled in a pile, too close to the leaping flames for comfort. Those boys were stripped to their smallclothes, and they were lashed together cruelly. The arms of each child had been tied in front of him, his wrists wrapped tightly with leather thongs. Each boy's arms had been tugged between his legs and lashed to the throat of the boy behind him. Any child who tried to ease his own aching shoulders was likely to strangle at least one fellow prisoner.

The children could not stand; they twisted about in a ghastly series of half crouches and desperate squats. Rani's own shoulders ached at the thought of their torture, and she tried not to stare into their pale, pale faces. Crestman, though, did not seem disturbed. He crossed to the largest of the bound boys and punched him hard on the arm, sending the blond child twisting onto his side, out of his dangerous equilibrium. As the boy fell, the soldier behind him choked for breath. That boy, in turn, pulled back, trying to ease the pressure across his windpipe. His motion served only to saw the harsh rope up between the legs of Crestman's chosen victim.

"Varner!" Crestman barked at the blond boy, his eyes glinting out of the black mask smeared across his cheeks. His words were more ferocious for breaking across his rasped throat. "You call yourself a soldier?" The captive only stared ahead, ignoring his bonds, unblinking. "I'm speaking to you, boy! Do you call your-self a soldier in the Little Army?"

"Yes."

"Then what sort of showing did you make today? What sort of fighting man do you think you are?"

Silence. Crestman knotted one hand, crashing his fist into Varner's face. Rani heard the crack of the prisoner's nose, and blood streamed down his bleached face. "I ask you again, boy. What sort of fighting man do you think you are?"

"A loyal one," Varner spat. "Davin needed someone on the walls to test his machines."

"Davin needed someone to *defend* the Swancastle! It does him no good to test his engines against a bunch of sniveling babes!" Rani could just make out the half-swallowed sobs of the other trussed-up captives. The larger group of boys, the black-painted ones, must have heard the sound as well, for they began to whis-per among themselves. "Da-vin. Da-vin."

Crestman dug his booted toe into Varner's side. "We might as well fight against kittens!"

"We did as we were ordered, Crestman." Varner's words were slurred by the blood that dripped from his nose.

"How can we trust you, Varner? How can the Little Army trust anyone weak enough to lose a *castle* to a group of boys?"

Varner glared at his tormentor, and he lifted his chin defiantly. "Enough, Crestman. Name our punishment. My men and I will meet it. We're loyal to the king."

Crestman scarcely hesitated before stepping back from the fire. "Free them," he barked, gesturing to two of his soldiers. The pair of victorious boys hooted as they cut the ropes that bound their captives. One of the released boys staggered to his feet and stum-bled a few steps away from the firelight, only to be harried back with the flats of his brothers' blades.

"Choose a man, Varner. Choose your best man."

The blond boy glared at Crestman, but he barely hesitated be-fore he said, "Stand forward, Monny."

Rani caught her breath as a boy stepped up to his leader's side. This must be the smallest child in all the Little Army! He could hardly be eight years old. The boy's red hair was darkened with sweat, wiry where it had come loose from his warrior's clout. Freckles stood out across his unmasked face.

"This is your best? This is the best you can offer King Sin Hazar?" Crestman's harsh laugh was echoed by his men.

"Monny." Varner barely whispered the boy's name, but the red-headed child nodded. Faster than Rani's eyes could follow, he hurtled his full weight at one of Crestman's guards, catching the older boy completely by surprise. Before the larger soldier could regain his footing, Monny had captured the boy's arrow-launching device. He scraped the knife-edged arrow across his erstwhile guard's throat, reached down to scrape some of the black paint from the older boy's face and deposit in on his own cheeks, and then he turned the weapon on Crestman. He closed one eye as he aimed the short bolt at his captain's heart; then he froze, testifying mutely to the damage that he could cause.

Crestman's soldier was swearing, sucking his breath between his teeth as his own sweat stung his slashed throat. Monny had moved carefully, though; the boy's wound was more bloody than deep. Rani watched Crestman register his approval, a slight lifting of his eyebrows and a slow nod of his head. "Drop your weapon, soldier."

Monny complied immediately, shouting out, "In the name of King Sin Hazar!"

The cry was taken up by Crestman's victors. "Sin Ha-zar! Sin Ha-zar!" The boys stomped on the ground with each syllable, and they moved forward ominously, encircling the unfortunate children who had been ordered to defend the Swancastle's walls.

Crestman barked his orders so that they fell between his army's cadence. "On the ground, boy! Spread your arms! Spread your legs!" Monny answered each order immediately, breathing heavily, but doing nothing else to betray any apprehension.

Rani stepped forward as Crestman signaled four of his men to his side. She had seen the cruelty of children; she had seen military discipline at its worst—in the Brotherhood of Justice, infractions were considered blood debts. Before she could speak, though, before she could distract Crestman from his deadly mission, Mair gripped Rani. The Touched girl shook her head once and dug her fingers into the meat of Rani's arm.

Meanwhile, Crestman gave a curt nod, and each of his four soldiers knelt beside the redheaded child, putting his full weight on a limb. Crestman waited until his men were settled before he turned back to the assembled soldiers. He thrust one fist into the air, momentarily stilling their chant of the king's name.

"King Sin Hazar relies on his soldiers to be the best in all the land! He relies on us to serve his cause, easy or hard, just or unjust, right or wrong. King Sin Hazar rules Amanthia by the right of all the Thousand Gods. By all the Thousand Gods, King Sin Hazar will come to rule the world!"

The army cheered Crestman's words, all of them but Monny and Varner. Crestman drew his short sword, brandishing it above his head until the boys fell silent. The captain's eyes glowed from behind his mask of black soot; the paint had smeared down his face and across his lips. "Sin Hazar demands our complete faith. When we do not understand a command, it is because we are only soldiers, because we are not king. Long live King Sin Hazar!"

"Long live King Sin Hazar!" rose the boys' shouts. Monny's voice rang out, shrill and piercing, loudest of all the children. Rani swallowed hard, her heart pounding as she dreaded whatever would happen next.

Crestman stepped over the redheaded boy, scarcely acknowledging his own kneeling soldiers. The captain came to stand chest to chest with Varner. The defeated boy glared at his leader for a moment, but then dropped his eyes. Crestman took the vanquished soldier's hand, closed it around the hilt of his own curved sword. He waited until Varner had accepted the weapon, until the boy had met his eyes.

"Shave him."

"What?" Varner laughed, the sound incongruous in the charged air beside the bonfire.

"Shave him."

Varner laughed again and crossed to the restrained Monny. He knelt beside the boy and shook his head, raising the curved blade to the child's sweat-dulled red locks. "In the name of Sin Hazar," he began, and Monny smiled, too.

"Not his head," Crestman interrupted.

"Not—"

"The king has enough soldiers. He needs more nightingales, to sing to him. To ease his mind, as he plans our next battle." Monny had frozen beneath his captors' hands, his grin still gaping incongruously against his filthy skin. "Geld the boy."

Varner stared at Crestman. "You're mad."

"I'm your captain, soldier! I'm the king's voice on this battlefield!"

"But he's just a boy! He's too young even to *be* in the Little Army!"

"He showed his own bravery, and his willingness to follow his king's orders. Are you going to take that away from him with your cowardice?"

"You don't know what you're asking!"

"I know," Crestman answered evenly. "Believe me, soldier, I know."

Rani shuddered at the grim words, at the confession painted behind the statement. Crestman had faced his own test. Sometime in the past, he had held his own blade, or arrow, or garrotte string. Captain Crestman had already passed the challenge he set for his men.

Even without black paint, Varner's face contorted into a mask, his mouth stretched into a gaping hole, his broken nose smashed beyond recognition. "Don't make me do this," he whispered. Rani could barely hear his words above the crackle of the fire, above the murmur of the waiting Little Army.

"*I* don't make you do anything, soldier. The king makes you. The king *commands* you. In the name of Sin Hazar!"

As Crestman must have planned, the boys took up the cry, pounding their feet against the earth, shouting the king's name as loudly as they could. Rani felt the hillside shake beneath them, the very ground trembling beneath the Little Army.

Crestman stepped back, away from the fire, away from Monny. Varner staggered toward the pinned boy, falling heavily to his knees.

Crestman's loyal soldiers did not flinch; they maintained their grip on Monny's limbs. Varner's hands shook, and now tears glistened on his cheeks, mixing with the slimy trail of blood from his nose. He raised Crestman's knife, offering it like a prayer to the Thousand Gods, and then he reached out with his free hand, seizing Monny's smallclothes and slashing through the cloth with a single motion.

Monny panted like a trapped animal, his breath whistling between his teeth. Every boy in the Little Army stared at Varner, watched as the vanquished soldier raised a blade against his own brother.

Every boy watched Varner, but Rani watched Crestman. She saw the captain measure his men. She saw him follow the path of his own sword, his own blade flickering above a sacrificial child in the firelight. She saw him weigh fidelity and trust. And she saw him snatch a breath of midnight air.

"Hold!" The word exploded from Crestman's mouth like the stone walls of the Swancastle cracking down onto the field. "In the name of King Sin Hazar, hold your blade!"

Varner snapped like a cut bowstring, falling across Monny's chest. The soldier's sobs wracked his body; he gasped for air like a drowning man. Monny did not even attempt to move; instead, he stared up at Crestman with a fierce glint that Rani could not read, that she could not translate to either love or hate.

Crestman stepped forward, into the firelight, into the deadly silence that had replaced the chanting Little Army. "In the name of King Sin Hazar, I spare this boy. Fetch a calf! We'll have fresh meat to celebrate our victory! Fresh meat as a gift from our king! A gift from Sin Hazar!"

It took only a moment for the boys to regroup, for a bawling calf to be brought from the holding pen on the other side of the Swancastle. Rani did not bother to watch as the animal was sacrificed, as its blood was caught in an iron pail, for Shea to use in making sausages. Rani did not witness the hide peeled back from the steaming meat, and she did not see the boys carve away flesh to roast in the fire.

Instead, she watched Crestman strip off his cloak. She watched the captain cross to Varner and settle the garment across the still-weeping boy's shoulders. She watched Crestman raise the edge of the cloak, wipe away some of the mess from Varner's face. The captain reached out for Monny as well, touching the boy's forehead once. "In the name of King Sin Hazar," Crestman murmured, but Monny flinched from his hand.

Crestman nodded, as if he had received the response that he expected, then he helped Varner to his feet. He took the boy to a log and settled him comfortably. Crestman tucked his own cloak in carefully, as if he were a nursemaid, and then he called over another soldier, ordered fresh meat and watered wine brought to the blond boy.

Once he had seen Varner settled, Crestman staggered off into the night, wrapping his arms about himself to ward off the chilly wind that had begun to blow across the hillside. Rani started to climb to her feet, to go after the boy, but Mair's hand clamped around her wrist with a fierce force. "I told ye i' th' king's palace, Rai. Ye canna trust anyone i' Amanthia."

"But—"

"'E's dangerous, Rai."

"He's frightened. And he's filled with remorse."

"'E's bound these boys t' Sin 'Azar better than any oath could 'ave. 'E's dangerous."

Rani pulled her wrist away from Mair and limped away from the fireside, ignoring the invitation of roasting meat, ignoring the ache in the back of her throat, ignoring the memory of Crestman, who had looked back at his private, untold torture as he ordered Varner to act. Instead, Rani remembered her own past, her own longing to join a group. She recalled the innocent blood that she had shed to further that goal.

She knew the pain of belonging. She knew Captain Crestman of the Little Army, even if she could not, would not, go to his side.

8

Hal stood in the embrasure of the nursery, staring down at the courtyard through the mullioned window. It had been months since he'd been in this room, in the chamber that he had shared with Bashi and his four half sisters, the apartments that he had shared with Rani when she first came to the palace. A few minutes earlier, when Hal had strode in, the nurses had looked up from the princesses' morning meal. They had needed only one glance at the king's face, one glance at the knifelike shards of wax that jutted from the parchment in his hands, and they had fled, taking the princesses and leaving Hal alone.

All alone. On his own. Blood and bone.

Consciously refusing to read the parchment letter again, Hal scooped up a doll that the youngest princess had been holding. He smoothed his thumb across the toy's wooden face, down the silky locks of horsehair. Rani had owned a doll when she had been designated First Pilgrim. She had offered up the poppet on the dais in the cathedral, cementing her oath to her king, to the Defender of her Faith.

Defender of the Faith. Remember the wraith—

No! No more rhymes!

After Rani had settled in the castle, after the horrific events that had cost her her brother and set Hal on his throne, Rani had confided to him that she had dreaded parting with her past, that day in the cathedral. She'd been loath to hand over the final bond with her mother and father, with the family that had sheltered and loved her as she had grown up within the City walls. Of course, the old king, Shanoranvilli, had known nothing of a child's hopes and desires. He had accepted the doll with an incredulous laugh, propelling Rani forward on her quest.

On her quest. To her rest. Death is best.

Death *is* best.

Why hadn't Shanoranvilli refused the childish offering? Why hadn't the old king mandated that Rani could not be the First Pilgrim, that she was too young? Maybe, then, Rani would still be alive. Shanoranvilli might still sit on his throne. Halaravilli might be left alone in the corner of this very nursery, playing with his soldiers, lining up his toys. Playing like a boy. Any little ploy.

Anything other than reading this parchment, reading it again, and knowing that it reeked of death. Death for Rani. Death for soldiers, who would fight to avenge the merchant girl. Death for Bashi, who had brought them all to such straits. Death for Hal, most likely, who would be hunted down by the Fellowship of Jair for rebelling against their orders, even if he somehow survived his war in the north.

For Hal had no option now. He and Sin Hazar had engaged in a stilted exchange of letters, two traveling in each direction. The king of Amanthia had made it clear that he desired nothing more than to return Rani to Morenia, along with Mair and Bashi. Sin Hazar claimed to be worried, though, afraid that he could not guarantee safe passage of his hostages. He believed that the journey could only be secured if he were allowed to move his troops into northern Morenia, into the rich borderlands between the two kingdoms.

Hal had refused, of course. As king, he could not permit entire divisions of armed men to encamp in his territory. Instead, Hal had suggested that the three hostages be returned on the next available ship, with no further questions, no further threats between the parties.

Sin Hazar had countered with a straightforward request for ransom. Gold, jewels, cartloads of iron—the king had served up a long list of demands. He noted that such wealth was necessary if he were to continue building his expensive campaign against the Liantines, across the ocean. He implied that he would not hesitate to direct his men to easier targets if he could not send them overseas. He would send his army south, to Morenia.

Again, Hal had refused. Again, he had demanded the return of all three prisoners, adding a brazen threat to harry the Amanthian border with all the troops at his disposal. And he had demanded proof that the prisoners were alive—proof that Rani Trader was treated well as Sin Hazar's captive.

Now, standing in the nursery, holding the reply to his most recent demand, Hal found himself acting without thinking, without planning, without consciously making any decision at all. His fist flew up, smashing through the window's fragile, bubbled panes. He was too high in the castle to hear the glass shatter on the courtyard stones below. The wind immediately grasped the advantage Hal had created, and its bony fingers pried into the nursery, stealing Hal's breath.

At least the cold drove away the voices, silenced the chittering swirl deep in his brain. Hal raised the letter once more, grasping it firmly against the wind's tug. He forced his eyes to read each letter, each ornate word copied out by some unknown scribe.

"To His Majesty, King of all Morenia, greetings from your loyal subject Ranita Glasswright. I have received your missive, and am honored by your concern for my well-being. Please know that I am treated well in the house of Sin Hazar, that he has provided me nourishment and succor. You asked me a question in your letter, and I provide you an answer: Dalarati. Dalarati was the person who first suffered at a Trader's hand in the cause of our Fellowship. You will know by my answer that I am well and protected by King Sin Hazar. While I would rather be in Morenia, I understand that I must stay in Amanthia for a while longer, while you and the king work out your affairs of state. I am honored that I can serve in this small way, keeping watch while you negotiate for my freedom and the glory of your kingdom. In the name of all the Thousand Gods, I remain your most loyal subject."

The letter's author had worked hard to capture Rani's tone, her characteristic stumble over phrasing more formal than anything she had ever learned in the Merchants' Quarter. Whoever had written the letter knew that Rani would address Hal more as a friend and companion than as her liege lord. And the writer had known about the Fellowship, at least about the martyred Dalarati. But the writer had missed two key facts.

First, Dalarati had *not* been the first member of the Fellowship murdered by a Trader. There was a darker history behind the Fellowship's battles, a history that had almost broken Rani when she learned its deadly secrets. Her own brother, Bardo, had murdered one of the Fellowship of Jair, long before Rani ever learned of the secret cadre's existence. Bardo had executed Treen, a Touched woman.

Even if Rani had somehow misconstrued Hal's question, even if she had somehow failed to understand that he would never have summoned her personal guilt about Dalarati's demise, Hal knew that Rani had not penned the letter that he held. For Rani would never call herself Ranita Glasswright, not of her own volition. She had vowed to restore the glasswrights' guild, but she would not call herself by her guildish name until she had built a new house, until she had found masters and journeymen to restore the guild that had been destroyed so unjustly. "Ranita Glasswright" would never have written from Amanthia.

And so Hal could only conclude that Rani was dead. Murdered at Sin Hazar's hand, perhaps. Maybe she had fallen to wounds she had suffered as Bashi dragged her north. Innocent victim of a grippe—what difference did it make? Rani was gone, and Sin Hazar was trying to hide the fact. Keep Hal trapped. All life sapped.

Hal leaned his head against the stone embrasure, letting the rough wall scrape across his flesh. Rani had pledged her fealty to him here. She had decided to join him, to turn back from the horror that she had witnessed. She had trusted him, here, in the nursery. And he had betrayed that trust. He had let Bashi spirit her away; he had let her be taken by force to an enemy's lands.

He had lost her—sister, Pilgrim, Fellow, gone. Midnight doubt swirled through his brain, colder than the air from the courtyard.

"Your Majesty!" Hal started at the summons, whirling to face his squire, who stood only an arm's length away.

"Farsobalinti?"

The youth bowed at the sound of his name, grimacing as if he disliked interrupting his king. "I'm sorry, Your Majesty. I would not have called you again, if you hadn't ordered me to summon you when the council is met."

"Call me again?"

"Aye, Your Majesty. I spoke to you from the door, and again from across the room." The squire looked uncertainly at his liege, at the parchment that Hal had crumpled in his fist. "Perhaps you've taken cold, Your Majesty. I'll call the glaziers to fix that window. The nursery should be secure."

Glaziers. The glaziers' guild would never be rebuilt now. Hal and all his followers would have to rely on glasswrights hired away from other lands, on craftsmen lured to work in a land that had only meant death and dishonor for their kind.

"Aye, Farso." Hal lapsed into his friendly nickname for the squire. No reason to frighten the boy. No reason for Farso to realize yet that his life was on the line, that armies would soon be marching, that Sin Hazar was more ruthless even than Hal had feared. Still, Hal's throat almost closed as he whispered, "The nursery should be a safe place."

The squire waited for a long minute, staring at his liege with obvious concern. "Er, Your Majesty. Your council awaits you. You asked me to let you know when they'd been assembled."

Hal forced a smile onto his face, even though he knew that the expression must look like a skull's rictus. He tried not to frighten one of his few allies in court. Not to alienate a loyal sword arm. Hal turned his back on the embrasure, on the courtyard that he had overlooked with Rani two long winters past. "Let us go, then. We shouldn't keep the council waiting any longer than necessary."

"Yes, Your Majesty." The squire reached for the nursery door, but then hesitated. "Um, my lord. . . ." Hal followed the boy's gaze, saw that he still held his sister's poppet. He turned back to set the doll on the bench beside the window, wasting a moment to smooth its silky hair. He reached up to close the wooden shutters, to lock out the prying wind.

"Let us go, then, Farso. Let us address the King's Council."

As they walked through the palace hallways, Hal heard the voices in his mind. They abandoned their typical rhyming, settling for cataloging his failures. He had failed to lead his people since Shanoranvilli had died. He had failed to see the threat in Bashanorandi. He had failed to protect women he was pledged to keep safe. He had failed to negotiate with Sin Hazar. He had failed to settle peacefully a border conflict that could destroy his young reign. He had failed he had failed he had failed. . . .

Hal could not meet his lords' eyes as he walked to his seat at the head of the council table. The jabbering voices grabbed hold of each councillor's name, twisting the long chains of syllables into dark poems. Hal clenched his hands into fists. The voices could only harm him here. They could only make the council rise up against him. The rhymes that had kept him alive to the age of seventeen might destroy him now, if he did not find the strength to banish them, to beat them back, to summon silence.

Silence.

Only when Hal had settled into his ornate chair did he trust himself to look out at the table, to survey the lords who attended him. Duke Puladarati was there, of course, leaning forward with both elbows on the table. The old regent was arguing with his neighbor, forcing a point with vigor and a maimed hand, as if he still held the power of the Crown within his grasp.

Tasuntimanu was present as well, halfway down the table, swaddled in the dull brown cape that he favored over his domain's flashy purple and silver. The brown did not hint at the scheming behind that placid face, did not suggest the thoughts that leaped beneath the Fellow's balding pate. Although Hal allotted the nobleman a long survey, Tasuntimanu did nothing to give away his thoughts; he did not so much as flick a glance at Duke Puladarati. Very well, then. Let the conspirators continue their game—it would matter little in the face of the news that Hal bore.

Continuing his review, Hal was relieved to see that Lamantarino was present as well, wheezing at the foot of the table. The old man's eyes teared up, and he repeatedly dragged a rag beneath his long nose. Hal imagined that he could hear the old man's breathing at this distance, hear the catarrh that scarred his lungs. No matter. Lamantarino had spoken kind words to Hal. Lamantarino might be the closest thing the king had to an ally in the entire council.

Before Hal could call the meeting to order, Tasuntimanu rose and bowed stiffly. "Are you well, Your Majesty? You look pale."

"I am well, Tasuntimanu," Hal forced himself to reply, marveling that he could speak above the voices, speak like a normal man.

Tasuntimanu nodded gravely, showing his bald spot as if he were offering up fealty, and intoned, "May the Pilgrim Jair look upon you and keep you in good health, Your Majesty." The benediction would merely sound like piety to the other councillors, but Hal understood the message. Tasuntimanu was taking no chances that Hal might forget his bonds to the Fellowship.

Well, Hal had sworn many oaths, some aloud, and others only in his heart.

"May all the Thousand Gods watch over this council and be praised," Hal answered. He was encouraged by Tasuntimanu's grimace. The man understood their unspoken exchange, Hal's refusal to give way to Jair in all things. Before Hal could lose his nerve, before the voices could begin their whispering again, he turned to his other lords.

"Well met, my lords," Hal said, settling both hands on the table. As he pinned the crumpled parchment against the oaken surface, he hoped that he would assume some of the table's bulk, that he would appear more imposing before his noblemen. "Be seated."

He watched as the nobles settled into their chairs. When an uneasy silence had sifted over the assembly, Hal raised the crumpled parchment in one trembling hand.

"I have had a letter, my lords, from the court of Sin Hazar."

"From the king's own hand?" Puladarati demanded immediately, and Hal resisted the urge to clear his throat like a nervous schoolboy. He reminded himself that Puladarati was no longer regent, that Hal no longer owed the bluff general any special obligation.

"A letter that purports to be from Lady Rani," he clarified. He knew that he should not give Rani her title, that he should not provoke his councillors, not now, with so much at stake. Nevertheless, he could not keep the honor from his lips, could not help but bring her some shred of dignity. Who knew what shame her body had suffered before she succumbed to Sin Hazar? Rani had been loyal to Hal's cause; she had been one of his first subjects to accept his rule, to realize that the king spoke more than tricksy riddles. He would honor her with words in this council chamber and with his sword on the battlefield.

Puladarati scowled; Hal could not tell if he objected to Hal's choice of title or to the message behind it. "Purports, Your Majesty? What does the merchant girl say?"

That was fine. Let Puladarati sneer, let him remind the council of Rani's station. Hal needed someone to feed him questions, to draw out his plan. He would use Puladarati, as he would any other tool. "She says that she is well and protected by Sin Hazar. She says that she is honored by the messages sent by this body."

"Then Sin Hazar is treating her as a noble hostage."

"Nay, Your Grace. Lady Rani is dead."

If Hal had hoped to provoke a spectacle with his solemn pronouncement, he was not disappointed. Several of the lords exclaimed aloud, and at least one blasphemed the Thousand Gods. Hal waited to hear Rani's name, waited to hear a single one of his nobles protest the murder of an innocent girl, but that desire was not filled. Rather, the council was united in decrying the insult to *Hal*, the threat to Morenia.

"Your Majesty, how can you be certain?" Puladarati at last made himself heard above the tumult. The man's tone was strong and steady, almost pedantic. Hal wondered suddenly if the old warrior had known the contents of the parchment all along, if the grizzled fighter already knew what had transpired in the north.

"There is no doubt. In my last letter north, I asked Lady Rani a question that only she could answer. The words in this reply are fair, and they shape an honest guess, but they do not answer my question correctly. An impostor hopes to make me believe that the lady still lives."

"And what question did you ask, Your Majesty?" Puladarati pushed.

Hal met the old soldier's eyes directly. "I'll not divulge that, Your Grace. It was a secret between Lady Rani and myself." Again, an explosion down the table, a rustle of whispers and invocations, blatant outrage that a noble—a king!—should hold secrets with a mere merchant girl.

Puladarati raised his voice to be heard above the outcry. "Yet you'd have us act based on that secret. You'd have us fight your battle without knowing the terms."

"I'd have you stand loyal to your king, man!" Hal pounded the table, letting a little of his emotion rock his voice. "I'd have all of you stand loyal to your king!"

Before Hal was ready to continue, Tasuntimanu leaned forward, his flat face creasing in disbelief. "You tell us that an impostor is writing from Amanthia. Are you ordering us to fight in the north, then, Your Majesty?"

Well, Hal had thought that he'd be the one to broach the subject. "That's precisely what I'm saying, my lord."

"In the name of Jair! Winter is fast upon us!"

Hal heard the warning, heard Tasuntimanu's dagger-sharp reproach on behalf of the Fellowship. He also heard the chittering voices—winter is fast, the die is cast, Hal could not last. He dared not hesitate, dared not give the voices a chance to break through his consciousness. He forced his own voice to a steadiness that he did not feel. "In the name of Jair, that's why we need to fight now."

Tasuntimanu gaped, giving Hal the break he needed to continue. "Our spies have reported Sin Hazar's troop movements for months. He has amassed a mercenary army outside his city, and it's made no sign of dispersing as the winter sets in. Despite reports that Sin Hazar's treasury is nearly empty, he is obviously paying those men steadily, keeping them loyal, keeping them focused. They're bound to demand more, though, as the winter progresses. As the rivers freeze and the ground grows rock-hard, as the hired men question their long months of useless service, we must attack. We cannot wait until the spring, until new life and new energy endanger our own men."

"In the name of Jair—"

"Jair has nothing to do with it!" Hal pounded the table, ignoring the gasps of his lords, who were shocked by the royal blasphemy. "This is about *men*, Tasuntimanu! Not about Pilgrims, not about gods. This is about whether Morenia will survive until next winter."

Tasuntimanu retorted, "This is about a merchant brat named Rani Trader."

"This is about a subject of your liege who was kidnapped! This is about a foreign king who was willing to murder a hostage, a *girl*! A king who was willing to disguise murder with a fair hand and forged words. This is about *honor*, Tasuntimanu. *My* honor as a man, and as a king. And your honor as a councillor— you and all who sit at this table, saying that you uphold justice."

Hal's heart pounded; blood beat through his temples with a rhythm stronger than any babbling voices. He clutched the edge of the table, willing himself to breathe, willing himself to think of the words that would inspire his councillors, would make them see justice and right, and not just a boy-king teetering on the edge of crisis.

"Begging your pardon, Your Majesty." The voice was cracked, so wispy that Hal almost didn't hear it above his own harsh breathing. "May an old man speak?"

"Aye, Lamantarino." Hal acknowledged the ancient advisor with a wave of his hand.

"This matter is not entirely without precedent. We have faced such perfidy at this table before." Several of the councillors shifted toward the far end of the table, craning their necks to make out the ancient lord's speech. As if he recognized that he must work to be heard, the trembling Lamantarino clambered to his feet. He clutched the edge of the table, apparently unconscious of how he parodied his young king. "Years ago, Your Majesty, before you were born, before Lord *Tasuntimanu* was born, your father faced such a decision."

Hal knew that he should not question one of his councillors, not at this table, not before all of his lords, unless he already knew the answers he would receive. Nevertheless, he could not help himself. Hoping he was not walking into a trap, praying that the ancient councillor was on his side, Hal asked, "What are you speaking of, Lamantarino? What happened to my father?"

"In the first year that King Shanoranvilli—may Jair guide him in the Heavenly Fields—took the throne, messengers came from the western edge of the realm, from the Sacred Grove, where only the king is allowed to hunt. They said that a white stag had been found in the Grove, a magnificent beast, with eighteen points. Your father was young then. By Doan, we were all young then!" The god of the hunt was a young man's god, and Lamantarino's explosive exclamation took its toll, leaving the ancient councillor gasping. One of his fellows passed him a goblet, and wine was red as blood on the old man's lips when he managed to continue.

"We rode out in the autumn and hunted that beast for a fortnight. Three times, we glimpsed him in the woods, and once—one night—we saw him standing at the top of a hillock. His antlers were tremendous; they would have crushed an ordinary stag, but he bore them proudly. Your father, Your Majesty, lost three quivers of arrows trying to get that beast, but at last he had to turn back to this city, to the kingdom that needed him."

Lamantarino shook his head with wonder, as if the hunt had been only the year before. Hal tried to imagine his father riding after a stag, sleeping out under the stars, a young man. He was unable to summon the image; even his earliest memories of Shanoranvilli were of a king worn down by age and the weight of his kingdom.

"That winter, as the snow filled the courtyard and the entire kingdom slept, King Shanoranvilli received a . . . gift. It arrived on a dray, covered in green and gold, the colors of Brianta, which lies to the west of the Sacred Grove. Your father lifted off a heavy cloth of samite, and he found the stag's head waiting for him. Its broken antlers glittered as if they were caught in new snow, like diamonds in the coldest silver setting. The Briantans had killed the stag and mutilated its horns."

Lamantarino drew a shuddering breath against his outrageous story, and even now, decades later, the noblemen grumbled that their king had been so insulted. "King Shanoranvilli wasted no time. He forgot that it was winter. He forgot that the ground was covered with snow. He forgot that he had a kingdom asleep, a kingdom that needed him to plan for spring. He gathered up his loyal men and coursed his hounds all the way to his western border. He found the poachers, and he executed them on midwinter eve." The old councillor raised his reddened eyes, caught his king's gaze down the length of the table. Lamantarino's voice was steady as he proclaimed. "Your father preserved the honor of his kingdom, Your Majesty. He preserved *your* kingdom, using his coursing hounds to honor the memory of that noble stag."

Coursing hounds. Noble stag.

Hal stared at his aged councillor, his jaw jutting forward with amazement. This was all fiction, all a rousing story! Lamantarino was intentionally riling up Hal's loyal councillors, reminding them of Shanoranvilli's glory, driving them toward Hal's goal. Let them think they're the noble stag, but treat them like the coursing hounds! That's what Lamantarino had said—that was what he'd *done*, helping out the fledgling king who needed deft guidance.

Hal nodded incredulously as Lamantarino wheezed his way back to his chair. As a fable, the story was unassailable. What councillor could argue that a human life—an innocent female hostage's life—was worth less than a stag's? Who could speak out against Hal leading his men north, winter or no? "My thanks, good Lamantarino. It's all too easy to remember the great Shanoranvilli who sat this chair for decades, and yet forget that he was once a young man, once a young king, who needed to fight to secure honor and justice in his kingdom."

Lamantarino inclined his head, as if he'd received some benediction in the name of all the Thousand Gods. He collapsed into his chair, spent as if he had run miles to deliver his tidings. It was Duke Puladarati who spoke next, who broke the reverent silence in the hall. The regent's voice echoed against the stone. "Then you will ride, Your Majesty? You will take back the honor of your kingdom?"

Hal swept his gaze over the table, measuring the tension in each of his councillors. He let his eyes come to rest upon Tasuntimanu before he replied. "In the name of Jair," he said, forcing irony from his voice, "could I do anything else?"

Rani caught her breath as she stepped near Davin's worktable, momentarily forgetting the creeping itch down her leg. "But how can you know how much to carve away? Do you grind off the same amount each time?"

Davin did not answer until he had lowered his sand-covered cloth to the table. "It's different for every type of glass. Cobalt grinds differently from red. They're both softer than clear glass."

"But what about clear glass that's stained? Does paint make it harder or softer?"

Davin nodded as if she had asked some shrewd question. "You understand the point, girl. It depends on what the paint is made of. Lead-based paints eat away at the glass, making it more brittle. Even I break lenses, if I try to grind them out of lead-painted glass."

"But why would you? You can't see through the lens if it's covered with paint."

"Foolish girl!" Rani recoiled from the old man's sudden rage. His squinting eyes flashed from deep in his wrinkled face, from the obscure tattoo that Rani still could not decipher into one of the northerner's castes. "You waste my time with your questions! If you aren't even *trying* to think of answers yourself, why should I be bothered?"

In the past fortnight, Rani had become accustomed to the old man's sudden tirades. They were a fair price for the lessons that she was learning, the instruction she had gained in pouring glass and carving it and making it meet her needs. As Davin spluttered and grumbled, Rani set her shoulders, staring at the lens that the old man had been working. Why would he want to paint glass and then curve the lens? What would be worth the paint, worth weakening the glass in the first place?

All of a sudden, Rani remembered Davin watching the assault on the Swancastle. She thought of the notched instrument that he had used to measure something about the walls, or about the hole that the boys had dug. Of course! She could paint *measurements* on the glass, not obscuring it completely. The paint would etch its way into the surface, weakening the glass, but it would leave behind useful guidelines. Then, Rani could grind the glass into a lens, using the paint that remained to help her measure what she saw, to help her calculate distances brought near by the lens. . . .

"You'd have to keep your hand very steady as you paint the lines, or else they'd be useless," Rani mused. "If they weren't perfectly even, your mistaken distances might be worse than knowing no distances at all."

"Aye." Davin spared her a rare grim smile. She had deciphered the mystery. That one, at least.

"What's that glass for?" she pushed. "What are you making?"

"A flying machine."

Rani sighed—that was Davin's standard answer when he did not wish to be disturbed. Before she could rephrase her question or think of something else to draw out the old man, the giant bird—the macaw, Davin called it—began to squawk from its perch. "A flying machine! A flying machine!"

"Quiet, you beast!" Davin threatened. "Quiet, or I'll pluck you bald!"

"Pluck you bald! Pluck you bald!"

The macaw captured Davin's tone precisely, and Rani could not bite back her laughter. She had realized after only a few days in the cottage that the wondrous bird could not actually speak *new* thoughts; it could only recite phrases it had memorized, mimicking its teacher precisely. Rani had spent hours while Davin was out with the Little Army, trying to get the bird to say her name. "Rani Trader," she had repeated over and over, taking care

to keep her intonation uniform. "Rani Trader." The bird had refused to learn the lesson.

Now, Davin set down his grinding tools with an exasperated
sigh. "I don't have time to play nursemaid to a girl. Get out of
here and let me finish my work."

Rani left with a cheerful smile, stopping to snag a pocketful
of small apples from their bowl by the door. "Finish my work!
Finish my work!" the macaw croaked as she headed down the
path toward the Swancastle.

Even though it was nearly winter, the sun streamed down on
the hill beneath the castle, and Rani let her cloak fall back from
her shoulders. Her leg was bothering her less—the wound had
not reopened for two days, and the reddened, puckered flesh on
either side of the brutal scab had not spread. Shea and Davin
had both insisted that she spend ridiculous amounts of time lying
on a pallet, keeping her wound elevated, letting it suppurate. The
old woman had forced bitter teas down Rani's throat, claiming
that they would help cool the fever that burned just beneath the
surface of her blood. Rani had given up asking when she would
be fit to ride; she contented herself with learning about glass-
work and spying on the Little Army. It would only be a couple
of days now, she promised herself, and then she would be well
enough to flee Amanthia, to ride to Morenia, and Hal, and freedom.

As Rani approached the mined walls of the Swancastle, she
saw that the Little Army was hard at work. A score of boys
stormed the south side of the castle, where the curtain wall was
still intact. They kept advancing a few feet and then falling back,
reworking their approach to take advantage of every tuft of grass,
every stone on the hillside. They were drilled by two of Crestman's lieutenants.

Rani could glimpse more boys inside the Swancastle. Through
the gap in the curtain wall, she could make out at least a dozen
soldiers scaling the inner walls, stretching for handholds, for
footholds. The boys were bound together with a sophisticated
system of ropes and pulleys; Rani could see the tangle anchored
around one of the merlons at the top of the wall. Another of

Davin's inventions, she surmised, and she watched for a moment until she could decipher how the ropes slid over each other, how they acted as brakes to keep the climbers from tumbling all the way to the ground when they lost their grips. The pulley system would be useful for glasswrights, Rani realized. Glaziers could use the suspended ropes to avoid erecting expensive and risky scaffolds when they needed to work on glass that was already installed in high places.

Even as Rani filed away the thought for her future guild, she noted that the remaining soldier boys were gathered around Mair, clustered close to the center of the castle keep. The Touched girl was exclaiming, "Now pay attention, Mon! If you can't figure out which hand I've put the stone in, then you'll never be able to follow my *knife*." As Rani watched, Mair lifted a pebble from the ground. She displayed it to the boys flamboyantly, and then wove it over and under her fingers, hiding it behind one palm and then the other, tucking it between her thumb and her first finger and retrieving it on her next pass.

The boys watched, enraptured, but Rani could trace the stone without difficulty. This sleight of hand was a standard trick of the Touched, a game that Mair had encouraged her troop to play often. Mair's children had used the game both to master their skills at theft and to resolve petty disputes, such as who would get to sleep under the warmest blanket or who would get to drink first from a newfound keg of ale.

"All right," Mair exclaimed, closing both hands and offering them to the boys. "Where's the stone?"

Monny bit his lip and darted a glance at each of Mair's fists. Rani saw that the Touched girl was trying to lead him toward her left hand; she had let her thumb bulge forward a little, as if it were driven out of place by the rock. Monny caught the position as well, and Rani watched him measure his options for several heartbeats before he made his decision, pointing at Mair's right hand.

"Are you certain?" Mair teased. The boy nodded solemnly, his clouted hair bobbing. His eyes stayed glued to her fists as if she might somehow cheat him. "The lives of your company could be riding on this, Mon."

"I'm sure," the boy said tensely. Mair shook her head and opened her right hand, showing only empty air. "That's impossible!" Monny exclaimed. "Show me the other one!"

Mair started to shake her head as Rani came up behind the children. "It's not in her other hand," Rani declared. "It's up her sleeve."

"It can't be," Monny argued. "I watched her pass it over her fingers, and under her thumb!"

"Mair?" Rani prompted, and the Touched girl lowered both hands, letting the stone fall out of her sleeve.

"Show me again!" Monny demanded, pushing his fellow soldiers out of the way and moving so close to Mair that his nose almost touched her hands. The Touched girl laughed and shook the pebble between her palms, starting the game anew.

"You know her well." Rani started at Crestman's voice, swallowing hard before she turned to face the boys' captain.

"Well enough not to be fooled by a few simple tricks."

"Then you know her well enough to understand why she calls him Mon, instead of by his name."

Rani considered her answer for a moment, measuring how much she was willing to tell this enemy soldier. "She calls him by a Touched name."

"Touched?"

"Like she is. One of the casteless, from our home. They have short names. Monny reminds her of the children in her troop, so she calls him Mon."

"Like she calls you Rai?"

"Aye."

"Then you're also . . . Touched?"

"I've lived in all the castes. I've gone by many names."

"But that isn't possible, not in the south."

"Just as it isn't possible for one of you northerners to be spared the fate of your birth?" Rani looked pointedly at the scar on his face, at the place where a tattoo should have marked his own caste. He acknowledged her question with a taut shrug, and she decided to reward him by answering at least part of his question. "I was born Rani Trader, a merchant girl. That's the name I use now."

"A merchant name."

"Aye. Like your own. 'Crestman' would be a merchant's name in Morenia."

"And Sin Hazar?"

Rani paused, unsure of her response. "Sin is the name of a Touched. Hazar is a merchant name. The two together name a guildsman."

"But not a king?"

"Sin Hazar is not the king in Morenia! Not now or ever." Rani's words spilled out like lead pouring from a crucible, and she whirled away from Crestman. How dare he insinuate that Morenia would fall? How dare he imply that Sin Hazar would conquer all that she knew and held dear?

Crestman caught up to her as she limped across the burnt grass where the bonfire had burned. "Lady Rani! I meant no disrespect! I only asked a question."

"Your question could only *mean* disrespect! You know nothing of my land! You know nothing of loyalty to a crown, nothing of the price one pays to save a kingdom!"

"Nothing, my lady?" Crestman's question was soft, so soft that Rani had to look at his face. His eyes, though, were not on her. Instead, he stared at a place just outside the burnt fire-ring, the place where Monny had lain the night the Swancastle fell.

"So you torture boys and make their fellows chant a king's name. That doesn't mean you've paid a price."

"I'm a captain in the Little Army, my lady. I've paid for the privilege of rank."

The words were so fragile, the memories so raw, that Rani could only ask, "What?"

For a moment, she thought that Crestman would not answer. Then, he pulled words from somewhere deep inside him. "They took me from my village. I was eight years old. It was springtime, and the river ran high, above my village. We lions were playing, trying to get bark boats to shoot the rapids. The suns were all busy planting. I don't know where the owls were—probably off with the priests. But we lions were all alone."

Rani watched Crestman's eyes take him back to the riverbank, to the village. He'd been eight—scarcely as old as Monny, then.

"When the Little Army surrounded us, we thought that they were other lions, maybe from another village. We'd heard that there were soldiers on the road, of course. We knew that Sin Hazar was planning a war, that he needed all his loyal lions to join together. That's why we were playing with the boats, so that we could learn how to fight the Liantines on the open ocean.

"They rounded us up before we knew what was happening. They had swords, real iron swords. And bows. Not the wrist braces that Davin has made—full bows, with long arrows. One of us lions . . . resisted, and they shot him, straight through his heart. He fell into the river, face down."

Crestman's cheeks had paled as he spoke; his scar stood out like a frozen pond. "They made us march, all day and night, with only short breaks for sleep. After a few weeks, we did not know where we were or how to return home, even if we could have escaped. They called us cowards, called us bed-boys and whores. We ran into other groups, and we learned that they weren't just taking lions. There were suns on the road, and owls. Even a swan or two, boys who were too young to have gone off with the other swans for training."

"All taken from your parents," Rani breathed, the horror blending with her own loss.

"Actually, that part wasn't terrible. We Amanthians all leave our homes when we reach the right age, all but the suns. That's what it means to be born under a night-sign. You leave your parents, your brothers and sisters. You go live with other lions, or owls, or swans."

"But this—"

"This was worse. This was going before we were ready, before we'd learned what we needed to do. And we weren't going to learn from other lions. We were learning from animals." Crestman shook his head and raised his finger to the scar on his cheek. "The first thing they did was remove our tattoos, so that we wouldn't bond with our fellow skychildren. They used a knife, and four boys held us flat. They burned us to stop the bleeding."

Rani's hand moved of its own volition, rising from her side to touch Crestman's face. He flinched as if she held a live coal, but he did not draw away. She ran a finger along the smooth flesh, her belly twisting as she thought of a child's pain, a child's terror. "But Sin Hazar!" she protested. "He still wears his swan tattoo. He and all his men are still marked."

"Aye," Crestman agreed. "The king has different plans for his grown supporters. He does not need to tear *them* from their roots. There is strength in the skycastes. Strength that the Little Army fears."

"Is it truly an army, then? An entire army made of boys?"

"After its own fashion. We're divided into platoons. Ten boys, serving under one lieutenant. Four platoons in a division, led by a captain. Back in the camp, there are no grown soldiers at all, not even someone like Davin to lead the forces. Older boys taught us to march, to count cadence, to fight. Nothing very different from what a lion would have learned."

"Except?" Rani picked up on the words he had not spoken.

"Except that they bound us in ways a lion is never bound. They taught us to fear and to love, and to love most the ones we feared most. Whenever we found something to cherish, they took it from us."

"Cherish? What is there to cherish in a military camp?"

"You'd be surprised." Crestman's voice was thick with bitterness. "The captains, boys of fourteen or fifteen, kept hounds to go hunting. In the spring, the bitches whelped. There were dozens of pups. The captains gave them to us boys, to the newest recruits. We were fools—we thought that we had finally found favor.

"We lived for those pups, dragged them into our tents, carted them around the camp. We named the dogs, we fed them from our plates. We turned them into the families we'd left behind, treasuring them all the more when the older boys mocked us.

"But one night the officers woke us, well after midnight. They'd painted their faces black, so that only their eyes glinted in the torchlight. They pulled us from our beds, naked and shivering, and they made each of us wrestle a captain, a boy nearly twice our age. As each of us lost, we had to hand over our dog. We had to forfeit our most valuable possession. And then, the victors gave us each a knife, pressed the weapons into our hands, even when we would have dropped them by the fire."

Crestman stared at the burnt-out circle of the bonfire, as if he were watching the scene he described, as if he could see it acted out before him. "They had their longbows trained on us, and they shot one boy who refused to hold his knife. I picked up my blade. I knew what I was supposed to do. My captain must have told me. He must have given me an order. I pulled back my dog's head, and I slashed its throat. One quick cut, and that animal was meat."

As Rani caught her breath, Crestman opened his hand, as if he were letting a knife fall to the ground. "He was meat, and we were soldiers. Good soldiers who followed orders. The captains ordered us to bring the dogs to the cook-tent, and they made us butcher them. They made us put the meat into a kettle, and they made us take turns stirring the stew. They made us eat, every bite, until the kettle was empty."

Tears were streaming down Rani's face, tears of loss and remembrance. She, too, had killed upon command. She, too, had murdered to belong.

But Crestman did not weep. He stared at the circle in the grass, and he finished his tale. "We saluted the king after that meal. After every meal, and when we rose and when we slept, before every maneuver on the battlefield. We offered up thanks to the Little Army, to our officers and our brethren. And when the next recruits arrived, we held the bows and trained our arrows on their hearts."

"But why? How could you?"

"How could we not? For the Little Army, there is no other world. We have no caste, our sky-signs are gone. Our parents could never take us back, not after the things we've done. The only one who values us is King Sin Hazar. He's the one who sought us out, after all. He's the one who trained us and fed us.

He's the one who lets the captains go on raids, to bring us food
and clothes and women."

"Women?" Rani breathed.

"Girls," Crestman corrected himself. "For the victors, of
course. All the riches go to the victors. But the finest job of all—
the best mission in all the Little Army—was left to only a few."

"And what was that?" Rani asked, hating herself for asking
the question, hating herself for wanting to know.

He smiled crookedly. "We led the raids on other villages. We
brought in the newest recruits to the Little Army, always killing
one to set an example, two if the boys were particularly dense."

"How could you do it? Why didn't you flee?"

Crestman's laugh was so harsh that it raised gooseflesh on
Rani's arms. "Flee? It took me months to gain the courage to do
just that. I plotted and planned and waited until we were on a
raid at the farthest edge of the Little Army's territory. I crept off
in the darkest hours of the night and I ran, hiding my trail in
every way that the Little Army had taught me.

"I needed food, though. And it was my fate to try to steal it
from an old woman, from a woman who looked at me like my
own dam would. If I could find my own mother. If she's even
still alive."

"Shea."

"Aye. That old sun made me believe that I could be free. She
made me believe that I could escape the Little Army *and* the rest
of Amanthia. But she lied. I'm here. And I'm surrounded by boys
who believe, who will kill to preserve the Little Army.

"Davin gave me shoes. He spared my life, even though he
knew I was a traitor; he knew my stories were lies. He put me
in charge of the Little Army, and I could do nothing to save myself. And since I didn't have pups to build boys' loyalties, I used
the next best thing. A child." Crestman's voice broke at last, and
he spat out the last word like a bitter seed.

Rani's injured leg was trembling, stressed by her standing for
so long. Her words shook as well. "They *made* you do it!" she
exclaimed. "They gave you no choice!"

"We all have choices. They put the knife in my hands, but I

had a choice. I still do." Crestman lifted his hand, holding it as if he cradled a long, curved blade. He raised the invisible weapon to his throat, slashed across with a force that would have left him headless if the blade had been real. He stared at his fingers, and a bitter laugh tore from his lips.

"No!" Rani cried, and she fumbled for his hands, covered them with her own. "No! You can make other choices!"

"I don't know any other choices! I've forgotten them! They were carved away, like my sky-sign was carved from my face!" Crestman's fury broke into a wordless howl. He reached for the scar on his cheek, raking his flesh with his own short-bitten nails. Rani grabbed at his wrists, trying to pull his hands down. It took all her strength to lower them to her waist, and the motion pulled him closer to her. She forced her words into the narrow space between them with all the precision of a prayer.

"Listen to me, Crestman! Listen! You made one choice—a choice to live. You can make that decision again. You have the power. You can bide your time and find the right place. You can leave the Little Army, maybe even deal it a death blow as you go. You can. I *know* you can."

She felt his strength tremble down his arms, the brute force that had propelled him past his fellows to the rank of captain. He yanked his hands free, grasped her shoulders as if he would push her away. Then, before she even realized what was happening, he lowered his face to hers. His lips were hot on her own, and she caught her breath in surprise.

She tried to pull back, but he gripped her too tightly. She stiffened her fingers, pushed against his chest. Before she could push him away, though, before she could escape, she heard hoofbeats on the grass behind her. Crestman must have heard them as well, for he leaped back as if he had been stung, as if Rani had dashed ice water in his face.

Gasping, Rani looked up to identify her rescuer. Her gratitude, though, turned to horror as she saw the richly caparisoned horse, as she made out the rider, sitting high in his saddle. She edged away from Crestman, scarcely thinking to brush the back of her hand across her swollen lips.

"Greetings, Ranita Glasswright. Hail and well met, you traitorous wench."

Rani felt Crestman stiffen beside her, but she barely realized that his grip was on her arm as he turned to the horseman. "Bashi," she whispered, in the brilliant sunlight beside the ashes of the bonfire.

9

Sin Hazar waved away his bodyguards as he stepped into his guest apartments. The king leaned against the ornately carved stone doorway, tilting his head to get a better look at the mirror across the room. "The swan looks good on you, Bashanorandi."

The prince started like a rabbit, and he barely managed to strangle his squawk of surprise. His face bore the desperate expression of a squire caught testing his master's sword. Just before the youth managed to paint a swaggering leer across his features, Sin Hazar could read his childish pleasure that the king had called him by his full name.

Really! Felicianda might have been occupied with trying to steal the southern throne while she was in Morenia, but she could have spared a *little* time to make sure that her brat was presentable! The boy was easier to twist than Briantan leather. Sin Hazar stood to his full height and moved into the chamber, watching the boy swallow nervously and lick his lips.

"My thanks, Your Majesty."

"The swelling should go down in a few days."

"Oh, it's not bad, Your Majesty. I expected more pain."

That was not what the priest had reported to Sin Hazar after tattooing the young prince. The religious said that Bashanorandi had flinched from the needle, whining and ultimately requiring a second application of stipple-leaf. Did the foolish boy think that the priest would not report to the king after the operation? Or did that southern bastard expect his flattery to win out, regardless of the truth? Did Bashanorandi believe that the king of all Amanthia could be so easily manipulated?

"Let's see." Sin Hazar strode across the room, taking a grim pleasure in the clap of his bootheels against the smooth wooden floor. He pinched Bashi's chin between his thumb and forefinger, tilting the boy's head to better catch the light. The priest *had* done a good job—enough of a swan's wing to mark the boy, but not so much as to overtake his face. Sin Hazar had given strict instructions not to make the tattoo too large. There were enough superstitious Amanthians who continued to equate expansive tattoos with power in a caste.

Of course, Sin Hazar had worked those superstitions to his own advantage. His peoples' false beliefs had led the king to have a second wing tattooed on his face, spreading his swan marking across his eyes like a mask. He had explained away the additional tattoo by proclaiming it a royal prerogative, and he'd made sure that the work coincided with his coronation, years before. There was no way to measure the value of a second swan's wing, but it couldn't hurt. No, it certainly could not hurt.

"Stop pressing it," Sin Hazar ordered his nephew. "You'll only irritate the skin more." Even though he could not mask the note of exasperation in his voice, he was pleased to see his nephew's hand plummet to his side. Good. At least the boy was willing to listen to reason, even if he failed to show the sense of a newborn coney. Sin Hazar forced himself to jest, "We'd hate for our court to say that we marred you, boy. We'd hate to be accused of ruining your handsome face."

He hadn't meant anything by the words as he said them; he'd actually intended to put the boy at his ease. The statement, though, made Bashanorandi tense as if spiders scurried across his flesh. He swallowed hard, and his eyes darted to the king's in the mirror. Sin Hazar remembered the conversation that his guard had reported, the fight between Bashanorandi and that cursed Touched girl.

What was her quaint phrase? That the boy was kneeling close enough . . . Well, the image was vivid, if not quite true. Sin Hazar

had other playthings; he hardly needed the attentions of an un-
schooled boy.

Nevertheless, what *would* it take to manipulate the prince?
What would it take to make Felicianda's boy do his bidding?
Certainly, Bashanorandi had been eager enough to pursue royal
favor—he'd practically wet himself at the opportunity to gain his
swan tattoo.

Sin Hazar could not resist the urge to press a little harder. He
stepped behind Bashanorandi, trapping the youth between his own
broad chest and the mirror. "Of course, your new-marked face
is the least of your attributes, hmmm? Your mission to the Swancastle served you well. You've tightened your muscles, sitting on
your horse." The king raised his hand to Bashanorandi's neck,
catching the soft flesh between his thumb and forefinger. He
rubbed gently, caressing the boy as he would one of his
wolfhounds. With his other hand, he traced his nephew's silken
sleeve, feeling the rigid forearm, pretending to measure the wrists
that had reined in royal stallions.

Sin Hazar held fast to Bashanorandi's gaze in the mirror, quirk-
ing an eyebrow at the heated flush on the youth's face. "We
would let you stray from our keep more often," Sin Hazar purred,
almost ruining the effect by laughing at the boy's discomfiture,
"if we could always be assured of such beneficial results."

"No, Your Majesty!" The boy's throat bobbed at Sin Hazar's
dangerous grin. "I mean, I did not stray! I did as you asked! I
retrieved Davin and brought him back to court, along with the
division of the Little Army. And Ranita Glasswright and Mair,
too! I did not—"

"Relax, cousin." The boy leaped like a flushed quail as Sin
Hazar leaned forward to whisper in his ear. "We were not ac-
cusing you. You have served us very well, so far." Sin Hazar
paused for a moment and then dropped the royal plural. "I expect you to do more in the future."

Even if Sin Hazar had not kept his hand on the boy's neck,
he would have sensed Bashanorandi's leaping pulse. The youth
tensed as if each muscle longed to carry him from the chamber;
his breath came in short, desperate gasps. If Sin Hazar *had* been

inclined to collect attentions from a boy, he had to admit that Bashanorandi's pathetic terror might have been intriguing. The boy ruined it all, though, by swallowing hard and lowering his gaze from the mirror. When he spoke, Sin Hazar could barely hear him, even though they stood cheek to cheek. "Th—that would please me, Sire."

Sire. . . . The boy might be frightened, might have felt forced to defend his manhood to the Touched wench, but he was willing to offer up that very bond he found so distasteful. Ah, Felicianda. . . . How could a girl of such headstrong pride have whelped such a pitiful specimen? Still, knowing that he could control Bashanorandi through shame at his admission, if nothing else, Sin Hazar permitted himself a malevolent smile. He settled one finger against the fresh swan tattoo that reddened his nephew's face, pressing hard enough that he was certain to cause the boy some pain. "Well. We'll see what arises. Now, if you're well enough, perhaps you'll do me the honor of accompanying me."

"Certainly, Sire!" Bashanorandi's smile was like a kicked dog's eager whimper. "Where are we going? Off to see the Little Army?"

"I think not," Sin Hazar replied wryly. "First snow has started, and I see no reason to tour a filthy, stinking camp." He turned on his heel, fully aware that he had not answered the boy's question. That was fine. Let Bashanorandi wait. Let him wonder. Let him trail behind his king, trying to remember not to raise questing fingers to the silvery wing that spread across his cheek.

Sin Hazar accepted his guards' salutes as he strode through the hallways, letting Bashanorandi trail behind. The king took pleasure in his long stride. He had decided that his next meeting would best take place in the stone chamber, deep beneath the palace stronghold. After all, that was where Sin Hazar's maps were kept, and all the markers of his armies. That was where the traitors from the south would best appreciate his might.

As expected, Al-Marai was waiting for him, beside the detailed battle map. The general held out an ermine-lined robe for his king, and Sin Hazar let his brother settle the garment about his shoulders. Yes, the stone chamber would be icy as a grave for the next several months. Still, the rich fur served two purposes—it kept the draft from creeping down Sin Hazar's neck, and it reminded Bashanorandi of Amanthia's wealth. The boy crossed his arms over his chest, surreptitiously rubbing his hands against his sleeves in an attempt to generate some warmth.

Sin Hazar pretended to be interested in the map, circling about the miniature pieces, fingering one of the boats that appeared to be en route to the east. Only when Bashanorandi had begun to study the map as well did Sin Hazar draw back, crossing to the tall, carved chair at the top of the board. Best that he face his prisoners in comfort.

He was pleased to see that Bashanorandi moved to stand beside him, taking up a squire's position without being ordered. The boy tried to keep out of reach, but he watched Sin Hazar with the nervous eyes of a ground squirrel. The king resisted the urge to reach out one hand, to trace a seam on the boy's leggings. *That* would create chaos, he was certain.

Sin Hazar settled for nodding toward Al-Marai. "Bring in the prisoners."

The lion transmitted the order to the guards at the door, then he unsheathed his massive curved sword. With his beard curling across his chest and his gaze turned to stone, he made a terrifying barrier to the map room. The arriving prisoners eyed Al-Marai warily, edging into the chamber like unbroken colts. They were so intent on the obvious threat of the unsheathed sword that neither immediately noticed Sin Hazar.

The king cleared his throat. "Lady Ranita. Lady Mair."

Both girls started, whirling to face the king. Sin Hazar saw the instant that they took in Bashanorandi, the scant moment it took for each to label the boy a traitor. Ranita Glasswright spared some attention for the map as well, measuring the troop placements as if she would report them to that southern upstart of a king.

The girls were bedraggled. Both sported dark circles under their eyes, as if they had not slept in weeks, and Ranita favored her leg as she crossed the stone chamber. Ink tracery around their eyes mimicked fading sun tattoos.

Sin Hazar had issued precise orders when Bashanorandi

dragged the girls back to his city. Ranita and Mair still wore the boys' clothes they had at the Swancastle. Their jerkins and leggings had been none too clean to begin with, and the uniforms certainly had not been bettered by a night spent in the royal dungeons. The garments were pulled out of shape by the iron chains around the girls' waists, the manacles that cut into their wrists and the loops that linked their ankles. Sir Hazar might have been made a fool of once, but he was not going to give these miserable wenches a chance to escape again.

Ranita Glasswright shot a single glance at her companion before she began to berate the king of all Amanthia. "Your Majesty, we expected better hospitality than these chains, in your storied castle."

"We are not accustomed to letting traitors roam our hallways free."

"Bashanorandi stands beside you, and he bears no chains."

"Our cousin is not a traitor, Lady Ranita. Not by the laws of Amanthia."

"Likewise, Lady Mair and I cannot be traitors to Amanthia. We are not subject to her laws. We are sworn to the house of ben-Jair, and we demand that you return us to King Halaravilli at once!"

"Brave words for a captured spy!"

"Spy!" The girl was shocked.

"Aye. What other reason could you have to leave our fine accommodations here in Amanth? Why else would you seek out our secret military encampment, study a division of our prize soldiers training with one of our greatest military advisors? You clearly plotted your escape from our hospitality with the goal of learning our military secrets. It would not surprise us to learn that that was the underhanded goal of your embassy in the first place."

"Embassy!" Ranita exclaimed. "Your Majesty, we offered no *embassy*. We were abducted and brought to Amanthia against our wills. Once imprisoned here, we did as any loyal Morenians would. We tried to flee for our homes."

"We did not give you leave to flee."

"Precisely! Your Majesty, you refused to treat us fairly! You refused to let us even walk in the garden, much less pen a missive to King Halaravilli!"

"We permitted you to attend a feast, didn't we?"

Ranita's response was an immediate blush. Sin Hazar swallowed his amusement. These youngsters were so full of passion. The king leaned forward in his chair, pointing a finger at the girl. "We attempted to honor you, Ranita Glasswright. We sat you at our left hand, and we ordered our servants to feed you the finest morsels from our table." Remarkable! The girl was actually writhing in her chains! He had thought her made of sterner stuff. Sin Hazar lowered his voice and addressed her as if they were alone in the chamber. "I danced with you, Ranita Glasswright. I touched the folds of your balkareen—"

"Leave her alone!"

Sin Hazar barely swallowed his surprise as the Touched girl stepped forward. "Lady Mair?"

"She danced with you because she had no choice. She was a guest at your table. She was required to eat and drink, if she did not want to provoke a battle."

"*You* could not be bothered to attend our feast, Lady Mair. We hardly think that you are qualified to instruct us on what happened there."

"There's no one who'll dare to instruct you, is there?"

Incredible! This casteless southern brat had the nerve to insult her elders, her betters, the one person who held complete power of life and death over her! Sin Hazar raised a hand to summon Al-Marai, but he caught the words in his throat as Ranita stepped forward.

"Please, Your Majesty." She twisted into the most elegant curtsey that her chains would allow. "My lord, Lady Mair is merely angered because she wants to return home. She and I both. Please, Your Majesty. Just let us assure King Halaravilli that we are safe. Let us send him a letter, so that you and he can begin your negotiations."

"Well, *that* has been done in your absence."

"Your Majesty?"

"We have assured Halaravilli that you are alive and well. Our negotiations should conclude in short order. Assuming, of course, that the king places the same value on your life that you apparently think he will."

The Touched wench snapped out a question before Lady Ranita could fashion a polite reply. "How did you manage that? How did you offer an assurance, when we were not available?"

"Perhaps we should clarify our statement, my lady. Halaravilli never asked about *you*. Your safety seemed of little concern to the king of Morenia." Sin Hazar could not keep from smiling as the girl blanched. He let one jeweled finger trace the outer edge of his swan tattoo. Let her think about that for a moment. Let her ponder Al-Marai's sword and the weight of her chains. . . .

Ranita cleared her throat, and asked tentatively, "What *did* you say on my behalf, Your Majesty?"

"Halaravilli asked a question, and Bashanorandi gave me the answer." Sin Hazar spared a fond glance for his nephew. The boy basked in the royal approval, even as both girls registered disgust. "Bashanorandi was confident of the reply, so a scribe wrote it up as a letter from you."

"And will you share the question with me, Your Majesty?"

Sin Hazar shrugged. No reason not to. No reason not to let the little fool see how easily he had penetrated the southerners' game. "He only wanted to know which Trader first slew a member of the . . . mmm, what was it, Al-Marai?"

"The Fellowship, Your Majesty." The lion bowed as he supplied the response.

"Ah, yes, the Fellowship. How could I have forgotten? My sister would never forgive me. If, of course, she were in a position to forgive anyone." He permitted himself a feral grin as he made a holy sign across his chest, in honor of Felicianda. "Bashanorandi here clarified that Trader was your family name." He glanced at the prince, scowling as he realized the boy was fingering his tattoo again.

"How did you know the answer?" Ranita turned a shocked gaze on Bashanorandi. "Bashi, how did you know what Hal wanted to hear?"

"Do you think your Fellowship can't be penetrated?" the prince spat. "You think you keep yourselves so well hidden! You and Mair and Hal and all the rest. I've had a man on the inside of your precious Fellowship, reporting every one of your meetings."

"E—Every meeting?" Rani stammered. "Your man must be highly placed. He must have been with us for quite some time. Most of the Fellowship hardly remembers Treen."

"What!" Sin Hazar bellowed, even as his pathetic nephew repeated the name. "What did you just say?"

"Treen. She was the first Fellow slain by—" Ranita obviously realized the import of her words, and she swallowed heavily.

"You're bluffing!" Bashanorandi screamed. "Your Majesty, she's making this up! She wants you to believe that I made a mistake!"

"Silence, fool!" Sin Hazar barely resisted the urge to slap his whining nephew. "Lady Rani, I warn you. You have only just begun to experience the hospitality of the Amanthian army. I can place you in a stone chamber so far beneath the earth that the rats won't hear your cries for mercy. I can have you tortured in a hundred ways before spring comes."

"Your Majesty, you can do those things, but that won't change the truth. My brother, Bardo Trader, murdered a member of the Fellowship when I was scarcely a babe. He executed Treen. Hal knows this. He knows the answer to his own question."

"But Dalarati!" Bashanorandi squeaked, his face deadly white beneath the irritated red and silver of his new tattoo. "You murdered him with your own hand."

What difference does it make, Sin Hazar wanted to bellow. What difference does it make who killed whom in the warrens of your filthy southern city! What did it matter that Ranita Glasswright had dispatched a soldier, when her brother had killed someone else *first*? Sin Hazar snatched Bashanorandi's arm, yanked the boy so hard that his thighs came to rest against the king's carved chair.

"You told me. You said that you knew the answer to the question."

"I—I thought I did!"

"I asked if you were certain."

"I was!"

"I told you that an entire kingdom rode on your answer!"

"I knew that! I knew that Ranita murdered Dalarati! I knew that they were both in their cursed Fellowship! I knew that— Please, Sire, you're hurting me!"

Sin Hazar swore and threw the boy away from him. "Leave me! All of you! Out of here!" The guards swept forward to conduct Ranita and Mair back to their cell, gathering up their clanking iron chains with clumsy hands. Bashanorandi fidgeted like a nervous cat. "Out of here, boy, or I'll have you thrown over the castle wall!"

Bashanorandi scuttled away, scarcely bothering to look behind him as he cleared the doorway. The other soldiers filed from the room, but Sin Hazar held up a rage-shaken hand as his brother started to close the heavy stone door. "Al-Marai, you may stay."

"Your Majesty." The lion bowed formally and remained by the door, watching warily as Sin Hazar climbed to his feet. The king paced beside the map table, not seeing the complicated swirl of mercenaries and ships, the bright gold markers for the Little Army.

He had asked for a simple fact. He had told the boy to be certain. He had said that they could make a diversion. He had checked for the truth. He had asked a second time and a third.

And the boy had lied.

No, not lied. Lying required thought, required a calculating mind. The bastard was too stupid for that.

The boy had launched a war, as surely as if he'd shot an arrow across a field. Launched a war that Sin Hazar would not be prepared to fight for at least six months.

"I want to kill him."

"Yes, Your Majesty."

"I want to flay him, inch by inch."

"Yes, Your Majesty."

"I want to feed him his own flesh, salted on the bone. I want to carve that cursed swan tattoo from his face with a spoon and mark the flesh beneath with a hundred-rayed sun. I want . . ."

Sin Hazar let himself run down, then he crossed to the table at the side of the room. His hand shook as he poured a cup of wine, and the clatter of the flask against the goblet almost made him throw the drink across the room. He didn't though. Instead, he drank deeply.

"Al-Marai, we're going to be at war in less than a month. And this one will be real—against Morenia."

"Yes, Your Majesty."

"This won't be the silly squabble we've been noising about in Liantine. Not some shadow victory of the Little Army."

"No, Your Majesty."

"These battles are going to be real. Fought on Amanthian soil. Fought against true warriors. Fought before we've bought our full army of Yrathi mercenaries. Fought before we *know* we can crush that southern idiot."

"Yes, Your Majesty."

"Enough of that, fool! I'm not asking for you to squawk agreement like some macaw! I'm looking for your guidance! I'm looking for your advice!"

"Certainly, Your Majesty. My first advice is that you drink another cup of wine."

"You sun-born, pox-ridden, mangy excuse for a lion—"

"My second advice is that you finish cataloging my failings, so that I can decide if I'm honor-bound to fight my brother to my death on the eve of war, when he most needs my counsel."

Sin Hazar actually managed a grim smile. He crossed to the map, picking up a handful of blood-red markers that had not yet been deployed. "Six months. That's all I needed. Now, it doesn't matter if that royal upstart comes by land or by sea—we're going to need more Yrathis."

"We can buy more men, Your Majesty."

"You're talking about Teleos?"

"Aye. The slave trader will pay enough for us to purchase more mercenaries. He'll definitely buy the girls."

"How many? And how soon?"

"I had my men look into it, after we last discussed the slaver's bargain. We can easily gather up three score, to send with the

next shipment of the Little Army. Maybe five, if we send an urgent message to our recruiters in the field."

"One hundred girls."

"To start with, Your Majesty. There are enough little whores
hanging about the camp now to make up more than half the shipment. Those girls already believe the Little Army are heroes.
They shouldn't give us much trouble if we tell them they're going
along to help Your Majesty's troops win the war."

"Three score whores, gathered here already! I had no idea we
treated the Little Army so well."

"Only the best for Your Majesty's forces."

Sin Hazar swallowed a tight smile as he stared at the map,
beginning to place crimson markers to represent Halaravilli's
likely troops. "That won't be enough, you know. We'll need an
entire division of Yrathi mercenaries, if we need to defend by
sea *and* by land."

"We can buy the Yrathi, Your Majesty. We'll have them in
time. We'll start by having the recruiters bring in two score girls.
The impressment squads are fairly far-flung right now, at the
edges of your holdings. That's probably just as well—we might
encounter some resistance from folk who don't understand the
demands of this war."

"Don't understand . . ." Sin Hazar rubbed a hand across his
face and sighed. "Can we do it, Al-Marai? Can we gather enough
in time?"

"I have no doubt, Your Majesty. The girls will be easier to
break than the boys. We can . . . encourage them more forcefully.
Their ultimate loyalty once they're sent to Liantine is less important."

"When do we send Teleos the first shipment?"

"In three weeks, Your Majesty."

"Very well. I expect one hundred girls by then."

"One hundred and two, Your Majesty."

"Two?"

"Certainly. Lady Ranita and Lady Mair can no longer serve
a purpose in your court. Halaravilli believes them dead. We might

as well make them dead to the world. And turn a little profit be-sides."

Rani blinked in the bright sunlight, looking around at the walls of the stockade. They stood almost twice as high as a man, and the inside surfaces had been planed smooth. The Little Army was as neatly imprisoned as if they were the pitiful cattle that had originally occupied the pen.

Mair came to stand beside Rani, swearing softly under her breath. "Well, we wanted out of the dungeons."

"Aye. But not for this."

Following the confrontation in the map room, Rani and Mair had spent the better part of a fortnight huddled in one of Sin Hazar's cells. They'd been restricted to bread and water, starvation rations, as if they were the ones responsible for Sin Hazar sending his fateful letter. They'd been forced to huddle together at night, shivering against the chill that seeped through the stone. They'd demanded ink and parchment and a messenger to ride to Halaravilli, but they stopped their requests when they tired of hearing their guards laugh. They'd asked for an audience with the king, only to be told that Sin Hazar did not bother himself with the refuse in his dungeons.

That royal neglect proved benign, compared to the scene that stretched before them now.

A village of tents crowded the stockade, weathered canvas flapping in the wind that stole over the log walls. True winter had gripped Amanthia, and snow had fallen three times in the past week. While a good part of that snow had drifted against the tents, the pathways underfoot had been churned to icy mud. Only the day before, Rani had slipped as she made her way past the one gate in the stockade. She had fallen hard, slamming her knee against the frozen ground, and she'd sprawled on her belly, trying to catch her breath. For one terrible moment, she'd thought that her wounded leg had been torn open.

One of the guards had looked down from his post, and his laughter was harsher than the whining wind. "On your feet, girl! I'm not off my shift until moonrise! I can't accept your favors till then!" When Rani had glared at him, the man had laughed again and called down, "At least turn on your back, then. Make it easy for the Little Army."

Rani had cursed Cot, scrambling to her feet and limping to the interior of the tent camp. Not that the god of soldiers appeared to pay much attention to anything happening inside the stockade, she had muttered to herself as she nursed her aching leg. The guards were ostensibly posted to protect the Little Army from spies and raiders, to keep the fighting children safe in the final days before they shipped out for Liantine. It had not taken Rani long to realize, though, that the men kept watch with their backs to the plain outside the stockade. The king's lions guarded with their swords turned against the Little Army. The soldiers were posted to protect the children from freedom, nothing more.

As the wind picked up, Rani and Mair turned back to the tiny tent they had commandeered. The shelter was small, but it was precious because it nestled against the stockade wall, cutting down on the wind's prying fingers. Only the night before, Rani had had to fight off another girl, who had thought that she would bring one of the boys into the tent. The other girl had not given up until Mair had awakened. Together, Rani and Mair had pulled the intruder's hair and administered some well-placed kicks, making the little slattern realize that there were easier dosses to be found.

There were nearly four score girls who roamed about the stockade. Most were eager to share their blankets with the boys of the Little Army—eager because they believed that they might escape the stockade, or because they hoped that the boys actually cared for them, or because the girls no longer remembered any other life.

Rani grimaced as she shook out her blanket, settling its scratchy wool about her shoulders. "It just gets colder and colder. Yesterday, I spoke with one girl from north of here. She said that it can get too cold to snow."

Mair shrugged. "That might be a blessing. It'll be worse on the ocean."

"Is it certain then? Are we definitely going?"

"They say we ship out next week. After Kel's feast day."

"We'll all be calling on Kel, feast day or no." Rani paused to think a brief prayer to the god of the sea. No reason to rile him, to make him think that she did not take his power seriously.

"There'll be a few more voices raised in prayer, once we're on the boats. A new group of girls is supposed to arrive this afternoon. That will make more than five score of us."

"How do you know these things?"

"A Touched girl has her ways," Mair answered mysteriously. Rani shrugged. She didn't care enough to learn the truth. Mair pouted in mock disappointment, then said, "There's something else. We're supposed to test Davin's new engine before we leave."

"And what is that?"

"A flying machine."

Rani sighed with exasperation. "Fine, Mair. I don't care if you don't answer. Couldn't you just say that you don't know?"

"I'm not telling tales, Rai. He's made a flying machine."

"So we'll all offer up prayers to Fairn and fly across the ocean?" Rani snorted.

"I don't know that the god of birds has anything to do with it. I've heard the boys talking, though. Mon says he's been in the harness."

Mon. Of course. *That* was how Mair got her information. The entire division from the Swancastle was now encamped in the stockade. They had marched up during the time that Rani and Mair were held in the dungeons; they'd been summoned by Bashanorandi on his fateful mission.

Mair had found Mon the first morning that she and Rani had been freed from the dungeons. Mon said that Davin had accompanied them north, carting along all sorts of equipment and tools. The Swancastle had been abandoned entirely; the old wizard had even dragged his macaw with him.

Before Rani could comment on Mon being harnessed to the flying machine, a furious clatter rose outside the tent. Neither girl jumped; they'd already become accustomed to life in a military camp. The sound of a sword beating against a leather-bound shield was as ordinary as birdsong. "Bread line! Bread line!"

Rani shivered and considered staying in the tent, huddling under her blanket *and* Mair's. The bread was always dry, anyway, and it tasted more of acorns than of wheat. "Go ahead, Mair. I'm going to sleep."

"You'll come with me, Rai. I'm not going to let you get weak from hunger."

"As if the bread would help with that," Rani grumbled, but she allowed the older girl to pull her to her feet. They took a moment to wrap rags about their fingers, to pull their itchy cloaks closer around their shoulders.

By the time they crossed to the middle of the camp, a long line had formed. As usual, the biggest boys had pushed their way to the front, joking—when they bothered to make any excuses—that they needed their strength to serve the king, to serve him on the battlefield and in their beds. As if bearing testimony to the boys' crude words, a handful of girls was scattered among the soldiers, clinging to their protectors with fingers that seemed too thin, gazing upon them with faces that were too pinched.

As usual, Mair provided a rallying point for other girls, for the ones who had not yet pledged themselves as bed warmers for the Little Army. With an occasional snarl and a grim voice, Mair led her troop through the ranks. Rani watched her redouble her efforts when she realized that there was soup as well as bread. Lan, the kitchen god, must be smiling on them today.

Even with Mair's assistance, though, the soup was gone by the time Rani got to the front of the line. Her disappointment was bitter across the back of her throat, and she started to turn away. Before she could back up from the rough boards, however, she was startled to find an entire loaf of bread placed in her cloth-bound hands. She looked up at the server, as if to ask if there were a mistake, and she found herself staring into Shea's eyes. The old sun managed to twist a smile across her lips. She spoke with the weary fortitude of a woman who cannot recognize defeat, who cannot distinguish loss from the brutal beating of daily life. "There you go, Rani Trader. Bread to tide you over until the night."

The old woman had come north from the Swancastle with the

boys; she had journeyed with Davin and Mon and Crestman and the others. She seemed to have made it her mission to watch over the children in the stockade, serving every meal with the grim kitchen wenches from the mercenaries' camp. Shea seemed oblivious to her stark surroundings. More than once, Rani had watched her gather up one of the smaller children, comforting a frightened girl or cajoling a boy who had turned an ankle on the ice. Shea was the only servingwoman who spoke to the children, the only one who seemed to realize that the Little Army needed any form of care and attention beyond basic feeding.

Rani muttered her thanks and took the bread, moving out of the line so that she could chew in peace. Mair was occupied with resolving a dispute between two of the new girls, dividing up their bread in something approaching fairness.

As Rani watched Shea smile at the smallest children, at the weakest ones who had followed in Rani and Mair's wake, she realized that the old woman might be able to help her. The sun might help Rani and Mair escape. After all, she didn't spend her nights in the stockade. She could raise an alarm among the Amanthians, let them know what was really happening behind the log wall. She could smuggle in bows and arrows, weapons that had been forbidden to the confined Little Army. What would it take to convince the sun to try?

"She won't do it." Crestman! By all the Thousand Gods, the captain seemed to appear out of nowhere all the time. Rani started guiltily and palmed the remains of her bread before she looked up into Crestman's face. He was studying her intently, and he shook his head as he sighed. "If you ask her, you'll just frighten her and give yourself away."

"Ask who?" Rani demanded belligerently. "What do I have to give away?"

"You want out of here as much as the rest of us do."

"You don't sound much like a loyal captain of the Little Army." Rani softened her sneer by remembering to look around, remembering to make sure that no one overheard her. She had spoken with Crestman several times since she'd been thrown into the camp, and all their conversations ended this way: she wanted to argue with him, wanted to make him understand the folly of his acquiescence. Standing beside him, she could not help but envision his horrific confessions, his tortured tale of recruitment for the Little Army. She remembered his words, and then the frantic heat of his lips on hers, the flaming touch of his fingers through her sleeve when Bashi had discovered them.

Now, she shivered in the shadow of the stockade, and Crestman looked down at her, concern painted across his face. He hesitated only a moment and then offered her his leather cup. There was still soup in it, broth that tantalized with both heat and aroma. Rani wanted to decline, she wanted to push it back toward the boy, but her fingers closed around the leather as if they had a mind of their own. As she swallowed the warm, salty liquid, she tried not to think that Crestman's lips had touched the cup before hers.

Crestman nodded toward the sunwoman. "All I'm saying is not to rely on Shea. It's all she can do to save you a crust of bread. She thinks of all of us as her children. She's a good sun, but she isn't meant for this. This is too much for her."

"A good sun would help restore some order to the world."

"Order, for her, is following the swans. It always has been. Sin Hazar bears a swan tattoo, and he has commanded the Little Army into this camp, and so she acts on that command."

"But the *girls*, Crestman. Surely we aren't part of that master military plan."

"Of course you are. Oh, perhaps not you and Mair. You've become trapped in larger games. But the king has a purpose for the Little Army, and for the girls who serve us."

"Us? Then you've forgotten your attempt to flee?"

"I've forgotten things that are dangerous to remember."

"Sin Hazar has an army of grown men. What does he need with children?"

"The Little Army has skills those fat old men have forgotten. You saw us take down the Swancastle. Just wait until you see the next machine that Davin has built."

"The flying machine?"

"I'm not at liberty to say more."

"Crestman! Mair's already heard about it from—from some of the boys."

Crestman's voice hardened, and he looked away, over Rani's head. "I'm a captain in the Little Army. I have loyalties."

"Loyalties, like when you fled to Shea? Like when you lied to Davin's boys?" Rani managed to keep her voice low, but her words shook with bitterness.

"You don't know what you're saying!" Crestman complained. "I told you those things because I thought that I could trust you."

"You *can* trust me, Crestman! You can trust me to help you, to help *us* break out of this camp. If we make it to Morenia, you'll never need to fear the Little Army again!"

"I fear no army, Ranita Glasswright."

"Don't call me that."

"That's what King Sin Hazar calls you, isn't it? That's your name."

"No, lionboy." He flinched at the appellation, and she swallowed a cruel, victorious smile. "That isn't my name. I'm Rani Trader. I'm Rani Trader until I keep the oaths that I swore, until I rebuild the glasswrights' guild."

"You'll be Rani Trader for a long time, then. There's not much chance that you'll rebuild any guild while you're on a ship to Liantine." His words were etched in acid, and she realized how deeply she had cut him by naming his caste. Before she could apologize, before she could make things right, Mair loped up.

"We're wanted at the gates, Rai."

"Us?" For just an instant, Rani imagined that she and Mair were to be set free, that they were going back to Morenia, to Hal.

Mair crushed that hope by spitting into the slushy mud. "Aye. There's a new group arriving. All girls, apparently. We've got to help them settle in before the Little Army gets involved."

Crestman shifted uncomfortably, but he did not contradict Mair. Rani sighed as she followed Mair to the gates.

The entire camp had gathered for the diversion. Sin Hazar's guards were particularly nervous, glancing out at the plain, and then inside the corral at the milling youth. More than one man had trained his bow on the children, and Rani could breathe in the tension like the stench of the latrines. "Mair," she whispered uneasily, but Crestman was already taking action.

"All right, men!" he called, and the boys in the Little Army immediately turned toward his steady voice. "Into formation! We'll greet our newest recruits like soldiers; we'll show them what we're made of!"

"But Crestman," a gangly lieutenant complained, "they're only *girls*. There's not a soldier in the lot."

"Times have changed, man," Crestman answered evenly. "The girls are a part of the Little Army, and we'll treat them with the respect that they deserve."

"A lot that means," the lieutenant sneered.

"What was that?" Crestman snapped.

"Nothing," the boy answered, nodding reluctantly at his own soldiers, who fell into a ragged line. Crestman let the infraction go, turning his attention to the gate.

Rani stepped up with Mair, swallowing hard as she felt the guards' bows swing toward her. Slowly, she brought her hands out from under her patched cloak, displaying her rag-wrapped fingers as if to convince the soldiers that she was benign. The fighting men cranked open the stockade gate, leaving a gap scarcely wide enough for one girl to sidle through.

Mair stepped forward as that first child entered, and she raised her arms in a manner that Rani knew was intended to placate the soldiers, even as it welcomed the newcomer. "Hail, sister," Mair called out. "Welcome to the camp of the Lit—"

"Tain!" Rani heard the cry like the twang of a bowstring. From the corner of her eye, she saw Crestman tense, watched him take a single, helpless step toward the gate. Before he could reach the entrance, though, a body hurtled past him, shoving him out of the way as if he were nothing more than a pile of kindling. "Tain!"

Shea fell upon the startled girl. The old sun threw her arms around the newcomer's neck, dragging her forward, pulling her past the stockade gate. Shea was sobbing and shouting, brushing back the girl's hair, asking questions and not waiting for answers.

The girl, tall and proud, had crumpled at the sight of the old sun, and now tears streamed down her cold-pinched face. More girls edged into the enclosure, stopping dead at the spectacle that greeted them, the sunwoman and the sungirl clinging to each other in the sea of mud.

Rani stared in confusion, gaping with the rest of the children, and then she turned to Crestman. He was shaking his head, his eyes blank with dismay. His hands clenched and unclenched, useless at his sides. "Who is it?" Rani hissed. "Who is this Tain?"

Crestman only shook his head and looked back at the gate. A handful of girls had entered the enclosure, each one smaller than the one who had gone before. Obviously, they had formed a plan outside the enclosure; they had sent their tallest and strongest first into the lions' den.

Rani felt the tension grow among all the children, the awe and disbelief at the youth of these newest recruits, shocking even to the Little Army, who had seen so much. The last of the girls eased into the compound, and the entire assembly stared in awe.

The final newcomer could be no more than six years of age, a babe by any calculation. A swan tattoo glinted by her right eye, capturing light from the steely sky. Rani felt the bread that she had eaten rise in her gorge, and she reached out to clutch Crestman's steely arm. He did not acknowledge her touch, though. Instead, he watched Shea look up from the sobbing Tain.

Rani saw the sunwoman glance across the courtyard, saw the light of recognition in her eyes as she acknowledged each new girl. The blade of horror, though, as she saw the youngest child was like a dagger plunged through Rani's chest. "Serena," Shea whispered, the name strangely clear in the silent stockade.

The sunwoman held out her arms to the little girl, stretching to reach her across the mud and muck. "Serena, child." The swangirl ran to the old sun, burying her face in the old woman's skirts. Shea began to smooth her hair, running her fingers through the filthy blond tangles. "Don't cry, Serena. You'll be all right. You're safe, Serena. We're all together again. You'll be fine, my poor, poor Serena."

Rani shivered at the old sun's lies.

10

Hal rested his muddy boot on a boulder that sat outside his tent flap, and he looked at his foot soldiers with eyes far older than his seventeen years. "What am I doing, Lamantarino? How can I possibly think that these men are a match for Sin Hazar's?"

The old man followed his king's gaze over the straggling soldiers and his head shook. Hal could not tell if the motion was from palsy or disagreement. "War's a strange thing, Your Majesty. The king who leads the most men into battle is not always the victor. You have to remember the other rules of war—choosing the location of your battle, the timing of your fight."

"I haven't forgotten, Lamantarino. I hardly *could* forget, with my honored lords drilling those rules into my skull since I took the throne."

"We only teach you so that you can lead us to victory, Your Majesty."

"Aye, Lamantarino." Hal scuffed at the gravel underfoot, adding dust to his trail-worn boots. He sighed. "I didn't mean to complain. It's just that I don't have any *control* over the coming battle. Sin Hazar will decide where we fight, and he'll decide when. I've barely had a chance to summon my own men from their villages and crofts. We'll march and set siege and make demands. And we'll starve, with winter fast approaching."

"Now *that's* unlikely, Your Majesty. The Amanthians will have gathered in their harvests. Their tithing barns must be bulging."

"Don't try to comfort me with a nurse's words, Lamantarino! You've heard our spies' reports, even before we decided to come up here. There are entire provinces starving, whole Amanthian villages that have yielded to ghosts and the Thousand Gods. We won't likely find tithing barns to feed our men. The Uprising crippled this land a generation ago, and it hasn't recovered yet."

"Ah, yes, Your Majesty. Well, we might as well return to the City, then. We might as well head back to the call of the Pilgrims' Bell, tucking our tails between our legs and hoping that Sin Hazar doesn't follow."

"Don't mock me, Lamantarino!"

"I'm not mocking you, Your Majesty. I'm merely reminding you of the weight of the crown. A weight, I might add, that your father bore before you, and in worse straits."

"Aye, so you say every chance you get. But my father did not need to confront Yrathi mercenaries. This morning's spies confirmed that Sin Hazar has dozens of hired swords, and he's recruited his Little Army. The rumors of Amanthia's power are true."

"Ah, yes. The rumors. They say that a captain in the Little Army is only promoted after he lies with his own sister and slits her throat while she still warms his bed. They say that the soldiers fight on no rations, feeding on the power of the Thousand Gods. They say that the Little Army can fly over bulwarks and drop stones the size of men's heads."

"Lamantarino, you're laughing at me."

"No, Your Majesty, I'm not laughing. Not laughing at all. I'm trying to make you hear the *reason* behind the words that you speak. The Little Army is just that—an army of children. They may be children who have been tortured, they may be children who are trained. But they are still boys. You can defeat them if you draw upon your own knowledge."

"I *have* no knowledge, Lamantarino! I'm a boy-king who has never led my men into battle. I've barely reviewed them at parade."

"You're King Halaravilli, son of Shanoranvilli ben-Jair!" Hal jumped at the steel in the old man's voice. "Your father led his men into battle when he had only seen two-and-twenty winters. He defeated the Liantines in his very first engagement. He fought bravely throughout his life. Only fifteen years ago, he led his men against Amanthia, and he defeated the northerners then. That's why Felicianda came to your court."

"And look where *that* has left us."

"Your Majesty, you're looking for someone to make this journey easy, to make the coming battle safe. If you ask for the impossible, then you're doomed to disappointment."

"I'm not asking for the impossible!" Hal protested. "I'm asking for justice. I'm asking for what I'm due, as a king anointed beneath the eyes of all the Thousand Gods. I only want what is right and fair."

"Now *there* is a demand worthy of a king." Lamantarino turned to face Hal head-on, ignoring the wind that tugged at his grey beard. "Listen to me, Your Majesty. Let me tell you a secret that will change the way you rule your entire kingdom."

Hal caught his breath and leaned closer to the old man. Expectation tensed his shoulders, made his heart pound. "Yes?" he whispered.

"The world isn't fair."

Hal's rage was a physical thing, a smothering eiderdown that threatened to cut off his breath. He spluttered and tossed his head. "What sort of lesson is that!" he managed to exclaim.

"It's the truth, Your Majesty. The world isn't fair, and if you're going to insist on acting as if it is, then you *will* lose the coming battle. Sometimes people fight unfairly. They hire massive armies when their treasuries should have been bled dry. They commandeer forces of children they have no business impressing. The world isn't fair."

Hal barely pushed down his urge to berate the old man. Of course he knew the world wasn't fair! Of course he knew that there were men who took advantage of others. What did Lamantarino think he was? Some sort of babe?

Rather than spew words that he knew he would regret later, Hal stalked away, throwing himself through the flap of his tent. A brazier burned in the center of the ground, warming the air and lending a smoky aroma to the shelter. Hal was still standing with his hands extended over the coals, dredging up witty retorts to Lamantarino's "lesson," when Farso ducked his head into the tent.

"Your Majesty?"

Hal looked up at his squire's troubled tone. "Yes, Farsobalinti. What is it?"

"I'm sorry, Your Majesty. Earl Tasuntimanu insists upon seeing you. He's waiting outside."

"Did you tell him I'm not seeing anyone?"

"Of course, Your Majesty. His Grace says that he bears a message for you. He says that you must hear what he has to say before we break camp."

"Very well, Farso." Hal sighed, realizing how exhausted he was. This business of raising the Morenian countryside was draining, all the riding through villages and towns, all the ordering and cajoling and manipulating his vassals. Now, to have to face one of his sworn councillors, one of the men that he should be able to *assume* was an ally, but whom he knew he could not trust. . . . "Send him in."

Hal drew his dagger from his waist, deciding that he'd rather have his hands busy when Tasuntimanu entered. He pared away a troublesome nail, then grasped the weapon's hilt, testing its weight as if he were not already familiar with the blade. Farso ducked into the tent, holding the flap behind him for Tasuntimanu to enter.

"Your Majesty," the squire said. "The Earl Tasuntimanu."

"Thank you, Farso. You may wait outside."

"Your Majesty?"

"You heard me. The earl and I will speak alone."

Farso did not look happy with the instructions, but he stepped outside of the tent. Tasuntimanu waited until the heavy flap had fallen back into place before he turned his placid gaze on Hal. Mud had dried on the man's boots, testimony to the messy path the soldiers had churned. The earth was the color of Tasuntimanu's dull hair, his calm eyes. The earl's tone was deceptively mild as he said, "It can be so hard finding a loyal squire, Your Majesty."

Hal swallowed his angry retort and forced himself to say levelly, "I doubt you've come to discuss my choice of servants, Your Grace."

"No, Your Majesty. I come in the name of Jair, blessed be the First Pilgrim."

"Blessed be the First Pilgrim," Hal agreed, aping the holy sign that Tasuntimanu made across his chest. "Let us avoid misunderstandings, my lord. Do you speak for yourself or for others?"

"I speak for myself *and* others, Your Majesty. I speak with the hope of bringing peace before many men lose their lives in battle."

"Tasuntimanu, I am not the one who has challenged that peace. I am not the one who executed noble hostages before I could even begin to count a ransom from my enemy."

"Rani Trader was not noble, Your Majesty. Nor was Mair."

Hal swallowed his anger, tamping down the rage that threatened to spill into his hands. Instead, he forced himself to look up at Tasuntimanu, to gaze into the noble's muddy eyes and try to understand the logic that coursed behind them. "Tell me, Tasuntimanu. Explain to me why you devote your life to the Fellowship of Jair."

"The Fellowship brings meaning to life, Your Majesty," Tasuntimanu replied without hesitation. "It permits me to act in ways that I know are right, in ways that the First Pilgrim would command. The Fellowship brings order and reason to a world that has no order and no reason."

"And how does it feel to accept that Fellowship blindly, when it could turn on you in an instant?"

"Your Majesty?" Tasuntimanu honestly seemed confused, unable to comprehend the question.

"How does it feel to embrace a Fellowship that throws its own members to the dogs? How can you stand here and purport to tell me about order and reason, when your own order and reason would leave two of our company unavenged?"

Tasuntimanu blinked and shook his head. "Vengeance is not necessarily the goal of Jair, Your Majesty." The earl gestured with his pudgy hands, clenching and unclenching them as if he could mold an answer from the brazier's smoke. "Jair has a picture greater than we can perceive, Your Majesty. He has a plan that we cannot know."

"And yet you purport to understand his commands, here, on the edge of battle?"

"*I* purport to know nothing, Your Majesty. I only bring you the words of another. My only purpose in asking for this audience was to remind you of the wisdom of our sister."

"Our sister?"

Tasuntimanu looked pointedly at the tent flap. "Do you want me to name her, Your Majesty? Is it worth the risk?"

Hal shook his head in disgust. No. No need to name Glair. No need to state facts known by both of them. "Enough, Tasuntimanu. Enough sparring. What message do you bear?"

"I have been ordered to tell you this, Your Majesty. You have disobeyed the Fellowship by declaring war on Sin Hazar. You have disobeyed the Fellowship by raising your army. You have disobeyed the Fellowship by marching north and leaving the City. The Fellowship has given way to you in all these things, because it wants you to remain king of Morenia; it wants your people to have faith in you, to support you. But the Fellowship can only be pushed so far. You must not raise a weapon against the king of Amanthia. You must not murder Sin Hazar."

Hal's head jerked up at Tasuntimanu's tone, at the bare command that sparked across his final words. "Murder, my lord? That's a strange word to hear on a battlefield. That's a strange description for the execution of a criminal who has ruthlessly exploited innocent children."

"I'll not play word games with you, Your Majesty. If you kill Sin Hazar, then the Fellowship will see you punished."

Hal let his disdain flood his retort. "And what sort of punishment is that, Tasuntimanu? Will you slap my wrist and send me to bed without any supper? Your Fellowship seems to think I'm nothing but a child."

"*Our* Fellowship thinks that you are headstrong, and that you do not know everything that is at risk in this game you play."

"Then tell me! Tell me what is at risk, that I should let my northern enemy run rampant! Tell me what is at risk, that I should leave the death of two of our people unavenged! What does the

Fellowship want, Tasuntimanu? What are its secrets? What are its goals?"

Tasuntimanu blinked, as if Hal's exclamations were a surprise, but then he continued as if he'd never been interrupted. "*Our* Fellowship thinks that you must be reminded of the dangers in the greater world, the forces that are stronger than any one of us, even than a king. *Our* Fellowship thinks that you need to remember the rules of this engagement—the rules and the penalties and the costs."

"And if I don't yield to your threat?"

"The Fellowship of Jair set you upon your throne, Halaravilli ben-Jair."

Hal stared at the man's placid face, marveling at the utter dispassion with which he uttered treason. "Go ahead, Tasuntimanu. Finish your threat. I want to be clear, so that there is no doubt left between us. Complete your sentence."

"The Fellowship of Jair set you upon your throne, and we will see you removed, if necessary."

"I could have you drawn and quartered, merely for uttering such a threat."

"Aye, Your Majesty. You could. You could have me flayed, and feed my body to your hounds. But that won't stop our Fellowship. There are members you do not know, names you cannot name. You can kill me, but you can't save yourself, not if you stray from our Fellowship in this."

"Leave me!" Hal bellowed. "Leave this tent!"

Tasuntimanu took his time completing a proper bow, then departed. Hal found himself standing over the brazier, ridiculously still holding his knife, grasping his dagger in hands that trembled like an ancient crone's. He swore and thrust the blade back into its sheath.

He had known that the Fellowship had goals, that they had hopes and dreams for Morenia, for all the world. But what *would* they gain by keeping Sin Hazar on his throne? What *was* the advantage of protecting a child-murdering, treacherous bastard? How long would Hal last in the world that the Fellowship labored to create? How long would he last, if he ignored Sin Hazar's threat?

Hal thought that the day could hardly grow worse, but that was before the company began its long trek north. Precipitation began to fall, stinging needles that were halfway between rain and sleet. Hal hunched forward on his stallion, miserably drawing his cloak nearer as he surveyed the line of men strung out along the road. A part of him longed to give up for the day, to call a halt and order his tent erected, to huddle over a hot brazier and drink mulled wine.

That half, though, would do no good for his foot soldiers, for the entire army that was dependent on stealing from the country-side as it worked its way out of Morenia and into Amanthia. Hal set his teeth and squinted into the driving wind.

And even the weather was not the worst thing about the day. As Hal peered down the road, he could make out Puladarati riding at Tasuntimanu's side. The leonine councillor was clearly preaching to his fellow—once, Hal even saw the older man reach out his three-fingered hand and grip Tasuntimanu's reins, jerking the placid councillor closer. Hal could imagine the plotting words that passed between the men, the conspiracies that were hidden by clopping horses' hooves and the screaming wind.

Hal thought about riding forward and breaking up the con-spiring pair. He held back, though, trying to bide his time. He wasn't ready to challenge his advisors. Not yet. Not until he was certain that his other lords would stand beside him.

On the long, lonely ride, Hal forced himself to ruminate on a new circle of questions. Was he merely leading this army to re-venge Rani Trader's death? Or was he fulfilling his obligation to root out a known traitor, to bring Bashi to heel? Could Hal rule Morenia complacently, knowing that a wolf howled on her north-ern flank, a wolf that had already flashed its teeth? Hadn't Hal sworn his vows to the Fellowship well after he had sworn his princely vows to protect Morenia and keep her people safe? Did he have any choice but to ride north and face whatever awaited him? Or was he merely leading this army to revenge Rani Trader's death?

The king's thoughts were not any brighter when Tasuntimanu and Puladarati strode up to him in the gloaming evening light. Hal had watched the camp being set up around him; he had studied the early sunset that bled crimson across the horizon. "Your Majesty," the silver-maned duke said, bowing low. Tasuntimanu mimicked the gesture a moment later.

"Aye." Hal resented needing to move his hand closer to his knife; he resented fearing for his safety in the face of one man who had been his regent and another who was his sworn brother in the Fellowship.

"The men have marched far today. We'll cross the Amanthian border at dawn."

"Aye."

Puladarati gave his king a curious glance, settling one gloved hand on the hilt of his sword. The tooled-leather gauntlet disguised the man's missing fingers, but Hal did not forget for one moment that the old nobleman had shed blood for the Crown. For the old Crown, for Shanoranvilli. But not for the boy who currently sat the throne.

"Your Majesty, I recommend that you order an extra ration of meat for all the men. It will do them good to have their bellies full, and they will be cheered by your consideration."

"An extra ration? When we have no idea how long it will take us to march through Amanthia?"

"Precisely, Your Majesty. Your spendthrift gift will make them believe that all is well."

Hal started to argue out of habit, but then he realized that the nobleman was right. It *would* do the men good to see that their king cared for them, was concerned about their hunger and their fatigue. And if they found no food in Amanthia, one day's meat would hardly make a difference. "Very well. Order the extra ration distributed."

Puladarati bowed again and gestured toward Tasuntimanu. "Will you see to that, brother councillor? Oh, and Your Majesty—should I spread word that you'll review the troops tonight? Will you make your way through the campsites?"

What in the name of all the Thousand Gods were Puladarati

and Tasuntimanu plotting? Did they have a cabal ensconced within the soldiers? Were they waiting to lure Hal into a trap under cover of night? Did they plan to kill Hal before Morenia was even left behind?

Puladarati cleared his throat, as if to remind Hal that he waited for a reply. "I only ask, Your Majesty, because it would raise morale. It would make the men that much stronger for the skirmishes that are certain to begin tomorrow."

There. Hal was left without a choice. Glaring at Puladarati, Hal agreed. "Yes, then. I will review the men, after they've eaten their double ration of meat." He could not help noting that Tasuntimanu inclined his head toward Duke Puladarati before skulking off into the night, as if the old silver-haired man were still the regent, still the voice of the king. Hal breathed a prayer to his ancestor Jair, wishing for guidance even as he longed to be back in the City, back in the palace, back in his own chambers, where he knew how to defend himself against men who would murder one king and set another upon the throne of all Morenia.

Shea looked up automatically from the bread line, a smile freezing across her face. "No, Serena. There isn't enough bread for everyone to have two pieces."

The little swangirl pouted, a frown puckering the narrow space between her fair eyebrows. "But I'm still hungry."

"Everyone is hungry, child."

"But I'm a swan!"

The four words rang out through the camp, loud enough that Shea winced and looked about at the adult soldiers on the stockade walls. "Hush, child!" When Serena's lips started to tremble, Shea came around the table. "I'll have none of that here! Swan or lion, owl or sun, it makes no difference in the Little Army's camp."

"But Tain said—"

"Tain said what she thought was true. Look around you, child. Do you see all these boys? Do you see how none of them has a tattoo?" Serena nodded reluctantly. "There are soldiers who would take away the girls' tattoos as well."

"But—"

"Serena! These men want to take their knives to your face! They want to hold you down in the snow and carve the swan's wing from your cheek! They want to make it so that there is never another swan, not you or anyone else! Now take your bread and go to your tent, and leave me alone!"

As Shea caught her breath, astonished at her outburst, Serena gaped at her. Shea could see the protest written on the girl's face, her challenge that she, *she* had been the only swan in the cottage. *She* had decided Crestman's fate.

Well, just look at how that decision had turned out, Shea wanted to grumble. Just look at what had come to pass after Serena made her murderous choice.

Shea clambered back to her feet and returned to the bread table, only to find that all of the meager provisions had been distributed. She was about to gather up her apron and pull her cloak closer about her shoulders when the strange southern girl came running up to the bread line. "'Urry, Shea!" The newcomer had lapsed into her odd outlander speech, the slurring that took over her words when she was excited.

"What is it, Mair?"

"They're openin' th' gates! They're lettin' us out!"

"What? Why would they do that?"

"Davin's goin' t' test 'is flyin' machine! Mon's already i' th' 'arness! 'Urry! Ye dinna want t' miss it!"

Shea waddled after the girl, pushing her way through the crowds of the Little Army. Sure enough, the guards *were* letting the children ease outside the stockade walls. They only let one child emerge at a time, though, and adult captains stood on the outside, harrying the young soldiers into straight, orderly ranks. Grown men held bows, with arrows cocked between their fingers, the strings half-pulled to their ears.

The girls, newly added to the Little Army, were slow to form their lines. They did not understand how to follow the adult officers' harsh orders. Shea watched with a touch of pride as Tain helped some of the youngest comply with the barked commands.

Shea automatically sought out Crestman, hunting for his blond braid in the crowd. In the past two months, the boy had grown several inches, and he now stood nearly a head taller than most of the little soldiers he chivvied. Her chest swelled with pride as it always did when she watched him do his job. She had been right to save the boy. She had been right to rescue the lion.

But what about Hartley, a voice whispered at the back of her mind.

What about Hartley? According to Tain, King Sin Hazar's recruiters had come upon Shea's old cottage early one morning. Tain had been dribbling meager grain into water, preparing to stir the thin gruel, when she heard the boy soldiers crash out of the woods. At first, Tain had thought that Shea had returned, leading Crestman and some of his fellows to the cottage. The sungirl had grumbled at the thought of yet *more* mouths to feed.

Tain only realized her mistake when the cottage door crashed in, tearing from its brittle leather hinges. The invaders had quickly looped ropes about the oldest sungirl, binding her arms to her sides. Tain had closed her fist about the meal she was pouring into the water; hours later, she had let Serena lick the grainy mush that had formed in the palm of her hand.

But during that morning, during the long hour when the sun rose and the water boiled away in the cauldron, the soldiers had rounded up Tain's children, Shea's children. The boys were carved away from the girls, and lengths of rope were looped around everyone's hands. A few children were gagged as they protested the invasion. Hartley, though, had been permitted to speak, permitted to command his lions into orderly submission.

The lions had listened, yes, but the owls had tried to work their debates. Torino had stepped to the middle of the floor, tilting his head quizzically at the soldiers. "Premise," he chirped. "It is unnatural for children to bind children in an undeclared battle."

There had been no time for another owl to reply, no time for Hartley to order Torino to silence. One of the Little Army raised his bow with a casual gesture, sighting down his arrow as if he were playing. The bow twanged, and Torino fell on the hearth, his rib cage pierced by a tufted stick, by a shaft that had looked neither long nor dangerous, until it pierced a child's chest.

If Shea closed her eyes even now, she could imagine Torino twitching on her neatly swept cottage floor. She could see the little owl struggling to draw a breath, trying to structure his final premise. She could see her other children, huddled in horror, in terror. Shea shook her head, desperate to drive away the image. It had already happened, days before. There was nothing she could do now. The girls had been marched out of the cottage, driven to King Sin Hazar's capital without time to sleep, to mourn.

And the boys? Shea did not let herself think of the boys, left behind in the cottage, bound at wrist and ankle. Certainly Father Nariom would have come from the village. Certainly the priest would have found the boys before they became too hungry. Too thirsty. Too cold. Certainly the boys were alive and well, living happy lives near the village they had always known, because the king had already met his quota for male soldiers in the Little Army.

So Shea had heard the grown soldiers say. Teleos, the mysterious general who would command the Little Army on its passage to Liantine, had declared that he needed no more boys. He wanted only girls, to balance his male troops.

Shea's sons had been spared. They still lived, back at her cottage.

She could not let herself believe otherwise.

And so, Shea followed her daughters, edging out of the stockade gate and taking up a position at the front of the Little Army, near the strange southern girls who had elbowed their way forward through the ranks.

A monstrous contraption spread across the plain outside of the stockade. Shea could make out four wings—two large ones and two smaller ones, all folded backward like the flying apparatus of a parchment moth. Between the wings was a narrow platform, a harness fashioned out of thin, whiplike tree branches. The narrow limbs had been stripped bare of leaves and wrapped many times around with strong, light willow bindings. The harness was surrounded by a thicket of ropes and pulleys; strange knobs of polished wood studded the contraption.

Davin stood beside the machine, scowling at his device. His

aged hands reached out to test the engine, tugging at a rope in one place, kicking at a strut in another. All the time, he muttered to himself, glancing back and forth from the construction to a series of parchment rolls. Those rolls refused to be constrained in the growing breeze, and more than once, Davin swore as he wrestled with a wayward sketch.

Each time the old man exploded in anger, a ripple ran through the assembled Little Army. Shea picked out a few of the boys that she knew, soldiers who had been stationed at the Swancastle. They eyed Davin with an excited eagerness; they knew the old man's ways, and they understood that they were about to see some novel invention.

As Shea watched, Crestman walked around from the far side of the moth-machine, leaning over the figure strapped into the willow-wrapped harness. It took Shea a moment to recognize Monny. The child's flame-red braid was pushed under a leather cap. His freckled features were animated as he spoke to Crestman, gesturing over his shoulder at the folded parchment wings. Crestman shook his head and tugged at one of the wooden knobs, moving the entire engine forward a pace. Monny gripped a leather handhold above his head and responded vehemently.

Glancing at the bemused guards, Shea moved closer to the arguing boys. The back of her neck itched as she felt the grown soldiers' arrows train upon her, but she forced herself to stand straight, to walk as if she had no care in the world. She was the closest thing either of those boys had to a mother, and it was her job to smooth over their dispute.

Crestman was scowling as he picked at one of the rope lashings. "I'm telling you, soldier, it's not safe. I won't have one of my men risking his life on some unproven flying machine."

"Aw, Crestman, you don't know what you're talking about. Davin says it's safe, and that's good enough for me. He added glue to the cross braces, so you can't complain about that anymore."

The captain looked as if he were going to rebuke his rebellious soldier, but he settled for saying, "Davin's opinion is a little suspect, don't you agree? He has something of an interest in this."

"Davin's interest is in serving King Sin Hazar." Monny turned his freckled face toward Amanth's walls, as if offering up his fealty. A look of surprise and amazement spread across his features. "Cor! Look, Crestman! It's the king himself!"

Shea followed the boy's excited finger. Gazing across the plain, she could make out a dozen horsemen wrapped in heavy winter cloaks, accompanied by a standard-bearer. The dragon of Amanthia billowed on the breeze of their fast ride.

"On your knees!" cried one of the adult soldiers behind Shea, and the Little Army dropped in fealty as the king and his company rode up in a flurry of hoofbeats. Shea eased her tired bones to the ground, halfway between the flying machine and the girls from the south. She took a moment to be grateful that the frozen earth was covered with only a dusting of snow; it had not yet been churned to freezing slush by passing feet.

King Sin Hazar drew up in front of the company, curbing his stallion with an iron hand on the animal's bit. The horse pranced in front of the Little Army, mincing sideways and snorting at a sudden gust of wind. Shea glanced up through her eyelashes to view the king.

He wore a cloak lined with ermine. The white fur framed the king's blue-dyed riding leathers, making the man seem larger than any possible life. The king of all Amanthia wore supple leather boots that reached to his thighs, and his spurs were washed with gold. As Shea caught her breath in astonishment at her sovereign's power and force, she realized that the Amanthian dragon was painted on his chest, glittering black lines tracing across his broad metal breastplate.

Shea could barely bring herself to gaze upon her liege's face. His dark hair was loose, flying on the wind in stark contrast to the clouted boys in the Little Army. A golden crown was on his head, and a handful of flat-cut diamonds and rubies glinted dully from the metal. The king's beard was even darker than the hair on his head, and his lips were as bright as cherries in the cold winter air. But it was the king's *eyes* that made Shea's heart beat fast—those eagle eyes that took in more than any mere man could see. King Sin Hazar's gaze flashed across the Little Army like a furrier measuring a sable.

Shea saw the king count up the neat lines of boys, and she noted the precise instant that he registered the girls. For just one heartbeat, the royal gaze lingered in its sweeping perusal, and Shea feared that *she* had attracted royal scrutiny. Then she realized that the king was looking behind her, at the two southern girls, Mair and Rani Trader. The king maneuvered his stallion to stand before the outlanders, and for just an instant, Shea thought that he would speak to the maidens.

They must have thought so as well. Both girls raised their eyes to the king, acting as if they were swanchildren. Shea caught her breath as Rani Trader took a half step forward. The girl actually drew breath to speak, made as if she would reach up for the royal stallion's bridle. Before she could act so inappropriately, though, Mair caught at her arm. Rani tugged herself free and lashed an angry glance at her friend, but by the time she turned back to the king, he had edged his horse farther down the line.

When King Sin Hazar spoke to the Little Army, he did not single out the two forlorn southern girls with purloined sun tattoos on their cheeks. Instead, he cheered his royal forces, his dedicated soldiers. "Well met, Little Army!" the king proclaimed. "You bring honor to all Amanthia!"

There was a moment's hesitation, but then the captains led their boys in a round of cheers. A few of the girls joined in, hesitantly adding their treble voices to the rollicking greeting.

"As many of you know, our campaign is moving forward!" Again, cheers. "You will be the first in a new wave of battles against Liantine, against the upstart eastern kingdom that refuses to bow its neck to our mighty Amanthia." Pandemonium surged on the field.

The king gestured his standard-bearer forward. The young squire who held the banner dipped it toward the king, taking care to let the long pennant catch the wind. The dragon's tail streamed out over Sin Hazar's head. "We are pleased to see your loyal arms raised to fight for us, Little Army. But even more importantly, we are pleased to see that our greatest advisor, our wisest councillor, has created a new weapon to use against Liantine."

The king turned in his saddle and inclined his head toward Davin. The old man managed to look up from his scrolls long enough to accept the royal salute. He even remembered to hide his scowl as a gust of wind tugged at the winged machine behind him. Monny swallowed a yelp as the moth-engine started to lift from the ground, and Crestman grabbed rapidly at one of the ropes that tethered the strange construction.

King Sin Hazar continued as if there had been no disturbance. "Lord Davin has crafted many a novel invention. Some of you have seen the mining equipment that he created, the engines that will eat the very earth from beneath Liantine's walls. Today, all of you will bear witness to another device, a most magnificent engine that will bring the Little Army supremacy over *all* our enemies. My lord Davin!" King Sin Hazar bowed slightly in his saddle, making the gesture extravagant by letting his ermine cloak billow behind him.

"Your Majesty," Davin muttered distractedly, and then he stepped over to the mothlike machine. "Boy! Don't waste your king's time!"

Monny shrugged his shoulders elaborately, forcing Crestman to step back. The freckled boy grinned at the Little Army, and Shea remembered when her own Pom had smiled with that much pride, when he had known that much confidence. Her own lion-boy had looked at her just like that, with his eyeteeth too long, his grown, adult teeth in a child's mouth.

Davin grabbed Monny's shoulder and pushed him back in the willow-covered harness. The child adjusted a pair of straps that cut over his shoulders, but the old man was not satisfied with the lay of the restraints. Davin pushed the boy to the very back of the harness and cinched the shoulder straps tightly, pulling twice more until Shea could see that the leather cut into Monny's shoulders. Then Davin wrapped two more lengths about the child, securing his wrists to the moth-machine. Again, he pulled sharply at the restraints, tightening them enough that Monny tensed with the pain.

The process went on, with Davin tying Monny to the shorter, back wings of the machine, linking the parchment membranes to the boy's feet by cinching tight knots about Monny's ankles. The left rope refused to fall to the old man's satisfaction, and he retied it three times, each time sawing deeper into Monny's flesh. On the last attempt, the child actually caught his tongue between his teeth, stifling his cry.

Leave him be! Shea wanted to scream. Leave him alone! She held her tongue, though, remembering that she was not the one who could speak against the old man. She was only a sun, a sun far away from her own orderly home. Who was she to speak out against the king's own councillor? Who was she to question a swan's desires?

As if to reward Shea's sudden realization, Davin stepped back from the flying machine. He threw his arms up over his head, and he cried, "Go, boy! Fly her to the clouds!"

Monny waggled his arms and legs, moving his limbs as much as his constricting bonds would permit. Each motion caught the ropes, stretching them tighter against the boy's flesh. Monny's face pulled into a mask of concentration; his eyes squinted closed with the strain of coordinating his limbs. His jaw tightened as if he were carved of wood, and beads of sweat popped out among his freckles, even though his breath plumed in the freezing air.

"Come on, boy!" Davin bellowed. "We've been over this before. Ach! Stop it, you fool! You'll tangle the lines! No! No! Let your arms down!"

Monny collapsed against the willow-wrapped harness, and the parchment wings of the flying machine rattled down around him. Davin stormed over to the boy, swearing fluently as he cuffed the child. "We've practiced this, boy! You know you have to move both arms at the same pace. Both arms, and both legs, but not at the same time. You'll never keep her stable if you try to open all four wings at once!"

Monny started to gasp some protest, but the old man continued his invective. "I don't know what you could have been before the Little Army stooped to take you in! You don't have the strength of a lion, and you lack the common sense of a sun. In the name of all the Thousand Gods, you're too stupid to be an owl, and I won't even insult His Majesty by implying that you might have been a swan!" The entire time he ranted, Davin relashed the ropes, tightening the bonds between Monny and the machine. The boy accepted his punishment in silence, his dark eyes glinting with suspicious moisture as the old man worked.

"There!" Davin exclaimed at last. "Let's see if you can follow simple directions this time."

It took only an instant for Monny to foul the lines again. Davin's face was nearly purple as he stepped forward. This time, he reached up to the king's standard-bearer, snatching the squire's riding crop from his boot. He stormed over to Monny with murder in his face, laying about the boy's arms and legs with the crop, as if he would flay away the snagged ropes. Monny tried to protect his face, but his futile gestures only tangled the lines further, pulling one entirely off its pulley.

Shea took a half step forward, a cry rising in her throat. "He's only a boy!" she started to yelp. Those four words resonated through her entire body, shaking down her hands. Shea threw a wild glance at Crestman, remembering how she had hoped to protect him from her orphans with the same invocation. She had wanted to save Crestman, but she had lost him to the Little Army, just as she had lost Hartley, had lost her own Pom. Monny might be only a boy, but childhood was no safeguard against brutal, bloody death.

As if to underscore Shea's realization, Davin slashed the riding crop across Monny's face, laying open a stripe beneath the boy's eye. Only when the blood had begun to seep over the child's freckles did the old man step back, panting as if he had rowed a boat all the way to Liantine. As Monny hung in his ropes, trussed like a chicken, the old man began to reset the lines, tying them one more time, adjusting them over the tricky pulley.

When the moth was restrung, the old man turned to the Little Army. "You!" He pointed a bony finger at Crestman. "Yes, you! Stop your gaping and step up here." Crestman swallowed a grimace of distaste and walked to the point that Davin indicated. The boy darted a quick look at his king, but seemed cowed by the stony gaze he found there. Davin pushed on Crestman's shoulders. "Kneel down. Get where he can see you. There! Now, I want you to count the arm strokes. Like this. Stroke! Stroke!"

Crestman waited a moment to get the proper rhythm, and then he took up the chant. The first time he barked the command, his voice quavered, but then he fell into the pattern. Shea remembered standing beside the Swancastle, listening to the boy count for the mining machine. Crestman had led the Little Army to victory then. She only hoped that he could do as much here.

Davin nodded as Crestman settled into the cadence, and then he looked out over the assembled children, his gaze darting like a snake's tongue. For just an instant, Shea thought that he was going to settle on Serena, that he was going to order the swangirl to assist him. Shea started to step forward herself, to volunteer so that she might spare her littlest orphan, but Davin growled and shook his head. Instead, he pointed a bony finger at one of the southern girls, at Mair.

"You! No, no! Don't kneel in front of him. That'll just be confusing. There you go. Off to the side. Let's hear you! Even, girl, even! In *between* the boy's count. Louder! Louder!"

"Come on!" Mair shouted between Crestman's count. "Come on!"

In reply, Monny sawed his legs back and forth, activating the back wings of the moth-machine. Crestman raised his voice, as if to remind the boy to control the front wings. "Stroke! Stroke!"

Mair shortened her command to keep the timing straight. "Mon!" she cried. "Mon!"

Shea saw the syllable register with the little boy. She saw the way he arched his back, the way he caught his breath in his narrow chest. Crestman shouted; Mair replied. Monny bit his lip and swept his hands up and down, swaggered his legs back and forth.

And slowly, ponderously, the flying machine began to move.

At first, the parchment wings strained, up and down, back and forth. They hovered on the edge of taking flight, tightening, shimmering, like a new-sprung moth trying to dry its wings, fresh from its slimy caterpillar shell. Then, Monny grunted like a boar, and the flying machine left the earth.

Afterward, Shea could not say how long Monny flew. She knew that he rose in the air, that he circled around the Little Army, spiraling higher and higher. She knew that he landed once and took off again, that he absorbed Crestman and Mair's chanted cadence and flew into the sky without error. She knew that he caught a rope between his teeth and tugged with all his might, releasing a rain of pointed darts over the empty field.

Shea heard the Little Army cheering as if it had already conquered Liantine. She saw King Sin Hazar throw back his head and laugh with abandon. Her own heart pounded, soared, as if she were strapped into the flying machine herself.

Only when Monny was back on the ground did Shea look at Crestman and Mair. The lionboy was staring intently at Monny, clearly fighting back his own tears of pride, pride that one of his soldiers should have accomplished Davin's impossible feat. When Monny brought the flying machine down, crashing roughly onto the frozen field, Crestman immediately sprang toward the child, stripping the ropes from his arms and legs, pummeling his back in victory.

Mair, though, did not leave her post at the edge of the Little Army. The southern girl remained on her knees, her hands clenching and unclenching into fists as she whispered, "Mon! Mon!" Before Shea could step forward, before she could settle a hand on the girl's shoulder, Rani Trader crossed to her friend.

Rani knelt beside Mair, grabbing hold of the girl's hands and stilling their automatic movement. Mair seemed to come out of a trance as she turned to her fellow outlander. "He's done it, then," she managed to whisper, and Shea could barely make out the words over the tumult of celebrating children.

"Aye," Rani nodded. "He's done it."

Mair shook her head and stared across the field at the rioting Little Army. "May all the Thousand Gods have mercy. Davin's done it. He's created a flying machine."

11

Hal stared out at the smoke billowing up from the castle walls, and he tried not to think about the flames that would chew away at other castles, the pyres that would purify corpses before this war was over. He imagined the cries of men cut down on the battlefield, of women and children trapped behind the curtains of fire.

He wondered if the northerners had granted Rani a pyre, or if they had set her corpse into the ground to rot. He muttered a prayer to Tarn, the god of death, in hope that Rani had already made it past the Heavenly Gates, that she already walked with her family, with Hal's own father, Shanoranvilli, who had come to love the merchant girl like a daughter.

Hal returned to the present bonfire with a slight start. He was wandering more and more frequently, following his thoughts down long paths, only to be jerked back to the army and the endless march north. Looking around to see if anyone had noticed, Hal saw Puladarati rein in his horse a few paces away and bow low in the saddle. Soot streaked the leonine councillor's face, darkening his silver mane and beard. Tasuntimanu rode beside him, also reining in his mount, also making a bow toward his liege. Hal had grown accustomed to seeing the two councillors together; Tasuntimanu had become the older nobleman's shadow. At least that made Hal's life easier; there was only a single threat to watch.

Only a single threat. Why bother, why fret? Death loomed like a debt.

Puladarati spoke, apparently unaware of Hal's dark thoughts.

"Your Majesty, we've set fire to the castle walls. The stone will be too hot for anyone to approach for at least three days."

"Explain again why we've done this, Puladarati." Hal's voice was weary, but he took the time to put steel behind his words. The former regent had managed to erode Hal's scant trust with his raging commands about the abandoned castle. Why was it so important to burn a pile of stone? What was the man trying to prove, and to whom? How much longer could Hal keep Puladarati leashed? And what would Tasuntimanu do, once open battle was launched?

"Your Majesty, we need to show these Amanthians that we're a force to be reckoned with."

"So we prove that by burning a castle they're not currently occupying."

"You've heard the villagers as we ride through the countryside. They worship this place, as if the Thousand Gods resided here."

"It's a *building*, Puladarati. It's a pile of stones."

"It's a symbol, Your Majesty. These northerners, they put great stock in symbols. You've seen the tattoos on their faces. They think that the swans are destined to guide them in all things. If we destroy this heap of stones, then they'll realize we can destroy the people who had it built. We can bring down the swans who lead them." Puladarati flexed his maimed hand within his glove, and Hal resisted the urge to draw his cloak closer about his throat.

The regent's restlessness had bred on the long ride north; Hal could almost sense his urge to pace, his desire to be moving, even though he sat his horse steadily in his high saddle. Puladarati clearly longed to be free of restraint; he longed to be free of his bonds to the Morenian crown. Hal darted a glance at Tasuntimanu and read a similar restlessness in the eyes of his brother from the Fellowship of Jair.

If the northerners did not get Hal, his own men were likely to, before he ever returned to Morenia.

Hal forced his voice to steady reasonableness. "If this symbol is so important, then why was it left unattended? Why were there no guards at this castle, no soldiers, not even any villagers?"

Puladarati looked at the smoldering hillside and shrugged his shoulders, the gesture rippling down his arms like a mantle of impatience. Tasuntimanu, though, was the one who spoke, as if he were the voice of the older councillor. "I can't tell you that, Your Majesty. You saw the wall when we arrived. You saw the evidence of mining."

"Aye. And I'm still waiting to hear who else might have had an interest in undermining an Amanthian castle. Especially one that housed the precious northern swans. It would be one thing if the wall was ruined during the Uprising, but these stones fell only a few weeks ago." Before Hal's lords could reply, a shout went up from the woods at the base of the hill. Hal wheeled his stallion around in time to see a half dozen of his soldiers harrying a man before them, a massive giant with the broad shoulders and leather apron of a blacksmith. The prisoner's hands had been lashed behind his back, and fresh cuts bled down his face.

"Your Majesty!" panted the captain as he forced the giant forward. "We found this man in the woods. He was hiding beneath an oak tree, near the smithy."

Before Hal could address the prisoner, another soldier stepped forward, swatting the man across the backs of his knees with the flat of his sword. "On your knees before your betters, oaf!"

The blow was insufficient to force the man down, but the smith clambered to a kneeling position of his own volition. When he twisted his head to look up at Hal, his dark tattoo stood out in the afternoon light. Hal saw the rayed sun and wondered again at the intricate castes of these northerners. Wouldn't it make more sense for this giant to serve as an Amanthian lion? Wouldn't his broad shoulders and his smith-trained hands make him a perfect farrier for the royal troops? In Morenia, such a man would certainly have been recruited to the soldier caste, even if he had not had the good fortune to be born to such a station. It was foolish, this northern tattooing. What could they hope to gain by cementing a man's station at his birth, by governing his life by something as meaningless as which stars were in the sky at the moment that he came into the world?

Hal sighed and swung down from his stallion. He planted his feet and drew himself up to his full height before speaking. "What is your name, man?"

The smith raised his eyes at the question, but he made no attempt to answer. Hal's troops surged forward at the insulting silence, and the king lifted one gauntleted hand, both to warn the prisoner and to control his own soldiers. "Name yourself, smith, or I'll have my men carve a name for you, in stripes across your back." The giant only shook his head, hunching his shoulders in what might have been a shrug, if his hands had not been cinched so tightly behind him. Hal stepped forward, ignoring the angry murmur of his troops. "Do you understand me, man?" The smith took a moment to think about the words before he nodded slowly. "Then tell me your name."

Again, the massive shoulders worked, and Hal wondered at the strength that rippled through those muscles. He doubted that the simple ropes catching the smith's wrists would be sufficient restraint if the man were determined to escape. Hal nodded permission to one of his guards, and the soldier nestled the point of his sword between the giant's shoulder blades. The smith cringed at the contact, and then he opened his mouth, as if he would at last be obedient. "Maaaahhhhh," he bellowed.

"Your name, man!" Hal commanded.

"Maaaaaahhhhh!"

At Hal's flicked glance, the soldier pushed harder with his blade, digging deeper into the smith's muscled back, and the tone of the man's single syllable raised in desperation. Nevertheless, he made no attempt to form words; his throat did not work around syllables. Hal raised a hand in disgust. "Hold, man. He's clearly not able to answer my question."

Puladarati sidled closer to his king, speaking softly enough that only Hal could hear. "Not *able*, Your Majesty, or not willing?"

Hal looked at the crimson-kissed sword blade sported by the giant's guard, and he made his tone as cold as the wind that blew steadily across the hillside. "Not able, I believe, Lord Councillor." He raised his voice to his soldiers. "Keep that man under heavy guard. I don't want him escaping and warning the Amanthians of our approach. We'll bring him with us when we proceed north tomorrow."

The giant let out a bellow then, tossing his head as if desperate to speak. He strained at his bonds and moaned meaningless syllables. A wild look flashed from his eyes, and he managed to twist himself loose from his captors, only to throw himself at Hal's feet. The king drew back from the writhing giant in horror, staring as the smith's hands clenched and unclenched like the mouth of a giant insect.

"Stop him!" Hal bellowed. "Get a gag in his mouth!"

It took five men to wrestle a gag between the smith's teeth, and Hal's own jaw was clenched by the time they led the creature away. Even as the king strode to his own tent in the center of the camp, his heart was pounding, and he could not get the animal echo of the man's screams out of his ears.

The smith had been desperate to communicate, terrified by something.

Hal tried to drive the horror away with a glass of mulled wine, but he found that his belly twisted around his dinner of rough stew. He refused Tasuntimanu's request for an audience as he took his evening meal, even when the councillor sent word "in the name of Jair." Hal had no desire to hear how the Fellowship disapproved of this journey. He did not want to hear that he was risking all for Rani's memory, for vengeance of a companion who was gone forever.

In addition, Hal had to deny entrance to Puladarati before he extinguished his candle and reclined on his cot. The former regent was easier to send away; he did not call upon the First Pilgrim to plead his case.

Hal lay awake long into the night, listening to the camp sounds around him and the crackling fire that chewed away at the swans' castle on the top of the hill. He fell asleep at last, breathing in the stench of woodsmoke and melting stone.

The morning dawned, cold and grey. Winter had Amanthia in

its teeth, and Hal could not drive away his shivering as he splashed water across his swollen eyes. He wasted little time mounting up, and he watched from the comfortable safety of his stallion as his men struck camp. Waves of heat still shimmered from the collapsed castle, and the former safehold slumped black and grim, like slag from a mine. Hal forbade himself to dwell on the stones that had been sprayed down the hill when they arrived, the unanswered mystery of why the castle walls had been breached, and recently. No Morenian force had penetrated this far north; the Amanthians had worked this harm upon themselves, and more than a decade after their Uprising. But why? Why destroy a perfectly good curtain wall of a castle honored and respected by all the local peasants? What had Sin Hazar meant to prove?

There were so many things about these northerners that Hal did not understand.

The sun was well over the horizon by the time the Morenian army began its slow march north. Haunted by the smith's obvious terror, Hal had issued orders that the prisoner was to travel with the vanguard. Even as Hal issued his commands, Puladarati frowned disapproval. "Is that wise, Your Majesty? The smith clearly does not want to lead our forces north. He must know something we do not. Put him at the back of our forces, where he can work no mischief."

"And when did I start taking orders from enemy prisoners?" Hal's rebellion was hot, immediate. If Puladarati wanted the prisoner at the rear of the army, that was the one place Hal could not trust the smith. What sort of fool did Puladarati think Hal was? Why should the king put a potentially murderous giant *behind* his own back? Better to lead the way with such an enemy, to keep him fully in view. Better to let any lurking compatriots realize they must harm their own colleague before they could get to the Morenians. Hal spurred his stallion forward before his former regent could protest further.

The forest loomed on either side of the road. Even though the bare limbs of the trees looked like shattered bones, Hal was grateful for the starkness of winter. He could see some distance from the path, several yards into the tangle of shrubs and trees. In the summer, he imagined, this would be fertile ground for an ambush.

In the winter, though, it was strangely beautiful. There were forests in the south, certainly, even forests that Hal had ridden through during the past two winters, when he'd been allowed to set his own royal schedule, to make his own decisions. But the trees in the south did not seem to grow as tall; their branches did not spread as wide. In fact, Hal thought as he glanced at the forest surrounding him, these northern trees were an entirely different species, or at least they housed different species.

Giant nests sat in the trees, abandoned by birds who had clearly chosen to flee the winter's cold. The nests were great, rickety affairs, pulled together of twigs and leaves, looking like children's playthings as they huddled in the crooks of branches. Here and there, Hal fancied that he could make out the glassy swell of an egg, abandoned months ago by some haphazard parent.

There! That nest had a *cluster* of eggs left in it, smooth surfaces glinting in the morning sunlight. Hal reined in his horse and reached for the spyglass that was tucked into his saddlebags. What sort of bird would go to the trouble of making a nest—and such a large one!—only to lay eggs and abandon them?

"Your Majesty? Is something wrong?" Lamantarino pulled up beside the king, following the royal glance toward the trees. The old man's voice creaked as much as his saddle leather. Hal was pleased to see his father's friend; the ancient advisor had been feeling ill the day before and had pleaded exhaustion before he stumbled to his tent at the edge of the Morenian camp.

"Nay, Lamantarino. Nothing wrong. I'm just curious."

"Curious? About what, Your Majesty?"

"See that tree there? And the nest at the crook of the branches?" Lamantarino turned stiffly in his saddle. The ancient man had to squint to make out the nest that Hal indicated, and he jutted his head forward on his thin neck, looking for all the world as if he belonged in a nest of his own. "There are eggs in it."

"Eggs? It's the middle of winter, Your Majesty!" Lamantarino answered with a tone reserved for annoying children. The old man's head shook with palsy and blooming exasperation as he gathered up his reins. His voice was peevish as he exclaimed, "You shouldn't play with an old man's failing sight, Your Majesty. Just you remember, your father would be as old as I—older, by a year."

"No, Lamantarino! Here, look through my glass. You'll see what I mean!"

Hal leaned forward in his saddle, stretching to pass the old man his spyglass. The distance was too great, though, and Hal had to dig his heels into his stallion's sides. The horse hesitated a split second before responding, a hesitation that saved Hal's life.

Afterward, he could not have said what happened first. There was a noise, louder than any thunder. There was a flash of fire, brighter than the noonday sun. There was a wave of heat, hotter than any pyre. And there were horses screaming in agony and men bellowing in terror. The entire forest came alive with flames and fleeing men, chaos exploding beneath the trees.

Lamantarino cried out as the fire burst forth, and for one horrendous moment, Hal thought that the ancient man was the source of the conflagration. He saw the old advisor's hair kindle about his head, blazing into stinking orange flame, fire that spread down the old man's arms, devouring his moldering robes, crackling across his fingers. Hal screamed Lamantarino's name and pounded his heels into his stallion's sides, desperate to reach the burning man, frantic to save the councillor who had first stood by his side.

Hal's stallion, though, was maddened by the fire, terrified by the smoke. The beast reared up on its hind legs, pawing the air as if it intended to shred the curtain of fire that surrounded it. The fire and smoke enraged the beast, and the horse took off down the forest path, ignoring Hal's shouted commands, ignoring the king's bootless attempts to saw back on the reins. Hal had only the vaguest impression of his army surrounding him, of other pockets of flame and stench, of men fighting with their beasts and of foot soldiers rioting as they pounded down the forest path. Then, there was a huge pit that stretched the width of the trails, a mouth yawning as if it would swallow up the entire southern army.

Hal's steed was rushing forward too quickly; the king had no hope of reining in the beast before it reached that jagged maw. Instead, he hunched low over his stallion's mane, tucking in his elbows and cinching in his knees. He felt his horse's muscles tighten beneath his saddle, sensed the pounding desperation as the beast leaped toward safety.

The stallion's back legs caught below the edge of the pit, and the huge animal strained to pull its hindquarters up the crumbling slope. Hal leaned forward, as if by strength of will alone he could drive the animal out of the gaping hole. The stallion threw back its head and screamed as the earth slid from beneath its hooves, but then it found the strength to make one more lunge, and Hal was free of the pit.

It took a full minute for the king to master his stallion, and even then, Hal had to dismount to return to the edge of the hole. Chaos reined on the other side. Smoke billowed up in great choking clouds, and fire chewed away at tree branches, gnawing on trunks. Hal gaped at the insanity, desperate to find Lamantarino, refusing to accept that a flame-licked pile of blackened flesh could be all that remained of a loyal fighting man and his mount.

Horses crashed into the woods on either side of the path, screaming their terror, risking their narrow legs as they plunged away into the forest. Men bellowed their pain. Officers shouted orders above the noise.

One sound, though, penetrated all of that maelstrom. Hal heard it almost beneath his feet, rising from the pit as if from the den of all the Thousand Gods. "Maaaaaaaaaahhhhhhhh! Maaaaaaahhh-hhhh!"

Hal edged up to the gaping hole in the path. The giant black-smith lay on the ground, his right leg bent at an unnatural angle under his body.

Hal's heart clenched in his chest, and he turned to order his soldiers to help the poor, mute unfortunate. Before he could bark a command, though, he managed to make out the smith's hands, could see that the man had burst his bonds and torn himself free from his restraints just as Hal had feared that he might the day before. Now, the smith tugged on two long pieces of rope, raising them over his head and waving them about with pitiful squawks.

Hal followed those lines with his eyes, tracing them through the smith's convulsing hands, along the edges of the pit. He saw that the ropes snaked up nearby tree trunks; they fed over a complex system of pulleys. One rope twisted into the remnant of a bird's nest, the charred strands looping across to another tree that now smoldered as if it were trapped in the wreckage of the castle behind them.

And Hal understood.

The pit had been a trap, a trap that the smith must have known about. Once he'd been forced to march north with Hal's forces, once he'd realized that his wordless pleading would gain him nothing with the southern army, he must have decided to employ the hidden engines against the Morenians.

It was all so simple, the northern army's plot. How difficult could it have been for the enemy army to disguise a pit across the path? A loose framework of sticks and some scattered earth, a few dried leaves. . . . The smith had tumbled into the pit and burst his bonds, catching at the engines' rope triggers. Those ropes had connected to the nests, to the strange eggs. And when the glassy eggs were crashed against each other, they had set loose their fire.

Set loose their fire. Give way to ire. Lamantarino's pyre.

As the chaos began to die down, Hal could smell camphor and pine pitch, alcohol and some sharp, acidic reek that he could not name. And meat. The sickening, oily stench of burnt meat and leather and hair.

The Morenian army had fallen into the trap, like children falling into bed at the end of a long day. Hal looked across the pit at the chaos that had been his army. He could just make out the charred remains that had been Lamantarino, that had been his father's trusted companion. Hal had betrayed that old man; the old councillor had died thinking that his young king played a trick on him, mocked him for his age and his failing vision.

"Maaaaaaaahhhhhhhh!" The smith was still bellowing from the pit, still brandishing the ends of the ropes, tugging as if he were ringing the Pilgrims' Bell back home. Hal looked at his men across the gaping hole, at the officers who were barking orders, mustering men, trying to create order out of the burning, stinking chaos. "Maaaaaaaaahhhhhhhhh!"

The smith had done this. Begun this. Won this.

Hal whirled away from the edge of the hole, striding down the path to the cluster of his men who had already managed to work their way through the charred and treacherous forest, who had wound around behind him onto the undamaged stretch of the road traveling north. Impossibly, Duke Puladarati stood at the front of the group, and the leonine councillor stepped forward immediately. "It's not as bad as it looks, Your Majesty. We'll be able to muster a full company on this side of the pit, and there are men who must have been at the back of our group, beyond the range of that demons' fire."

"A bow."

"Your Majesty?"

"I want a bow. A bow and an arrow."

"I'm sorry, Your Majesty, I don't understand. Let's move down the path. I don't think that these trees are likely to catch fire, but there's no reason to take chances."

"This isn't a chance, it's a certainty. Give me a bow." Just let me go. He reaped; I'll sow.

Puladarati started to protest, but Hal glared at him and extended one gloved hand. The duke swallowed a comment, nodded gravely and turned to the soldiers that milled behind him. "You heard your king! Where's an archer!"

It took a moment for a man to scramble forward, a moment when the air was full of the cries of terrified horses, the stench of burning flesh. The archer who stepped to Puladarati's side bowed to Hal. "Y—Your Majesty."

"Give me your bow." Sow. Sow.

"If it please Your Majesty, I'll shoot at your command."

"It pleases me to have your bow."

The archer handed over the curve of yew wood, and then he

ducked under the strap of his quiver, proffering the arrows to his liege. Hal took one and turned on his heel, striding back to the edge of the pit.

"Maaaaaaah!" The smith started his tirade again as Hal stepped into view. The crippled giant still held the ropes, still tugged at them as if he would ignite the firestorm all over again. "Maaaaaah-hhh!"

Hal raised the bow, turning it for just an instant so that the smith would be certain to recognize the weapon. Then he nocked the arrow to the string, taking care to sight down its length. His hands shook like an old man's, like Lamantarino's. Lamantarino, destroyed so foolishly, after a long life of faithful service. Roasted like a joint of meat, after serving Hal's father. After serving Hal.

Joint of meat. Deadly heat. Despicable feat.

Hal brushed his fingers over the arrow's fletching and breathed a prayer to Bon, the god of archers. "Ma—" the smith began, but his cry was cut short as he realized his danger.

Only then did the giant drop the rope triggers. Only then did he fight to pull his broken leg beneath him, to scramble toward the far side of the pit. Only then did he catch his fingers on the earthen edge, try to hoist his weight upward.

Hal settled his own, far more meager weight on the balls of his feet, sighting down the arrow and waiting for the smith to turn around. The giant tried three times to heave himself out of the pit, but he failed repeatedly, unable to gain a solid purchase with his damaged leg. On the last attempt, he lost his footing on the crumbled earth that had slid back into the pit, and he slipped, sprawling on the filthy ground. He scrambled onto his back, trying to force his broken leg beneath him. Blood had soaked through his leather apron, and earth was smeared across his face as he supported himself against the pit's wall.

"Maaa—" he started to wail. And Hal let his arrow fly. It caught the smith in the mouth, traveling past his teeth and into his skull, moving with enough force to throw the smith's head against the earthen wall.

King Halaravilli did not wait for the corpse to collapse into the hole. Instead, he turned to Puladarati and handed back the

bow. "Gather the men together. Let's count our wounded and regroup, on this side of the pit." As Hal withdrew, the chittering
voices rose up like flames, chewing away at the corners of his
mind.

Rani swallowed hard and reminded herself to breathe deeply.
Had she been this ill on the trip up the coast, on Bashi's ship?
She could not remember back that far, could only vaguely recall
that those sailors had told her that the ocean had been calm, that
the sea had been smooth. By anyone's definition, though, the current waters were roiled; there were constant swells that rocked
the boat from side to side, tossing it with enough force that Rani
could only keep her balance by grabbing hold of one of the ropes
strung along the side of the craft.

Looking out at the grey sprays of seawater, Rani could not
help but think of the silvery dolphins she had seen with Bashi.
Those leaping fish—they *were* fish, whatever Bashi had said about
their birthing live young—might have been at home in these
seething northern seas, might have found games to play in the
wake of Rani's ship. But those fish had been destroyed by sharks.

A shiver ran down Rani's spine, and she thought again of the
dozens of children huddled belowdecks, vulnerable to those
bloody sharks' mouths if the ship were to founder. There were
nearly one hundred and fifty members of the Little Army on her
craft, and a companion boat tossed on the waters just visible to
Rani's left, bearing another eight score soldiers.

None of this made any sense, she thought for the hundredth
time. None of the Little Army's planning made any sense at all.

Preparations for the journey to Liantine had moved much more
rapidly after Monny had demonstrated his ability to operate the
flying machine. The adult soldiers had swept through the stockade on the plain outside of Sin Hazar's city. The children had
been given a few minutes to gather their belongings, and then
their tents had been struck, their portable city destroyed.

The children had been assigned to the boats randomly. Mair
was supposed to be on the other craft, but she had darted across
the divide on the docks, squirming her way into the crowd of

children surrounding Rani before the guards could react. The soldiers had not been happy at her disobedience, but they were powerless to act—they could never have picked out one child from another. To Sin Hazar's adult soldiers, the children were all interchangeable parts in one of Davin's war machines.

So, Rani and Mair were on one boat, along with Crestman and Monny and dozens of other soldiers. Tain and Serena, the girls from Shea's cottage, had been assigned to the other craft. Rani had watched Shea's face crumple as she realized that Crestman could not watch over her daughters.

In fact, the old sunwoman had begun to scream at the grown soldiers, to fight her way to the front ranks of the children. She had been ordered back, the threatening words reinforced by a soldier's heavy hand on his sword. When Shea had still refused to comply, the adult captain had ordered her bound and gagged.

That action had stirred up all the children, but the little swangirl, Serena, was particularly rebellious. She had planted her hands on her narrow hips and ordered the grown soldiers to release her mother. The men had laughed and looped a few lengths of rope around the child's shoulders, securing her arms to her sides. They had tossed her onto the other boat with a nod and a laugh, threatening to gag her when she shrieked to all the Thousand Gods.

Those threats stuck with Rani as the Amanthian ships cut through the ocean. She heard them, over and over, as she braced herself against the railing, and she shivered at the words that had not been spoken, at the story behind the threats. The Little Army might give itself a proud name, it might proclaim itself one of King Sin Hazar's strongest tools on the eve of war, but it still consisted of children. Children who could be silenced at a grown soldier's whim. Another shiver convulsed Rani's shoulders.

"You're not dressed for the cold."

"Crestman." Rani turned to face the captain. "We girls weren't issued cloaks by the quartermaster."

"Ah, you're supposed to find your comfort in a soldier's arms." Crestman laughed as he undid the clasp on his own garment, settling it around Rani's shoulders.

"Precisely." Rani wanted to sneer and give back the gift, but it was too warm across her shoulders. She managed to stop her teeth from chattering.

"If you're that cold, Rani Trader, you should go belowdecks."

"It's worse below."

"It's warmer."

"If you can stand the stench. I'd rather shiver in the cold than be warm in a stinking sickroom." As if to test her point, the ship lurched into a particularly deep trough, sending up a freezing spray. Rani swore under her breath. She did not want to be sick in front of Crestman, did not want to see the mixture of revulsion and pity on his face. And she did not want to soil his fine cloak. When she thought that she had mastered her rebellious belly, she turned to face him and said, "You know that we don't stand a chance against the Liantines."

"Don't stand a chance? What do you mean? You saw my men at the Swancastle! You saw how we undermined the walls. Once we meet up with the other Amanthian troops already in Liantine, there will be no stopping us. Besides, we have the flying machine."

"Aye, the flying machine. And Monny. A little boy for you to manipulate in your battles."

"He's a soldier, Rani Trader."

"He's a tool that you used, like your sword or your dagger. You don't care that he'll risk his life at your command! You don't care that he'll be strapped in with willow withes and strands of rope!"

"Davin says the machine is safe."

"Davin doesn't care if it's safe or not! He only wanted to prove that he could build a flying machine! He just wanted to make one of his drawings come to life! Why do you think he chose you and Mair to call the count?"

"Our voices are different. He chose us because Monny could hear which of us was calling."

"Did he? Or did he choose you because the pair of you have become Monny's captains? Monny would succeed for you and Mair, or die trying! Davin *used* you, Crestman. He used you, and he'll continue to do so, as long as you let him."

Crestman started to protest, but his words caught in his throat, choking him as if he'd swallowed a fish bone. Rani let her challenge freeze on the air between them, and she started to turn back to the ocean water, to the open, endless plain of salt waves.

Out of the corner of her eye, though, Rani caught a flash of movement on the raised forecastle at the front of the ship. She knew that Teleos, the ship's captain, kept his quarters there. The children had been told on the first day that they were forbidden to mount the short ladder to the upper deck. Nevertheless, a furtive flicker registered in the grey light. No sailor would move that rapidly or harness the foggy patches of shadow that effectively. Without consciously realizing the fact, Rani knew that she had glimpsed Mair, had just made out the Touched girl darting from the captain's cabin.

It was important that no one else see Rani's companion. No other children were on deck, and the sailors were occupied with the business of driving their vessel through the tossing seas. That left Crestman as the only threat, Crestman as the only person who could alert the Amanthians to Mair's presence where the Touched girl had no business.

Rani forced an earnest smile across her face and pitched her voice low enough that the boys' captain had to step closer to hear her question. "What are your orders, Crestman? How are you supposed to use the flying machine? What are the boys going to do when we arrive in Liantine?"

"We'll follow the rest of the Little Army. We'll do whatever they tell us to."

With a shiver, Rani thought of the training she had witnessed on the grounds of the Swancastle, Monny's brutal torture. At the same time, she remembered Crestman's urgent words when he'd spoken to her the following day, on the edge of the castle clearing, his description of his indoctrination in the Little Army. Without intending to, Rani remembered Crestman's lips on hers, and her belly clenched, but she did not know if she was reacting to the nearness of the captain, or the memory of his kiss, or the sudden toss of the ship on the ocean. "The rest of the Little Army?" she forced herself to ask, remembering Mair, remembering that she had to keep Crestman's attention engaged. "How many of you have already been shipped to Liantine? How many do we expect to meet in the port?"

"I don't know for certain."

"I'm not asking for the king's recruiting rolls!" Rani let a little acid slip into her words. Why did Crestman insist on misunderstanding everything she said? "I meant in general. Approximately how many children has Sin Hazar shipped overseas to fight for his cause on foreign soil?"

Crestman waited for long enough that Rani thought he would not answer. His hands tightened on the wooden railing, and he braced himself against a particularly high wave, ducking his clouted head as the spray broke over the side. Rani longed to look over her shoulder, to see if Mair was still on the forecastle, but she restrained herself, managing instead to splutter against the salt spray.

When the ship had righted itself, Crestman turned to Rani and sighed as if he were preparing for a winter storm. "There have been at least five score ships, in the past two years."

Five score. . . . Their own vessel held one hundred and fifty children, could have held more if they'd been forced into even closer quarters belowdecks. Rani's mind boggled at the notion. Fifteen thousand soldiers? Fifteen *thousand* children sent to Liantine?

"But that must be all the children in Amanthia!"

Crestman shrugged. "Most of the boys."

"And how has the Little Army fared?" Crestman did not respond, gazing out at the ocean, and Rani thought he must not have caught her question above the crash of the waves. "What has the Little Army accomplished in the east?" she pushed. "What battles has it fought? *What do they expect us to do?*"

For a moment, she thought that he did not answer because he did not trust her. She saw him start to form words, start to phrase a reply, but then he swallowed hard and clenched his hands on the ship's railing. "I don't know."

"What?" His admission surprised her enough that she forgot she'd started this conversation just to distract him. She didn't know what she'd expected to hear—that Crestman had been ordered to lead his boys into certain death? That they were expected to storm the Liantine port like rats off a ship? That they were supposed to run with torches into the city, spreading chaos and mayhem? But to hear him admit ignorance . . . "How can you not know?"

"I'm a captain, Rani Trader, a captain in the Little Army. I'm a soldier. I follow orders. I doubt you can understand what that means."

Rani's thoughts raced back to her own life in the City, to the time she'd spent jumping from caste to caste before she'd been dragged north to Amanthia. She remembered living in the Soldiers' Quarter and following orders issued by the King's Guard. And she remembered believing herself a member of the Brotherhood of Justice, following the commands of a shadowy hierarchy, when she did not know the reason, did not know the meaning behind the battles that were fought around her.

For just an instant, Rani could see a Zarithian blade, her own prized dagger. The knife had been a gift from her father, one of the few treasures that she had carried with her when she'd journeyed from the safety of her family's shop. She had valued the dagger almost more than her own life, and she had been proud to use it, to defend herself when she'd thought that she was threatened. Even now, she could see crimson blood coating the Zarithian blade; she could hear the labored breathing of the soldier she had executed, *murdered* because she'd been ordered to do so.

Now, standing beside the Little Army's scornful captain, Rani looked down to see her hands clenched into fists, her nails digging into her palms. Half crescents of blood seeped through her flesh, and she forced herself to meet Crestman's eyes. "I understand orders. I understand following commands of a superior. And I know that those orders can be wrong, Crestman. I know that orders can be deadly."

Before he could offer up some protest, Rani caught the glimmer she'd been waiting for, a glimpse of a lithe shadow slipping down the ladder to the hold. Mair had finally finished her Touched prowling on the forecastle.

Rani turned her attention back to Crestman, saw him weighing her solemn words, but suddenly she was sickened by their discourse. She did not want to hear a soldier talk further of blood and war. She did not want to remember her life in the Soldiers' Quarter, the mistakes she had made. Rani darted under a startled Crestman's arm and scrambled for the ladder that led down into the hold, down into the darkness and the stench where the Little Army waited.

She was gasping, taking care to breathe through her mouth, by the time she reached the bottom. There were only two torches that burned beneath the deck, guttering in iron-shielded frames so that they could not kindle the entire craft. Rani squinted in the dim light, willing her vision to adjust. She was fumbling for the cloak at her throat, desperate to remove Crestman's garment in the overheated hold, when someone closed a hand around her wrist. Rani gasped.

"Calm yerself, Rai. It's only me." Mair loomed out of the darkness, her face looking like a cadaver's in the flickering shadows and the blue light that crept down the rickety ladder.

"What were you doing, Mair!"

"Doing? What do you mean?" The Touched girl was striving for a light tone, but Rani could hear a catch in her voice.

"I *saw* you! I saw you leave Teleos's quarters!"

"Hush!" Mair hissed the command and dragged Rani into a darker patch of shadow, as far as possible from the ladder, from the fresh air, from spying ears. Rani longed for some pungent, cleansing aroma—ladanum, anything!—to block the stench of the hold. "Watch yer tongue, Rai!" Mair's voice was tight.

"Mair, what were you doing?"

"Nothing more than creeping about the Nobles' Quarter, back home in the City," she said, but her breeziness was strained across her words. "I was seeing if there was anything we needed to know about our ship's captain, anything that will help us."

"And what could you possibly have learned that was worth

the risk? Do you *know* what Teleos would do if he caught you spying?"

Mair ignored the latter question, but she answered, "I learned that Teleos is supposed to collect gold bullion for his delivery of the Little Army."

"What?" Rani struggled to process the words, to make sense of Mair's whisper.

"Teleos is supposed to hand us over to the Liantines, and they will *pay* him with bars of gold. He gets to keep four bars, and the rest he must return to Sin Hazar."

"But we're supposed to *fight* the Liantines!" Rani's stomach lunged upward, even as the ship rolled over another enormous swell. She forced herself to take deep breaths, settling her panic before she forced out words. "We're being sold. We're slaves."

"That's the way it looks," Mair confirmed grimly. "This isn't the first shipment Teleos has made. He's become a wealthy man ferrying children across the sea."

"Fifteen thousand children . . ." Rani breathed. Slavery. Bondage. The Little Army was nothing but a sham, then, designed to enrich Sin Hazar so that he could further whatever nefarious plans he had crafted. All the talk of the Little Army and child soldiers . . . All of that was a carefully crafted screen. Rani was heading toward Liantine, a slave trapped in the hold of a ship. "Mair, we've got to do something! We'll get the girls to rise up with us. They'll help us escape."

Mair snorted. "Escape? You watched those girls in the camps! You can hear them now, rutting like sows. They've already been recruited to the Little Army. They're here to serve your precious Crestman's boys, wherever they might have to go, and don't fool yourself otherwise."

"He's not *my* Crestman!" Rani and Mair had avoided this fight for days, for all the time that they'd been stuck in the stockade outside Sin Hazar's city.

As the ship lurched into yet another deep trough, though, Rani could not think straight, could not ask herself the right questions about the Little Army. About the girls in the camp. Nothing made sense down here in the stinking hold, not as her mind reeled with the discovery that Teleos was a slaver, that she and Mair were mere goods to be delivered. Rani could not think with the sounds of creaking ropes and moaning boards around her. And not with the other sounds in the hold—a smothered giggle, a scarce-masked grunt.

Fifteen thousand children in Liantine. Fifteen thousand slaves, disappeared. And those had been boys, hardened in the Little Army's camps. What would happen to the girls following in their footsteps—untrained girls, without weapons, or experience, or even a hint of battle training?

"But Crestman wouldn't let—" Rani began.

"How much control will Crestman have, when we're greeted by archers at the port? How much power will he have, when one of his boys is shot, as an example? When one of the girls is collared and chained, or worse, on the very dock?"

Rani swallowed hard, fighting against the reek of salt and fish and unwashed bodies. For just an instant, she could remember standing beside Sin Hazar, dancing with him at his cursed feast. Her breath was tight in her chest, as it had been when she'd been bound by the nareeth, by the queer, restrictive northern garments. Rani remembered the flush that had spread across her cheeks as Sin Hazar danced with her, the way she had responded to his silky words.

Even then, he had been using her. He had been exploiting her the way he intended to exploit all the girls on this ship, all the children in the Little Army.

She had been spared his touch that night in Amanthia, the night that she had escaped with Mair. Whatever she had thought she wanted, whatever she had thought was right, she had escaped with her honor, her faithfulness to Morenia and Halaravilli intact. She wasn't about to lose that honor now, not on this ship, and not on the Liantine shore.

They had three days before they were supposed to arrive in Liantine. Three days before they would be pawned for gold. For gold that could buy weapons, buy grown mercenaries who would be used against Halaravilli, against Morenia, against her liege. "We've got to do something, Mair."

"And what do you suggest, Rai?"

"We've got to gather the girls together. We've got to explain."

"The girls!" Mair snorted. "There may be five score girls all told, on both these ships, only about sixty of them here. What can we do with sixty girls against the Little Army and all the grown soldiers? Those boys believe they're on a mission, appointed by their king! And there are Sin Hazar's men, too, more than half a dozen of them, guarding us."

"We have to try," Rani vowed. "Come on. Let's head toward the ladder. There's a breeze, and we'll be able to think more clearly." When Mair did not move, Rani plucked at her arm. "I won't be used, Mair. I won't be a bed warmer or a slave or a weapon against my king."

"I don't know that you have the choice, Rai."

"We've all got choices." Mair started to protest again, but Rani merely shook her head, dragging her friend over to the ladder and the tendrils of fresh air that curled down from the deck. "No, Mair. We've all got choices. Some of them are just harder to see than others."

12

Sin Hazar removed two ship-markers from his map, scooping up the carved pieces as if he intended to throw them across the board, like dice sealing his fate. Instead, he turned toward his nephew, tossing the wooden carvings to the unsuspecting Bashanorandi. The boy let one of the pieces clatter to the floor, and he scrambled to retrieve it before it could roll toward the drafty hearth. Felicianda's boy, on his knees before his uncle . . . Well, it was an amusing start for a strategy session. Suppressing a tight smile, Sin Hazar turned his focus to his brother. "Well, Al-Marai. Two fewer issues to worry about."

"Aye." Al-Marai moved to the foot of the board, cocking his head, as if to get a better perspective.

"Those ships should reach Liantine within the next three days," Sin Hazar mused. "Our profit on the goods will let us buy another score of Yrathis. What does that bring our total to? Eight hundred?"

"Give or take."

Sin Hazar was annoyed that his brother replied without a trace of emotion. This was a time to celebrate! The notion of impressing the girls—that had been inspired by the Thousand Gods! Why, if the recruiters gathered up girls throughout the winter . . . Sin Hazar would have another—what?—five ships to send to the Liantines? Another fifty Yrathis added to his troops? Al-Marai should be a touch more enthusiastic. He should at least *pretend* that he cared about the looming battle. "Perhaps, brother, you'd like to switch sides now." Sin Hazar kept his voice dry, but he watched the general tense at the words.

"I'd fall on my sword, if my liege but suggests it," Al-Marai replied automatically, and his hand reached for the curved blade that hung from his waist.

"Yes, yes," Sin Hazar waved off the formula, directing a scowl toward the now-hovering Bashanorandi. No reason to drag the boy into this, to make statements that would have to be backed up in front of prying eyes and ears. "What's wrong, Al-Marai? What are you not telling me?"

"Nothing's wrong, Your Majesty." Al-Marai kept his hand on his weapon as he strode up the side of the map. "Nothing that we can't fix."

In a flash, the general reached out for the board, shifting pieces to move the Morenian army closer to the capital, close to Sin Hazar himself. Still dissatisfied with the map's display, Al-Marai shook his head and reached into the gutters at the side of the painted board. He extracted three more crimson pieces, markers for the upstart Halaravilli's army. Al-Marai settled them on the board beside the other pieces, shook his head, and moved the entire mass of crimson markers still farther north, so that they were within two days' march of Sin Hazar.

"Surely you jest." Sin Hazar kept his dry cynicism with an effort.

"There's no jest here. I've just received our most recent scouts' reports."

"But there's no way that southern dog can have that many men! It's wintertime! He would need to muster his entire kingdom!"

"Perhaps we were misinformed about the number of his standing forces." Al-Marai flicked a glance toward Felicianda's bastard.

Sin Hazar followed his brother's gaze and restrained a shrug of irritation. "Bashanorandi." The name was clearly a command, but it still took the boy a moment to step up to the map. What had the creature expected, when he insisted on joining his uncles in the stone chamber? That he could sulk in the corner like a child denied sweets?

"Your Majesty?" Bashanorandi bowed as he stepped up to the table, but he avoided meeting Sin Hazar's eyes.

Ah, Felicianda had much to answer for. . . . Had she truly expected to set this child on her southern throne? If so, perhaps she had remained more dedicated to her homeland Amanthia, to her family, than Sin Hazar had ever expected. He could have overrun *Bashanorandi's* kingdom with the effort it took to swat a fly.

"You've heard your uncle. There are more troops approaching from the south than we expected. You told us that we would find no more than a hundred men on horse, and merely ten companies of foot soldiers."

"Th—that's what I thought, Your Majesty." Bashanorandi darted a tongue over his chapped lips. A nasty habit, that. It made him look like a lizard, an appearance that was not disputed by his eyes' furtive dart toward the map board. The new swan's wing tattooed on the boy's cheek twitched nervously.

"And what was your base for those estimates, Bashanorandi?"

"There were exercises set for us by our tutors, back in Morenia." The boy closed his eyes and caught his tongue between his teeth, sighing deeply as if he were trying to remember a complex calculation. "They said that in the first year of Shanoranvilli's rule, he marched north to Amanthia. He raised troops along the way. One hundred men on horse, he had, and he gathered ten companies—"

"At the beginning of his reign!" Sin Hazar exploded, smashing his fist down onto the table in fury. The army markers jumped, and three units of foot soldiers collapsed on their sides. "How long did Shanoranvilli sit his throne, boy?"

"F—for sixty years."

"And what Amanthian borders changed during that time?" Bashanorandi stared at him as if he spoke the language of the Thousand Gods. "Didn't he become the lord of the Eastern March?"

"But, Your Majesty, I did not know how to calculate other figures!"

"Didn't he become lord of the Eastern March?" Sin Hazar repeated, ignoring the pitiful protest.

"Yes, Your Majesty." Bashanorandi hunched his shoulders unhappily.

"And didn't he annex the Southern Reach?"

"Yes, Your Majesty."

"And didn't he become overlord of the Pepper Isles?"

"Yes, Your Majesty. But there aren't many people there, not more than a few hundred."

"Not more than a few hundred!" Sin Hazar bellowed, and his fists closed in his nephew's royal blue tunic. He felt the boy's heart pound beneath his hands as he drew the whelp close, near enough for Bashanorandi's nervous breath to brush across his own lips. He squeezed the boy and hissed, "Not more than a few hundred! But how many more people declared their loyalty to your father, when he could provide them with a safe route to the spices?" He shook the boy hard enough that he could hear teeth chatter together. "How many more of your merchants swore fealty in the southern part of your father's realm? How many more soldiers bear the Morenian lion on their shields?"

"I—I don't know! P—Please, Your Majesty, you're hurting me!"

Sin Hazar swore and twisted the boy's tunic tighter between his hands, gathering up the silk folds until the cloth sawed into the vulnerable flesh at the front of the boy's throat. The soft skin was bared like a lover's, and Sin Hazar saw fear in the boy's pleading eyes, blue eyes so like Felicianda's.

What a miserable excuse for a prince!

Felicianda would never have tolerated such abuse from Sin Hazar! Even if she had made the same stupid mistakes, even if she had failed to take into consideration the most basic elements of statesmanship, she would have fought against her elder brother's punishment. Anger would have flashed from her blue eyes, pure rage. And then she would have twisted in his grip, even if the movement cut off her breath even more. She would have fought like a coney in a snare, and she would have stomped on his toes. . . .

But Felicianda was gone. Dead. Executed as a traitor. All for trying to place this waste of a boy on her southern throne.

"Your Majesty." Sin Hazar barely heard the words, scarcely registered the murmur. Nevertheless, Al-Marai took a step forward, distracting Sin Hazar from his fury. The king did not bother to look at his brother as he brought himself back to the stone chamber, to the map that was riddled with false markers.

Instead, he twisted his hands a fraction tighter, sawed the fabric just a little deeper into his nephew's soft throat. And then he released Bashanorandi.

The boy collapsed to his knees, retching. He leaned forward to support most of his weight on his hands, gasping for air as if he were a fish pulled from the ocean depths. Sin Hazar reined in the temptation to dig a booted toe into the boy's side. Better to ignore the brat. Better to leave him out of the affairs of men.

Instead, Sin Hazar turned back to the board, reaching out with a steady hand to pick up the foot-soldier markers that had been toppled. "Very well, then." He might have been discussing nothing more perturbing than an overcooked goose at the dinner table. "Tell me, Al-Marai. How long will it take for these southern troops to arrive on our doorstep? And what must we do to crush them?"

Al-Marai did not waste time glancing at his gasping nephew. Lion that he was, he'd never had a great love for Felicianda. Sin Hazar knew that she'd grasped a swan's right to command when she was only a little girl. Many times, Sin Hazar had watched Felicianda order around their older brother with a vicious cruelty, making a swan's demands of Al-Marai that Sin Hazar himself had never dared. Sin Hazar had always remembered the power behind his lion-brother's sword arm. Sin Hazar had been no fool.

And now, Sin Hazar watched Al-Marai discard Felicianda's whelp, rubbing his soldierly hand across his lion tattoo, as if the general were reminding himself of his true purpose in the Amanthian court. "Here," Al-Marai said, pointing to one of the new markers. "They've already cleared the Swancastle."

"And what about the toys that Davin said he'd leave behind?"

"Oh, he left them, Your Majesty. They did their work. We es-
timate that Halaravilli lost ten of his nobles, and at least three
score foot soldiers."

"Seventy men?" Sin Hazar frowned. "That's all? Davin said
they'd be destroyed entirely."

"Seventy men, but we've made them afraid. They're sending
out scouts now, studying everything on and off the road."

"S—Seventy Morenians murdered?" Sin Hazar had not noticed that Bashanorandi had risen to his feet, had come back to
the map. He *did* note, though, that the boy kept his distance. The
pup was frightened of his royal uncle; he clearly had no intention of standing close enough to be seized again, even if he *had*
dared to voice a foolish, sentimental thought.

Sin Hazar ignored the child's incredulity and shot his next
question at Al-Marai. "And how many men did we lose in Davin's
maneuver?"

"None, Your Majesty. Only a sun, the smith who launched the
trap." Al-Marai nodded at the map. "It was an excellent ploy.
The southerners were stung by an insect they'd never seen before, and now they're wary of anything with wings."

"Anything with wings . . ." Sin Hazar heard the undercurrent
of disagreement in Al-Marai's tone. "You still think I'm wrong
to send the flying machine to the Liantines, don't you?"

"Not *wrong,* Your Majesty."

"But it's a choice you would not have made."

"I would have kept the machine here, to defend your city
walls."

"But Davin can make me another. He's already working on
it. Besides, the Liantines have offered enough gold for the contraption that we can procure *another* ten Yrathis."

"So you've said."

Sin Hazar glanced at Bashanorandi; he was annoyed at being
challenged in front of the boy, however obliquely. "Al-Marai,
we've been over this a dozen times. The Liantines will pay."

"They've honored their obligations so far, Your Majesty. But
the Liantines do not control Yrath. We may not be able to procure the mercenaries, even with Liantine gold."

"But who is offering more money than we?"

"So you've argued before, Your Majesty."

"Al-Marai, you certainly can't be afraid that that upstart rebel of a southern king is going to out*spend* us? You can't think that he's going to buy the Yrathis out from under us?" Sin Hazar forced himself to laugh in ridicule at the concept. From everything they'd heard, from Bashanorandi and more reliable spies, Halaravilli could not afford to smelt weapons for his men. How was he going to purchase the finest soldiers that money could buy?

"Nay, Your Majesty. We've seen nothing to indicate that he can afford the Yrathis."

"Then what is it, Al-Marai? What are you not telling me?"

The lion took a deep breath, then flicked his glance toward Bashanorandi. He seemed to be asking Sin Hazar a question, begging permission to speak plainly in front of the southern brat. Sin Hazar waved an exasperated hand, but Al-Marai still swallowed hard before he managed to meet his liege's eyes. "Your Majesty, we can't guarantee that the southerners will be stopped before they reach the city. They make decisions as if they're mad! They torched the Swancastle, and the countryside is afraid."

"The Swancastle was an undefended pile of stones! Our own *boys* undermined the walls!"

"Aye, but the sound of a stone wall falling does not carry. Smoke can be seen for leagues."

"What are you telling me? Do you think that I'm in *danger*?" Sin Hazar's voice broke on the last word, from disbelief or rage, even he could not have said.

"I don't think that you're in serious danger. I don't think that your life is on the line. Nevertheless . . ."

"Nevertheless, what? What are you trying to say, Al-Marai?"

"I think that you should take out the *Golden Dragon*. I think that you should command this war from the sea."

Sin Hazar gaped at his brother. Go out to sea? Admit to fear?

Al-Marai was the first lion in the history of Amanthia to conceive of setting up an alternative command post during war. They'd talked about it often enough—the *Golden Dragon* had become Al-Marai's pet project over the years. The general had always championed the notion of a palace that could be maneuvered about the open seas, providing secrecy and safety. . . . Sin Hazar could use pigeons to send messages to a half dozen landbound outposts. He could launch smaller craft from the deck of the *Golden Dragon*; he could issue orders to his crack troops, all from a safe distance.

And all Sin Hazar needed to do was admit that he was afraid. "The *Golden Dragon* . . ." he said, sampling the taste of the ship's name, sampling the flavor of retreat.

"Aye, Your Majesty. It would permit us to test my theories. You could try now, before you *need* to. Cement your command for the future. For you know that next year, we'll be turning our attention away from the south. Once you have Morenia under control, you'll be looking toward Liantine in earnest. Knowing our capabilities on the open sea will be important there."

"But who would stay behind to command my forces on land?"

"I would, Your Majesty."

Sin Hazar gazed at his brother, warmed by the automatic reply. He flicked a glance toward Bashanorandi, to see if the brat was absorbing the lesson. The boy's eyes were locked on Sin Hazar, his hand raised to his throat, massaging the angry red line where his tunic had cut across his windpipe. There was a message behind that cornflower gaze, an expectation that Sin Hazar would accept Al-Marai's offer. Would accept the escape.

Al-Marai persisted. "War is fraught with danger, Sire. I'll stay behind. We'll work well together."

War is fraught with danger. And what sort of king would Sin Hazar be if he ran from that danger? One glance at the sniveling Bashanorandi answered that rhetorical question. "I'm sorry, Al-Marai. I will not flee a battle, even to test your *Golden Dragon*."

"But Your Majesty—"

"It would look like cowardice to my people, no matter how much you and I might know that it is not."

"My lord—"

"I'll brook no dispute on this."

"But, brother—"

"Aye," Sin Hazar cut him off, before Al-Marai could make some demand that could not be denied, some last-ditch plea backed by blood. "*Brother.* We have battles to fight. Kingdoms to protect. A war to win. I will not let you harvest all the glory, here on land, while I am pampered and bored on the *Golden Dragon.*" Sin Hazar smiled as he reached out for Al-Marai, clasping his brother's strong hand across the map as Bashanorandi looked on with transparent jealousy. Sin Hazar chose his words to cut as deeply as he could. "Let's study how we'll defeat these southern bastards."

Rani gathered the cloak closer about her shoulders, leaning her head back so that the soft cloth brushed against the nape of her neck.

"Are you ready, Rai?"

"Aye," Rani muttered, opening her eyes to look at Mair. "Are you certain you shouldn't lead this?"

"I don't have Crestman's ear. In the end, he's what matters."

"Aye. And you're sure they won't believe us if we just tell them the truth? They won't recognize the danger and fight to turn the ship around?"

"Would you? If you'd been dragged into the Little Army, or you thought you loved a boy who had been? Would you believe a pair of southern traitors who don't even talk like proper suns?" Mair leaned forward and grasped Rani's wrist. "If you don't have the stomach to follow through, you're better off not even beginning."

"I know that," Rani said. Of course she'd be better off not beginning. She'd be better off not on this tossing, rocking boat. She'd be better off not in Amanthia at all. She'd be better off if she'd stuck with her promises, if she'd worked on rebuilding the glasswrights' guild and ignored all the pomp and intrigue of living as a noble in Hal's court. She'd be better off if she'd never taken her falcon out, if she'd never tried to fly Kalindramina on that autumn afternoon that seemed like a lifetime ago.

But she *had* flown her falcon, and she'd been carried off to the north. And now, if she did not act quickly, she was going to be sold into slavery in Liantine, slavery or worse. Rani sighed. "I'm ready. Call them over, and I'll do my part."

"All right then. May Cot watch over us."

"Cot?" Rani almost managed a grin. "I don't know that the god of soldiers has anything to say about this mission. More like Quan."

"Not *all* the girls are harlots."

"Not all of them, no. But enough for our plan to work. Or so we can hope." Rani grimaced and pulled herself to her feet.

At least the ship had stopped tossing so violently. Crestman had even called the Little Army up onto the deck for an afternoon of military maneuvers, announcing that he wasn't about to have his company arrive in Liantine out of shape and lax in military discipline. From down in the hold, the girls could easily make out the drumbeat of the boys' feet on the wooden deck, the crash and tumble of the soldiers going through their exercises. They'd already been at it for a long time; Rani dared not delay anymore.

Mair lit one of the precious rushlights from the torch on the wall and began to walk among the girls. "Are you all right there?" she asked of one of the youngest. "Come with me. You, there. Let's gather over here. We need to talk, girls. We need to make our own preparations to help the boys. We need to help the Little Army."

More of the girls gathered about than Rani had expected. At first, she'd been afraid that Mair would only be able to attract the very youngest, the ones who were too small for even the most desperate of the boys to bother with. Some of the older girls, though, left off their whispering and giggling, coming to join the ragged circle around Rani.

As the girls pressed around, one of the oldest—Suditha, Rani remembered—settled between Rani and Mair. Rani started to shift position, to maneuver closer to her Touched ally, but she caught Mair's shake of her head and returned to her seat on the floor of the hold. Suditha sank beside her, her owl tattoo close enough that Rani could have traced the lines with her finger.

The Amanthian girl was oblivious to Rani's interest, though; she was occupied only in raking her fingers through her long, fiery locks. The action was sufficient to remind Rani that Suditha had taken up with one of Crestman's lieutenants. The girl was one of the first who had warmed to her role in the boys' camp, and she had embraced her position—and her soldier—eagerly. As Rani waited for the other girls to settle into a close circle, Suditha reached out and touched her tight-woven cloak, the cloak that Crestman had settled around Rani's shoulders when she had stood on deck. "That's a nice garment there."

"Aye," Rani said, and she drew it closer about her shoulders.

"My Landur would have given me his, but he's up on deck."

"Of course," Rani said neutrally.

"My Landur says that he'll give me a fur-lined cloak when all this is over. After the war. When he's had his share of the gleanings."

And he'd give her a silk gown, Rani thought bitterly. And velvet slippers. And a golden fillet for her hair. If he could buy their way out of chains. Rani had thought that owls were trained in thinking, in proper logic, but there was no limiting what lies a girl would tell herself when she was lonely and frightened and far from home.

Rani held her tongue while the other girls settled down. When she finally did speak, she purposely pitched her voice low enough that everyone drew closer. "We're drawing nigh to Liantine, ladies. We're nearing Liantine, and the Little Army is preparing to fight. There's something you should know, though. Something that all the Little Army needs to hear."

Rani looked at the earnest faces around her, flickering in the rushlight. Their tattoos stood out on their pale faces. Suditha's owl, and a handful of lions. Two swans, on the edge of the crowd, and suns. So many suns. Swallowing hard, Rani turned to Mair and spat out the protest they'd rehearsed. "I can't do it, Mair. I can't betray my people."

"You don't have much choice, now, do you?" Mair's condemnation was immediate; her words dripped with scorn.

"But Mair, I grew up in Morenia! I was raised in the shadow

of King Halaravilli's palace! Halaravilli was like a brother to me!"

"A brother, was he? Tell me about Halaravilli's brothers, Rai. He's lost three of them, hasn't he? And under mysterious circumstances, to say the least. . . ."

Rani swallowed hard at Mair's insinuating tone. She knew that she had to continue with this charade. She had to sway the girls. But the words sounded so much like treason. . . . They felt so much like betrayal. "Ach," she breathed, and then forced herself to voice, for the benefit of the Amanthians: "I know you're right, Mair. It's just that I *trusted* him. I thought King Halaravilli would come to save me."

"He has greater interests than you, you little fool!" Mair's anger sounded real, and the shock on Rani's face wasn't feigned. "He's marching north, through Amanthia. He has a throne in his sight, not some caste-jumping girl, not some fool who dreams of rebuilding a broken guild. Even now, he's likely at the Swancastle, billeting his men in the great hall."

"No one could take the Swancastle!" That, from one of the girls in the shadows at the edge of the circle. Even as Rani reeled from the viciousness of Mair's attack, she swallowed a smile—the first bait was taken.

"Aye, no one *could* have," Mair answered the girl. "Once, long ago in the history of your people. But after the Little Army finished its training, after they'd used the Swancastle to learn how to protect all Amanthia, it was left undefended. It was ripe for Halaravilli's army to pluck."

"How can you know that?" Suditha whirled toward Mair, tossing her red hair over her shoulder as if it were a weapon. "How can you, a southerner, know *anything* about the Swancastle? How can you know how we Amanthians do things?" Again, Rani swallowed a smile. The owl had spoken her lines as if she'd memorized the script for this play.

Rani took up her cue, forcing Suditha to whirl back around. "We learned it while we were at court, Suditha. I learned it sitting at Sin Hazar's side."

"You were never with His Majesty!"

"Ah, but I was. I wore a nareeth and a balkareen, and I danced with King Sin Hazar at a feast held in my honor." The heat of Rani's memories burned behind her words, and she leaned toward the hungry girls. "I ate at the king's table, and I drank from his cup. He pledged to me that he would conquer Morenia, and then we danced in front of all his lords."

Rani heard the tears behind her speech, the emotions that she thought she'd strapped down within her. What did it matter, though? How were the girls to know that Rani longed to murder King Sin Hazar, not bed him?

"So why aren't you with His Majesty now?" Suditha had opened another door without even realizing it, and Rani swallowed hard, pushing down the crimson bloodlust that welled up in her chest. Let the Little Army think that she longed for the king. Let them think that love, not hatred, drove her back to the Amanthian shore.

"I had no choice. I was carried away by events and misunderstandings. Besides, the important thing is not what I learned with your king. It's what I knew before I ever arrived in Amanthia, long ago, when I was in Halaravilli's court. The important thing is what I learned before I came to love King Sin Hazar."

There. That caught them. That snared them.

"Don't say more, Rai," Mair warned, and Rani could hear the double meaning of her words—the false warning that the girls were meant to hear, and the hidden one that reminded Rani that the girls were about to buy her story, fit and whole, if only she did not push them too far. Mair continued, "There's no going back, if you tell these girls more."

"There's no going back, even if I don't." Rani took a deep breath and gathered Crestman's cloak about her shoulders. "Ladies, Halaravilli poses more of a threat than just marching his soldiers into the Swancastle. The king of Morenia has men who are loyal to him, here in the north. Halaravilli has agents who are already stationed in Amanthia, agents close to King Sin Hazar."

"That's ridiculous," snorted Suditha, even as other girls gasped in horror. "His Majesty has spies whose sole job is to root out Morenian agents, to discover them and execute them like dogs."

"Is it ridiculous? Is it so very strange?" Rani let the passion of her lies carry her to her feet. "You Amanthians are marked at birth. You're tattooed with your caste, marked as swan or sun, lion or owl." Rani watched as more than one hand was raised to a cheek, as more than one girl thought of her station beneath the Amanthian skies.

Rani continued: "But in Morenia, it's different. I was born as Rani Trader, a merchant, by the way my people count things. But I changed my caste. I bought my way into the glasswrights' guild. I left the guild and became a soldier, then one of the Touched. I joined the nobles. Like First Pilgrim Jair, I changed my life."

"First Pilgrim!" Suditha retorted. "Jair was a man, not a god. The Thousand Gods never intended men to live in castes like you southerners!"

"They may not have intended it, but that's the way of my people. And that's the way that looked inviting to some of you northerners."

"To us? To whom?" Suditha's challenge was bald, as stark as the owl that flickered across her cheek in the rushlight.

"To Al-Marai."

The girls' collective gasp was like a wave striking the ship, but Suditha recovered first. "Al-Marai? The king's own brother?"

"Aye. The king's brother. The brother who was born before him, who was born first, but bears the mark of a lion. In my home, firstborn Al-Marai would have been the king. He would have commanded *all* Amanthia, not just its armies. But here, because of the time of night when Al-Marai was born, because of when his mother pushed him, screaming and puling into the world, he is nothing but a general."

"A general who will beat you southern invaders into submission!"

"A general who has already decided to join the southern invaders!" Rani's declaration rang out against the rafters of the hold. Her breath came in panting gasps, and she grabbed hold of

Suditha's patent incredulity to plant her final lie. "A general who has sold his birthright for the hope of changing castes."

Rani's heart pounded as she watched Suditha fight her disbelief. The other girls were silent, studying the scene before them as if they watched a play. Suditha swallowed hard and said, "Premise. Al-Marai is the brother of King Sin-Hazar and loyal to Amanthia."

Rani answered as if she'd been born to the northerners, but she employed the skills she'd learned in the south, the tricks that she'd learned masquerading through all the castes of her youth. She joined the debate as if an owl's tattoo were painted across her cheek. "Counterpremise. Al-Marai is a man, who is controlled by jealousy and passion like any other man."

Suditha's throat worked as she looked at the other girls in the hold. She clearly wanted to respond as an owl, wanted to find the cold, logical argument to dispatch Rani's words. She wanted to believe in Al-Marai, in King Sin Hazar, in the order that she'd been taught since her birth. But she had no tools to force faith into her story.

Suditha swallowed hard and sank back on her heels, a gesture that Rani chose to interpret as submission. After a quick glance at Mair, Rani spoke to the other girls. "Al-Marai is a man. A man who will betray his brother. A man who will open the palace gates to King Halaravilli, who will hand over Amanthia, *unless*—" Rani stopped, and the girls leaned toward her. "Unless we let His Majesty know of the danger."

"But how can we do that?" The question came from the center of the cluster of girls, and it was met with a bevy of nodded heads.

"We can turn this ship about. We can return to Amanthia. We can let the Little Army march into the king's courtyard and alert him to the danger."

"You lie!" Suditha had come to her feet again. Tears coursed down her cheeks, and she pointed a shaking finger at Rani. "You stand there and tell us lies!"

"How have I lied to you, Owl?"

"If you knew this, if you knew that King Sin Hazar was in danger, you would have spoken before you boarded this ship!"

Rani eyed the owl steadily, and the words came to her as if she were tutored by Hin, the god of rhetoric. "Premise: I did not know my heart until I boarded this ship."

"Counterpremise," Suditha spat. "Your heart is in Morenia, with your upstart Halaravilli."

"Premise," Rani answered evenly. "My heart is with the Little Army. With its captain, Crestman, who serves my one lord and king, Sin Hazar." Rani let her arms fall to her side, let Crestman's cloak drape over her Little Army rags.

Rani read Suditha's face as if the owl were a parchment scroll. Suditha was jealous of Rani. She doubted her own soldier, Landur. She longed for a simple garment. She longed for true love. Rani whispered, "I found my heart, Suditha, and I spoke as soon as I knew the truth. This goes beyond owls and premises and counterpremises. This is love, Suditha."

The owl's lip quivered, but she kept her voice steady. "And what would you have us do? You and your cloak and your love, what would you have us do?"

There. The hook was set.

"I'd have each of us spread the word within the Little Army. I'd have us explain what must be done. I'd have us gain the attention of the soldiers in every way we know, so that they listen, so that they hear and they understand. And then I'd have this ship turn about. I'd take us back to Amanthia, so that we can save King Sin Hazar."

"Are you mad? We'll be in Liantine in three days!"

"Aye," Rani nodded. "Three days. That doesn't give us much time, does it?"

"Why don't we just wait? Why don't we reach Liantine, and the Little Army can fight the king's battles there?"

"If the Little Army is forced to fight its way through our enemies in Liantine, we won't return to Amanthia in time to save the king. King Sin Hazar will fall to Morenia. It will be too late."

As Rani finished speaking, a giant shout went up on the deck of the ship. She knew that sound—the Little Army had finished its maneuvers for the afternoon. Crestman would set them one last task; he would send them running about the ship's deck, for five laps or ten. Then the boys would come hurtling down the ladder, down to the hold.

"What do you say, girls of the Little Army? Are you willing to fight for your king? Are you willing to convince your men?" Rani heard footsteps pounding the deck; the boys were running their last footrace. "Will you save Amanthia?"

Will you save *yourselves,* Rani thought. Will you spare us all a life of slavery and shame?

The first of the boys darkened the passage abovedecks, his shadow long and flickering across the hold. Suditha looked up as if she'd had a visitation from all the Thousand Gods. "Yes," she whispered. "Yes!" The other girls joined in her cries and moved forward to greet the returning army, to draw the boys into the shadows.

Rani gasped for breath, more than a little unnerved that she had cut things so close. Mair came to her side, and whispered, "I didn't think you were going to get them in time."

"I didn't either."

"We're not done yet. There'll be boys who need convincing beyond anything the girls say. There are boys enough who've kept themselves warm on these winter nights, without the help of our girls."

"Just as there are girls who've kept to their own bedrolls. Talk to them, Mair. You're the best at that."

"And you?"

Rani only sighed and gestured with her chin toward the deck. "I've got to bring him around. Without Crestman, we'll never succeed." She strode toward the ladder and climbed up on deck, before she could lose her nerve.

The sun was bright as it cut across the ocean, boosted by the occasional curl of a wave. Rani caught herself squinting, and she tried to force her eyes open wide, but they watered in the late-afternoon gold. Irritated, she glanced about the deck, taking a moment to locate Crestman.

He stood alone, at the prow of the ship. He leaned out over

the carved wooden balustrade, as if he would drive the ship to Liantine with the power of his thoughts alone. A wisp of hair had come undone from his tight clout, and his face was still red from the exercises he'd set for his men. His breath puffed onto the air, like a dragon's white smoke. As Rani approached, the breeze carried the healthy rankness of his sweat.

"You're working hard to keep your army in shape," she said.

"Aye. It was hard to stay fit in the stockade. No room for maneuvers. Not much better here." He was still panting, and she wondered what deadly tricks he'd shared with the boys, what useless moves they'd practiced, which would only guarantee them violent executions as rebellious slaves in Liantine.

"Crestman, you should take back your cloak. You'll catch your death in this breeze."

"I'll go below in a moment." He made no movement, though, and Rani told herself that his staying at the prow was an invitation, a gift from the gods. Forcing herself to ignore the tossing deck of the ship, she found a foothold and hauled herself up to stand beside Crestman. He automatically reached out to steady her, and she let his hand brush against her arm.

She'd done this before. She had masqueraded as a girl in love with a boy. She had lain in wait in a man's bed, eager to trap him. Eager to kill.

No. This was different. Crestman was only a boy. Only a soldier in the Little Army. He was not Dalarati, not a full-grown warrior, no matter his command over his boyish troops. Crestman was not one of the Fellowship of Jair. And Rani did not need to kill him. She only needed to convince him, to bring him around to her way of thinking. She did not need her knife.

"We'll be in Liantine in three days," she forced herself to say.

"Aye."

"And the Little Army will do battle."

"Aye."

"As soon as you're told what that battle will be."

"I told you, Rani. I'll wait for my orders."

"You know they aren't coming! You know that something is amiss!"

"I know that I'm a captain in the Little Army."

"Is that always your answer? Is that always your excuse?"

"Rani, you don't know what you're talking about."

"Did they carve out your brain, when they carved away your lion tattoo? Go ahead, Crestman! Go ahead and strike me! I'm only asking the question that you've been asking yourself since you returned to the Little Army! They took you from your family; they made you fight with other boys. They carved away your sky-sign. They killed your dog, and they forced you to eat its flesh. What makes you think that King Sin Hazar is watching out for your welfare? What makes you think that Liantine will be a safe place?"

"I'm a soldier, Rani. I don't ask for safety!"

"Do you ask for death?" The tears that had come close to her eyes when she spoke of Sin Hazar's seduction were back again, forced down her cheeks by her pounding heart. "Crestman, is that what this is all about? You wanted to escape from the Little Army, but you were not able? You couldn't leave when you came across Shea, so now you'll let the Little Army orchestrate another sort of escape for you?"

"Are you calling me a coward, Rani Trader?"

His hands gripped her arms, and even through his cloak, she felt the fury tremble through his body, the raw rage that coursed untapped in his flesh. She remembered the passion that had spilled into his embrace before, the fire when he had kissed her on the hill below the Swancastle. She raised her chin defiantly. "*Are* you a coward?"

For just an instant, she thought she'd pushed too hard. She thought that he would toss her over the railing, throw her to the sharks and all the other fishes. She watched his jaw tense, watched the wisp of hair that had fought free of his battle clout. His face flushed crimson, raw with fury, except for the stark white patch of the scar stretched beneath his left eye.

Rani raised her hand to touch that scar. It was cool against her fingertip, impossibly chilled when the boy-soldier before her was so enflamed with war and fear and honor. She whispered, "I *know* you're not a coward. Crestman, I know!"

He crushed her against him, completing the embrace that Bashanorandi had interrupted on the grounds of the Swancastle. Rani was startled by the strength of his arms as he pulled her against his chest, and she gasped as he crushed his lips to hers. Her heart pounded, harder than it had when she'd stood up to Suditha, harder than when she'd danced with King Sin Hazar. Harder than when she'd betrayed Dalarati, so long ago in faraway Morenia.

She struggled to pull her head back enough that she could whisper against the corner of his mouth, against his cheek. "Crestman, I know you're not a coward. And I know you're not a fool." She raised a single finger to trace the edge of his scar. "You know that something is not right with Liantine, that you're delivering the Little Army into danger. And you know that a king who would place children in danger is not to be served." He started to speak, but she lowered her finger to his lips, stilling his words. "King Sin Hazar has built the Little Army to serve his purposes, but his purposes are not war. Not war against Liantine. He wants *Morenia*. He wants to conquer Hal and Morenia, and all the southern lands. The Little Army is merely a tool to accomplish that, like Davin's mines or his flying machine. Sin Hazar will let all of you perish, as readily as he would have let Monny die, as easily as he let thousands of his subjects die during the Uprising."

She felt the fight go out of Crestman, felt it die with his passion, and a part of her longed for him to take her back in his arms. She wanted the feel of him against her chest; she wanted his fingers to tangle in her hair. But she knew that she had succeeded when she heard him ask, "What are you saying?"

"Only what you already know. The Little Army is being sent into danger, a greater danger than any battle. Sin Hazar would sell the Little Army as slaves, sell us to the Liantines."

"How can you know this!"

"Mair saw papers in Teleos's cabin. Teleos receives four gold bars if he delivers the entire ship of children."

Rani watched as he thought through what she said. She saw him measure the truth, fit the pieces together. He *knew* there was something wrong; he *knew* Liantine was not a safe harbor for the Little Army. His words were barely audible as he said, "What would you have me do?"

She was almost afraid to answer him. "Order the ship turned about. Return to Amanthia. Help King Halaravilli fight Sin Hazar."

He swallowed hard, and she knew he was weighing his loyalty, weighing his devotion to his king. He'd already fought this battle, though, months before, when he had decided to flee the Little Army. He had deserted Sin Hazar before he knew the full truth about the Little Army, when he had only thought that Amanthia fielded a monstrous corps of children, children run wild. Rani watched as Crestman regained the conviction that had brought him to Shea's cottage in the first place. When he spoke, she knew that he had decided to set aside the Little Army, to turn his back on Amanthia, once and for all. "This ship's captain will hardly listen to me, not with gold bars and the wrath of Sin Hazar weighing against me."

"He'll listen to a hundred armed soldiers who tell him where to sail."

"A hundred boys."

Rani shook her head. "A hundred soldiers in the Little Army."

"What about the other ship? Its captain will hardly let us escape Liantine."

"We can turn about in the night. The other ship won't know until dawn. Even then he'll probably think that we're ahead of him, just over the horizon."

"And what's to keep Teleos from turning about tomorrow night? He'll want to be paid, paid for all of us."

"You can pledge enough gold to make the change worth his while."

"My commission in the Little Army hardly provides me with that," he managed wryly.

"Ah, but King Halaravilli can. He'll pay for our safe delivery. You can promise Teleos twice what he was earning from Sin Hazar. Twice those wages, plus a surcharge for the safe delivery of Mair and me."

"You're confident, for a southern wench."

"I know King Halaravilli."

Crestman shook his head, staring out over the ocean, at the invisible Liantine shore. "The rumors at the port, before we took ship, said that the Morenians are already approaching Amanth. They say that the southerners burned the Swancastle. We can't be sure where we'll meet up with your king."

Rani's heart soared. They would turn the ship about. They would head toward Amanthia, then home. "No," she tried to mask her elation. "But if we return to one of the ports just south of Amanth, we can find him—either setting siege to the city or marching toward it. We'll find Hal."

"Hal," Crestman repeated.

"King Halaravilli," Rani supplied dutifully.

Crestman paused before asking, "And my men? How do I convince the Little Army that turning back isn't cowardice?"

"You won't be challenged by them. I've already taken care of that. Me, and Mair, and the other girls. We've told them that we must return to save Sin Hazar, to protect him from his brother's treacherous alliance with Morenia."

Crestman stared at her, a slow smile breaking across his face. "And I suppose you've already figured out how we'll defeat Sin Hazar, when he learns that it's actually the Little Army that has turned traitor?"

"Not yet." Rani smiled back. "You're the captain in the Little Army. I wanted to leave you something to work on."

13

Rani stood in Teleos's cabin, trying to look at the ship's captain with the aplomb of a lady in King Halaravilli's court. It was hard, however, when she was clothed in the rags of the Little Army, and when she had to fight her rebellious belly, and when she was so very, very tired. Perhaps, though, her appearance mattered little; the ship's captain was in the middle of a heated debate with Crestman.

"This is a war, boy," the captain was saying. "And you are in open mutiny against your king."

"This is no war. It's a business transaction. You're taking my men to Liantine to sell us. My men, and the women under my protection. Only soldiers can mutiny, and the Little Army is nothing but a horde of slaves."

"You're dreaming, boy!" Nevertheless, Teleos glanced nervously at his two bodyguards, at the bare scimitars that curved to either side of him.

The Little Army had begun its rebellion in the middle of the night, rising up against the unsuspecting and unprepared sailors on Teleos's vessel. They had managed to throw four of the king's guards overboard, taking the lions by surprise with more than a dozen boys choreographed to dispatch each guard. The Little Army had tied up the remaining four of Sin Hazar's men, taking the men's long swords to bolster their own meager weaponry. Teleos's sailors, watching the fate of the king's trained fighting men, had not put up any significant resistance. Instead, they had looked to their master for instruction, for reason in the face of a midnight battle against children.

And Teleos had summoned the leaders of the children to a parley, agreeing to meet with Crestman and Rani and Mair in his cramped cabin. He had insisted, though, that they be disarmed, and he had kept his own guards close at hand. The slaver looked worried, and a sheen of sweat stood out across his face. His dark beard looked oiled.

Crestman took a step closer to the slaver's table, and he lowered his voice to a growl. "My dreams might become your nightmares."

Rani wondered at the captain's bravery. Or his stupidity. He had no weapon; he had no steel to back up his threat.

"What do you mean, boy?" Teleos countered, and Rani saw the muscles in his arm tense. He was almost ready to signal his men, almost ready to order the Little Army put in its place.

"He means that we can work together, Your Grace, if we choose to," Rani interrupted, ignoring the fact that Crestman had intended nothing of the sort. "We can work side by side, and both get what we want. Or we can fight and both lose our goals."

Crestman glared at Rani, even as the slaver turned to her in surprise. The bearded man asked, "And who are you?"

Rani considered giving her name, letting the slaver know her true identity. But there was no advantage in letting him know that she was a merchant, that she was accustomed to bargaining for what she wanted. For what she needed. "I'm a member of the Little Army, Your Grace, just another slave for your men to unload on the Liantine docks. But for the right buyer, I can be worth far more. To Morenia, for example, I'm worth gold. An entire ingot."

Teleos's amusement overcame the suspicion in his dark eyes, and he laughed aloud, drawing out a large kerchief to swipe at the rivulets of sweat that trickled down to his collar. "An entire ingot, for a girl? A man could have his way with you for a few copper coins." The slaver flicked his eyes down her chest dismissively, shaking his head when he got to her narrow hips.

"King Halaravilli ben-Jair will pay for me!" Rani shouted, and she was pleased to see the slaver blanch. "The king of all Morenia will pay to see me safely returned to him. He'll pay for me, and for my companion, Mair, and for Crestman, too. And he'll pay for every one of the children you hold on this stinking tub."

The humor in Teleos's eyes was replaced by a frown. "There's no reason to go maligning my ship, now."

"King Halaravilli could buy this ship ten times over, before the sun rises."

"Aye, any king can spend more than a poor, hardworking sailor. But how do I know he'll pay for *you*? A wise man hoards his gold."

"A wise man knows the value of goods before he bids, and he spends what's fair to get them." The banter of bargaining stirred Rani's blood. She'd been born to this life. She'd been born to argue for a fair price. She'd just never thought that she'd be forced to do it for her own freedom, for her own chance to return to Morenia and the life she'd *chosen*, as a glasswright.

"How do I know you aren't making up your entire tale?" Teleos mopped at his face again. "How do I know you're not some gutter scum who came to the Little Army because you like spreading your legs for a horde of randy boys?"

Crestman made a strangled noise in his throat, and his hand shifted to where his sword would have hung. Rani, though, merely brushed her fingers across his sleeve and shot a glance to Mair. The Touched girl understood the unspoken message and shifted closer to Crestman's other side, leaning toward the captain to whisper calming words under her breath.

Rani had to swallow once before she was certain her voice would be level, but when she spoke, she had mastered a merchant's dispassion. "Set your price, procurer." It was Teleos's turn to choke on a reply. "Set your price for me. For me and for Crestman, for Mair and the rest of the Little Army."

"Six hundred bars of gold."

Rani gaped, completely unprepared for such a sum. Before she could even think to counterbid, Mair squawked, "That's ridiculous! Ye were only supposed t' get four bars fer th' entire shipful o' slaves!"

Teleos barely spared the Touched girl a glance. "My life was not at risk when I bargained over a shipful of slaves. When King

Sin Hazar learns of my failure to deliver the Little Army, my life will be worth nothing. Not in Amanthia, and not in any port across the sea. He'd have me killed before spring."

Rani struggled to counter the argument. Six hundred bars. . . . She had been prepared to commit Hal's treasury, prepared to bind the king to pay even an unreasonable amount of money for her release, for her and the rest of the children. But six hundred bars. . . . Hal would need to levy taxes on his people; he would need to call in debts from his nobles. Six hundred bars would cripple Hal's treasury, would hamstring his entire rule.

"Three bars each for the three of us," she finally said, "with the rest of the Army tossed in. That's more than twice what you expected to gain, and you don't have to complete the ocean crossing."

"Nine? You must think me a fool. Show these children back to their bunks." Teleos waved a dismissive hand at his guards and turned toward a stack of parchment correspondence.

"Another nine, then, for the rest of the Little Army."

"Eighteen bars of gold. And my life in the balance."

Crestman stepped forward before Rani could respond. "Eighteen bars of gold, when you would otherwise have four, you bastard. Eighteen bars of gold, and my army does not turn upon your men."

Teleos scarcely spared Crestman a glance, directing his words to Rani. "Fifty bars."

"Twenty-five."

"Twenty-five." The slaver nodded. "And the Little Army stays on board until you return with my payment."

Crestman spluttered, "You can't keep one hundred and fifty children hostage!"

"Speak to your colleague, boy. The term is 'collateral.' "

Crestman darted a glance at Rani, but she merely nodded. The slaver was protecting his investment, like any good merchant. She made her voice as cold as golden coins. "We'll bring your money by the new moon."

The slaver laughed for the first time. "By the new moon! By the new moon, Sin Hazar will have my hide stretched across the gates of Amanth! By the new moon, the seas will be too rough to cross to Liantine. I'd have no way to recoup my losses, to bring the Army to Liantine, if you fail. You'll have my payment by moonrise the day that we put into port, or I go back to sea, with all the Little Army."

Crestman protested before Rani could craft a proper reply. "We have to *find* King Halaravilli! He could be anywhere between the Swancastle and Amanth!"

"Rumor puts him within a day of the city. You'd best start looking for him on the Amanth Plain."

Rani saw the pattern spread out before her, as clearly as if it were drawn on a whitewashed table back at the glasswrights' guild. Teleos was setting them impossible odds. They needed to avoid capture by the Amanthians. They needed to find Hal. They needed to convince the king of Morenia to pay vast amounts of gold to free an army that had been trained to attack him. "We'll need a week," she said.

"One night."

"Two."

"One. My ship is well-known. As soon as we're spotted, Sin Hazar's lions will be on us like vultures on carrion. We can only stay hidden for a night, if we go into a port close to Amanth."

One night. They could never succeed. They could never find Hal and return with the gold that Teleos demanded. They weren't likely to be able to return even with a royal pledge. Rani nodded, though, as if she were accepting Teleos's explanation. "We'll need a fourth to help us then. We need the boy called Monny."

Rani saw Crestman look at her oddly, but then he nodded as well. He understood that they were going to fail. He knew that the Little Army was going to be forfeit. Monny, at least, should be spared the passage to Liantine; he should be spared a lifetime as a slave.

Teleos waved his hand. "One night. If we don't see you by sunrise, we lift anchor and head east."

Crestman finally spoke. "And we need the flying machine as well. To get the Morenians' attention."

"The flying—?" The slaver cut off his incredulous exclamation and pursed his lips in his shiny beard. "Fine." He shrugged, spreading his hands to indicate his generosity. "And the flying machine."

Rani nodded and tried not to think of all the children who were huddled beneath the deck. She tried not to think of the girls who were even now rewarding their soldiers for rising up against their Amanthian guards. She tried not to think of the lies that she had told those girls, the stories that she had woven to get the ship back to land with the least amount of bloodshed, with the fewest lives lost.

All of her manipulations were likely to be for nothing. Suditha, Landur, all the other children . . . If Rani could not do the impossible, if she could not find Hal and convince him to pay Teleos's extortion, the Little Army would be heading back to Liantine.

Nevertheless, they now had *some* chance, a single ray of hope.

Crestman and Teleos shook hands over their bargain, and the three children were escorted from the crowded cabin. Mair took one look at Rani's face and darted belowdecks. The Touched girl would tell the Little Army what had happened. She would tell them that the ship was turning about, that they were heading back to King Sin Hazar. She would tell them that Rani and Crestman had been successful.

Before Rani could follow her friend, Crestman gripped her arm. With his free hand, he tilted her face, moving her about so that the moonlight bounced in her eyes. "It's not easy to do what you did in there."

"What I did? I struck a bargain."

"Aye. You bargained with children's lives. You bargained to save the four of us, even though the currency you paid was children's lives."

Rani swallowed hard. Four was such a small number. "I chose to get us back to Amanthia. I chose to give us a chance for freedom, a chance to reach Hal."

"You acted like a general."

Rani stared at the captain as his words prickled across the nape of her neck. She shook her head, wondering if she could possibly make him understand. "Not like a general, Crestman. Like a merchant, making my best bargain. Or . . . or like a guild-mistress. I chose what was best for my people, over all, when I had next to nothing to bargain with. I did what had to be done."

There was a chance, after all. A shadow of a ghost of a vestige of a chance. They might find Hal. He might agree to the twenty-five bars of gold. He might spare the Little Army.

A sailor cried out in the night, and Rani felt the ship begin to turn about. The great sails swelled with wind, and the craft creaked as it shifted its heading from Liantine back toward Amanthia. Rani swayed as the ship lurched, but Crestman tightened his grip on her arm, steadying her. "We've begun, then." His voice was grim.

"Aye." She matched his tone. "And may Doan help us find King Halaravilli."

She whispered the prayer, almost losing the name of the god of hunters in the sounds of the wind and the waves, and the sigh of the soldier standing beside her.

Hal knelt before the makeshift altar in his tent, bowing his head against the sharp wooden edge of the platform. He had tried to pray all evening, tried to pull words together to exorcise the demons that so often whispered in his mind. Nothing worked, though. Nothing brought him the peace of his childhood prayers, his appeals to the simple gods of love and family, of nobles and playthings. Whatever words he spoke, whatever prayers he prayed, Hal kept seeing the mute smith splayed against the wall of the earthen pit, mouth gaping around the quivering shaft of an arrow.

"Hail, Roat, god of justice," Hal began again. "Look upon me with favor, great god Roat. Know that I have acted to further your ways among men. Know that I have tried to bring your wisdom to my actions."

Words. Empty, formulaic words.

Was it justice for a man to be cut down, when he had merely acted in service to his king? Was it justice to forfeit a single life for the three score and ten who had been murdered by those impossible glass eggs? What about the twisted genius who had conceived of the eggs? What about the king who had commanded him? Where was Hal to find justice on a cold winter night, as his troops besieged a strange northern city?

And even that siege wasn't certain to bring justice, in the end. Hal's army was encamped outside the gates of Sin Hazar's capital, spread out on the plain, just beyond reach of an expertly shot arrow. They had effectively cut off the merchants' road into the city; they had severed Sin Hazar's landward supply routes.

There was nothing Hal could do, though, about the sea. He had only a handful of ships at his command. They had taken up their positions in Sin Hazar's harbor, but there were too few to cut off the Amanthians completely. Sin Hazar would be able to sneak in fish and supplies, run any number of craft around Hal's blockade.

Realizing that his attention had wandered from his prayers once again, Hal stifled an oath. As if in reply to his scarce-swallowed curse, he heard cloth shift behind him. Farsobalinti must have entered, ready to help him prepare for bed. Fine. Enough of this kneeling, of this self-abasement. If the gods wanted to send Hal wisdom, they could find him in his dreams.

"Ach," he spoke aloud, and settled one hand on the altar as he clambered to his feet. "Farso, it's colder tonight than it was *last* night. Why didn't we march south when we had the chance?"

"Aye, Your Majesty. If you had marched south, things might have been so much simpler."

Hal whirled at the voice, so much deeper than Farso's boyish tenor. "Tasuntimanu."

The councillor bowed slightly, his broad face impassive. "Sire."

"Where is Farsobalinti? What did you do to my squire?"

"Nothing, Your Majesty. I told him to take a walk, to go warm his hands over one of the campfires. I told him I would serve you this evening. I've come to speak with you privately, Sire. As one man to another."

Hal started to call for his guards, but he stopped. If Tasunti-manu had meant to murder him, the earl could have cut Hal down while he knelt at prayer. There must be something else the coun-

cillor wanted to achieve. Hal took the precaution of moving behind the altar, placing the wooden stand between them. He wished
that he had his sword at his side, but he had left the weapon
across the tent, tossed carelessly onto his low cot when he had
decided to pray. Hal forced a shrug into his words, and asked,
"What do you want, Tasuntimanu?"

"I've been trying to speak with you for nearly a fortnight,
Your Highness."

"I've been busy commanding a war."

"Not too busy to meet with Lamantarino."

"May he walk the Heavenly Fields," Hal said piously, making a religious sign across his chest.

Tasuntimanu followed suit, but he spoke before his hand had
dropped to his side. "Not too busy to meet with Lamantarino, or
your other councillors."

Hal sighed. "I did not mean to avoid you, Tasuntimanu." He
hoped that the honest fatigue in his voice would be enough to
mask the lie.

"If I only wished to speak to you for myself, Your Majesty,
that would be one thing. But I come on behalf of others. Others who cannot abide your silence."

"Others?"

"Aye." Tasuntimanu stepped up to the altar, settled his broad
hands across the wood surface. Hal drew his own fingers back,
reluctant to allow the nobleman so near his flesh. "I speak for
the Fellowship, Your Majesty. I come to you in their name."
Tasuntimanu studied Hal's face and apparently did not find the
recognition he sought. "The Fellowship of Jair," he prompted.

"I understood you, man."

"You made promises back in the city, Your Majesty. You told
Glair that you would seek my counsel before you took action."

"I was not given the *opportunity* to consult you, Tasuntimanu.
When I learned that Lady Rani had been executed, I needed to
act immediately. I needed to bring my armies north, to avenge
the lady. To preserve the honor of my kingdom."

Tasuntimanu leaned forward and grasped Hal's wrists. The
king jerked back by reflex, fighting to free his hands, but the no-

bleman only tightened his grip. His spatulate fingers dug into Hal's flesh, pulled the king forward until their faces were only inches apart. "Did you, Your Majesty? Did you need to ride north?"

"I am a king," Hal lashed out, "anointed before the Thousand Gods! Remove your hands, or I will call my guards."

"You were a member of the Fellowship before you were king," Tasuntimanu replied, but he loosened his grip. "We remember the oaths you swore, even if you have forgotten them."

"I forget nothing, my lord." Hal flexed his arms and let his cloak fall more naturally about his shoulders. "*Nothing.*"

Tasuntimanu studied him for a moment, shaking his head with grim disapproval. "This did not need to be so difficult, Your Majesty. If only you had permitted me to speak with you earlier, before we traveled this far north. Before you set siege to Amanthia." The nobleman stepped back, letting his weight fall on his heels. "The Fellowship of Jair commands all its members not to interfere with its business in Amanthia. You must order your men to break camp at dawn. Break the siege and return to Morenia."

Hal started to laugh with incredulity. "Break—" he began, but trailed off as he realized that Tasuntimanu was not smiling. "You're actually serious! You think that I can just ride south for the winter and ignore the fact that my brother is a traitor behind the walls of that city. You think that I can just forget that they executed Rani Trader! Rani, and presumably another member of the so-called Fellowship, Mair."

"You're the king of Morenia. You can do whatever you want."

Hal spluttered in disbelief. "Do you realize what my men would do? How long would I last on the throne of Morenia, Tasuntimanu? I'd be cast down before we got back to the city."

"You exaggerate, Your Majesty."

"Not by much."

"It may be difficult, Your Majesty, but you must accept my word that it is necessary. We could have avoided this unpleasantness if you had listened to me in Morenia. If you had permitted my counsel before."

"There was no way to avoid this!" Hal hissed. "Bashanorandi would have turned traitor whether I sought your counsel or not! Rani Trader and Mair would have been murdered by that Amanthian monster if I prostrated myself before Glair or not! Your Fellowship could not change what has happened here!"

"*My* Fellowship, Your Majesty?" Tasuntimanu let his own voice spark. "It is *our* Fellowship, Sire! *Our* Fellowship. And it is *our* plans that you will destroy if you persist in this siege. Years of hard work, a treasury emptied of gold, all for naught! All so that you can get your vengeance for a treacherous bastard, a Touched wench, and a dead-and-buried merchant brat!"

Not buried, Hal wanted to argue. Not consigned to a frozen northern grave. Surely Sin Hazar must have granted Rani a pyre.

Granted a pyre. Purifying fire. Murder for hire.

Hal managed to focus his attention past the voices, concentrate on the true thrust of Tasuntimanu's words. "Years of work and countless gold? What has the Fellowship done, Tasuntimanu? What have you orchestrated, and only now deigned to tell your king?"

The councillor glanced at the tent flaps, as if he had just remembered that the night was passing, that the stars were rising and setting, and dawn would come all too soon. Dawn, or Farsobalinti, or some other petitioner, to take away Halaravilli. A light kindled in Tasuntimanu's eyes as he replied, "The Fellowship, Your Majesty. It's larger than you think. We have brethren in all the kingdoms, east and west, north and south of Morenia."

"Glair said as much."

"Aye. But she stopped short of telling you that the Fellowship has a plan, a dream of uniting all the kingdoms under one leader. We await the Royal Pilgrim to gather all the lands under the banner of Jair. The Royal Pilgrim will guide all his people in the ways of the Thousand Gods."

Hal heard the words, heard the worshipful tone, but he wasn't impressed. He had surmised at least that much of the plan when Glair first told him of the Fellowship's shadowy reach. "And how does my treacherous brother fit into your schemes? How can it possibly help the Fellowship to let Bashanorandi live? To let two ladies' deaths go unavenged?"

"Prince Bashanorandi is a tool, Your Majesty. As were Rani and Mair. As are you and I. We all pale in significance to the Fellowship, to the power of Jair. Blessed be the Pilgrim."

"Blessed be the Pilgrim," Hal muttered in annoyance, making the appropriate sign to spur on Tasuntimanu's confession.

The councillor's words fell more rapidly as his religious fervor rose. "We may all be tools, but we pale in significance next to Sin Hazar. The Amanthian king is strong, you know. He is fearless, and he rules his kingdom with an iron fist, with plans to advance his holdings far and wide."

"You need hardly remind me," Hal said dryly. "I'm aware of my enemy's strength." He paused for a moment and felt a tumbler click into place. "Wait! What are you saying? Does the Fellowship intend *Sin Hazar* to be its Royal Pilgrim?"

"No!" Tasuntimanu's protest was almost too hasty; he exclaimed like a man awakening from a nightmare. His breath came faster as he protested, "Not Sin Hazar! He would be too strong, and he does not walk the paths of the Thousand Gods."

"Then why preserve his kingdom? Why forbid me to fight him?"

"The Fellowship has already arranged to do away with Sin Hazar. All our actors are in place. If you call Sin Hazar out to battle, you risk upsetting plans that have been more than a decade in the making."

"But if *I* don't stop him, who will?"

"The Yrathis."

"What?" The answer was so unexpected that Hal could not believe that he had heard properly. "Tasuntimanu, you listened to our spies' report this afternoon. Sin Hazar has surrounded himself with mercenaries—there must be seven hundred of them. Even the Fellowship can't have bought off seven hundred Yrathi mercenaries."

"Not seven hundred, Your Majesty. We only needed to turn a handful. Fewer than a dozen, all told." Hal felt the confusion on his face, knew that he must look like a fool. Tasuntimanu leaned forward and enunciated his words as if he spoke to a child, but he packed a lifetime of passion into each word. "We bought the men closest to the throne. The Fellowship has purchased Sin Hazar's own guard."

A chill convulsed Hal's spine, but he could not say what made him more afraid—the notion that the Fellowship had enough funds to corrupt Yrathi mercenaries, or the thought that the Fellowship could penetrate clear through to a king's—any king's!—inner circle. "But will that be enough?" he forced himself to ask. "Will Al-Marai be any easier to manipulate, for your purposes?"

"Al-Marai?" Tasuntimanu looked confused.

"Of course. If you eliminate Sin Hazar, then his heir will take the throne. His brother is next in line."

Tasuntimanu laughed mirthlessly. "How little you know of these northerners, Your Majesty! Al-Marai is a lion, a soldier. He'll never sit on the Amanthian throne. Sin Hazar's crown will pass to the male child closest in a swan's line of descent. If Sin Hazar dies without issue, then Amanthia passes to—"

"Bashanorandi." Hal traced the answer a heartbeat before Tasuntimanu could complete the diagram. "Felicianda's son would take the throne."

"Aye. And Bashanorandi will be a weak king. He'll be a king the Fellowship can manipulate at will. When we open the door to war with the Liantines in a few years, Amanthia will fall like a child's toy soldier."

Hal listened to his councillor, to a man discussing the toppling of kingdoms with the dispassion of an equerry setting forth thoroughbred bloodlines. "So when Bashi dragged Rani up here . . ."

"The Fellowship rejoiced. We had thought we would have to tempt Bashanorandi to flee north, maybe even abduct him and drag him here. You see, after two years of doing nothing in your court, Bashanorandi seemed to have accepted his fate. Some of us argued that you must be forced to banish him, regardless of any sentimental notions you harbored in your father's memory. But First Pilgrim Jair blessed us, in his infinite wisdom. Bashanorandi made his move, just as we cemented our bonds with the Yrathis. We've hardly needed to pay a month's extra wages to keep the mercenaries in our employ."

A mechanical part of Hal's mind noted the gloating tone in Tasuntimanu's voice. A fine bargain the Fellowship had struck, and economical besides! How admirable for the Fellowship. "But Bashi did not come up here alone. He abducted Rani and Mair."

"Yes, Your Majesty." Tasuntimanu sounded perplexed.

"And Rani Trader and Mair belonged to your Fellowship!"

"They were sworn to our ways, yes."

"But did they ever know the sacrifice they made? Did they ever know your plans for the Amanthian throne?"

"Of course not, Your Majesty. We weren't ready to share the dream of the Royal Pilgrim with all our members. It would have become common knowledge in a fortnight."

Hal heard the explanation—clear, simple, beyond debate. Part of him wanted to cry out, to denounce the Fellowship's folly. They were twisting people's *lives*! They were manipulating living, breathing people, people who were sacred to the Thousand Gods!

But another part of Hal was numbed by the beauty of their plan. Conquer Amanthia from within. Set a puppet on the throne. Use the Amanthian caste system against the kingdom. How much the Fellowship saw. . . . How much they understood!

"And if I challenge Sin Hazar, then all your plans fall apart."

Tasuntimanu nodded, and a smile broke across his broad face for the first time during this exchange. Hal felt as if he were a slow pupil who had finally grasped a lesson, a sensation that was only heightened by his councillor proclaiming, "Precisely, Your Majesty!"

"If I conquer Amanthia, then it becomes part of Morenia. *I* take Sin Hazar's throne. Not Bashanorandi."

"You see why we cannot let that happen! Not with the outlay from our treasury to purchase the Yrathis. Not with the years we've spent measuring the Amanthians. Not with our plans for the Liantines."

Hal saw more than that. He saw the unspoken threat behind Tasuntimanu's words. If the Fellowship intended to let Hal stay in power, if they intended to let him rule Morenia for his natural life, then they would be content to let him add Amanthia to his kingdom. They'd be content to let him win the current battle and revel in the spoils.

The Fellowship had other plans for Hal.

The king shook his head in disbelief, wondering how he could have been so foolish, how he could have trusted the shadowy body of plotters. He forced himself to say, "And you expect me to concede, just like that."

How had he ever believed in the Fellowship? How had he trusted their machinations? Yet, even as he marveled at their manipulative evil, Hal realized that he had long known the Fellowship's willingness to tinker with monarchies. He'd accepted their assistance blithely enough when his own throne was on the line. He'd welcomed the Fellowship when they had helped to destroy Felicianda's treacherous plot in Morenia.

Enough. It was time to end this farce. Hal planted his hands on the altar and squared his shoulders as he leaned toward Tasuntimanu. "I'll never give in to your Fellowship, Tasuntimanu."

"Your Majesty?"

"You are right. I *should* have spoken with you more in Morenia. I should have spoken with you often on the long trail north. I should have made it perfectly clear that I will never—*never!*— permit the Fellowship to dictate how I rule my kingdom."

"Your Majesty, you must not say such things. It is dangerous to speak in absolutes."

"Dangerous? Let me explain danger, Tasuntimanu. It is *dangerous* to threaten me. It is *dangerous* to foment rebellion. It is *dangerous* to speak treason to the king of all Morenia!"

Tasuntimanu reacted faster than Hal had thought possible. One moment, the man was standing before him, fat and placid, his pudgy hands easy at his side. The next instant, he had unsheathed his sword and lunged across the altar.

If Hal had not reflexively stumbled backwards, he would have been decapitated by Tasuntimanu's blow. "Guards!" Hal bellowed, putting all his rage into the cry. "Guards! To me!"

Tasuntimanu gasped like a madman, swinging his sword

wildly. "Danger! Danger, you say!" He upset the altar and swiped again at Hal, who darted behind a camp chair. The king fumbled for his knife, desperate to make his way to his bed, to his own sword. He had no breath to waste in calling again for his soldiers. Tasuntimanu bellowed, "You have not *known* danger, Halaravilli ben-Jair!"

The councillor smashed through the camp chair, tangling his blade in its slotted back. Hal leaped to the side and tripped over a chest, a low casket that supported a map of the Amanthian capital. Hal fumbled for a weapon, for a pointer, anything at all. His fingers closed around a clay oil lamp, jostling the wick and splashing hot oil onto his palm. For just an instant, he recoiled from the searing kiss of the wick, and then he hurled the lamp toward Tasuntimanu. Droplets of oil cascaded through the air, raining down fire on the councillor.

As Tasuntimanu roared in rage and pain, Hal lunged over the chest, scrambling at last toward his cot and his sword. Then, the tent was full of armed men, echoing with the clatter of commands, the clang of sword on sword. "Beware!" Hal exclaimed from the cot, even as one of his soldiers sprawled on top of him, protecting him from the Fellowship's insane messenger. "He's mad!"

Hal craned his neck to see over his defender. One soldier used his own sword to catch at the hilt of Tasuntimanu's, pulling away the councillor's weapon. Two other guards dived forward, seizing the traitor's arms and forcing him to the ground. The earth crushed out the last sparks from the oil lamp, leaving behind the stench of burnt wool and singed hair. Yet another guard knelt in the middle of Tasuntimanu's back, setting a mailed fist across his neck.

Only after the traitor was further subdued with a pair of sharp jabs delivered to his lower back did Hal succeed in pushing off his protector. The king's chest seemed too small for his pounding heart as he fought for his feet, and he gladly seized his guard's hand, grateful for the assistance. He was vaguely aware that his palm was singed; his side was bruised. The breath was knocked

clear from his lungs, though, when he saw which man had in-
terposed his body to save his liege. "Puladarati!"

The old councillor was gasping for his own breath, his lion's
mane of grey standing out around his face as if he'd been caught
in a storm. "Aye, Your Majesty."

"But—I thought—"

"My liege, you're injured!" The former regent snapped out a
command to one of the soldiers, ordering the chirurgeon to be
summoned. Before the medic could arrive, Puladarati guided Hal
to a camp chair, his large hands gentle as he eased his king to a
sitting position. "Breathe deeply, Sire. You've only had the wind
knocked out of you."

"Only—" Hal paused to gasp, a reaction that was made even
more necessary by Puladarati sinking down before him, kneeling
like the most humble of supplicants in the House of the Thousand Gods. Before Hal could act, the silver-haired councillor had
pulled a silver-chased dagger from his well-worn boot.

Even as Hal registered that the older man was offering up the
weapon, was turning the hilt toward his king and resting the
sharpened edge against his own forearm, Hal recognized the blade.
It had been his father's long ago. It had belonged to King
Shanoranvilli, one of the treasures of the old king's line, supposedly passed from father to son. "Your Majesty," Puladarati intoned, ignoring the stunned look that Hal knew painted his own
face. The duke glanced toward the restrained Tasuntimanu, his
eyes sharp as daggers. "I failed you, by letting that . . . that traitor gain access to your person in the dark of night. I've failed
your father and let fall the faith he placed in me. I am not worthy to bear his gift. I am not worthy to serve you, Your Majesty."

"You—" Hal was still having trouble breathing, still finding
it difficult to piece together the fragments before him. His hand
pulsed where it was burned, and he was only now able to fill his
lungs against the shooting pain in his side. Shaking his head, he
reached out and settled his unburned palm upon the hilt of the
silver-chased dagger. In a flash, he could picture his father, imagine the old king giving up the blade to his most trusted of re-

tainers. "Puladarati, I thought that you . . . that you and Tasunti-manu . . . I thought—"

The leonine councillor's eyes widened for a moment, and then a slow smile spread across his face. "And I thought that you were a rebellious boy, who was reluctant to take advice from his elders. Even when those elders mistrusted some of your closest councillors. Even when those elders appointed themselves to watch over your councillors, to stay close to the danger."

A hot wave washed over Hal's face, a steaming mixture of shame and gratitude, all coated with searing relief. "My father chose you, Puladarati. I should have known. . . ."

"Aye. And if all princes listened to their fathers—" Puladarati grasped Hal's arm, holding him upright against the sudden darkness that swooped across his vision. The old man's three-fingered grip was as firm as iron. "Steady, Sire! Here. Sip this. It's wine."

"Your Grace—"

"Drink, my prince. It wasn't so long ago that I was your regent—I can still force this down your throat, if you don't follow my orders." Hal heard the gruff affection in the man's voice, saw the smile in his full beard. The first sip of wine brought a steadiness to Hal's breathing, a balance to his whirling head.

"Very well, Duke Puladarati." Hal looked to his other soldiers, to the other loyal men who surrounded Tasuntimanu. "I'll drink it down. But not until you get that cursed traitor out of my sight."

Puladarati bowed and gestured a command to the soldiers. "My pleasure, Your Majesty. My most extreme pleasure."

14

Rani's breath plumed as she looked out over the Amanth Plain. Campfire embers still glowed softly, and there were occasional jangles of harness and exclamations from soldiers who should have been asleep. Glancing at the stars, Rani could see that it was nearly midnight. There were precious few hours before sunrise, before sunrise and Teleos's return to open water with the Little Army.

Crestman's cloak was a welcome warmth across her shoulders. As if the young soldier heard her thoughts, he eased close beside her and whispered. "Not much farther. Their guards should stop us soon."

"Are you *certain* this is the right thing to do?" Rani scarcely mouthed the words. "How will they react to strangers, arriving in the middle of the night?"

"Not well." Crestman shrugged, settling his hand on his dagger. He had retied his hair as the foursome huddled at sunset, newly come to shore after Teleos's ship had put into a harbor just south of Amanth. The clout stretched the skin beside his eyes, and he looked far younger than he had on the ship three nights before, when he had argued with Teleos about the fate of his soldiers.

That battle clout kept Rani worried; she feared that she and her companions would be taken for Amanthian agents as soon as they reached the Morenian camp. What would happen if the guard refused to take them to Halaravilli? What would happen if some overeager soldier decided to rid his king of an Amanthian threat, acting before Rani could identify herself?

But what would happen if they stayed here till dawn, doing nothing?

Rani raised her chin and exhaled sharply. The steam from her breath rose like a beacon in the starlit night. "All right, then. Let's greet Halaravilli ben-Jair."

She led them into the camp with more confidence than she felt. Ten steps. Twenty. A hundred. She could make out a crimson banner farther down the road, barely stirring in the nighttime breeze. She knew there was a lion on the pennant; if the moon were closer to full, she could pick out Halaravilli's sigil. Another ten steps. Another twenty.

"Halt!" Even though Rani was expecting the command, she jumped, biting off a shriek. "Who dares disturb the camp of King Halaravilli ben-Jair?"

"It is I, Rani Trader, a friend of the house of Jair. I come with allies to help His Majesty, King Halaravilli."

In the space of a few heartbeats, torches were brought. Soldiers shouted orders, and rough hands seized Rani and her companions. They were hustled through the awakening camp, chivvied forward with the pressure of sharp steel points. Rani consciously kept her hands visible in front of her; she ordered her steps to calm smoothness. She would not give these nervous men any excuse to harm her.

Slowly, steadily, she turned her head and saw that her three colleagues marched behind her. Crestman had adopted her example, keeping his hands in plain view, well away from the hilt of his short sword. At Rani's glance, he moved up to walk beside her, setting his eyes directly ahead, as if he were marching to his death. Mair, on the other hand, had an amused smirk on her lips. She might have been nothing more than a Touched girl, playing out some midnight game in the streets of the Morenian capital.

Monny made Rani nervous, though. He kept glancing at his guards, darting his gaze about as if he were preparing to attack one of the soldiers. He had been told the truth about their return, and he had vowed to fight Sin Hazar under the command of his captains, of Crestman and Mair. Nevertheless his hands twitched open and closed, and Rani feared that he would make some nervous guard act without thinking.

Mair must have seen the danger as well; she dropped back until she was even with the boy. Once she had the child's attention, she extended her hands before her with ostentatious ease, setting an example of studied innocence. Monny scowled, but then he followed suit. He was no fool. He had received his orders, and he would comply.

Rani was no longer shivering by the time the foursome reached the center of the Morenian camp. Rather, her blood beat hot in her cheeks, as if her face were a beacon that beamed to the gates of Sin Hazar's city. She heard the growing murmur in the camp about her as men awakened their fellow soldiers. Her name traveled from stranger to stranger—Rani Trader, Rani Trader. There was the occasional addition of other names—Rai, or Ranita, or Ranimara—and one or two of the soldiers seemed to recognize Mair. But most of the attention was for Rani.

Beside her, Crestman began to hold back. Surely, she had told him that she was known to the king, that she had lived in the palace in Morenia. But he had apparently not absorbed that part of her story. The captain of the Little Army began to look at her sideways, awe flicking across his face.

Rani, though, did not have time to reassure Crestman. Before she was ready, before she had decided what she would say to Hal, she found herself in front of an ornate tent in the center of the camp. Lion banners hung at either side of the entrance. More than a dozen men stood on guard, hands on bared swords. Their protective presence was bolstered by six giants who stood at attention beside the entrance of the tent, iron pikes planted by their sides. The heavily guarded tent could only belong to King Halaravilli.

By some blessing of the Thousand Gods, Rani knew the leader of the king's guard. "Birilano," she said, inclining her head as if she had happened to encounter the soldier in a garden outside the palace.

"Lady Rani!" He sounded astonished, more surprised than even her sudden appearance could account for. His amazement was rapidly explained as he blurted out, "We were told that you were dead, my lady!"

Sin Hazar. The Amanthian king must have spread lies to account for Rani's lack of letters to Morenia! No wonder Sin Hazar had thought that he could banish Rani to Liantine. No wonder he had been so certain of his plot!

"No," Rani murmured, beginning to understand just how underhanded her opponent was. "I'm still very much alive. And here to see His Majesty."

"King Halaravilli sleeps, my lady. There was a . . . commotion in the camp earlier tonight, and he did not find his bed until late in the night."

A commotion? Well perhaps that explained the extra guards, the added excitement among all the soldiers they had passed. Before Rani could frame a courteous reply, Monny pushed his way forward. "Well we haven't slept either, soldier. The lady requests an audience with her liege!"

"Monny!" Rani and Mair both grabbed for the boy, even as a pike was lowered in his direction. Mair pulled the squirming redhead back to her side, tugging at his arm for good measure. Crestman looked daggers at his soldiers but did not speak.

Rani cleared her throat. "Birilano, this child is rash, but he does speak the truth. We urgently need to speak with King Halaravilli. More than seven score lives hang in the balance. Lives of children."

A flicker of emotion crossed the old soldier's face, but he shook his head. "I'm sorry, my lady. Duke Puladarati gave the strictest orders. It would mean my commission if I let you pass. We can send for the duke, though. If he grants you permission—"

Even as Rani started to structure some civilized plea, Monny twisted free from Mair's grasp. The child darted past Rani, howling like a cat in season. Oblivious to swords and pikes, he hurled himself at the entrance to King Halaravilli's tent.

The soldiers reacted immediately. Rani was thrown to the ground, one man straddling her back and two more pinning her arms. She yowled and tried to twist away, but she was firmly pinned. She saw that Crestman and Mair were similarly captured;

one of Crestman's captors took the added liberty of throwing a gauntleted arm across his windpipe, stretching his neck back until his eyes rolled up into his head.

Monny was seized at the threshold of the tent. One soldier grabbed him from behind, snapping an arm across his throat. Two more leveled pikes at his belly, and three swords were lowered with deadly precision. For all the weaponry focused on him, Monny gave no sign of heeding the danger—he continued to howl word-less threats, squirming and twisting and fighting to drag himself closer to Hal's tent.

Rani struggled to draw a breath against the soldier who strad-dled her, trying to fill her lungs enough that she could cry out an order to the boy. Before she could make herself heard, though, another voice rang across the plain. "*Hold!*"

Monny cut off his howl in mid-scream, and Rani sensed the soldiers above her bowing their heads. "What nonsense is this? Why can't my guards follow a simple order and let me sleep?"

Hal stood in the doorway of his tent, tunic rumpled and cloak thrown back over hastily strapped-on armor. His great sword pointed before him, the gleaming point directed at Monny's throat. "Who is this?" Hal demanded. "What *child* has invaded this camp?"

"Your Majesty," began Birilano. "I'm sorry, Your Majesty. I tried to keep them from awakening you! I knew you'd issued or-ders—"

"Who *are* these people?" Hal took a threatening step toward Monny. "What's your name, boy?"

"I'm Monny," the child announced. "Rani said that she needed to see you, and these men said she couldn't. Your Majesty," the boy added, clearly as an afterthought.

"Rani!" Hal lunged forward, planting the tip of his sword against Monny's throat. A drop of blood welled up, black in the torchlight. "What do you know of Rani?"

"My lord," Rani managed to squeak at last.

Hal whirled upon her, and even from a distance, she heard his breath catch in his throat. He dropped his weapon as if it were a snake, using his hand to trace a holy sign across his chest. "Tarn save us from ghosts who walk among us!"

"No ghosts, Sire!" Rani's words lit an ember of longing in Hal's face. She pressed on. "Sin Hazar has lied to you, Your Majesty. Only one of his many crimes."

"Rani. Rani Trader."

"Aye, Sire." Hal's hands flicked in a command, and the soldiers who had pinned Rani dragged her to her feet. She managed a shaking curtsey. "Alive and at your service, Sire."

For a long minute, Hal was unable to speak. Rani could see that exhaustion had carved the flesh from his bones, exhaustion or worry or fear. Dark circles stood out beneath his eyes, as if someone had rubbed pitch beneath his lashes. For just an instant, Rani flashed back to the Hal who had been her inquisitor when she had been required to answer for her sins back in Morenia, and she wondered where that boy-king could have gone. The youth who stood before her now was infinitely older, wiser, sadder.

Hal raised a pale hand toward Rani, summoning her to move closer. She met his eyes and took a step, barely flinching when the king's finger traced the sun drawn upon her cheek. "Rani," he whispered.

There was a thicket of emotions behind the word. Rani's heart leaped in her chest, pounding so hard that it made her gasp. She leaned toward Hal, her teeth catching her lower lip as his single inquisitive finger was replaced by his palm. She closed her eyes as she tilted her head, letting his caress linger on her cheek.

Finally, when she felt her knees trembling, when she doubted that she could whisper a reply, she swallowed hard and drew back from Hal's touch. There were battles to be fought, after all. Children to be saved. Kingdoms to be won.

Nevertheless, she wished that Hal had followed her when she moved back; she wished that she could feel his flesh against her cheek one more time.

Before either of them could speak again, Duke Puladarati pushed his way through the guards. "Your Majesty, I've just heard! My lady!"

There was a flurry of activity, and Rani found herself ushered

into the tent. Monny was hurried behind her, along with Mair and
Crestman. Rani made introductions all around, fighting to be heard
over Monny, who was trying to explain to Crestman that he had
not intended to be disobedient, that he had only been trying to
get the king's attention. Rani spoke rapidly, explaining how she
and Mair had found themselves with two soldiers in the Little
Army, breaching the perimeter of Hal's camp, but there were too
many questions, too much commotion, too many interruptions by
the soldiers and Monny and Puladarati.

"Silence!" Hal finally made himself heard above the chaos.
"Puladarati! Take these others from my tent. See that they are fed
and given warmer clothes. I'll speak with Lady Rani and learn
her tale."

"Your Majesty." Puladarati bowed, his grey hair flying. "I'll
see these others attended to, but you should not be alone with
Rani Trader." At Hal's protest, the former regent raised his hand,
three fingers summoning attention. "We still do not know how
Rani came to be in these northlands, months ago. Need I remind
you that your own falcon-master was murdered when Rani disappeared? We do not know that Rani Trader is a friend to your
throne."

"I will not waste time arguing with you, my lord. Leave whatever guards you deem I need, but get these other people out of
my tent." Puladarati grumbled, but he appointed a half dozen soldiers to stay with the king. He made a show of choosing the
largest and most sinister of the guards. Only when they had taken
up their watchful stance, weapons bared and faces impassive, did
Puladarati begin to escort Monny and Mair away.

Crestman, though, struggled to stay behind. "I would stay with
Rani," he growled, reaching by habit for the sword that had already been removed from his waist.

"I'm fine, Crestman," Rani said levelly.

"But, Rani, there are armed men!"

"Go, Crestman." She saw the uncertainty in his eyes, the fear—
not for himself, but for her safety. She thought of the faith that
he had put in her, the faith that had turned him away from his
own king, from the Little Army. She forced her voice to a gen-

tle register as she admonished the boy-captain, "My king will not harm me."

Crestman cast one last anguished glance toward Hal, but he complied.

Hal watched the tent flap close behind Crestman. Rani saw unexpected emotions flicker across the king's face—she recognized surprise, and gratitude, and something that might have blossomed into jealousy if it were fed and watered.

Hal kept his gaze averted, his eyes fixed on the tent flap, and only when the silence had stretched a little too long did he force his words to steadiness. "That one is devoted to your cause."

"Then he is devoted to you, Your Majesty."

Hal sucked in a deep breath, and his voice was tight as he asked, "Why did you not send word to me?"

Rani wished that he would look at her. "At first, Sin Hazar would not let me. And when I escaped, I was with his Little Army. I could scarcely command a messenger to ride to their enemy." Rani took a step closer to Hal, ignoring the soldiers who tensed at her motion. She scarcely restrained herself from reaching for his hand. "Your Majesty, I did not know that Sin Hazar had lied to you. If I'd known, I would have managed, somehow, to get word to you."

Hal kept his head bowed, his eyes averted. Rani felt his mistrust like an icicle through her breast. Not mistrust that she would harm him—that had not been a fear since the heartrending moment when he had recognized her in the shadows outside his tent. No, he mistrusted her *words*. "Hal—" she started to say, and the king flinched as if she had struck him.

Thinking of the trials they had shared in Morenia, of the companionship that they once had known, of the heat of his palm against her cheek when she had stood outside his tent, Rani gaped in pain. "Your Majesty, forgive me! Be not angry with me for Sin Hazar's evil!" He stiffened but did not meet her pleading eyes. "Please, Hal!" A sob broke from her lips on the last word, and she raised her hand to dash away furious tears.

Before she could wipe her face, though, Hal stepped closer. He caught her wrists in a surprisingly firm grip. His lips quivered as he tightened his grasp, stretching the skin until she felt it bruise against her bones. "I heard the voices!" Hal whispered. "*They made me believe that you were gone.*"

"V—Voices, Your Majesty?"

"Aye." He nodded as if she should understand him, but then a look of wonder spread across his face. "I heard the voices through all these long months, but now they're gone. They left when I confronted Tasuntimanu. They did not speak after I faced him down!"

"Tasuntimanu?" Rani asked, uncomprehending. Could Hal mean their colleague in the Fellowship of Jair? But what could the Fellowship have to do with voices? And how could Rani ask, with a dozen soldier-ears listening to every word? To be certain that they spoke of the same man, Rani said, "In the name of Jair. . . ."

"Aye," Hal agreed. "In the name of Jair. Tasuntimanu, and Yrathi mercenaries, and . . ." He finally met her eyes, pinned her with a burning gaze that held mystery and truth and deep, dark suffering. In his eyes, though, she also saw another emotion: determination. She raised her chin a bit, in response to the bold power that steeled her liege.

As if recognizing her salute, he raised her hands between them and brushed his lips across their tanned backs. Rani felt the caress like a sweep of silk down her spine, and she shuddered as she forced herself to hold his depthless gaze. She leaned closer as he whispered, "We have much to talk about, Rani Trader."

"Aye, Your Majesty, but we haven't much time."

"Time? We've the better part of winter, I'm afraid. My army has set siege to the Amanthians, but our blockade won't hold. They'll get goods by sea."

Rani shook her head as she let Hal draw her over to two low camp chairs. Urgency bubbled up beneath her heart, and she started to tell him of the Little Army and Teleos, of Liantine and the slave markets. "Your Majesty, we have until sunrise to get back to the harbor. Otherwise, seven score children will sail into slavery."

*   *   *

It took Rani nearly an hour to tell Hal all that had happened in Amanthia. She forgot about the listening guards as she related what she had suffered, from Bashanorandi kidnapping her on the hill outside of the City, to her queasy journey north, to settling into Sin Hazar's court as a hostage.

As she related her tale, she sensed the soldiers' disbelief. She went a long way toward restoring their trust, though, when she showed Hal the long angry scar that twisted along her leg, remnant of the sword that had plunged into the hay wagon as Rani and Mair huddled to escape from Sin Hazar. The scar, and her passion, and Hal's unyielding faith—by the time Rani was through with her tale, the soldiers had relaxed their vigilant stance, had begun to mutter among themselves of pride and revenge.

Two of the guards even vied with each other to lead a hastily assembled expedition to the harbor south of Sin Hazar's capital. Hal ordered twenty men to collect Teleos, to bring the slave trader into camp.

"We bargained with him in good faith!" Rani objected.

"Aye, as good a faith as one can have in a thief, a slavemaster, and a procurer." Hal nodded to the soldiers. "Bring him here, but leave the Little Army, under ample guard. We won't test their loyalty to their Morenian liberators. Not yet." As the guard started to slip out of the tent, Hal called out one more instruction. "Bring the flying machine as well; have men carry it here at double speed."

Then Hal began his own tale. He related the battles that he had fought in his council chamber, how he had argued that he must lead his army north. Several times, the king glanced at his remaining soldiers, and Rani understood that there were bits he was not telling, information that could not be shared in public. Nevertheless, it took him hours to relate all that had transpired in her absence. He concluded by reciting fresh intelligence from one of his scouts. "And so," Hal ended, "it seems that some of the Yrathi mercenaries are prepared to turn against Sin Hazar."

"Are we certain that they've been bought off? Can we trust your scouts' sources?"

"By Jair, we have no choice!" By Jair. Then the Fellowship

was definitely involved. Well, Glair could manipulate Yrathi mercenaries, if anyone could.

There were more secrets. Rani could see them carved across Hal's cheeks, rubbed into the shadows beneath his eyes. She longed to linger with him beside a cheery hearth, sipping mulled wine and talking, as they had spoken in the long days after King Shanoranvilli had passed through the Heavenly Gates. But time was a luxury they could not afford on the Amanth Plain. There'd be time enough to talk if they survived the coming battle.

As if to underscore that thought, a soldier ducked into the tent and bowed low.

"Your Majesty, the flying machine is here."

"Already? Then, what, it must be nearly dawn?"

"Yes, Your Majesty. An hour off or so. The soldiers bringing the slaver should be here shortly after sunrise."

Hal nodded and gestured for Rani to lead the way outside the tent. The air was freezing. Rani felt it catch in her lungs, prickle at the corners of her eyes. By the time she had walked with Hal to the northern edge of the army's camp, her fingers were numb.

She was grateful to see that Puladarati had followed Hal's orders to the letter: Crestman, Monny, and Mair were clustered on the leading edge of the camp, each swathed in a crimson-dyed woolen cloak. Someone had even managed to find the newcomers matching woolen mittens, although one of Crestman's lay on the frozen ground by his feet.

The youth was leaning over the flying machine, frowning at the spindly structure. He gestured for a nearby soldier to lean in closer with a torch. "There's something off with the harness, here." He glared at the contraption, and the Morenian moved even closer with his flickering light. "Careful, man!" Crestman exclaimed, pushing the guard's arm back. "This thing is held together with glue and a prayer! The joints will burn like oilcloth if you get that thing too close!"

The chastised soldier swore softly, shaking his head as Crestman made some adjustment to the rigging. It was several long minutes before the straps fell to his satisfaction, and he still frowned at Monny as he instructed the boy: "Lean back, Monny."

"What are you doing?" Hal finally asked, unable to keep silent any longer.

Before Crestman could reply, Duke Puladarati stepped forward from the shadows that surrounded the mothlike machine. "Your Majesty, we think it best to surprise the Amanthians with their own creation. While you were conferring with Lady Rani, your generals have held their own conference. We are agreed that we must use the flying machine, now, before Sin Hazar sees it from the city walls."

"We haven't had a chance to think this through!" Hal protested. "Why can't we just cover the thing, and make our decision later?"

"We've been encamped outside the city for nearly a week, Your Majesty. You can be certain that the Amanthians know every corner of our camp; they've watched us through their spyglasses since we settled here. They'll see some large machine, even if it's under wraps. They'll know something is amiss."

"Then place it in a tent!"

"To what end, Your Majesty? If the Thousand Gods have seen fit to send us the contraption, we'd be fools not to use it."

"Even if we know nothing about it? Even if we've only just learned of its existence?"

The burly councillor sighed. "Your Majesty, you know that we've been searching for a means into the city." When Hal did not respond, Puladarati held up his maimed hand, gesturing with one finger. "We've considered mines, but we haven't been willing to risk your men." The councillor extended another finger. "We've cut our battering ram from the forest and dragged it into camp, but again, we dared not risk the men who would be exposed for the time—for the *days* it could take—to break the city gates." He extended his last digit, gesturing with his deformity toward the flying machine. "This creation appears to us as a gift from the gods."

"What exactly do you plan?" Hal's curiosity was winning out over his caution.

"Just this, Your Majesty. The boy, there, will be strapped in. . . ." The duke settled his good hand on Hal's shoulder and guided the king to the edge of the cluster of people. Rani could not make out the rest of his words, but she could hear his tone—reasoned, calm, confident.

She turned her attention to the flying contraption.

"There you go," Mair was crooning, as she cinched a band across Monny's chest. "Is that tight enough? No? How about that?"

"Is this truly necessary?" Rani asked. "Can't we at least wait until daylight?"

Crestman spared her the quickest of glances. "You heard the old man. We spoke with the generals while you consulted with the king." Rani heard the seeds of jealousy in his voice, and she swallowed a hundred arguments. "All the soldiers are agreed. We should attack at dawn. The light will be trickiest then—the Amanthians won't be able to see well to shoot Monny down, but he should be able to make out his targets."

"Targets?"

Crestman sighed at her uncomprehending tone. "Do you still think this is a toy? It's a weapon, Rani. One of Davin's finest. Monny should be able to take out the guards at the gate. The soldiers stationed in the towers, too, on either side of the gate."

"But we aren't ready to attack! This is happening too fast!"

Crestman started to snap a reply, but Mair stepped up to Rani's side. "Too fast for what, Rai? Hal's men have been here for a week. Their supplies won't last forever. They came north to fight, not to freeze on an icy plain."

"But they didn't even know about the flying machine until we appeared!"

"They knew they needed to get into Sin Hazar's city. Why should they care how the gates are opened?" When Rani still refused to back down, Mair grabbed her arm. "Hal's generals are agreed. Puladarati will convince the king. You know this must be done, Rai. Are you going to help us or just stay in the way?"

"I—" Rani started to protest, but then she stopped herself. There was no need to argue every point. She was back with King Halaravilli, back with the army of Morenia. She no longer needed to make every decision to save herself, to save Mair, to save an army of children. Relief uncoiled beneath her heart like a fern frond in spring, and Rani asked, "What can I do?"

Crestman grunted. "Check the arrows. Make sure that they're all pointed down, with the fletching undisturbed." Rani stepped up to the machine, ducking under the wings to follow Crestman's instructions.

She had just completed her inspection when Hal returned from his conversation with Puladarati. The king's interest was clearly captured by the flying machine, and he walked all the way around the contraption. The sky had begun to pale in the east, a blush of grey leaching across the star-speckled blackness. The light wasn't much, but it was enough for Hal to make out the machine's joints, to study its folded parchment wings. When he had completed his survey, he asked Crestman, "Are you ready, then? It's nearly dawn."

Crestman ignored the question, reaching out instead to tug at the thicket of leather straps and willow strips that surrounded Monny. He ran his hand down one membranous wing, refolding a flap so that it lay even with the ground. "Mair?" Crestman asked, and the Touched girl nodded from the other side of the device.

"Yes," Crestman finally said, turning back to Hal. It took him a moment to swallow and add, "Your Majesty."

Hal nodded and settled a hand on Rani's arm, as if he were going to protect her from the flying machine. Or as if he were staking claim to her. "Very well then." He turned his attention to the pale Monny. As he faced east, the boy's freckles could just be made out in the growing light. "May Fairn bless you, soldier. Fairn and all the Thousand Gods."

Rani let Hal guide her back several steps as Crestman and Mair crouched beside the flying machine. She could hardly believe that everyone around her was so calm. This was the battle she had longed for, while she was held captive in Sin Hazar's court. This was the battle the flying machine had been made for.

As the eastern sky melted to pearl, Crestman and Mair began to call their count.

"Stroke!" Crestman urged. "Stroke!"

"Mon! Mon!" Mair added, timing her orders between Crestman's exclamations.

Monny's face tightened in concentration, and he flapped his

arms up and down. He caught his tongue between his teeth, and then he began to move his legs, sawing them back and forth, in rhythm with Mair's chant.

Rani felt Hal's fingers dig into her arm, cutting deep into the flesh above her elbow. "By Fairn!" the king exclaimed, and Rani felt a little of his wonder, of the astonishment that she had first known when she'd seen what Davin's engine could do.

And then Monny lifted the flying machine from the ground. He flapped the wings a dozen times, sending ripples of freezing air over the gaping Morenians. Rani's hair blew back from her face, driven by the wind the machine created. Monny rose into the freezing dawn, pumping higher and higher, until he was even with the towering city walls.

Rani stepped forward, dragging Hal with her until they stood beside Crestman and Mair. Crestman had stopped his cadence as soon as Monny rose up, but Mair was still whispering, the one repeated syllable barely audible amid the pluming smoke of her breath. "Mon. Mon."

By the time the giant moth moved over the city, the sky had bleached to dirty grey. Rani could make out the giant wings flapping up and down; she imagined that she could see Monny's fierce expression. His eyes would be half-closed with concentration, his arms rigid like boards.

For one heart-stopping instant, the flying machine swooped lower, and Rani caught her breath. Even as the great moth recovered and climbed again, Rani wondered at how light-headed she felt. Monny must be exhausted as well; he also had not slept for the entire night, and for the long, trying day before. Rani hugged her arms closer about her chest, ignoring the ache that bloomed in her muscles as if she were commanding the moth herself.

As the grey light faded to dull white, Rani saw six soldiers materialize in silhouette at the top of the city gates. The men stood in full battle gear, their helms donned and their heads tilted up as they studied the demon-bird that hovered above them. Rani could just make out cries from within Sin Hazar's city, and then she saw more guards flood the walls. Crestman had been correct when he said that soldiers would storm to defend the towers; at least a dozen men scrambled over each stone construction.

Monny clearly saw them as well. Rani caught her breath as the boy swooped lower with his flying machine. She imagined she could see him twist his head, pulling back on the leather strap that he held between his teeth. In the tricky light of first morning, Rani could make out the dark rain of arrows released from beneath the drab, mothlike wings.

As the first round was set free, the flying machine leaped higher, relieved of some of its weight. Many of the steel arrow tips managed to find their homes. Men bellowed in pain, loud enough to be heard on the plain below. Rani saw one guard fall from the gate, tumbling backward to land on the hard ground outside the city.

Monny swooped in again, heading to the east tower for his next attack. Rani imagined that some of the men must have taken cover, but Monny released another volley of arrows.

Now, men were cheering in the Morenian camp, chanting Halaravilli's name as the flying machine wrought its havoc. Monny seemed to be borne aloft by those cries; he flapped his wings with powerful downstrokes. He soared higher, sailing across the gates, coming to hover over the west tower. One beat. Two. Rani imagined the boy beginning to tire. Even Monny must yield to exhaustion at some time. She thought of his pulling the leather strap one last time, twisting his neck to release one final volley of arrows.

There! One last rain of deadly black fell upon the tower. A guard bellowed as he fell, half-in an embrasure, half-sprawled against the side of the tower. The Morenian army erupted into another round of cheers. Every soldier was now awake and pounding sword on shield. Foot soldiers who had nothing but pikes beat their weapons against the ground, screaming victory as the sun finally blushed the sky to full, bloody dawn.

"MON!" Mair screamed above the clamor, and Rani heard the frantic note, the sudden, sharp despair.

By the time Rani looked back to the city walls, she felt as if a lifetime had beat away. A figure stood on the western tower, mounted on a stone merlon, silhouetted against the bloody dawn. Rani could just make out a bow, arched against the bright sky.

For one horrible moment, Rani remembered another bow, another battle fought, when she had been nothing but a naive apprentice, staring up at her guild's handiwork in the cathedral. Then, a bow had brought disaster, had brought murder and treachery and the destruction of all the family Rani had ever known.

Now, sick and desperate, Rani turned toward Hal, saw that the king was studying the scene through a spyglass. Without thinking, she snatched the lens from his hands, raising it to her own eye. What she saw froze the prayer she'd been about to breathe.

The archer was Al-Marai. Sin Hazar's lion brother.

Monny must have seen the threat as well. The boy pumped his wings harder than before, forcing the machine to rise higher. His feet sawed back and forth, but somehow he had lost his rhythm, lost the careful balance that let him move forward. Rani saw the clutch of panic on Monny's freckled face, and she caught herself breathing, "Higher. Higher."

For even as Monny fought to control the flying machine, Al-Marai nocked an arrow to his bow. The warrior sighted down the shaft as Rani struggled to follow the line of the arrow, but her vision blurred. Swearing, she shook the spyglass and then returned it to her eye. The end of the arrow was still blurred, wavering in the dawn.

It took Rani another moment to realize what she was seeing. Al-Marai's arrow was alight, the flame bleached out against the morning sky.

As Rani watched, the lion made a slight adjustment in alignment. He pulled the bowstring to his ear, held it for a moment, and released the burning arrow.

The bolt shot true. Monny's arms were stretched above his shoulders, the moth wings at their apex. The arrow landed at a critical join in the upwind wing, kindling a tight knot of the glued framework. Orange flames blossomed from the glue, leaping across the stretched membrane and exploding up the dried willow bindings. As Rani screamed in horror, the fire raced across Monny's back, chewing into the other wing.

"Mon!" Mair cried again, the single syllable breaking like the flying machine.

Then, the flaming wings began to fold, twisted with the heat of their own burning. Rani watched as the child-soldier kicked once more, sending the moth leaping forward through the air. For a moment, she thought that Monny was trying to clear the wall, trying to land outside the city so that there was a chance, a prayer, that Hal's army could reach him, could save him. As she watched the winged machine arc down, though, she realized that salvation had never been Monny's goal.

Instead, the child swooped low, over the western tower. Al-Marai did not see the danger until too late; he must not have realized the searing pain that a child could endure. He must not have realized how well he had trained the Little Army, how well he had crafted a brave, strong soldier.

Monny caught the lion across the man's back, assaulting him with the full weight of the burning flying machine. The pair of warriors, child and man, toppled over the tower wall and fell atop the oaken city gates. The fighters' thrashing only served to fan the wings' final flames, and the gates themselves began to kindle.

Al-Marai and Monny were tangled in the flying machine, caught up in an inferno of burning leather and willow and rope. The gates had firmly caught fire by the time both man and boy were reduced to charred flesh. The flying machine crashed to the ground at the foot of the tower beside the gates, and the fire continued to chew its way into the wooden barrier.

Rani's belly twisted inside her, and she swallowed acid at the back of her throat. Before she could turn away, though, Mair was fighting to cross the plain, to run within range of Sin Hazar's archers.

"Mon!" she sobbed.

"No!" Rani tugged her arm free from where Hal still gripped her. She launched herself at her Touched companion. "Mair! No! You can't help him now! It's too late!" Mair twisted like a dragon on a pike, spitting and clawing at Rani. "Mair! Stop it! There's nothing you can do!"

Even as she fought with her friend, Rani was aware of orders issued behind her. The flames on the city gates were beginning to die down. Rani could see that the blackened oak planks still stood, but she knew they must be weakened, ready to tear from their iron hinges. As Rani gathered Mair closer, she heard Duke Puladarati issue orders for a battering ram to be brought forward.

Through the chaos, Crestman stood at attention. He did not lift a hand to help the soldiers behind him, to maneuver their massive tree trunk into position. He did not kneel beside Rani, help her to gather up the shivering Mair. He stood like a soldier, staring blankly at the city gates and the charred, blackened pile that had been two fighters.

Once the battering ram was in position, Hal strode beside the weapon, tossing his crimson cloak over his shoulders to display his gold-washed mail. Rani noted mechanically that dozens of men had taken up positions beside the ram. Hal began to exhort them to victory, telling them that they must make the most of a child's death, that they must cement the glory of Morenia.

Before Rani could bring herself to look again on Monny's blackened remains, on the one soldier from the Little Army who had offered up all to his king, a clarion call rang out. For just an instant, Rani was confused, thinking that the horn had blown in Hal's camp, to summon the men, to begin the battering ram's inevitable march.

Then, even as she realized that the metallic clangor came from atop Amanth's walls, she saw that the city gates were cranking open. They moved slowly, ponderously, as if the soldiers who operated the winches were afraid that the iron hinges would not hold. Nevertheless, the gates swung out, scraping aside the charred remains of boy and man and machine, until six men could ride abreast onto the plain.

It took Rani a moment to distinguish the company that did ride through the gap. She expected to see azure uniforms and Sin Hazar's dragon crawling atop the soldiers' helms. She expected to see the sprawl of lion tattoos across high cheekbones.

Instead, she could only make out blacked-scarred slashes across warriors' brows and glimmering cloaks of darkest midnight. Yrathi mercenaries—a dozen of them. They rode with their double-hooked pikes at the ready, bristling skyward like a deadly thicket. Each man had his sword bared as well, slung in Yrathi fashion from the pommel of his high saddle, ready to drive forward in an instant. The mercenaries' faces were implacable beneath their high helms, staring directly ahead, as if they did not see the battering ram, as if they were unaware of the Morenian soldiers who scurried away from their approach.

Sin Hazar's dragon banner floated in the middle of the company, rich cobalt blue mocking the bleached winter sky. Rani, by craning her neck, could make out the standard-bearer in the midst of the Yrathis, and she gasped as she recognized Bashanorandi.

So. The prince was reduced to a squire's job, wrestling with the long dragon banner to keep the standard firmly planted in his stirrup. He stared at the snapping silk with a concentration that bordered on religious devotion. The swan tattoo across his cheek stood out against his pale skin, accenting his ginger hair. His eyes watered in the stiffening breeze.

Behind Bashanorandi rode Sin Hazar, sitting tall and straight on his ebony stallion.

Without thinking, Rani strode to the front of the battering ram. She took her place beside Halaravilli as if she were destined to be there. For one fleeting instant, she longed for a horse, for anything to bring her on a level with Sin Hazar. But she had no mount. She had no shield, no sword. Nevertheless, she raised her chin in defiance.

Rani was vaguely aware of a barked order, and then she saw a company of soldiers fall into place around her. The armed men formed a semicircle about Hal and Rani, flexing their ranks to let Mair and Crestman pass through, and then Duke Puladarati.

Rani did not permit herself to think of how pitiful the Morenian troops looked, how insignificant the common southern soldiers were against Sin Hazar's splendid Yrathi contingent. At a hand signal from Puladarati, the Morenian guards bared their swords, turning their wicked blades toward the mounted mercenaries.

The two groups of warriors stood in stasis for only a moment, and then Bashanorandi kicked his mount through the Yrathian line. "Hail, Morenian scum!" Rani heard a lifetime of bitterness in the unchivalrous greeting, and she was not surprised to see Bashi's hateful glare directed at her before he turned his attention to his royal brother. "His Majesty, King Sin Hazar, King of all Amanthia, lord of the Iron March, and overlord of Aristine, orders you from this plain and commands you to return to your Morenian hovels. If you have taken leave of this plain by noon, he will show you mercy and not hunt you down like dogs."

Hal started to step forward, angry words patent on his face, but Duke Puladarati edged to the front of the group. He did not advance far, though, so that he would not have to look up too sharply at Bashi's mounted height. "So, boy. Do you lick your king's boots, as well as hurl insults on his behalf?"

"My name is Bashanorandi, and you'll address me as the prince I am!"

"I know your name. I know you're Felicianda's bastard, and I'll address you as a turncoat and a traitor."

Bashi's face paled to whey, and he gripped the Amanthian flag so tightly that the dragon swooped forward. "I am loyal to my true liege! I am loyal to King Sin Hazar!"

"Are you certain that's a wise choice, boy? Your Sin Hazar shoots down children as if they were geese!"

"Your *child* cost us our proudest general. Your child brought down Al-Marai, the bravest lion of the Amanthian house!"

"Al—" Puladarati started to retort, but Hal laid a hand upon his arm.

"Aye," Hal said, taking a single step closer to his brother and raising his voice so that it rang out clearly across the plain. "Bashanorandi, we cut down one your liege held dear. Well might your king mourn the loss of *his* brother, of Al-Marai. I, however, would not stop to spit on the grave of the traitor I called *my* own brother."

Bashi reacted faster than Rani would have thought possible. Bellowing his rage, he tossed his leg over his horse's back, shifting his grip on the dragon standard so that he brandished it like a pike, in fragile mockery of the still-silent Yrathi mercenaries.

He had already crossed half the distance to Hal, was already within a sword's length of the Morenian troops, when a cry rang out.

"Hold!" Sin Hazar's eyes flashed as he bellowed his command, and his lips disappeared within his beard. The king's left hand was stretched toward Bashanorandi, fingers rigid, as if he would cast a spell to freeze the boy. "Hold, I say!"

"Your Majesty," Bashi spluttered, spittle flying from his lips as he turned back toward his liege.

"I'll not command you again!"

Bashi opened his mouth to protest, but then he took in the Yrathi mercenaries, noted that the three front riders had lowered their pikes toward him. He suddenly seemed to realize that he was unhorsed, and on the edge of enemy troops. The tail of the dragon banner trailed across the ground, drifting close enough that Rani could have stomped it with her booted foot. With a convulsive shudder, Bashi uprighted the standard and planted it beside his own foot, as if he had intended, all along, to stake claim to this territory for his king.

If Sin Hazar appreciated the gesture, he gave no sign. Rather, he switched his attention from the trembling bastard prince to Hal. "Halaravilli ben-Jair, you trespass on our lands. We will grant you until noon to begin your retreat. We do not wish to shed blood between your house and ours, in honor of our blessed sister, who has gone to walk among the Thousand Gods. For Felicianda's memory, we will let you retreat to your borders."

"Felicianda was a traitor," Hal spat. Rani could not help but think his words would carry more weight if he were mounted on a horse, if he could look Sin Hazar in the eye. The Amanthian king evidently thought the same; he let his stallion jangle forward a few steps, forcing his Yrathi guards to edge up their own mounts. The motion only underscored Hal's danger.

"Felicianda was our sister, a swan, and a princess of the house of Amanthia!" Sin Hazar tugged on his ebony steed's reins. "I repeat, Halaravilli. You trespass on our land. We have ridden out to treat with you, so that you understand our men will *never* yield. Ride now and save yourself, or you will regret your decision when the fighting is done."

Hal's voice tightened. "Your army has already yielded. One boy in our ranks was able to take down your greatest general, your Al-Marai."

"Do not speak his name!" Sin Hazar's face twisted into a mask of fury, and Rani began to understand why the king had ridden from the safety of his palace, why he had passed through his city gates to the vulnerable plain. Sin Hazar was maddened by his loss. He spat, "Do not speak the name of our brother, of the lion of Amanthia. You could not have *touched* him if you had not used our weapons. You stole our engine! Now, with your own weapons, you have no hope of winning any battle!"

"Nor can you, Sin Hazar." Hal's voice was deadly quiet in the freezing air. "Nor can you hope to win, or you would not have ridden out here. Al-Marai would be ashamed."

"By Jair, you try our patience, upstart prince!" Even as Sin Hazar's face darkened with rage, Rani's gaze was pulled toward his Yrathi escort. She could not be certain, but she thought a handful of the men had started at their employer's oath. Before she could be sure, Sin Hazar continued, "If you wish to speak of shame, Halaravilli, look at the dogs that trail behind you. Ranita Glasswright!" Sin Hazar pinned Rani with his ebony eyes. "Have you told your king that you feasted by our side? Have you told him that you danced with us in the darkest hours after midnight?"

Rani refused to acknowledge the blush that leaped to her cheeks. With all the prepossession she'd gathered in her years at court, she forced her voice to a steady treble. "I've told him that you sent me to a prison camp, my lord. I've told him that you meant to sell me as a slave. Me, and Mair, and Crestman. And Monny who lies dead, yonder. I've spoken the truth to His Majesty, in the name of First Pilgrim Jair."

There. She was certain that she glimpsed movement this time. It was nothing much, probably would not have been visible if she'd been on a level with the mounted men. But from her compromising angle, she could just glimpse the Yrathis' fists tighten on their reins. For a single instant, several of the mounts tensed, ready to move forward. Then, almost as soon as Rani recognized the motion, the mercenaries lapsed back into their vigilant formation.

Rani darted a glance at Hal, to see if he had also noticed. She thought that he had; she thought that he ducked his chin just a bit in her direction. But she was not certain until she heard his next challenge. "And by Jair, Sin Hazar, I believed my vassal. I believed every word that Lady Rani told me, when she said that you were craven enough to enslave an army of boys, to procure your kingdom's girls for the Liantines."

On the third voicing of the Pilgrim's name, Rani was certain. The Yrathis were reacting to Jair, responding to the holy name.

Oblivious, Sin Hazar threw back his head to laugh. "Enslave boys? Procure girls? You're a child yourself, Halaravilli ben-Jair! You're a child, if you believe that wars can only be won with honor and glory and sacred prayers to the Thousand Gods."

Hal shot a glance at Rani, sparing her one tight nod as she shifted her grip to the dagger thrust through her belt. Then Hal raised his chin in defiance and called out, "Not to the Thousand Gods, Sin Hazar. To First Pilgrim Jair!" Hal shouted his challenge: "To me, Yrathis, in the name of Jair!"

Chaos.

Eight of the Yrathis reversed their pikes, driving them into their brothers' mounts. Horses screamed. Men cursed. Sin Hazar swore in the name of all the Thousand Gods, wasting breath in a helpless explosion of rage.

Hal unsheathed his sword and plunged into the maelstrom, burying his weapon in the chest of Sin Hazar's stallion. The beast crashed to the ground, scarcely giving its master time to leap free.

Even as the Amanthian king fought his way clear of his own stirrups, he fumbled for his scimitar, screaming for the Yrathis he had purchased to protect him. Those mercenaries, though, were engaged in a deadly battle with their own brethren, two Fellowship-bought men battling every one who stayed loyal to Sin Hazar.

Rani saw the instant that Sin Hazar recognized his danger, the precise heartbeat when he knew that he was trapped. Swearing viciously, he jerked his curved sword free from its sheath, brandishing the weapon high above his head. He threw back his head and screamed out an Amanthian battle cry, a ululation that echoed off his city walls.

As Sin Hazar tore his gaze from the dispassionate sky, he pinned Hal with his depthless midnight eyes. Rani could read the madness in his features, the death-knowledge on his face. He knew he was surrounded by traitors. He knew that battle was futile.

Rani watched as the morning breeze stiffened, catching the edges of Hal's crimson cloak. The king of all Morenia raised his dripping sword, as if he would consecrate this encounter to all the Thousand Gods. Then, with a wordless cry, Hal swung his blade in a perfect arc.

Sin Hazar folded over the Morenian steel, barely managing to twist around and stare up at his rival. His eyes grew wide with shock, melted into stained pools above his twin swan-wing tattoos. The fingers of his free hand convulsed, clutching at the dreams that flowed away with his crimson blood—dreams of conquering Morenia and Liantine and more. His throat worked as if even now he would give orders to his men, issue commands to the sham of his Little Army. When he opened his mouth to speak, though, blood slicked his lips, and he fell hard to his knees.

Hal stepped back, tugging his sword free from the tangle of Sin Hazar's blood-drenched cloak. The rough motion brought Sin Hazar halfway up, and his arms rose as if to ward off further injury, jerking like broken wings. He collapsed back to the ground, managing a single convulsive breath as he swiveled his gaze up to Rani. He tried again to speak, but before he could form words, a horrible shudder overtook his limbs, his arms and legs trembling as if he were no more than a rag doll. He fell forward at last, and his blood poured onto the churned Amanthian soil.

Rani stared at the man who had wrought such havoc in her world, who had played with the lives of children and men alike. She watched as the breeze picked up, blew as if it were possessed by the last breath that sighed from the monster who had ruled the north. Sin Hazar's blue cloak lay sodden across his body, too soaked with blood to stir in the wind.

Only as Rani staggered back from the slain king did she realize that the Fellowship's eight Yrathi mercenaries had subdued their fierce brethren, murdering each of the soldiers who had fought to remain loyal to Sin Hazar. The Fellowship of Jair had gained a good bargain with its purchase of the ruthless soldiers. However much gold had been paid from the Fellowship's shadowy treasury, the cost had been a fair one.

At last Rani realized that Puladarati was screaming orders to his men, commanding that they close around their king. Hal stood tall above the body of his vanquished enemy, his own cloak thrown back from his shoulders, soaring on the wind like a mantle woven by all the Thousand Gods. His teeth were bared in a grim smile as he stared down at his bloody victory, and he held his crimson-slicked sword away from his own body.

Even as Rani fought to draw a breath, fought to step up to Hal's side, she caught a glimpse of motion. There, to the right— too fast for safety, for security.

Rani's dagger slapped into her palm, and she whirled with the ease that Mair had taught her a lifetime ago, in Moren's dangerous streets. Her knife drove home before she was even consciously aware that she had struck. She felt the moist pressure of meat and then the jarring crunch of bone. She twisted her dagger and pulled it upward, fighting to free the blade. And then, before she could register the gouts of blood that spilled across her clothes, before she could see Hal's fingers around her wrist, before she could feel Crestman pulling her back and hear Mair call her name, she looked at the body on the ground before her.

Bashi stared back, surprise bright in his cornflower eyes. As Rani took a step away she saw the traitor's own knife tumble from his dying fingers, topple harmlessly onto the ground. He opened his mouth to say something, and a bubble of blood floated across his lips. "Brother," he gasped, bursting the bubble, and then his face collapsed like a gate before a battering ram. His blood was hot on Rani's hands as she let herself be pulled away from the chaos and the murder and the victory.

15

Rani slipped into the great hall, surprised to find it empty of people. The last of Davin's crates were clustered at the far end of the room, near the dais where she had once sat with Sin Hazar. She was tempted to cross over and pry open the topmost box, dig about for some sort of treasure in the old man's collection of trinkets and toys. Before she could move, though, she was startled by the loud squawk of a bird. Her heart was still pounding as she turned to the near corner of the hall, to a cage that stood out of the draft.

Davin's macaw stared at her, tilting its head to one side and lifting up one of its claws. The bird picked between its toes with its thick, black tongue, all the time keeping a golden eye trained on Rani. She approached cautiously, edging up until she stood an arm's length from the cage. "Rani Trader!" she prompted brightly. "Rani Trader!"

The bird only squawked again and ruffled its azure feathers, shuffling about on its perch. "Davin's misunderstood," the bird croaked, giving an uncanny imitation of its ancient owner. "No one understands poor Davin."

"Aye, and no one will understand poor you, if you don't keep your mouth closed." Rani started at the old man's voice behind her; she had not heard him enter the hall. Nevertheless, he stood inside the doorway, his arms linked around a heavy, leather-bound book. Even though he rested the volume against his right hip, the top edge reached nearly to his chin.

"Davin!"

"Aye. What are you doing to my macaw?"

"I wasn't doing anything! I was just making sure it was ready to travel."

"Travel? That bird? He's not going south with us."

"Why not? You've loaded down three drays with everything else that you require."

"The winter air on the journey would kill him. Macaws were never meant to live this far north, and the draft along the way would freeze his lungs." The old man scowled, his brows knitting above his dark eyes. "And don't you comment on my drays. You let your king's quartermaster argue with me over what I pack. It was not my idea to move to Morenia."

Rani settled her hands on her hips. She'd heard enough of Davin's harping in the fortnight since Hal had occupied Sin Hazar's palace. "Don't complain, old man. You know that King Halaravilli has shown you mercy."

"Mercy? Making an old man ride for weeks during the middle of winter? Plucking an old man from his home?"

Rani refused to fight back. Instead, she set out her grim reply like winding sheets before a pyre. "King Halaravilli could have had you executed for what you've done. If not for you, more than three score Morenian men would be traveling in the middle of winter, making their way home to their wives and bairns!"

Davin pinned her with his steely eyes, gimlets that darted out from their fields of wrinkles. "Your king will never execute me. Not while he thinks I can create new engines for him. Besides, Rani Trader, your king is ready to admit what you will not. Morenia would have lost far more men, if not for me. My flying machine won the day."

Davin's flying machine. And Monny.

Rani dared not continue the battle, for fear that she would give way to the tears that still lingered close to her heart. Instead, she sighed. "What's that in your arms, Davin? King Halaravilli has told you he has no more space for your books."

"This one is not for me. It's for you."

"Me?"

Before Rani could make further reply, a dozen boys tumbled into the great hall. They were laughing and shoving each other, making crude jokes, but their amusement was cut short when they caught sight of Davin and Rani.

"My lord," said the oldest, flushing scarlet so that the scar across his cheekbone stood out like a white flag. "My lady."

Before either Davin or Rani could speak, Crestman strode into the hallway. "What's keeping you, boys? Those crates have to make it onto the last dray. Move—" The captain caught sight of the hall's other occupants, and his words stopped in his throat.

Davin cleared his throat with unaccustomed tact. "I was just instructing the boys," the old man lied. "I need them to help me repack some goods. I have herbs from swampy Brandir that must be sheltered from the cold."

Before Rani could argue, the old man moved away, setting his oversize book on a nearby trestle table. He began to bully the boys who had come to help him, ordering them about with the same irritability that he had shown when he housed the Little Army near the Swancastle.

Rani was left staring at Crestman. She caught her fingers opening and closing on the cloth of her robe, and she tried to remember a civil greeting.

"Crimson." He spoke first, after a painful pause. "It suits you."

For just an instant, she did not know if he referred to the color of her garment, or Hal's banner, or the blood that had streaked her hands on the plain outside the city gates. "Crestman," Rani whispered, wincing as the boys behind her started to heave crates about the room.

"Why won't you let me come?" the lion pleaded. "The Amanthian countryside is not yet safe! You need a guard."

"Hal can guard me. He has an army at his command."

"Hal."

"Crestman," Rani said miserably, "we need you here. If you don't stay behind to command the Little Army, they'll suffer."

"Command them? They're boys. There is no more Little Army."

"Precisely." Rani glanced over Crestman's shoulder, distracted by the youths' squabbling. Good-natured debate began to turn as one boy called another a filthy name. In seconds, knives were drawn and Davin's goods forgotten.

"Men!" Crestman's voice rang out across the hall. "I'll take your daggers and melt them down, same as I did with your swords!" The boys fell silent immediately, hanging their heads and scuffling their boots against the flagstones. "Now if you can't get these crates out to the courtyard, I'll find some soldiers who can!"

Crestman waited until the fighters had sheathed their blades, but then he took care to turn away before they went back to their assigned labors. Rani understood that this was the way he showed his trust. This was the way he let his soldiers know that he believed in them. She waited as most of the boys left, carrying crates out to the courtyard. The only noise left in the hall was Davin berating the unfortunate trio who had been designated to help him repack his herbs.

"Crestman," Rani said into the uncomfortably heavy silence, "they *listen* to you. Puladarati's men would have them strung up in a day. These boys must be reminded of the Little Army—they can't just be ordered to forget what happened. You can help them. You can teach them how to keep their pride while you prepare them to return to their homes."

The lion refused to meet her gaze, refused to acknowledge the truthfulness behind her words. Rani sighed and reached out a finger to trace the scar along his cheek. "It's a better life than Sin Hazar had planned for you."

"It isn't!" Crestman protested, and he grabbed her hand. His fingers were icy claws around her wrist. "It's the same life! Sin Hazar would have enslaved me to the Liantines, and your precious 'Hal' has bound me to his Morenians! What difference does it make?"

Rani trembled at the rage in his voice, at the hurt behind his words. "You wear no chains, Crestman. If you had been on the other ship, or on an earlier vessel, you'd be in shackles by now. In shackles or worse."

She watched him measure her words, watched him remember the other ship, the one that had not turned back from Liantine.

Fifteen thousand soldiers, all told, lost in the Little Army, and he was complaining about striding free in Sin Hazar's palace. She saw his grudging acceptance of her argument, his reluctant admission that he was better off in Amanthia. Beneath that resignation, though, she could still see anger. Anger and hurt and shattered trust.

"This will get easier," she urged. "When you begin to send the boys home, you'll see that you're making the right decision." Rani struggled to change the subject. "How is Shea doing?"

"Still the same. She's mourning those girls, her Tain and Serena. It was cruel for her to see them again, in the stockade, only to have them sent to Liantine. She'd lost them once, and she may never recover from having to let them go again."

"Don't give up on her, Crestman. She'll help you with the Little Army, especially with the girls. She'll help you send the children home."

"And when we're done? When all the Little Army is disbanded? What plans do you have for me then?"

"Crestman, I—"

Before she could fashion a lie, she was interrupted by a bass voice, booming from the doorway. "Lady Rani, King Halaravilli said that I should—. Ah. My lady." Duke Puladarati took a step back, swallowing his message and drilling his gaze into Rani's hand, into the wrist that was still encircled by Crestman's fingers. "Excuse me, my lady. The king instructed me to find you."

Crestman braved the duke's gaze. "I was just leaving, Your Grace." The boy paused deliberately and shifted his grip, moving his fingers to curl beneath Rani's palm. She let him raise her hand to his lips, struggled not to reveal a hint of emotion as he brushed a kiss across her flushed skin. "My lady," he murmured, and bowed before he strode over to the boys who still fumbled at Davin's belongings.

"Crestman!" Rani started to call out, but then she caught his name at the back of her throat. She swallowed hard and forced herself to face Puladarati.

"Yes, my lord," she said instead, and her voice sounded curiously high in her own ears. "You were sent to find me?"

"Aye. King Halaravilli wanted to know your preferences for tomorrow's feast."

King Halaravilli. . . . Hal had scarcely spoken to her since the bloodshed in front of Amanth's gates. Rani knew that he was purposely keeping to his appropriated apartments, that he was mourning the deaths of the men he had led north. There were so many. . . . The seventy soldiers who had been destroyed by Davin's glass eggs. The councillor, Lamantarino. Monny. Even Bashi, in a way.

Rani wanted to go to Hal, wanted to comfort him with words and understanding. She *knew* why he had acted, why he had endangered his kingdom and his vassals. She wanted to tell him that he had made all the right decisions, that she was grateful for her rescue, for the liberation of the Little Army.

She wanted to go to him, but she would not. She would wait until he wished for her company, until he summoned her to his side. He was her king, after all. Not her brother. Not more. Her king.

Until then, she would serve him as best she could. Struggling to turn her attention to the matter at hand, Rani asked Puladarati, "Tomorrow's feast?"

The former regent scowled and ran his maimed hand through his mane. His words were pointed, as if he were berating a young child. "After the Amanthians swear their fealty."

"Of course," Rani replied, shaking her head as she forced herself to focus on Puladarati's words. "What was the king asking about?"

"Would you have Lady Mair sit at the head table? Or should she be with His Majesty's generals?"

"I should think at the head table." Rani forced herself to turn away from the boys at the far end of the hall. "Puladarati, you're going to be the governor here. You can make these decisions without me."

"I tried to tell that to His Majesty, but he insisted that I consult with you. Just as he insists on everything else around here. He thinks he has to be involved with everything, decide every last detail. He thinks we'll judge him harshly if he hasn't decided who sits above the saltcellar."

Rani sighed. "Don't worry about him, Your Grace. He'll be more reasonable once we return to Morenia."

"Reasonable!" The duke harrumphed and shook his head. "I don't question his *reason*! I question the burdens he's taking on. He scarcely knows how to run a council meeting! Just because I'm no longer his regent doesn't mean that I can't assist him."

"Of course it doesn't." Rani struggled to put all of her reassurance into her tone. "Your Grace, he chose you to be his governor here precisely because you *have* assisted him. Who else could he trust to administer Amanthia? Sin Hazar's own lords must be watched over closely. It will be some time before their loyalty can be trusted, whatever oaths they swear tomorrow."

"He's only a boy, though! He needs me at his side, not leagues away."

"He's a boy who was man enough to lead an army up here. He was able to convince his council to ride. He broke the Little Army and Sin Hazar's regular forces. He has begun administering his lands with all the skills you've taught him."

The duke shook his head and his throat worked as if he wanted to continue to argue, but he stood a little straighter as he looked out over the hall. "I've got to get this room prepared for tomorrow's feast. We need fresh reeds on the floors, and the tables moved out from the walls. And we've got to get that old man's rubbish out of here."

"I'll take care of that, Your Grace. Davin is nearly through packing his belongings." Rani gestured toward the boys who were hefting the old man's crates, following Crestman from the hall. She shrugged. "If you see Mair, you can send her to me, and we'll make sure that the feast goes smoothly."

Puladarati started to argue, but he cut himself off. "Very well, my lady." He managed a scant bow before he crossed toward the door.

"Your Grace!" Rani called, and the burly councillor reluctantly turned back to face her. "You aren't being banished from Morenia. We'll see you in the south come spring, when Hal calls his first council meeting in the new year."

"That isn't far away," the proud man said grudgingly.

"No, Your Grace. It isn't far away at all."

Puladarati bowed again and took his leave.

"Well, you handled him like a tame pup," Davin grumbled, before Rani could smile with satisfaction.

"He's a good man, Davin."

"Aren't they all?" the old man asked caustically. "If you're quite through holding court, we can get back to the business at hand."

Rani started to bristle at the insulting tone, but she settled for a shrug and turned her attention to the large book that sat on the trestle. At Davin's waved invitation, she walked over to it, shifting it closer across the planks of the table. The book was even heavier than it looked; it took a solid effort to pull it near. "Why is it so heavy?" she asked, surprised that the old man had carried it so casually.

"That's lead about the binding." He gestured toward the tracery that sprawled across the cover.

"Of course," Rani breathed, belatedly recognizing the metal. She leaned closer to examine the binding. Upon inspection, the lead design was strangely familiar, carving up the underlying leather into distinct sections. The leather itself had been tooled with a series of different patterns. Some sections remained light and golden, seeming to leap forward from the surface. Others had been carefully stained so that they appeared to recede. The pattern was the work of a master. "It's like a window," Rani said, with dawning recognition. "A window in the cathedral."

"Aye. I had it from a master. A glasswright from the west."

"May I?" Rani's hand trembled at the edge of the volume. She had seen books like this back in her guildhall, back when she had served as an apprentice. Then, she had scarcely been trusted to wipe the dust from such treasures. She would never have been permitted to read a master glasswright's treatise.

"I brought it to you, didn't I?" Davin shook his head, as if he were doubting his decision, but then he waved his hand toward the volume. "Go ahead. There's no spell on it."

Rani caressed the edge of the cover and breathed a prayer to Clain before she dared to open the tome. There was a creamy page of parchment, extravagant in its blankness, inviting her to turn it over. She did so with a mounting excitement and leaned closer to the next page, picking out the words from their ornate script. "The Glasswrights' Craft, being a Treatise on the tempering and construction of all Things glass and the Ways of the master Glaziers."

"Not *all* things," Davin grumbled. "There's precious little on lenses there. But the book will tell you about making your own glass, about the fires you'll need and your tools. It has quite a lot on grozing irons and bits. And there's a useful section on dyes."

"We don't have anything like this in Morenia! All the treatises were destroyed with the guild."

"I'd heard as much. I suspect you can do something with this."

"I can." Rani resisted the urge to turn the page, to begin reading the treatise right there, in the middle of the hall. The smell of the leather, though, kindled in her memory all the reasons that she wanted to rebuild the glasswrights' guild. She thought of the windows she would craft, the glass creations that would capture the sacred rays of the sun and shape the very light itself. She would fill a dining hall with glowing illumination to inspire gaiety and nobility; she would soften a chapel with visions of light that would make the proudest man fall on his knees in worship of the Thousand Gods.... "Davin," she managed to whisper, "thank you."

"No," the old man said, raising his veined hands in protest. "Thank *you*."

"For what?" Rani was surprised.

"For proving that the flying machine worked. For helping them to use it as it was meant to be used—in a true battle."

Rani let the lead-embossed cover of the book fall back onto the creamy parchment pages. The book was blood-money, then, purchased with Monny's life.

For just an instant, she remembered ducking under the wings of the moth-machine, straightening the arrows, checking their fletching. She shivered, recalling the bitter cold that had crept up from the ground in the freezing predawn. She had let Crestman strap a little boy into a harness. She had stood by as Mair drove a child to his death. Rani had done nothing to save Monny. Nothing at all.

"That's all it was to you?" Rani asked Davin. "A test of one of your creations?"

Davin raised a hand to his cheek, to the unreadable tattoo that faded into his wrinkled flesh. "I'm an old man, my lady. I'm an old man, and I create things. The boy wanted to fly."

"The boy died!"

"And others live. Your King Halaravilli understands that. That's why he's invited me to Morenia."

"He invited you to Morenia because he could not trust you here." Rani wanted to cut Davin, to hurt him as badly as he had hurt her by summoning up the vision of Monny's death.

The old man only shrugged. "What is trust? I make my machines, and men use them. What difference does it make to me if *your* king uses them, or another? Besides, you were eager enough to learn from me when I told you about lenses. You did not hesitate to learn about painting glass and carving it to meet your needs."

Rani wanted to tell Davin that he was wrong. She wanted to tell him that he should swear loyalty to one king, and one king alone. She wanted to tell him that he was despicable, as worthless as one of Sin Hazar's forsworn mercenaries. But who was she to lecture a man old enough to be her grandfather? Who was she to rant against the only glass instructor she would find in all Morenia?

Besides, it *was* safer to keep Davin close at hand. And who knew what he might invent that could serve Halaravilli?

She reached out for the book, hefting it from the table and cradling it against her chest. "You'll take it then?" Davin asked. "You'll accept my gift, Ranita Glasswright?"

Rani took a breath to explain, starting to untangle the confusing thoughts in her head. Before she could begin, though, the macaw bated on its perch behind her. The bird thrust out its azure wings and cocked its head to one side. Rani was pinned by that golden gaze as the macaw proclaimed, "Ranita Glasswright! Ranita Glasswright!"

Silently, she nodded at Davin and turned to carry her treasure from Amanthia's great hall, to pack it away for her long journey home.

Please turn the page for
an excerpt from

SEASON OF SACRIFICE

by
Mindy L. Klasky

Coming in January 2002 from ROC.

Alana Woodsinger watched from the sloping beach as Reade raced along the cliff top, waving a branch high above his head. The five-year-old boy's clear soprano rang out over the crashing surf as he cried, "Hevva! Hevva!"

The meaning of the word was lost in time. Some of the People said that it came from the ancient word for spring; others said that it came from "herring." Still others said that it was the last remaining sound of the Unspeakable Names of all the Guardians.

Whatever the mystery, though, whatever the magic, Reade had strong lungs, and his natural energy was boosted by his pride that the fishermen had chosen him to be the huer at this first fish harvest of the season. That pride was even greater because Reade was performing the annual ritual in front of visitors, in front of Duke Coren and his men.

The duke . . . Alana tore her gaze away from the boy, seeking out the visiting nobleman. She swallowed hard against the by-now-familiar pounding of her heart. The duke had lifted one wry eyebrow when Alana told him of the traditions surrounding the first harvest. He had managed to convey tolerance and amusement without speaking a word.

Before Alana could find Duke Coren on the crowded beach, though, she was caught again by Reade's shouting hevva. His voice arced like a gull's cry as he waved his branch and guided his fishermen toward their first spring catch.

Nothing could be more mystical. Nothing could be more simple.

Exotic inland visitors or no, every year the first harvest began the same way, with the excitement of the young huer calling out to the boats that tossed on the icy water. Those same boats rose and fell, driving schools of silvery pilchards into newly repaired nets. Reade, like all the lucky, sharp-eyed children chosen before him, directed the frenzy from his vantage point on the cliff, signaling with his branch so that the last of the boats could close in around the fishes' dark shadows.

The men hauled in their nets, and Reade's voice was drowned out by the People's excited gabble as the first boats returned to shore. The little boy dropped his furze branch, his job complete. He scrambled down from the promontory and was quickly lost among the other children who whooped at the water's edge, helping the fishermen drag their laden nets to shore.

Alana resisted the urge to order the riotous youngsters back to the safety of higher ground. She made herself trust Teresa, Reade's mother, and the other young mothers who guarded their children with the caution of a seagoing people.

Of course, little Maida led the mayhem, jealous of her twin brother's prize place on the cliff. She was always determined to stir up mischief among the children, even those who were older and larger than she. Her shrieks of revenge as she chased Reade into the crashing surf were enough to make Alana's breath come short, but Reade fought back valiantly, grasping his twin by her ankle and pulling them both under a breaking wave's icy shower.

As Teresa strove to bring order to her wrestling children, Alana could not help but remember how she herself had frolicked on the same tongue of rocky sand not very long before. Now, though, she was required to wear the woodsinger's multicolored cloak, a riotous patchwork of the Guardians' colors—brown and red, blue and white.

The Guardians had chosen Alana. The Tree had called her.

Even as that thought raised the hairs at the nape of Alana's neck, she reached out reflexively for the Tree's consciousness. The giant oak had stood on the cliff above the beach since the Guardians had created this Age, since they had spun the world into being out of earth and air, fire and water. Even when Alana had been a child, even before she'd been called to serve as woodsinger, she had known that the Tree watched over the People, tangible symbol of the Guardians' spirit forces. The Tree watched over the People, and the People cared for the Tree.

Now, though, as woodsinger, Alana knew so much more. She knew that the Tree remembered the life of every single one of the People. It absorbed their stories with the words the woodsingers chanted, soaking up their lives like sunlight and water and earth. Year by year, the Tree added to its enormous girth, girdling itself in another circle of bark. The oak combined all the Guardians' forces—earth, fire, water, and air—to become the physical embodiment of those spirit forces that had created the world, that had created the People.

And year by year, the Tree added to its memories, drinking in more tales of the People. It recorded how the Guardians were worshiped. It recorded how the People lived. It recorded the holy and the ordinary—no detail was too small for the Tree to remember.

Even now, Alana could feel the giant oak's awareness tug at the back of her mind. It reminded her of another huer, generations past, one almost as young as Reade. It reminded her of another spring day, when the pilchard run had been so great that three boats were swamped, pulled over by the weight of the fish in their nets. The Tree reminded Alana that the People had lived this ritual for centuries, and it pulled at the woodsinger, luring her up the steep path to the top of the cliff.

The Tree wanted her to share the story of today's huer, of today's catch. It wanted to add to its store of knowledge.

Alana drew her patched cloak closer about her. Surely the Tree could be patient. It must be able to wait until she had tasted the first of the ocean's offering in this new season. She wasn't going anywhere, after all. She wasn't going to abandon the earthbound oak.

But the Tree was insistent, stirring deep inside her thoughts like the memory of a sweet dream after sleep has crept away.

Alana sighed and hefted her staff, tossing her red-gold hair over her shoulder. There would be time enough to feast after she had told the Tree of the spring harvest.

Reaching the oak, Alana shivered against the stiff breeze that skipped through the Tree's branches. Freshly unfurled leaves trembled in eager anticipation of news from the fishing expedition. Now that the pilchard season had begun, Alana would spend many long days by the oak. She had already begun to prepare the Tree for the fisherman's labors, breaking the earth above its massive roots, roughing up the ground to receive the new-caught fish that she would offer up in gratitude for past guidance, in hope of future support.

Breathing deeply from her steep climb, Alana set her staff on the ground and laid one long-fingered hand on the trunk's rough bark, as if she were calming her own pounding heart.

"Ah, the fair Alana seeks refuge by her tree."

She started at the unexpected voice, but managed to paste a smile across her lips before turning to the intruder. "Duke Coren."

No wonder she had not been able to find the nobleman on the beach! He must have been here on the cliff all along, watching Reade hue in the boats. Alana shrugged off a strange feeling of uneasiness at the break with tradition, at the interference the man might have created by being so near the huer. The harvest had been accomplished without any problem, she remonstrated with herself. All was well on the headland.

The woodsinger remembered to drop a curtsey, as a woman of culture might, a woman from distant Smithcourt. As she bobbed her head, she admonished herself not to notice the sun glinting on the embroidery that spanned the duke's broad chest. His coat of arms was picked out in splendid thread—a black background with a golden sun, all emblazoned with a bloody knife.

Alana's formal gesture made the duke laugh, and he threw back his mane of chestnut curls. His teeth were bright against his narrow lips, almost lost in his beard. His eyes half closed with amusement as if she had told a brilliant tale, and she reminded herself that he only meant to compliment her with his excess. His courtly manner made her nervous, though, and her fingers flew to her hair, anxious to do something, anything. She settled for twisting the silky strands into a loose knot against her neck.

The duke studied her for a long minute, as if he were measuring out grains of gold. His silent scrutiny made her even more uncomfortable than his laughter, but now she was blessed with the familiar flush of angry irritation. None of the People would ever be so bold, so insulting as to gape at the woodsinger. Even a child as young as Reade knew that the woodsinger could speak the secrets of the Guardians, the secrets passed on by the Tree. Even a child knew that the woodsinger was special. Different. Apart.

"My lord." She captured a hint of the headland's chill breeze in her words. "The wind is strong here on the headland. I'm sure you would be more comfortable on the beach. The feast should begin momentarily."

"Perhaps the feast is not what I had in mind." She barely made out his words, tangled in his beard and his inland accent. "Tell me, Woodsinger, why do your people call this the Headland of Slaughter?"

"That has been its name forever, since the beginning of this Age."

"But the name is so . . . harsh."

"Our lives are harsh, Your Grace. There have been terrible shipwrecks on the rocks below. Men have lost their lives when they sailed too close to shore." Even as Alana spoke the words, she felt the stories stir inside her mind. Yes, the Tree knew about those lost lives. It knew the People who had been forfeited to the sea, lost to the Guardians of Water. The Tree remembered.

The duke continued, obviously unaware of the swirl of stories that surged beneath Alana's thoughts. "And yet your people continue to live in the shadow of such tragedy."

"The People could live no other way, Your Grace. The Headland of Slaughter *is* our life." When he quirked an eyebrow skeptically, she fought an indignant blush at what must seem the simple way of fisherfolk. She continued vehemently, though, as if she needed to convince him, as if she needed to justify her People's ways, her own father's death. She shuddered and pushed away that story, the first story that she had ever sung to the Tree. When she spoke again, her voice quavered. "The sea makes us different from you inland people. For instance, you surely noticed that there are no dogs among us?"

She made the statement a question, and he nodded tersely before she continued. "And we made your men tie up their own dogs, far from our village. That is because of the Headland, because of a great storm that blew, decades before my own birth. Three ships foundered on the rocks, and bodies washed ashore for a fortnight. There were more corpses than the People could bury promptly—men and women and little children, too. The dogs got to the bodies before the People did."

Alana's jaw hardened with revulsion, and she swallowed against the sick taste that rose in the back of her throat. Her disgust was triggered by the Tree's recollection, by its instant retelling of the horrors, deep in her mind. She could smell the rotten meat on the beach, see the bloated corpses that trailed fine hair and tangled clothing. She could hear the snarling curs fighting for putrid morsels, snapping at each other for a reeking human hand.

The woodsinger raised her chin defiantly, as if the duke had challenged her. "We drove out every last dog from the village, Your Grace. They could not be tolerated with a life like ours."

"But dogs are useful, Woodsinger! They hunt; they herd. I should think you would keep them to ease your lives."

"Ease is not a luxury for fishermen. We'll never again see a dog gnaw a child's corpse. In fact, our children fear dogs more than you fear the sea."

"I do not fear the sea, Woodsinger." The duke's denial was automatic, but Alana noted the wary eye he cast toward the rocky beach.

"You should."

The nobleman ignored the warning. "But you, Woodsinger. You are more than a superstitious fisherwoman." Duke Coren's eyes glinted again with unruly energy, and Alana pretended that she chose to take a step backward. Letting her fingers trail against the Tree, she met the duke's penetrating gaze. He smiled as if he knew the trembling in her belly, and when he spoke, his voice was so soft that she had to lean close to hear him. "Tell me, Woodsinger. What exactly *is* your role among your people?"

"I serve the Tree, so that the Tree may serve the People."

"Serve the People?"

His laugh was a mongrel's harsh bark, and Alana swallowed the unfamiliar taste of scorn. Last autumn, when she had first donned her woodsinger's mantle, she would have felt the need to turn to the great oak immediately, to console it by singing of the People's faith. Now, she was wiser, and she knew that the duke's ignorance could not harm the massive oak.

"The Tree is not like those that grow in your ordinary inland forests." She sighed as she struggled for words to explain. "Oh, I don't know how to make you understand! The Tree is the embodiment of the *Guardians*, of the spirits that created the world, created us. The Tree *is* earth and air, fire and water. It is all the world around us. It lives for the People, and we live for it."

"Fair words, my lady. But what can a tree do for you, beyond offering shade in the summer and acorns in the fall?"

"The Tree holds all the history of the People!" Alana clenched her teeth in exasperation, knowing that she must sound like a superstitious child. She cast a quick thought into the deep pool of the woodsingers who had lived before her, plumbing the memories that the Tree held in trust. No ready words, though, shimmered to the surface of that murky darkness. No other woodsinger had fed the Tree stories about the frustration of describing the giant oak to an inland duke.

Maybe Alana could find a real answer in the unread tomes that filled her little cabin; maybe her sister woodsingers had recorded their lessons for ignorant outsiders there. Perhaps earlier woodsingers had chosen not to sing directly about inlanders' ignorance to the Tree, to protect the giant oak. Nevertheless, they may have recorded their wisdom in the leather-bound journals that crowded Alana's cottage. She would have to check, to learn. Left on her own for now, though, Alana tightened her voice and tried again.

"When a child is born, Your Grace, I bring it to the Tree. I

sing to the Tree of the newest member of our village, and it
learns. It remembers. When I rest my hand against the Tree's
bark, it . . . it speaks to me. I hear voices inside my head, voices
of all the woodsingers before me. They tell me things, tell me
stories of the People who have lived before."

The duke stared at her as if she were speaking gibberish, as
if she were a child telling hobgoblin tales by the fireside. She
raised her chin defiantly. "When I am with the Tree, I can see
the storm that gave the Headland its name. I can see the years
of good harvests and bad." She gestured toward the roots, toward the neat troughs that she had dug as the ground began to
thaw. "I bring the Tree some of our first harvest. I lay the fish
on the earth, and I cover it. The fish seep into the roots, binding the Tree to our fishing lives. The Tree remembers, and it
reaches into our lives, into my mind."

She could read the skepticism on his inland face, his patent
disbelief. She knew that he was going to say something, was
going to try to humor her as if she were a child telling a story
about talking conies or flying horses. She cut him off before she
could see scorn twist his lips. "The Tree is the core of our lives,
Your Grace! Every fisherman takes a piece of it onto his boat,
so that the Tree will know him and remember him if he does
not come home."

Her throat closed around those last words. She had not yet
found the strength to reach into the Tree's memories of her father,
into the stories sung by earlier woodsingers about her da. His
story ended with Alana becoming woodsinger herself, with the
death of old Sarira Woodsinger, who had tried to sing Alana's
father home, who had tried to save the fishermen from their brutal autumn storm. His story ended with Alana donning the
Guardians' patchwork cloak, taking up the title and responsibility of woodsinger.

Duke Coren's skepticism creased his forehead into a frown.
"A tree, remember? What sort of witchery is that?"

Alana forced herself to step away from the oak's quiet comfort, to stride to the outer reach of its branches. Her voice was

cold as she answered, "Perhaps, Your Grace, you will understand better if I show you."

Forcing down the chill behind her words, she began to chant deep in her throat, a soft sound like a mother's lullaby. Another breeze skirled through the new-green leaves, but she ignored it, opening her mouth to voice the hymn that rose within her. The tune was wordless, a whisper about the People's lives, about the festival that spread across the beach.

Alana sang of the long line of huers who had cried out from the Headland, of the fish that had just been caught. She sang of the strange men who had come with Coren, of the anger barely hidden behind their inland beards. She sang of the dogs that were chained well away from the People, and the power of the man who stood before her, and his skepticism about the woodsinger.

As she sang, a stillness fell over the hill. The breeze calmed in a pocket around the two humans and the Tree. The children's laughing cries on the beach below melted away, swirled into the sudden silence. Alana felt the Tree listen to her, felt it add her words to its great store of knowledge. Inside her mind and her heart, she sensed the massive oak measuring the request that she had not quite dared to make.

A single branch began to lower.

Her song turned into a laugh when she glimpsed Duke Coren's amazed face. She reached up toward the branch, and the Tree moved like a supple cat, curving to greet her and caress her cheek with a whisper of fragile leaves. She strode closer to the living wood, tracing the branch back toward its heart in the tree's trunk. She followed a path that was as thick as her wrist, her neck, her waist.

When she reached the limits of the great Tree's flexibility, she settled her hands on the rough wood. Her sung notes wrapped around the Tree's essence, melded with the living bark. For just a moment, her heart beat with the fresh sweetness of oaken sap, and her soul settled into an otherworldly calm, layer on circular layer of peace. She was no longer Alana Woodsinger, hoping to impress a worldly duke. For a single, timeless instant, she *was* the Tree, she was the living essence of the Guardians in all the world.

And then her heart beat again, and she was a woman once more, an ordinary woman standing beside a branch that quivered in a sudden gust of wind. She lifted her hand from the branch, and she was not surprised to see its valleys and peaks etched into her skin, carved over the lines of her own palm. She sighed and shook her head, not noticing when her hair fell free of its improvised knot. Coren appeared not to notice either, for he gazed intently at what the Tree had revealed.

"What in the name of the Four Winds is that?" His gruff surprise grounded Alana rapidly, and she bit back a smile at the skeptical finger he pointed toward the bark.

She barely had to touch the patch of wood to lift it from its nest. Perfectly symmetrical, the wooden globe was carved into an intricate star, tiny points striking out against the air like a night-black snowflake. As Alana turned the star before the duke's eyes, she saw his interest sharpen until it was as penetrating as one of the carved points.

She smiled. "The children call it a woodstar, but the real name is a bavin."

"A bavin?" He stumbled over the unfamiliar term.

"It's an old word. The first woodsingers learned to ask the Tree for them. When a bavin is lit, it burns without consuming the wood. Each boat we make receives a bavin. The woodstars are set in the prow, so that the Tree can track us out at sea. As woodsinger, I always know where my people are, by watching through the bavins."

"How many does the tree hold?"

"Hold?" The question puzzled her, startled her almost as much as the avaricious gleam in his eyes. She felt the Tree's sudden concern, its disquiet about the inlander's question. Unconsciously, she settled her hand against the fresh bavin scar, as if she were gentling a newborn colt. "We've never tried to find out."

"If I cut down this branch, would they just come rolling out?"

"Oh, no." Alana laughed uneasily. "The Tree does not contain bavins until we ask it to. Even then, it does not always give us woodstars. It must believe that we *need* a bavin before it makes the sacrifice." She realized that he could not understand until he had examined the Tree's gift, and she tossed the carved sphere to the man. She saw his surprise as his fist closed around the star, as he registered how light it was. "The Tree has chosen to give this one to you. Take it as a keepsake of your time with the People."

He stared at the bavin for a long minute before secreting it in a leather pouch that hung at his waist. When he bowed, she felt as if she were a noblewoman in Smithcourt's royal castle. She shoved away the uneasiness that the Tree swirled into her thoughts. After all, what could an oak tree know of nobility? What could it know of the king's distant court? How could any woodsinger have told the Tree about the strange ways of Smithcourt?

Duke Coren bowed fluidly. "And may I see you to the beach, my lady?"

She paused only long enough to caress the Tree, to thank it once again for its gift and to feel the balm of its comforting acknowledgment at the back of her mind. "I would be honored, Your Grace."

Such courtly words were foreign to the People, but Alana had practiced for nearly a fortnight, since Duke Coren had arrived, leading a train of packhorses laden with trade goods. After the visitors' troublesome guard dogs had been banished to the village's perimeter, the People had been pleased with the duke's riches. They longed for the smooth linen that Coren brought to trade; it was crisper and softer than their own rough wool. There were other items as well—trinkets of colored glass that pleased parents and children alike, hardened leather for shoe soles, and iron knives worked by near-magical smiths.

The people had no iron anywhere near the Headland. They needed to trade for all the metal they required, for cookpots and hardware for their boats and for precious knives. The People's need was one of the many incongruities of life on the Headland. Devoted as the People were to the Tree, to the living essence that combined all the Guardians' forces, they still needed to bargain for iron, for the other major gift that the Guardians had crafted when they created this Age. The People remembered the Guardians' ancient power over earth and air, fire and water; they knew the forged power of the dark metal that was not theirs. They consoled themselves with the force of the Tree, and they traded when they could.

During Duke Coren's visit, the People marveled that the nobleman wanted so little in exchange for the precious goods he brought. All he asked for were barrels of salt fish and oil, left over after the easy winter—those, and a handful of purple-and-white clamshell beads. The entire visit had carried the excitement of Midsummer Day, although it was barely spring.

That excitement was heightened by Duke Coren's proclamation that he traded in the name of the king. Of course, the Westlands were ruled by the distant king in Smithcourt, but no lord from so far inland had ever deigned to travel all the way to the Headland. The People had lived for generations as complacent, distant subjects, raising their cups to their absent liege. They enjoyed the fact that they were not ground under some noble heel on a regular basis, even if that meant that the price of iron remained high, that trade in linen and beads remained rare.

Nevertheless, the presence of a nobleman spurred a giddy excitement among all the People. There were even rumors that Duke Coren hoped to ascend to the Iron Throne when he returned to Smithcourt after this journey. After all, even the People had heard of the king's untimely death the previous year, of his passing without an heir. *That* gossip was strong enough to make the journey to the edge of the kingdom. Duke Coren supposedly claimed the crown because of the wealth that he had poured into the dead king's treasury, wealth from trading in lands so distant that the People could not imagine their names.

On the duke's first night in the village, when all the People were gathered about a warm hearth sipping ale, the nobleman had handed out presents. Excitement had fluttered beneath Alana's breastbone. She had told herself that she had no use for a silver brooch, and it was completely inappropriate for a strange man to proffer the sturdy linen sash that gathered the colors of the rainbow and nestled them about her narrow hips. Nevertheless, it would have been rude to decline his gifts. Besides, there was the village to think of—if she, the woodsinger, refused her presents, then the People could not accept theirs.

Therefore, she kept Coren's offerings, and she found herself drawn into conversation with the generous lord. He went out of his way to make her feel at ease, and she realized that he honestly wanted to learn about the People. He was an ambassador of goodwill, and it was her duty to pave his way among the fishermen. It was not *his* fault that she was drawn to him in ways that were not entirely proper for the People's woodsinger, especially not a woodsinger who had been called to her post before settling on a husband.

Alas, that was one seaside tradition that Alana was *not* going to divulge to Duke Coren. There was no reason for him to learn that she was sworn to a life dedicated to the Tree, that she would never be permitted to settle in a cottage with a man, to raise children, to divide her attention between a family and the Tree. Of course, if she had found her mate before being called to serve the oak, things would have been different. . . . The Tree would have made its choice, knowing her commitment to her family. But Alana had had no family when the Tree chose. She had had no distractions. The Tree would not tolerate her divided loyalty now. She would remain alone.

Through no fault of her own, she would remain alone.

Repeating that rule to herself even now, Alana stumbled as her hard-soled winter shoe turned on a stone. Before she could catch herself, Coren's hand was under her elbow, steadying her with a quiet strength. "Careful, my lady," he murmured, and she was startled by the sudden breathlessness that closed her throat. She forced herself to look down at the stony path, to focus on the earth underfoot. She thought she heard the duke chuckle beside her, but she refused to meet his piercing eyes.

His hand was still on her arm when they emerged from the scrubby ocean grass onto the beach. The People looked up in expectation, and a sudden hush fell over the crowd. Laughter and a reed flute's dancing notes slipped away in the crash of breakers. Alana saw the gossiping glint in Goodwife Glenna's eyes, and she jerked her arm away from the duke as if she'd been burned.

Goody Glenna was the oldest of the People. The crone's hearing might be going, but her eyes were sharp, and Alana knew the old gossip was recording this latest tidbit to share by the communal ovens on the next baking day. Alana sighed. She was already tired of the Women's Council watching her every move. She knew that she was not permitted a husband. She had accepted that she was sworn to the Tree.

"Alana!" The woodsinger whirled to face Sartain, the current leader of all the People. The Fisherman was short and muscular; like most of his folk, his body had been shaped by hauling nets heavy with fish. His back was stooped from years of repetitive labor, and his hands were horny pads, callused by decades of service on the People's coracles. Sartain's eyes were carved deep in his face, protected by a web of lines etched by sun and wind.

"Yes, Fisherman?"

"While you've kept our guest up on the bluff, the feast has been laid. We can't have the duke saying that the People lack hospitality, can we?" Alana heard a good-natured smile behind the Fisherman's sea-salt words. "Come, Woodsinger, let us begin the feast."

Sartain turned and led the way to the strip of firm sand, still dark from the ocean's tidal soaking. When a restless silence had once more fallen over the beach, the Fisherman spoke. "My People," he began, and then, with only a gull's cry for competition, Sartain stumbled through a few formulaic greetings, awkwardly daring to clap his hand on Duke Coren's shoulder. "Your Grace," Sartain continued with gruff modesty as he realized the presumption he had taken, "I would not bore you with an old fisherman's words. Merrick, stand forward and speak to the duke."

Alana watched Merrick flow beside the Fisherman with a stoat's grace, his teeth white against his dark skin and darker hair. Merrick was one of the few men among the People who had ever ventured beyond the Headland of Slaughter. Last year, he had journeyed inland to trade salt fish for precious iron and tin and to meet with the royal census takers, declaring how many men, women, and children lived beside the sea. Now, Merrick spoke for all those People, using flowery language to admit pride and gratitude.

Alana's breath caught in her throat as she watched the young man proclaim the People's hospitality. As if unconsciously, Merrick let the wind tug the edge of his cloak, flaring the fabric to accentuate his broad shoulders. The casual fist that he set against his hip was a subtle reminder of his strength, and Alana caught herself wondering for the hundredth time how his strong hands would feel against her flesh, against the naked skin of her back. . . .

She shook her head in annoyance. Of course she thought of the young fisherman that way—he did everything he could to make every girl in the village pine for him. It was certainly no coincidence last summer that he had not finished his bath when the girls came to draw cooking water for the Midsummer Feast. . . . He purposely used the village common to practice his fighting forms, wearing nothing more than his breeches as he swung about his smith-precious iron sword. He had his own reasons for tending the spitted lambs at the summer festivals, sweltering by the heat of the fire so that the flames drew out a glow on his bared chest.

Old Goody Glenna reveled in the attention all the girls paid to Merrick. Each day she found a new tale to tell, a story of the woe that had befallen some smitten slip of a girl when she accepted the sort of invitation that Merrick kept open. Alana, searching her knowledge from the Tree, knew that only a fraction of Goody Glenna's stories were true. Nevertheless, the young woodsinger also knew that it was her duty to keep the village girls in line.

She had intended to do just that, late last fall, when she had confronted Merrick for the first time since donning her woodsinger's cloak. With a grin, the man had admitted every one of his faults, casting his dark blue eyes toward his feet with a child's heart-stealing shame. Alana had caught herself wishing he would brush against her as he left the clearing, or better yet that he would not leave at all. . . .

Foolishness.

When Merrick finished his speech, Sartain invoked the traditional blessings of earth, fire, water, and air. With the Guardians' names still hovering over the People and their guests, laughter broke out. The young twins, Maida and Reade, recommenced their game of tag, and a drum joined the flute's rollicking voice, dancing amid the crash of waves.

After filing by the great iron cooking pots, Alana settled on a convenient outcrop of rock, a little removed from the crowds of boisterous people. She pulled her iron dagger from her waist, smiling at the rich present that her father had given her, long before he met the Guardians of Water.

Now, Alana used the treasured blade to salute her father with the sea's first harvest, carefully picking the flesh from a steaming pilchard. She was grateful that Sartain had led his early-morning fishermen to such bounty—all of the People were tired of the salt fish that had sustained them for the winter.

Sartain was clearly in a celebratory mood as well, for he ordered the young men to break out a barrel of apple wine. As Alana looked over the rim of her earthenware cup, she noted that Coren and his followers did not partake of the sweet, cool stuff. Perhaps their inland palate was accustomed to finer drink. It was a failing in the man, she mused, but not a deadly one.

"Hmphhh! He does not deign to drink our apple wine! Perhaps m'lord would prefer mead from the king's court!"

Alana did not need to turn about to chastise the complainer; she did not even need to listen to the woodsingers' quiet murmurs at the back of her mind to identify the speaker. "Hush, Landon. I think, instead, that he is loath to take something that we clearly hold so dear." She set down her dagger and forced herself to face the lanky young man. While she knew that Landon's long face *could* be pleasant, an ugly frown distorted his features now. A sea breeze chose that unfortunate moment to skip across his brow, stressing the fact that he had already lost the better part of his hair.

She frequently had to remind herself that Landon was only four years her senior. His cautious ways and his receding hairline lent him an aura of conservative seniority almost as great as Goody Glenna's. There was a time when Alana had found his maturity compelling. Things had not gone well, though, since the Winter Solstice, and the woodsinger delicately forced her thoughts away from a memory as prickly as the bavin she had just sung for Duke Coren.

Landon made that retreat easier as he grumbled, "I'm certain you would know about his thoughts, Alana. What secrets did he whisper to you by the Tree? Did you actually give him that woodstar you sang?"

"Were you *spying* on me, Landon? What I do with the Tree is no interest of yours!"

"The Tree belongs to all the People, Alana. Not to you, and certainly not to some cursed inlander. Look at him, the way the women wait on him! It's not like he's even eating the tidbits they offer."

"You sound like a child! What has Coren ever done to you?"

"Ah, so now he is 'Coren.' Not 'my lord' and not 'the duke,' but simply Coren."

"You know the People have never put much stock in titles! If I didn't know better, I'd think that you were jealous."

"Jealous? Not I, Woodsinger. I am nothing but a humble tracker, interested only in the welfare of our People. I live only to serve, following game to feed our folk when the Guardians of Water are not kind." His words were stewed in bitterness.

"You know that's not what I meant, Landon." If only she could take back the words that she had spoken on the longest night of the year. . . . As she'd stared at his offering of mistletoe berries, she had been so certain he would understand her. He *knew* that she was pledged to the Tree now, that as woodsinger she could have no husband.

Of course, Landon also knew the exceptions to the ancient rules. He knew that a married woman could keep her husband, keep her children, and still serve the Tree. He had argued that Alana should fight to change the rules, should broaden them to include a maiden who had found her true love but had not quite married before she was called to the Tree.

Alana had swallowed hard at the thoughts his arguments implied. She had averted her eyes from his mistletoe berries, from the creamy white confession that she had managed to ignore for months. Instead, she had chosen her words carefully, telling Landon that serving as woodsinger was a sacrifice. She must give up her freedom for the good of all the People. She must forfeit her decisions, so that she could offer up gratitude to the Tree that had watched over her since birth. She tried to explain that the Tree that had chosen her, had plucked her from the black-rimmed pit of despair after her father was lost to the Guardians of Water.

When Landon had refused to accept Alana's explanation of her duty to the Tree, she had been forced to point out that he was a hunter, a tracker, a man who lived his life looking *inland*, away from the Tree. Even if she had been inclined to overthrow generations of tradition, Alana had tried to say gently, she could not break the rules for him. She only just managed to avoid the true admission, the one that would have stung him beyond reason: Alana was not a smitten maid. She did not love Landon.

Now, the woodsinger took a deep breath to explain again. Before she could find the hackneyed words, though, she was interrupted by a flurry of activity on the far end of the beach.

For an instant she could not discern individual shapes in the confusion. Then she saw that the People were running, screaming, flinging about trenchers of food. As Alana glanced reflexively at the cliff, at the Tree, she saw clouds of dust billowing from the steep path to the beach. Swirled into the dust, screaming as if in battle, were the inlanders' great horses. The massive beasts were ridden by Coren's men, by dark-liveried soldiers who bellowed at the beasts, even as they hurtled toward the beach.

The shouting would have been disturbing. The sight of warhorses caparisoned for battle would have been frightening. The thick-throated battle screams of Coren's men would have been terrifying. But there was a greater horror coursing down the path to the beach.

There were dogs.

Dogs charged among the People, forcing grown men to step back in ingrained fear and revulsion. One mastiff ripped at Sartain's sleeve, and Alana saw the Fisherman pull back from the slavering jaws with his snarl of disgust. The dogs were the People's greatest nightmare, sprung to full life on the sandy beach. Alana leaped to her feet, hefting her oaken staff as if she could beat back the People's madness.

Before the woodsinger could move, a high-pitched scream ripped through the melee. "The inlanders are taking my babies! They're stealing the children!"

The anguish in the voice froze the People, and even as Alana recognized that Teresa was the source of the heartrending cries, she began to search the crowd for the twins, for the mischievous Maida and Reade. She found them before the others could react, but what she saw chilled her blood.

Maida was in the arms of Coren's lieutenant, struggling like a fish caught in a net. Her little body twisted and pulled, and she thrashed her head about as if she were determined to break her own neck if she could not be free. One well-placed kick landed against the inlander's armored solar plexus, but the man's strong right arm merely tightened across the girl's vulnerable throat, transferring his fury to the soft flesh and tiny bones. Maida kicked one last time, then slumped in the soldier's grasp.

Reade was tangled in Duke Coren's own arms, struggling with the terror of a trapped coney. Coren's beard jutted out like a broken tree limb, and his thin lips twisted in a snarl.

Before Alana could cry out, the duke raised a silver-chased dagger. The pommel was set with a heavy ruby that glinted across the beach, mirroring the bloody knife embroidered on Coren's chest. With the smooth gesture of a man dispatching a stubborn fish, the duke brought the hilt down, smashing into the tender flesh behind the boy's ear. Reade continued to struggle feebly, but the inlander had no trouble hoisting the child onto his huge destrier.

And then, as suddenly as it had begun, the terror was over. The People stared in ragged ranks as the soldiers swung up on their horses, leading their slavering dogs up the steep cliff-side path. Teresa's harsh sobs meshed with the waves, and a lone gull cried out as the inlanders rode off with the twins.

Look what's coming in August...

❑ HOMEFALL: Book Four of The Last Legion
by Chris Bunch

One of the fastest growing series in science fiction. Combat veteran Chris Bunch takes The Last Legion on their fourth and possibly final mission—undercover, under suspicion, and ultimately, exposed...

458419/$6.99

❑ REVELATION
by Carol Berg

Seyonne, the slave-turned hero from Berg's highly acclaimed *Transformation*, returns to discover the nature of evil—in a "spellbinding"* epic saga. (*Romantic Times*)

458427/$6.99

❑ SHADOWRUN #40: The Burning Time
by Stephen Kenson

Low-level programmer Roy Kilaro wants desperately to become an elite operative and experience some real action in the battles between the megacorporations. He gets what he wanted and more...

458397/$5.99

Prices slightly higher in Canada

Payable by Visa, MC or AMEX only ($10.00 min.), No cash, checks or COD. Shipping & handling: US/Can. $2.75 for one book, $1.00 for each add'l book; Int'l $5.00 for one book, $1.00 for each add'l. Call (800) 788-6262 or (201) 933-9292, fax (201) 896-8569 or mail your orders to:

Penguin Putnam Inc.	Bill my: ❑ Visa ❑ MasterCard ❑ Amex_____(expires)
P.O. Box 12289, Dept. B	Card#_____
Newark, NJ 07101-5289	
Please allow 4-6 weeks for delivery	
Foreign and Canadian delivery 6-8 weeks	Signature_____

Bill to:

Name_____

Address_____ City_____

State/ZIP_____ Daytime Phone #_____

Ship to:

Name_____ Book Total $_____

Address_____ Applicable Sales Tax $_____

City_____ Postage & Handling $_____

State/ZIP_____ Total Amount Due $_____

This offer subject to change without notice.   Ad # JanROC (9/00)